PRIZE STORIES 1980
The O. Henry Awards

EDITED AND WITH
AN INTRODUCTION
BY WILLIAM ABRAHAMS

DOUBLEDAY & COMPANY, INC.
GARDEN CITY, NEW YORK
1980

ISBN: 0-385-15106-3
Library of Congress Catalog Card Number: 21-9372

CONTENTS

PUBLISHER'S NOTE

This volume is the sixtieth in the O. Henry Memorial Award series.

In 1918, the Society of Arts and Sciences met to vote upon a monument to the master of the short story, O. Henry. They decided that this memorial should be in the form of two prizes for the best short stories published by American authors in American magazines during the year 1919. From this beginning, the memorial developed into an annual anthology of outstanding short stories by American authors, published, with the exception of the years 1952 and 1953, by Doubleday & Company, Inc.

Blanche Colton Williams, one of the founders of the awards, was editor from 1919 to 1932; Harry Hansen from 1933 to 1940; Herschel Brickell from 1941 to 1951. The annual collection did not appear in 1952 and 1953, when the continuity of the series was interrupted by the death of Herschel Brickell. Paul Engle was editor from 1954 to 1959 with Hanson Martin coeditor in the years 1954 to 1960; Mary Stegner in 1960; Richard Poirier from 1961 to 1966, with assistance from and coeditorship with William Abrahams from 1964 to 1966. William Abrahams became editor of the series in 1967.

Doubleday also publishes *First-Prize Stories from the O. Henry Memorial Awards* in editions that are brought up to date at intervals. In 1970 Doubleday also published under Mr. Abrahams' editorship *Fifty Years of the American Short Story*, a collection of stories selected from the series.

The stories chosen for this volume were published in the period from the summer of 1978 to the summer of 1979. A list of the magazines consulted appears at the back of the book. The choice of stories and the selection of prize winners are exclusively the responsibility of the editor. Biographical material is based on information provided by the contributors and obtained from standard works of reference.

INTRODUCTION

We are entering a new decade. *Prize Stories 1980* is the sixtieth volume in this annual series; and while longevity is not everything, it is something—at the least, an occasion to emphasize the continuing vitality of the story as a literary form, and its continuing attractiveness to some of our most gifted writers whether late in a distinguished career or at the point of starting out. I must ask the indulgence of regular readers of the O. Henry collections if I say again—as I have said more than once in these introductions—that the accessibility (or more precisely, the inaccessibility) of worthwhile stories to readers who would welcome them if they knew of their existence, seems to me a more serious problem than the quality and number of stories that are being written. In the latter respects we are as well off as we have ever been. I would like to think that the stories gathered here sustain the argument: surely a year that offers an achievement of the caliber of Saul Bellow's "A Silver Dish," to name a single instance, is reason enough for optimism as to the future.

Perhaps the problem of accessibility will remain unsolved. Perhaps it was a kind of naïveté to expect it should ever be otherwise, to fail to acknowledge that magazines reaching a large audience will be unlikely to pay much attention to the publication of stories when their sales pitch, geared to the needs of their audience, is seductively elsewhere. In that context, it seems appropriate (and long overdue) to speak in praise of *The New Yorker*, a magazine in which so many excellent stories are published each year—four, by Ann Beattie, Saul Bellow, Jean Stafford and Peter Taylor, are included in the present volume—that one tends to take it for granted. Perhaps that explains the number of intelligent readers with a declared interest in fiction who say, not apologetically but complacently, even snobbishly, "Oh, I never read the stories in *The New Yorker*," and go on, with no thought of being inconsistent, to describe the shortcomings of the stories they make a point of not reading. *The New Yorker*, appearing weekly, publishes more than a hundred stories each year (for which it pays, as writers are well aware, very generously), and if it sometimes has been guilty of inexplicable omissions and inclusions, such editorial lapses are venial. The standards over the years have been very high; the achievements and rewards, commensurate.

Fortunately, *The New Yorker* is not alone among the "large" magazines in its responsiveness to serious fiction (and not least to fiction in the comic mode, as in the stories of V. S. Pritchett and Woody Allen, and sometimes, Donald Barthelme). Still, I found it heartening, having assembled this year's collection, to look back for comparison to *Prize Stories 1970* and the lineup there of the "large" magazines from which stories had been chosen. In 1970: *The New Yorker, The Atlantic, Harper's Magazine,* and *Esquire.* Ten years later: still *The New Yorker, The Atlantic, Harper's,* and *Esquire.* But also *Cosmopolitan* and *Redbook* (both of which have been represented in the past), and *Yankee* (for the first time.) Taking statistics a bit further, I note that in the 1970 collection there were seventeen stories from thirteen magazines, nine from "little" magazines, eight from the four "large" magazines mentioned earlier. In the present collection: twenty-two stories, ten from nine "little" magazines, eleven from seven of the "large" magazines, and one from a magazine in an "in-between" category, *The New Republic,* which only rarely publishes fiction. However one chooses to interpret these figures, it seems to me an inescapable conclusion that the "little" magazines have become an important resource for writers and readers of the contemporary short story. From this it follows that at a time when an exceptional number of worthwhile stories are being written, they must be sought out, very often in unexpected or unlikely places. Of course *The New Yorker.* But also *Canto* and *Antaeus.* Of course the *Sewanee Review.* But also *Yankee* and *Cosmopolitan.*

Here, then, are the results of one such seeking out: stories by twenty-two American writers, fourteen of whom are receiving O. Henry Awards for the first time. As always, literary excellence has been the criterion; certainly I have not chosen these stories because they are exemplary or representative of trends or tendencies. Each is able to stand on its own, distinctive merits. And yet, once the stories are brought together, and placed, one hopes, to their best advantage, it is curious to see how their resemblances and diffcrences emerge more strikingly than one had anticipated, how, as it were inadvertently, one can begin to decipher trends, tendencies, themes, styles—the situation of the American short story at the end of the 1970s.

From that point of view, it seems to me cause for rejoicing that two of the undeniable masters in the older generation, Saul Bellow and Jean Stafford, should have returned to the story after a long absence—a recognition, I like to think, that there are qualities peculiar to the story that drew them back to it, a vigor and shapeliness that the shorter form allows and encourages and that one sees not only in *their* stories but in many others being written now. So that if there *is* a "tendency" that deserves notice, it is in this embracing of the full-fledged story, one that eludes both randomness in the telling and the constraints of some rigid preconceived formula, and moves naturally and fatefully to its inevitable ending. (An unexpected consequence is that one hesitates now to disclose the endings of many of these stories—readers ought to be allowed to experience them for themselves without didactic comment or a figurative tugging of the sleeve.)

I have said that in the return of Saul Bellow and Jean Stafford we had cause for rejoicing; but in Miss Stafford's case we must also mourn. "An Influx of Poets," so wiry, so inspired, so ruthless in its malice and candor, is the last of her stories to be published in her lifetime. In "A Silver Dish," Saul Bellow says of his hero, Woody, that he was "moved when things were *honest*. . . . He hated faking." It is a description that might well have been applied to Jean Stafford herself. She was "moved when things were *honest*," and it was her own hatred of "faking," one feels confident, that must have set in motion her pursuit of the bogus in "An Influx of Poets." What a set! And with what wit and fury she pinned her macho poets to the page! If Bellow, in "A Silver Dish," has written a magnificent tribute to the life force as it expresses itself in Woody and his father, Stafford has written a subtle, unforgiving, self-implicating and ultimately devastating indictment of those who are anti-life. In the climactic glimpse of the narrator and her poet husband at the story's end, we are shown a life-denying action that horrifies us by its cruelty, even as we accept its rightness, its inevitability.

Like "An Influx of Poets," "A Silver Dish" is the work of a

master. Both originate in a desire to recapture the past, whether real or imagined. Thereafter, resemblances cease: each artist follows his own adventurous way, responding to the possibilities of the story he has chosen to tell. In "A Silver Dish," that memorable account of a son and his father, so moving, so open and generous in the writing, Saul Bellow has succeeded at something rare and very difficult. He has created in this wonderful story a truly admirable, likable and sympathetic human being, with an unconstraint that has its beginning and its fulfillment in love.

WILLIAM ABRAHAMS

A SILVER DISH

SAUL BELLOW

Saul Bellow, born in Lachine, Quebec, Canada, of Russian
immigrant parents, grew up in Chicago and has lived there
for most of his life. He is the author of *Henderson the Rain
King, Herzog, Seize the Day, Humboldt's Gift,* and other
books. The recipient of quite a few awards, he received the
Nobel Prize in 1976.

What do you do about death—in this case, the death of an old father? If you're a modern person, sixty years of age, and a man
who's been around, like Woody Selbst, what do you do? Take this
matter of mourning, and take it against a contemporary background. How, against a contemporary background, do you mourn
an octogenarian father, nearly blind, his heart enlarged, his lungs
filling with fluid, who creeps, stumbles, gives off the odors, the
moldiness or gassiness of old men. I *mean!* As Woody put it, be
realistic. Think what times these are. The papers daily give it to
you—the Lufthansa pilot in Aden is described by the hostages on
his knees, begging the Palestinian terrorists not to execute him,
but they shoot him through the head. Later they themselves are
killed. And still others shoot others, or shoot themselves. That's
what you read in the press, see on the tube, mention at dinner.
We know now what goes daily through the whole of the human
community, like a global death-peristalsis.

Woody, a businessman in South Chicago, was not an ignorant
person. He knew more such phrases than you would expect a tile
contractor (offices, lobbies, lavatories) to know. The kind of
knowledge he had was not the kind for which you get academic
degrees. Although Woody had studied for two years in a semi-

nary, preparing to be a minister. Two years of college during the
Depression was more than most high-school graduates could
afford. After that, in his own vital, picturesque, original way
(Morris, his old man, was also, in his days of nature, vital and picturesque) Woody had read up on many subjects, subscribed to
Science and other magazines that gave real information, and had
taken night courses at De Paul and Northwestern in ecology,
criminology, existentialism. Also he had travelled extensively in
Japan, Mexico, and Africa, and there was an African experience
that was especially relevant to mourning. It was this: On a launch
near the Murchison Falls in Uganda, he had seen a buffalo calf
seized by a crocodile from the bank of the White Nile. There
were giraffes along the tropical river, and hippopotamuses, and ba-
boons, and flamingos and other brilliant birds crossing the bright
air in the heat of the morning, when the calf, stepping into the
river to drink, was grabbed by the hoof and dragged down. The
parent buffaloes couldn't figure it out. Under the water the calf
still threshed, fought, churned the mud. Woody, the robust traveller, took this in as he sailed by, and to him it looked as if the
parent cattle were asking each other dumbly what had happened.
He chose to assume that there was pain in this, he read brute grief
into it. On the White Nile, Woody had the impression that he
had gone back to the pre-Adamite past, and he brought reflections
on this impression home to South Chicago. He brought also a
bundle of hashish from Kampala. In this he took a chance with
the customs inspectors, banking perhaps on his broad build, frank
face, high color. He didn't look like a wrongdoer, a bad guy; he
looked like a good guy. But he liked taking chances. Risk was a
wonderful stimulus. He threw down his trenchcoat on the customs counter. If the inspectors searched the pockets, he was prepared to say that the coat wasn't his. But he got away with it, and
the Thanksgiving turkey was stuffed with hashish. This was much
enjoyed. That was practically the last feast at which Pop, who also
relished risk or defiance, was present. The hashish Woody had
tried to raise in his back yard from the Africa seeds didn't take.
But behind his warehouse, where the Lincoln Continental was
parked, he kept a patch of marijuana. There was no harm at all in
Woody but he didn't like being entirely within the law. It was
simply a question of self-respect.

After that Thanksgiving, Pop gradually sank as if he had a slow
leak. This went on for some years. In and out of the hospital, he
dwindled, his mind wandered, he couldn't even concentrate
enough to complain, except in exceptional moments on the Sundays Woody regularly devoted to him. Morris, an amateur who
once was taken seriously by Willie Hoppe, the great pro himself,
couldn't execute the simplest billiard shots anymore. He could
only conceive shots; he began to theorize about impossible three-
cushion combinations. Halina, the Polish woman with whom
Morris had lived for over forty years as man and wife, was too old
herself now to run to the hospital. So Woody had to do it. There
was Woody's mother, too—a Christian convert—needing care; she
was over eighty and frequently hospitalized. Everybody had diabe-
tes and pleurisy and arthritis and cataracts and cardiac pace-
makers. And everybody had lived by the body, but the body was
giving out.

There were Woody's two sisters as well, unmarried, in their
fifties, very Christian, very straight, still living with Mama in an
entirely Christian bungalow. Woody, who took full responsibility
for them all, occasionally had to put one of the girls (they had become sick girls) in a mental institution. Nothing severe. The
sisters were wonderful women, both of them gorgeous once,
but neither of the poor things was playing with a full deck. And
all the factions had to be kept separate—Mama, the Christian
convert; the fundamentalist sisters; Pop, who read the Yiddish
paper as long as he could still see print; Halina, a good Catholic.
Woody, the seminary forty years behind him, described himself as
an agnostic. Pop had no more religion than you could find in the
Yiddish paper, but he made Woody promise to bury him among
Jews, and that was where he lay now, in the Hawaiian shirt
Woody had bought for him at the tilers' convention in Honolulu.
Woody would allow no undertaker's assistant to dress him but
came to the parlor and buttoned the stiff into the shirt himself,
and the old man went down looking like Ben-Gurion in a simple
wooden coffin, sure to rot fast. That was how Woody wanted it
all. At the graveside, he had taken off and folded his jacket, rolled
up his sleeves on thick freckled biceps, waved back the little trac-
tor standing by, and shovelled the dirt himself. His big face, broad
at the bottom, narrowed upward like a Dutch house. And, his

small good lower teeth taking hold of the upper lip in his exertion, he performed the final duty of a son. He was very fit, so it must have been emotion, not the shovelling, that made him redden so. After the funeral, he went home with Halina and her son, a decent Polack like his mother, and talented, too—Mitosh played the organ at hockey and basketball games in the Stadium, which took a smart man because it was a rabble-rousing kind of occupation—and they had some drinks and comforted the old girl. Halina was true blue, always one hundred per cent for Morris.

Then for the rest of the week Woody was busy, had jobs to run, office responsibilities, family responsibilities. He lived alone; as did his wife; as did his mistress: everybody in a separate establishment. Since his wife, after fifteen years of separation, had not learned to take care of herself, Woody did her shopping on Fridays, filled her freezer. He had to take her this week to buy shoes. Also, Friday night he always spent with Helen—Helen was his wife de facto. Saturday he did his big weekly shopping. Saturday night he devoted to Mom and his sisters. So he was too busy to attend to his own feelings except, intermittently, to note to himself, "First Thursday in the grave." "First Friday, and fine weather." "First Saturday; he's got to be getting used to it." Under his breath he occasionally said, "Oh, Pop."

But it was Sunday that hit him, when the bells rang all over South Chicago—the Ukrainian, Roman Catholic, Greek, Russian, African-Methodist churches, sounding off one after another. Woody had his offices in his warehouse, and there had built an apartment for himself, very spacious and convenient, in the top story. Because he left every Sunday morning at seven to spend the day with Pop, he had forgotten by how many churches Selbst Tile Company was surrounded. He was still in bed when he heard the bells, and all at once he knew how heartbroken he was. This sudden big heartache in a man of sixty, a practical, physical, healthy-minded, and experienced man, was deeply unpleasant. When he had an unpleasant condition, he believed in taking something for it. So he thought, What shall I take? There were plenty of remedies available. His cellar was stocked with cases of Scotch whiskey, Polish vodka, Armagnac, Moselle, Burgundy. There were also freezers with steaks and with game and with Alaskan king crab. He bought with a broad hand—by the crate and by the dozen.

But in the end, when he got out of bed, he took nothing but a cup of coffee. While the kettle was heating, he put on his Japanese judo-style suit and sat down to reflect.

Woody was moved when things were *honest*. Bearing beams were honest, undisguised concrete pillars inside high-rise apartments were honest. It was bad to cover up anything. He hated faking. Stone was honest. Metal was honest. These Sunday bells were very straight. They broke loose, they wagged and rocked, and the vibrations and the banging did something for him—cleansed his insides, purified his blood. A bell was a one-way throat, had only one thing to tell you and simply told it. He listened.

He had had some connections with bells and churches. He was after all something of a Christian. Born a Jew, he was a Jew facially, with a hint of Iroquois or Cherokee, but his mother had been converted more than fifty years ago by her brother-in-law, the Reverend Dr. Kovner. Kovner, a rabbinical student who had left the Hebrew Union College in Cincinnati to become a minister and establish a mission, had given Woody a partly Christian upbringing. Now Pop was on the outs with these fundamentalists. He said that the Jews came to the mission to get coffee, bacon, canned pineapple, day-old bread, and dairy products. And if they had to listen to sermons, that was O.K.—this was the Depression and you couldn't be too particular—but he knew they sold the bacon.

The Gospels said it plainly: "Salvation is from the Jews."

Backing the Reverend Doctor were wealthy fundamentalists, mainly Swedes, eager to speed up the Second Coming by converting all Jews. The foremost of Kovner's backers was Mrs. Skoglund, who had inherited a large dairy business from her late husband. Woody was under her special protection.

Woody was fourteen years of age when Pop took off with Halina, who worked in his shop, leaving his difficult Christian wife and his converted son and his small daughters. He came to Woody in the back yard one spring day and said, "From now on you're the man of the house." Woody was practicing with a golf club, knocking off the heads of dandelions. Pop came into the yard in his good suit, which was too hot for the weather, and when he took off his fedora the skin of his head was marked with a deep ring and the sweat was sprinkled over his scalp—more drops than hairs. He said, "I'm going to move out." Pop was anxious, but he was set to go—determined. "It's no use. I can't live a life like this." Envisioning the life Pop simply *had* to live, his free life, Woody was able to picture him in the billiard parlor, under the "L" tracks in a crap game, or playing poker at Brown and Koppel's upstairs. "You're going to be the man of the house," said Pop. "It's O.K. I put you all on welfare. I just got back from Wabansia Avenue, from the Relief Station." Hence the suit and the hat. "They're sending out a caseworker." Then he said, "You got to lend me money to buy gasoline—the caddie money you saved."

Understanding that Pop couldn't get away without his help, Woody turned over to him all he had earned at the Sunset Ridge Country Club in Winnetka. Pop felt that the valuable life lesson he was transmitting was worth far more than these dollars, and whenever he was conning his boy a sort of high-priest expression came down over his bent nose, his ruddy face. The children, who got their finest ideas at the movies, called him Richard Dix. Later, when the comic strip came out, they said he was Dick Tracy.

As Woody now saw it, under the tumbling bells, he had bankrolled his own desertion. Ha ha! He found this delightful; and especially Pop's attitude of "That'll teach you to trust your father." For this was a demonstration on behalf of real life and free instincts, against religion and hypocrisy. But mainly it was aimed against being a fool, the disgrace of foolishness. Pop had it in for the Reverend Dr. Kovner, not because he was an apostate (Pop couldn't have cared less), not because the mission was a racket (he admitted that the Reverend Doctor was personally honest), but because Dr. Kovner behaved foolishly, spoke like a fool, and acted like a fiddler. He tossed his hair like a Paganini (this was Woody's addition; Pop had never even heard of Paganini). Proof that he was not a spiritual leader was that he converted Jewish women by stealing their hearts. "He works up all those broads," said Pop. "He doesn't even know it himself, I swear he doesn't know how he gets them."

From the other side, Kovner often warned Woody, "Your father is a dangerous person. Of course, you love him; you should love him and forgive him, Voodrow, but you are old enough to understand he is leading a life of wice."

It was all petty stuff: Pop's sinning was on a boy level and therefore made a big impression on a boy. And on Mother. Are wives children, or what? Mother often said, "I hope you put that brute in your prayers. Look what he has done to us. But only pray for him, don't see him." But he saw him all the time. Woodrow was leading a double life, sacred and profane. He accepted Jesus Christ as his personal redeemer. Aunt Rebecca took advantage of this. She made him work. He had to work under Aunt Rebecca. He filled in for the janitor at the mission and settlement house. In winter, he had to feed the coal furnace, and on some nights he slept near the furnace room, on the pool table. He also picked the lock of the storeroom. He took canned pineapple and cut bacon from the flitch with his pocketknife. He crammed himself with uncooked bacon. He had a big frame to fill out.

Only now, sipping Melitta coffee, he asked himself—had he been so hungry? No, he loved being reckless. He was fighting Aunt Rebecca Kovner when he took out his knife and got on a box to reach the bacon. She didn't know, she couldn't prove that Woody, such a frank, strong, positive boy who looked you in the eye, so direct, was a thief also. But he was also a thief. Whenever she looked at him, he knew that she was seeing his father. In the curve of his nose, the movements of his eyes, the thickness of his body, in his healthy face she saw that wicked savage, Morris.

Morris, you see, had been a street boy in Liverpool—Woody's mother and her sister were British by birth. Morris's Polish family, on their way to America, abandoned him in Liverpool because he had an eye infection and they would all have been sent back from Ellis Island. They stopped awhile in England, but his eyes kept running and they ditched him. They slipped away, and he had to make out alone in Liverpool at the age of twelve. Mother came of better people. Pop, who slept in the cellar of her house, fell in love with her. At sixteen, scabbing during a seamen's strike, he shovelled his way across the Atlantic and jumped ship in Brooklyn. He became an American, and America never knew it. He voted without papers, he drove without a license, he paid no taxes, he cut every corner. Horses, cards, billiards, and women were his lifelong interests, in ascending order. Did he love anyone (he was so busy)? Yes, he loved Halina. He loved his son. To this day, Mother believed that he had loved her most and always wanted to come back. This gave her a chance to act the queen, with her plump wrists and faded Queen Victoria face. "The girls are instructed never to admit him," she said. The Empress of India, speaking.

Bell-battered Woodrow's soul was whirling this Sunday morning, indoors and out, to the past, back to his upper corner of the warehouse, laid out with such originality—the bells coming and going, metal on naked metal, until the bell circle expanded over the whole of steelmaking, oil-refining, power-producing mid-autumn South Chicago, and all its Croatians, Ukrainians, Greeks, Poles, and respectable blacks heading for their churches to hear Mass or to sing hymns.

Woody himself had been a good hymn singer. He still knew the hymns. He had testified, too. He was often sent by Aunt Rebecca to get up and tell a church full of Scandihoovians that he, a Jewish lad, accepted Jesus Christ. For this she paid him fifty cents. She made the disbursement. She was the bookkeeper, fiscal chief, general manager of the mission. The Reverend Doctor didn't know a thing about the operation. What the Doctor supplied was the fervor. He was genuine, a wonderful preacher. And what about Woody himself? He also had fervor. He was drawn to the Reverend Doctor. The Reverend Doctor taught him to lift up his eyes, gave him his higher life. Apart from this higher life, the rest was Chicago—the ways of Chicago, which came so natural that nobody thought to question them. So, for instance, in 1933 (what ancient, ancient times!) at the Century of Progress World's Fair, when Woody was a coolie and pulled a rickshaw, wearing a peaked straw hat and trotting with powerful, thick legs, while the brawny red farmers—his boozing passengers—were laughing their heads off and pestered him for whores, he, although a freshman at the seminary, saw nothing wrong, when girls asked him to steer a little business their way, in making dates and accepting tips from both sides. He necked in Grant Park with a powerful girl who had to go home quickly to nurse her baby. Smelling of milk, she rode beside him on the streetcar to the West Side, squeezing his rickshaw puller's thigh and wetting her blouse. This was the Roosevelt Road car. Then, in the apartment where she lived with her mother, he couldn't remember that there were any husbands around. What he did remember was the strong milk odor. Without inconsistency, next morning he did New Testament Greek: The light shineth in darkness—*to fos en te skotia fainei*—and the darkness comprehended it not.

And all the while he trotted between the shafts on the fairgrounds he had one idea—nothing to do with these horny giants having a big time in the city: that the goal, the project, the purpose was (and he couldn't explain why he thought so; all evidence was against it), God's idea was that this world should be a love-world, that it should eventually recover and be entirely a world of love. He wouldn't have said this to a soul, for he could see himself how stupid it was—personal and stupid. Nevertheless, there it was at the center of his feelings. And at the same time Aunt Rebecca was right when she said to him, strictly private, close to his ear even, "You're a little crook, like your father."

There was some evidence for this, or what stood for evidence to an impatient person like Rebecca. Woody matured quickly—he had to—but how could you expect a boy of seventeen, he wondered, to interpret the viewpoint, the feelings of a middle-aged woman, and one whose breast had been removed? Morris told him that this happened only to neglected women, and was a sign. Morris said that if titties were not fondled and kissed they got cancer in protest. It was a cry of the flesh. And this had seemed true to Woody. When his imagination tried the theory on the Reverend Doctor, it worked out—he couldn't see the Reverend Doctor behaving in that way to Aunt Rebecca's breasts! Morris's theory kept Woody looking from bosoms to husbands and from husbands to bosoms. He still did that. It's an exceptionally smart man who isn't marked forever by the sexual theories he hears from his father, and Woody wasn't all that smart. He knew this himself. Personally, he had gone far out of his way to do right by women in this regard. What nature demanded. He and Pop were common, thick men, but there's nobody too gross to have ideas of delicacy.

The Reverend Doctor preached, Rebecca preached, rich Mrs. Skoglund preached from Evanston, Mother preached. Pop also was on a soapbox. Everyone was doing it. Up and down Division Street, under every lamp, almost, speakers were giving out: anarchists, Socialists, Stalinists, single-taxers, Zionists, Tolstoyans, vegetarians, and fundamentalist Christian preachers—you name it. A

beef, a hope, a way of life or salvation, a protest. How was it that
the accumulated gripes of all the ages took off so when trans-
planted to America?

And that fine Swedish immigrant Aase (Osie, they pronounced
it), who had been the Skoglunds' cook and married the eldest son
to become his rich, religious widow—she supported the Reverend
Doctor. In her time she must have been built like a chorus girl.
And women seem to have lost the secret of putting up their hair
in the high basketry fence of braid she wore. Aase took Woody
under her special protection and paid his tuition at the seminary.
And Pop said . . . But on this Sunday, at peace as soon as the
bells stopped banging, this velvet autumn day when the grass was
finest and thickest, silky green: before the first frost, and the
blood in your lungs is redder than summer air can make it and
smarts with oxygen, as if the iron in your system was hungry for it,
and the chill was sticking it to you in every breath—Pop, six feet
under, would never feel this blissful sting again. The last of the
bells still had the bright air streaming with vibrations.

On weekends, the institutional vacancy of decades came back to
the warehouse and crept under the door of Woody's apartment. It
felt as empty on Sundays as churches were during the week. Before each business day, before the trucks and the crews got started,
Woody jogged five miles in his Adidas suit. Not on this day still
reserved for Pop, however. Although it was tempting to go out
and run off the grief. Being alone hit Woody hard this morning.
He thought, Me and the world; the world and me. Meaning that
there always was some activity to interpose, an errand or a visit, a
picture to paint (he was a creative amateur), a massage, a meal—a
shield between himself and that troublesome solitude which used
the world as its reservoir. But Pop! Last Tuesday, Woody had gotten into the hospital bed with Pop because he kept pulling out
the intravenous needles. Nurses stuck them back, and then
Woody astonished them all by climbing into bed to hold the
struggling old guy in his arms. "Easy, Morris, Morris, go easy."
But Pop still groped feebly for the pipes.

When the tolling stopped, Woody didn't notice that a great
lake of quiet had come over his kingdom, the Selbst Tile Warehouse. What he heard and saw was an old red Chicago streetcar,

one of those trams the color of a stockyard steer. Cars of this type went out before Pearl Harbor—clumsy, big-bellied, with tough rattan seats and brass grips for the standing passengers. Those cars used to make four stops to the mile, and ran with a wallowing motion. They stank of carbolic or ozone and throbbed when the air compressors were being charged. The conductor had his knotted signal cord to pull, and the motorman beat the foot gong with his mad heel.

Woody recognized himself on the Western Avenue line and riding through a blizzard with his father, both in sheepskins and with hands and faces raw, the snow blowing in from the rear platform when the doors opened and getting into the longitudinal cleats of the floor. There wasn't warmth enough inside to melt it. And Western Avenue was the longest car line in the world, the boosters said, as if it was a thing to brag about. Twenty-three miles long, made by a draftsman with a T-square, lined with factories, storage buildings, machine shops, used-car lots, trolley barns, gas stations, funeral parlors, six-flats, utility buildings, and junk yards, on and on from the prairies on the south to Evanston on the north. Woodrow and his father were going north to Evanston, to Howard Street, and then some, to see Mrs. Skoglund. At the end of the line they would still have about five blocks to hike. The purpose of the trip? To raise money for Pop. Pop had talked him into this. When they found out, Mother and Aunt Rebecca would be furious, and Woody was afraid, but he couldn't help it.

Morris had come and said, "Son, I'm in trouble. It's bad."

"What's bad, Pop?"

"Halina took money from her husband for me and has to put it back before old Bujak misses it. He could kill her."

"What did she do it for?"

"Son, you know how the bookies collect? They send a goon. They'll break my head open."

"Pop! You know I can't take you to Mrs. Skoglund."

"Why not? You're my kid, aren't you? The old broad wants to adopt you, doesn't she? Shouldn't I get something out of it for my trouble? What am I—outside? And what about Halina? She puts her life on the line, but my own kid says no."

"Oh, Bujak wouldn't hurt her."

"Woody, he'd beat her to death."

Bujak? Uniform in color with his dark-gray work clothes, short in the legs, his whole strength in his tool-and-die-maker's forearms and black fingers; and beat-looking—there was Bujak for you. But, according to Pop, there was big, big violence in Bujak, a regular boiling Bessemer inside his narrow chest. Woody could never see the violence in him. Bujak wanted no trouble. If anything, maybe he was afraid that Morris and Halina would gang up on him and kill him, screaming. But Pop was no desperado murderer. And Halina was a calm, serious woman. Bujak kept his savings in the cellar (banks were going out of business). The worst they did was to take some of his money, intending to put it back. As Woody saw him, Bujak was trying to be sensible. He accepted his sorrow. He set minimum requirements for Halina: cook the meals, clean the house, show respect. But at stealing Bujak might have drawn the line, for money was different, money was vital substance. If they stole his savings he might have had to take action, out of respect for the substance, for himself—self-respect. But you couldn't be sure that Pop hadn't invented the bookie, the goon, the theft— the whole thing. He was capable of it, and you'd be a fool not to suspect him. Morris knew that Mother and Aunt Rebecca had told Mrs. Skoglund how wicked he was. They had painted him for her in poster colors—purple for vice, black for his soul, red for Hell flames: a gambler, smoker, drinker, deserter, screwer of women, and atheist. So Pop was determined to reach her. It was risky for everybody. The Reverend Doctor's operating costs were met by Skoglund Dairies. The widow paid Woody's seminary tuition; she bought dresses for the little sisters.

Woody, now sixty, fleshy and big, like a figure for the victory of American materialism, sunk in his lounge chair, the leather of its armrests softer to his fingertips than a woman's skin, was puzzled and, in his depths, disturbed by certain blots within him, blots of light in his brain, a blot combining pain and amusement in his breast (how did *that* get there?). Intense thought puckered the skin between his eyes with a strain bordering on headache. Why had he let Pop have his way? Why did he agree to meet him that day, in the dim rear of the poolroom?

"But what will you tell Mrs. Skoglund?"

"The old broad? Don't worry, there's plenty to tell her, and it's all true. Ain't I trying to save my little laundry-and-cleaning shop?

Isn't the bailiff coming for the fixtures next week?" And Pop rehearsed his pitch on the Western Avenue car. He counted on
Woody's health and his freshness. Such a straightforward-looking
boy was perfect for a con.

Did they still have such winter storms in Chicago as they used
to have? Now they somehow seemed less fierce. Blizzards used to
come straight down from Ontario, from the Arctic, and drop five
feet of snow in an afternoon. Then the rusty green platform cars,
with revolving brushes at both ends, came out of the barns to
sweep the tracks. Ten or twelve streetcars followed in slow proces-
sions, or waited, block after block.

There was a long delay at the gates of Riverview Park, all the
amusements covered for the winter, boarded up—the dragon's-
back high-rides, the Bobs, the Chute, the Tilt-a-Whirl, all the fun
machinery put together by mechanics and electricians, men like
Bujak the tool-and-die-maker, good with engines. The blizzard
was having it all its own way behind the gates, and you couldn't
see far inside; only a few bulbs burned behind the palings. When
Woody wiped the vapor from the glass, the wire mesh of the window guards was stuffed solid at eye level with snow. Looking
higher, you saw mostly the streaked wind horizontally driving
from the north. In the seat ahead, two black coal heavers both in
leather Lindbergh flying helmets sat with shovels between their
legs, returning from a job. They smelled of sweat, burlap sacking,
and coal. Mostly dull with black dust, they also sparkled here and
there.

There weren't many riders. People weren't leaving the house.
This was a day to sit legs stuck out beside the stove, mummified
by both the outdoor and the indoor forces. Only a fellow with an
angle, like Pop, would go and buck such weather. A storm like
this was out of the compass, and you kept the human scale by
having a scheme to raise fifty bucks. Fifty soldiers! Real money in
1933.

"That woman is crazy for you," said Pop.

"She's just a good woman, sweet to all of us."

"Who knows what she's got in mind. You're a husky kid. Not
such a kid either."

"She's a religious woman. She really has religion."

"Well, your mother isn't your only parent. She and Rebecca

and Kovner aren't going to fill you up with their ideas. I know your mother wants to wipe me out of your life. Unless I take a hand, you won't even understand what life is. Because they don't know—those silly Christers."

"Yes Pop."

"The girls I can't help. They're too young. I'm sorry about them, but I can't do anything. With you it's different."

He wanted me like himself, an American.

They were stalled in the storm, while the cattle-colored car waited to have the trolley reset in the crazy wind, which boomed, tingled, blasted. At Howard Street they would have to walk straight into it, due north.

"You'll do the talking at first," said Pop.

Woody had the makings of a salesman, a pitchman. He was aware of this when he got to his feet in church to testify before fifty or sixty people. Even though Aunt Rebecca made it worth his while, he moved his own heart when he spoke up about his faith. But occasionally, without notice, his heart went away as he spoke religion and he couldn't find it anywhere. In its absence, sincere behavior got him through. He had to rely for delivery on his face, his voice—on behavior. Then his eyes came closer and closer together. And in this approach of eye to eye he felt the strain of hypocrisy. The twisting of his face threatened to betray him. It took everything he had to keep looking honest. So, since he couldn't bear the cynicism of it, he fell back on mischievousness. Mischief was where Pop came in. Pop passed straight through all those divided fields, gap after gap, and arrived at his side, bent-nosed and broad-faced. In regard to Pop, you thought of neither sincerity nor insincerity. Pop was like the man in the song: he wanted what he wanted when he wanted it. Pop was physical; Pop was digestive, circulatory, sexual. If Pop got serious, he talked to you about washing under the arms or in the crotch or of drying between your toes or of cooking supper, of baked beans and fried onions, of draw poker or of a certain horse in the fifth race at Arlington. Pop was elemental. That was why he gave such relief from religion and paradoxes, and things like that. Now Mother *thought* she was spiritual, but Woody knew that she was kidding herself. Oh, yes, in the British accent she never gave up she was always talking to God or about Him—please-God, God-willing, praise-God. But she was a big substantial bread-and-butter, down-to-earth woman, with down-to-earth duties like feeding the girls, protecting, refining, keeping pure the girls. And those two protected doves grew up so overweight, heavy in the hips and thighs, that their poor heads looked long and slim. And mad. Sweet but cuckoo—Paula cheerfully cuckoo, Joanna depressed and having episodes.

"I'll do my best by you, but you have to promise, Pop, not to get me in Dutch with Mrs. Skoglund."

"You worried because I speak bad English? Embarrassed? I have a mockie accent?"

"It's not that. Kovner has a heavy accent, and she doesn't mind."

"Who the hell are those freaks to look down on me? You're practically a man and your dad has a right to expect help from you. He's in a fix. And you bring him to her house because she's big-hearted, and you haven't got anybody else to go to."

"I got you, Pop."

The two coal trimmers stood up at Devon Avenue. One of them wore a woman's coat. Men wore women's clothing in those years, and women men's, when there was no choice. The fur collar was spiky with the wet, and sprinkled with soot. Heavy, they dragged their shovels and got off at the front. The slow car ground on, very slow. It was after four when they reached the end of the line, and somewhere between gray and black, with snow spouting and whirling under the street lamps. In Howard Street, autos were stalled at all angles and abandoned. The sidewalks were blocked. Woody led the way into Evanston, and Pop followed him up the middle of the street in the furrows made earlier by trucks. For four blocks they bucked the wind and then Woody broke through the drifts to the snowbound mansion, where they both had to push the wrought-iron gate because of the drift behind it. Twenty rooms or more in this dignified house and nobody in them but Mrs. Skoglund and her servant Hjordis, also religious.

As Woody and Pop waited, brushing the slush from their sheepskin collars and Pop wiping his big eyebrows with the ends of his scarf, sweating and freezing, the chains began to rattle and Hjordis uncovered the air holes of the glass storm door by turning a wooden bar. Woody called her "monk-faced." You no longer see

women like that, who put no female touch on the face. She came
plain, as God made her. She said, "Who is it and what do you
want?"

"It's Woodrow Selbst. Hjordis? It's Woody."

"You're not expected."

"No, but we're here."

"What do you want?"

"We came to see Mrs. Skoglund."

"What for do you want to see her?"

"Just to tell her we're here."

"I have to tell her what you came for, without calling up first."

"Why don't you say it's Woody with his father, and we
wouldn't come in a snowstorm like this if it wasn't important."

The understandable caution of women who live alone. Respectable old-time women, too. There was no such respectability now
in those Evanston houses, with their big verandas and deep yards
and with a servant like Hjordis, who carried at her belt keys to the
pantry and to every closet and every dresser drawer and every pad-
locked bin in the cellar. And in High Episcopal Christian Science
Women's Temperance Evanston no tradespeople rang at the
front door. Only invited guests. And here, after a ten-mile grind
through the blizzard, came two tramps from the West Side. To
this mansion where a Swedish immigrant lady, herself once a cook
and now a philanthropic widow, dreamed, snowbound, while frozen lilac twigs clapped at her storm windows, of a new Jerusalem
and a Second Coming and a Resurrection and a Last Judgment.
To hasten the Second Coming, and all the rest, you had to reach
the hearts of these scheming bums arriving in a snowstorm.

Sure, they let us in.

Then in the heat that swam suddenly up to their muffled
chins Pop and Woody felt the blizzard for what it was; their
cheeks were frozen slabs. They stood beat, itching, trickling in the
front hall that *was* a hall, with a carved newel post staircase and a
big stained-glass window at the top. Picturing Jesus with the Sa-
maritan woman. There was a kind of Gentile closeness to the air.
Perhaps when he was with Pop, Woody made more Jewish obser-
vations than he would otherwise. Although Pop's most Jewish
characteristic was that Yiddish was the only language he could
read a paper in. Pop was with Polish Halina, and Mother was

with Jesus Christ, and Woody ate uncooked bacon from the flitch. Still now and then he had a Jewish impression.

Mrs. Skoglund was the cleanest of women—her fingernails, her white neck, her ears—and Pop's sexual hints to Woody all went wrong because she was so intensely clean, and made Woody think of a waterfall, large as she was, and grandly built. Her bust was big. Woody's imagination had investigated this. He thought she kept things tied down tight, very tight. But she lifted both arms once to raise a window and there it was, her bust, beside him, the whole unbindable thing. Her hair was like the raffia you had to soak before you could weave with it in a basket class—pale, pale. Pop, as he took his sheepskin off, was in sweaters, no jacket. His darting looks made him seem crooked. Hardest of all for these Selbsts with their bent noses and big, apparently straightforward faces was to look honest. All the signs of dishonesty played over them. Woody had often puzzled about it. Did it go back to the muscles, was it fundamentally a jaw problem—the projecting angles of the jaws? Or was it the angling that went on in the heart? The girls called Pop Dick Tracy, but Dick Tracy was a good guy. Whom could Pop convince? Here, Woody caught a possibility as it flitted by. Precisely because of the way Pop looked, a sensitive person might feel remorse for condemning unfairly or judging unkindly. Just because of a face? Some must have bent over backward. Then he had them. Not Hjordis. She would have put Pop into the street then and there, storm or no storm. Hjordis was religious, but she was wised up, too. She hadn't come over in steerage and worked forty years in Chicago for nothing.

Mrs. Skoglund, Aase (Osie), led the visitors into the front room. This, the biggest room in the house, needed supplementary heating. Because of fifteen-foot ceilings and high windows, Hjordis had kept the parlor stove burning. It was one of those elegant parlor stoves that wore a nickel crown, or mitre, and this mitre, when you moved it aside, automatically raised the hinge of an iron stove lid. That stove lid underneath the crown was all soot and rust, the same as any other stove lid. Into this hole you tipped the scuttle and the anthracite chestnut rattled down. It made a cake or dome of fire visible through the small isinglass frames. It was a pretty room, three-quarters panelled in wood. The stove was plugged into the flue of the marble fireplace, and there were par-

quet floors and Axminster carpets and cranberry-colored tufted
Victorian upholstery, and a kind of Chinese étagère, inside a cabinet, lined with mirrors and containing silver pitchers, trophies
won by Skoglund cows, fancy sugar tongs and cut-glass pitchers
and goblets. There were Bibles and pictures of Jesus and the Holy
Land and that faint Gentile odor, as if things had been rinsed in a
weak vinegar solution.

"Mrs. Skoglund, I brought my dad to you. I don't think you
ever met him," said Woody.

"Yes, Missus, that's me, Selbst."

Pop stood short but masterful in the sweaters, and his belly
sticking out, not soft but hard. He was a man of the hard-bellied
type. Nobody intimidated Pop. He never presented himself as a
beggar. There wasn't a cringe in him anywhere. He let her see at
once by the way he said "Missus" that he was independent and
that he knew his way around. He communicated that he was able
to handle himself with women. Handsome Mrs. Skoglund, carrying a basket woven out of her own hair, was in her fifties—eight,
maybe ten years his senior.

"I asked my son to bring me because I know you do the kid a
lot of good. It's natural you should know both of his parents."

"Mrs. Skoglund, my dad is in a tight corner and I don't know
anybody else to ask for help."

This was all the preliminary Pop wanted. He took over and told
the widow his story about the laundry-and-cleaning business and
payments overdue, and explained about the fixtures and the at-
tachment notice, and the bailiff's office and what they were going
to do to him; and he said, "I'm a small man trying to make a
living."

"You don't support your children," said Mrs. Skoglund.

"That's right," said Hjordis.

"I haven't got it. If I had it, wouldn't I give it? There's bread
lines and soup lines all over town. Is it just me? What I have I
divvy with. I give the kids. A bad father? You think my son would
bring me if I was a bad father into your house? He loves his dad,
he trusts his dad, he knows his dad is a good dad. Every time I
start a little business going I get wiped out. This one is a good little business, if I could hold on to that little business. Three people work for me, I meet a payroll, and three people will be on the

street, too, if I close down. Missus, I can sign a note and pay you in two months. I'm a common man, but I'm a hard worker and a fellow you can trust."

Woody was startled when Pop used the word "trust." It was as if from all four corners a Sousa band blew a blast to warn the entire world. "Crook! This is a crook!" But Mrs. Skoglund, on account of her religious preoccupations, was remote. She heard nothing. Although everybody in this part of the world, unless he was crazy, led a practical life, and you'd have nothing to say to anyone, your neighbors would have nothing to say to you if communications were not of a practical sort, Mrs. Skoglund, with all her money, was unworldly—two-thirds out of this world.

"Give me a chance to show what's in me," said Pop, "and you'll see what I do for my kids."

So Mrs. Skoglund hesitated, and then she said she'd have to go upstairs, she'd have to go to her room and pray on it and ask for guidance—would they sit down and wait. There were two rocking chairs by the stove. Hjordis gave Pop a grim look (a dangerous person) and Woody a blaming one (he brought a dangerous stranger and disrupter to injure two kind Christian ladies). Then she went out with Mrs. Skoglund.

As soon as they left, Pop jumped up from the rocker and said in anger, "What's this with the praying? She has to ask God to lend me fifty bucks?"

Woody said, "It's not you, Pop, it's the way these religious people do."

"No," said Pop. "She'll come back and say that God wouldn't let her."

Woody didn't like that; he thought Pop was being gross and he said, "No, she's sincere. Pop, try to understand; she's emotional, nervous, and sincere, and tries to do right by everybody."

And Pop said, "That servant will talk her out of it. She's a toughie. It's all over her face that we're a couple of chisellers."

"What's the use of us arguing," said Woody. He drew the rocker closer to the stove. His shoes were wet through and would never dry. The blue flames fluttered like a school of fishes in the coal fire. But Pop went over to the Chinese-style cabinet or étagère and tried the handle, and then opened the blade of his penknife and in a second had forced the lock of the curved glass door. He took out a silver dish.

"Pop, what is this?" said Woody.

Pop, cool and level, knew exactly what this was. He relocked the étagère, crossed the carpet, listened. He stuffed the dish under his belt and pushed it down into his trousers. He put the side of his short thick finger to his mouth.

So Woody kept his voice down, but he was all shook up. He went to Pop and took him by the edge of his hand. As he looked into Pop's face, he felt his eyes growing smaller and smaller, as if something were contracting all the skin on his head. They call it hyperventilation when everything feels tight and light and close and dizzy. Hardly breathing, he said, "Put it back, Pop."

Pop said, "It's solid silver; it's worth dough."

"Pop, you said you wouldn't get me in Dutch."

"It's only insurance in case she comes back from praying and tells me no. If she says yes, I'll put it back."

"How?"

"It'll get back. If I don't put it back, you will."

"You picked the lock. I couldn't. I don't know how."

"There's nothing to it."

"We're going to put it back now. Give it here."

"Woody, it's under my fly, inside my underpants, don't make such a noise about nothing."

"Pop, I can't believe this."

"For Cry-99, shut your mouth. If I didn't trust you I wouldn't have let you watch me do it. You don't understand a thing. What's with you?"

"Before they come down, Pop, will you dig that dish out of your long johns."

Pop turned stiff on him. He became absolutely military. He said, "Look, I order you!"

Before he knew it, Woody had jumped his father and begun to wrestle with him. It was outrageous to clutch your own father, to put a heel behind him, to force him to the wall. Pop was taken by surprise and said loudly, "You want Halina killed? Kill her! Go on, you be responsible." He began to resist, angry, and they turned about several times when Woody, with a trick he had learned in a Western movie and used once on the playground, tripped him and they fell to the ground. Woody, who already outweighed the old man by twenty pounds, was on the top. They landed on the floor beside the stove, which stood on a tray of decorated tin to protect the carpet. In this position, pressing Pop's hard belly, Woody recognized that to have wrestled him to the floor counted for nothing. It was impossible to thrust his hand under Pop's belt to recover the dish. And now Pop had turned furious, as a father has every right to be when his son is violent with him, and he freed his hand and hit Woody in the face. He hit him three or four times in mid-face. Then Woody dug his head into Pop's shoulder and held tight only to keep from being struck and began to say in his ear, "Jesus, Pop, for Christ sake remember where you are. Those women will be back!" But Pop brought up his short knee and fought and butted him with his chin and rattled Woody's teeth. Woody thought the old man was about to bite him. And, because he was a seminarian, he thought, "Like an unclean spirit." And held tight. Gradually Pop stopped threshing and struggling. His eyes stuck out and his mouth was open, sullen. Like a stout fish. Woody released him and gave him a hand up. He was then overcome with many many bad feelings of a sort he knew the old man never suffered. Never, never. Pop never had these grovelling emotions. There was his whole superiority. Pop had no such feelings. He was like a horseman from Central Asia, a bandit from China. It was Mother, from Liverpool, who had the refinement, the English manners. It was the preaching Reverend Doctor in his black suit. You have refinements, and all they do is oppress you? The hell with that.

The long door opened and Mrs. Skoglund stepped in, saying, "Did I imagine, or did something shake the house?"

"I was lifting the scuttle to put coal on the fire and it fell out of my hand. I'm sorry I was so clumsy," said Woody.

Pop was too huffy to speak. With his eyes big and sore and the thin hair down over his forehead, you could see by the tightness of his belly how angrily he was fetching his breath, though his mouth was shut.

"I prayed," said Mrs. Skoglund.

"I hope it came out well," said Woody.

"Well, I don't do anything without guidance, but the answer was yes, and I feel right about it now. So if you'll wait I'll go to my office and write a check. I asked Hjordis to bring you a cup of coffee. Coming in such a storm."

And Pop, consistently a terrible little man, as soon as she shut the door said, "A check? Hell with a check. Get me the greenbacks."

"They don't keep money in the house. You can cash it in her bank tomorrow. But if they miss that dish, Pop, they'll stop the check, and then where are you?"

As Pop was reaching below the belt Hjordis brought in the tray. She was very sharp with him. She said, "Is this a place to adjust clothing, Mister? A men's washroom?"

"Well, which way is the toilet, then?" said Pop.

She had served the coffee in the seamiest mugs in the pantry, and she bumped down the tray and led Pop down the corridor, standing guard at the bathroom door so that he shouldn't wander about the house.

Mrs. Skoglund called Woody to her office and after she had given him the folded check said that they should pray together for Morris. So once more he was on his knees, under rows and rows of musty marbled cardboard files, by the glass lamp by the edge of the desk, the shade with flounced edges, like the candy dish. Mrs. Skoglund, in her Scandinavian accent—an emotional contralto—raising her voice to Jesus-uh Christ-uh, as the wind lashed the trees, kicked the side of the house, and drove the snow seething on the windowpanes, to send light-uh, give guidance-uh, put a new heart-uh in Pop's bosom. Woody asked God only to make Pop put the dish back. He kept Mrs. Skoglund on her knees as long as possible. Then he thanked her, shining with candor (as much as he knew how) for her Christian generosity and he said, "I know that Hjordis has a cousin who works at the Evanston Y.M.C.A. Could she please phone him and try to get us a room tonight so that we don't have to fight the blizzard all the way back? We're almost as close to the Y as to the car line. Maybe the cars have even stopped running."

Suspicious Hjordis, coming when Mrs. Skoglund called to her, was burning now. First they barged in, made themselves at home, asked for money, had to have coffee, probably left gonorrhea on the toilet seat. Hjordis, Woody remembered, was a woman who wiped the doorknobs with rubbing alcohol after guests had left.

Nevertheless, she telephoned the Y and got them a room with two cots for six bits.

Pop had plenty of time, therefore, to reopen the étagère, lined with reflecting glass or German silver (something exquisitely delicate and tricky), and as soon as the two Selbsts had said thank you and goodbye and were in mid-street again up to the knees in snow, Woody said, "Well, I covered for you. Is that thing back?"

"Of course it is," said Pop.

They fought their way to the small Y building, shut up in wire grille and resembling a police station—about the same dimensions. It was locked, but they made a racket on the grille, and a small black man let them in and shuffled them upstairs to a cement corridor with low doors. It was like the small mammal house in Lincoln Park. He said there was nothing to eat, so they took off their wet pants, wrapped themselves tightly in the khaki army blankets, and passed out on their cots.

First thing in the morning, they went to the Evanston National Bank and got the fifty dollars. Not without difficulties. The teller went to call Mrs. Skoglund and was absent a long time from the wicket. "Where the hell has he gone," said Pop.

But when the fellow came back he said, "How do you want it?"

Pop said, "Singles." He told Woody, "Bujak stashes it in one-dollar bills."

But by now Woody no longer believed Halina had stolen the old man's money.

Then they went into the street, where the snow-removal crews were at work. The sun shone broad, broad, out of the morning blue, and all Chicago would be releasing itself from the temporary beauty of those vast drifts.

"You shouldn't have jumped me last night, Sonny."

"I know, Pop, but you promised you wouldn't get me in Dutch."

"Well, it's O.K., we can forget it, seeing you stood by me."

Only, Pop had taken the silver dish. Of course he had, and in a few days Mrs. Skoglund and Hjordis knew it, and later in the week they were all waiting for Woody in Kovner's office at the settlement house. The group included the Reverend Dr. Crabbie, head of the seminary, and Woody, who had been flying along, level and smooth, was shot down in flames. He told them he was innocent. Even as he was falling, he warned that they were wrong-ing him. He denied that he or Pop had touched Mrs. Skoglund's property. The missing object—he didn't even know what it was—had probably been misplaced, and they would be very sorry on the day it turned up. After the others were done with him, Dr. Crab-bie said until he was able to tell the truth he would be suspended from the seminary, where his work had been unsatisfactory any-way. Aunt Rebecca took him aside and said to him, "You are a little crook, like your father. The door is closed to you here."

To this Pop's comment was "So what, kid?"

"Pop, you shouldn't have done it."

"No? Well, I don't give a care, if you want to know. You can have the dish if you want to go back and square yourself with all those hypocrites."

"I didn't like doing Mrs. Skoglund in the eye, she was so kind to us."

"Kind?"

"Kind."

"Kind has a price tag."

Well, there was no winning such arguments with Pop. But they debated it in various moods and from various elevations and per-spectives for forty years and more, as their intimacy changed, de-veloped, matured.

"Why did you do it, Pop? For the money? What did you do with the fifty bucks?" Woody, decades later, asked him that.

"I settled with the bookie, and the rest I put in the business."

"You tried a few more horses."

"I maybe did. But it was a double, Woody. I didn't hurt my-self, and at the same time did you a favor."

"It was for me?"

"It was too strange of a life. That life wasn't *you*, Woody. All those women—Kovner was no man, he was an in-between. Sup-pose they made you a minister? Some Christian minister! First of all, you wouldn't have been able to stand it, and, second, they would throw you out sooner or later."

"Maybe so."

"And you wouldn't have converted the Jews, which was the main thing they wanted."

"And what a time to bother the Jews," Woody said. "At least *I* didn't bug them."

Pop had carried him back to his side of the line, blood of his blood, the same thick body walls, the same coarse grain. Not cut out for a spiritual life. Simply not up to it.

Pop was no worse than Woody, and Woody was no better than Pop. Pop wanted no relation to theory, and yet he was always pointing Woody toward a position—a jolly, hearty, natural, likable, unprincipled position. If Woody had a weakness, it was to be unselfish. This worked to Pop's advantage, but he criticized Woody for it, nevertheless. "You take too much on yourself," Pop was always saying. And it's true that Woody gave Pop his heart because Pop was so selfish. It's usually the selfish people who are loved the most. They do what you deny yourself, and you love them for it. You give them your heart.

Remembering the pawn ticket for the silver dish, Woody startled himself with a laugh so sudden that it made him cough. Pop said to him after his expulsion from the seminary and banishment from the settlement house, "You want in again? Here's the ticket. I hocked that thing. It wasn't so valuable as I thought."

"What did they give?"

"Twelve-fifty was all I could get. But if you want it you'll have to raise the dough yourself, because I haven't got it anymore."

"You must have been sweating in the bank when the teller went to call Mrs. Skoglund about the check."

"I was a little nervous," said Pop. "But I didn't think they could miss the thing so soon."

That theft was part of Pop's war with Mother. With Mother, and Aunt Rebecca, and the Reverend Doctor. Pop took his stand on realism. Mother represented the forces of religion and hypochondria. In four decades, the fighting never stopped. In the course of time, Mother and the girls turned into welfare personalities and lost their individual outlines. Ah, the poor things, they became dependents and cranks. In the meantime, Woody, the sinful man, was their dutiful and loving son and brother. He maintained the bungalow—this took in roofing, pointing, wiring, insulation, air-conditioning—and he paid for heat and light and food, and dressed them all out of Sears, Roebuck and Wieboldt's, and

bought them a TV, which they watched as devoutly as they
prayed. Paula took courses to learn skills like macramé-making
and needlepoint, and sometimes got a little job as recreational
worker in a nursing home. But she wasn't steady enough to keep
it. Wicked Pop spent most of his life removing stains from people's clothing. He and Halina in the last years ran a Cleanomat in
West Rogers Park—a so-so business resembling a laundromat—
which gave him leisure for billiards, the horses, rummy and pi-
nochle. Every morning he went behind the partition to check out
the filters of the cleaning equipment. He found amusing things
that had been thrown into the vats with the clothing—sometimes,
when he got lucky, a locket chain or a brooch. And when he had
fortified the cleaning fluid, pouring all that blue and pink stuff in
from plastic jugs, he read the *Forward* over a second cup of coffee,
and went out, leaving Halina in charge. When they needed help
with the rent, Woody gave it.

After the new Disney World was opened in Florida, Woody
treated all his dependents to a holiday. He sent them down in separate batches, of course. Halina enjoyed this more than anybody
else. She couldn't stop talking about the address given by an
Abraham Lincoln automaton. "Wonderful, how he stood up and
moved his hands, and his mouth. So real! And how beautiful he
talked." Of them all, Halina was the soundest, the most human,
the most honest. Now that Pop was gone, Woody and Halina's
son, Mitosh, the organist at the Stadium, took care of her needs
over and above Social Security, splitting expenses. In Pop's opinion, insurance was a racket. He left Halina nothing but some out-
of-date equipment.

Woody treated himself, too. Once a year, and sometimes of-
tener, he left his business to run itself, arranged with the trust department at the bank to take care of his Gang, and went off. He
did that in style, imaginatively, expensively. In Japan, he wasted
little time on Tokyo. He spent three weeks in Kyoto and stayed at
the Tawaraya Inn, dating from the seventeenth century or so.
There he slept on the floor, the Japanese way, and bathed in
scalding water. He saw the dirtiest strip show on earth, as well as
the holy places and the temple gardens. He visited also Istanbul,
Jerusalem, Delphi, and went to Burma and Uganda and Kenya on
safari, on democratic terms with drivers, Bedouins, bazaar mer-

chants. Open, lavish, familiar, fleshier and fleshier but (he jogged, he lifted weights) still muscular—in his naked person beginning to resemble a Renaissance courtier in full costume—becoming ruddier every year, an outdoor type with freckles on his back and spots across the flaming forehead and the honest nose. In Addis Ababa he took an Ethiopian beauty to his room from the street and washed her, getting into the shower with her to soap her with his broad, kindly hands. In Kenya he taught certain American obscenities to a black woman so that she could shout them out during the act. On the Nile, below Murchison Falls, those fever trees rose huge from the mud, and hippos on the sandbars belched at the passing launch, hostile. One of them danced on his spit of sand, springing from the ground and coming down heavy, on all fours. There, Woody saw the buffalo calf disappear, snatched by the crocodile.

Mother, soon to follow Pop, was being light-headed these days. In company, she spoke of Woody as her boy—"What do you think of my Sonny?"—as though he was ten years old. She was silly with him, her behavior was frivolous, almost flirtatious. She just didn't seem to know the facts. And behind her all the others, like kids at the playground, were waiting their turn to go down the slide; one on each step, and moving toward the top.

Over Woody's residence and place of business there had gathered a pool of silence of the same perimeter as the church bells while they were ringing, and he mourned under it, this melancholy morning of sun and autumn. Doing a life survey, taking a deliberate look at the gross side of his case—of the other side as well, what there was of it. But if this heartache continued, he'd go out and run it off. A three-mile jog—five, if necessary. And you'd think that this jogging was an entirely physical activity, wouldn't you? But there was something else in it. Because, when he was a seminarian, between the shafts of his World's Fair rickshaw, he used to receive, pulling along (capable and stable), his religious experiences while he trotted. Maybe it was all a single experience repeated. He felt truth coming to him from the sun. He received a communication that was also light and warmth. It made him very remote from his horny Wisconsin passengers, those farmers whose whoops and whore-cries he could hardly hear when he was in one of his states. And again out of the flaming of the sun would come

to him a secret certainty that the goal set for this earth was that it
should be filled with good, saturated with it. After everything preposterous, after dog had eaten dog, after the crocodile death had
pulled everyone into his mud. It wouldn't conclude as Mrs. Skoglund, bribing him to round up the Jews and hasten the Second
Coming, imagined it but in another way. This was his clumsy intuition. It went no further. Subsequently, he proceeded through
life as life seemed to want him to do it.

There remained one thing more this morning, which was explic-
itly physical, occurring first as a sensation in his arms and against
his breast and, from the pressure, passing into him and going into
his breast.

It was like this: When he came into the hospital room and saw
Pop with the sides of his bed raised, like a crib, and Pop, so very
feeble, and writhing, and toothless, like a baby, and the dirt already cast into his face, into the wrinkles—Pop wanted to pluck
out the intravenous needles and he was piping his weak death
noise. The gauze patches taped over the needles were soiled with
dark blood. Then Woody took off his shoes, lowered the side of
the bed, and climbed in and held him in his arms to soothe and
still him. As if he were Pop's father, he said to him, "Now Pop.
Pop." Then it was like the wrestle in Mrs. Skoglund's parlor, when
Pop turned angry like an unclean spirit and Woody tried to ap-
pease him, and warn him, saying, "Those women will be back!"
Beside the coal stove, when Pop hit Woody in the teeth with his
head and then became sullen, like a stout fish. But this struggle in
the hospital was weak—so weak! In his great pity, Woody held
Pop, who was fluttering and shivering. From those people, Pop
had told him, you'll never find out what life is, because they don't
know what it is. Yes, Pop—well, what is it, Pop? Hard to comprehend that Pop, who was dug in for eighty-three years and had
done all he could to stay, should now want nothing but to free
himself. How could Woody allow the old man to pull the intravenous needles out? Willful Pop, he wanted what he wanted when
he wanted it. But what he wanted at the very last Woody failed
to follow, it was such a switch.

After a time, Pop's resistance ended. He subsided and subsided.
He rested against his son, his small body curled there. Nurses
came and looked. They disapproved, but Woody, who couldn't

spare a hand to wave them out, motioned with his head toward the door. Pop, whom Woody thought he had stilled, only had found a better way to get around him. Loss of heat was the way he did it. His heat was leaving him. As can happen with small animals while you hold them in your hand, Woody presently felt him cooling. Then, as Woody did his best to restrain him, and thought he was succeeding, Pop divided himself. And when he was separated from his warmth he slipped into death. And there was his elderly, large, muscular son, still holding and pressing him when there was nothing anymore to press. You could never pin down that self-willed man. When he was ready to make his move, he made it—always on his own terms. And always, always, something up his sleeve. That was how he was.

WOMEN
IN A ROMAN COURTYARD

NANCY HALLINAN

Nancy Hallinan is the author of three novels: *Rough Winds Of May*, *A Voice From The Wings*, and *Night Swimmers* (1976). Her short stories have appeared in such diverse periodicals as *Cosmopolitan*, *The Smith*, and *Harper's Magazine*. She was born in London, England, and came to America at the age of seventeen and stayed. She now lives in New York City.

"Thieves?" Katherine said. "Thieves *again?*"

"*Ladri! Sì, ladri!*" Lucia cried, brandishing her string shopping bag.

Every day Lucia was robbed by thieves. The accusation never varied, and was actually a summons. Every day Katherine Cardew obeyed it and ran downstairs, hoping for a letter and a check, but prepared to listen to Lucia's ceremonial choler. Lucia was their landlady and therefore powerful. If not properly attended she might lock the hot water faucet or remove a fuse and plunge the house in darkness, or fill the refrigerator with fish. Today's diatribe had to do with the cost of American instant puddings, on which the landlady's old mother depended for her life. Katherine appreciated the high cost of living in Rome, and she naturally sided with the helpless, but today she was more anxious for herself. Two weeks, and no word from Daniel. She knew that the postman came at about his hour, ten chimes from the seminary up the hill. Then she noticed the pocket to Lucia's dress. It contained two letters.

"*Niente lettere?*" she asked, hinting.

Lucia continued her harangue. Katherine struggled to understand the connection between Lucia's mother's stomach and the post office strike, which had just begun or just ended. She waited in some suspense. Daniel had been gone for two whole weeks. They had quarreled before, but always made up. Now she felt a vague panic that maybe he'd gone forever, leaving her to manage two small children, one persecuted landlady and her dying mother, and the annihilating heat of a Roman summer. She pointed to Lucia's pocket.

"*Niente lettere?*" she repeated. "From the Signor Cardew?"

"*No. Non c'é niente!*"

Lucia clutched the letters to her bosom. Oh, the sinful films being made in Rome! *Sí!* The work of the American *studenti* and illicit relations in sleeping bags beneath the very portals of the Vatican! The poor Pope. . . . Katherine felt her mind buckle beneath Lucia's eloquence. She gave up trying to translate, and hoarded her strength in an effort at patience. She thought she glimpsed Daniel's handwriting, but the ink was an unfamiliar brown. Lucia continued. Oh, but the polluted Tiber! Katherine nodded.

"*Sí, Signora . . .*"

The Signora Lucia Felici wore a gold wedding ring embedded in a fleshy finger, but there was no mention of the Signor Felici, and Katherine guessed he'd run off years ago. Sometimes she doubted his existence altogether. Who would marry such a woman? Her eyes were small and black; her chin jutted out and its brown mole sprouted long hairs. Anger carved her features, and perhaps her hair. Lucia cut this black mop at whim, with a knife and without a mirror. She was huge, as though with child. Yet despite this maternal bulk she had a curiously virginal quality. She wore floral-patterned wraparound dresses, her heavy legs sheathed in mauve stockings. She could be thirty, forty, fifty.

"*Niente lettere!*" she said with sudden malice. "No letter!"

Lucia despised Daniel, possibly all men. But why was she so mysteriously persecuted? And why, in this country of long siestas, was she always rushing? She thundered up and down the stairs, carrying puddings, a bedpan, soiled linen. She rushed to the factory where she worked by the hour, making artificial flowers. She rushed to and from the market, carrying her string bag of bargains. Now she used the letters as a fan and denounced the summer sun. Katherine's patience vanished. It was no wonder Lucia lived alone and had no visitors. She was a spinster by choice, angry at the whole universe.

"*Niente, niente lettere!*"

Lucia fanned herself vigorously. Katherine felt humiliated, watching. Lucia had the letters and the largess. Lucia could grant privileges or refuse them; her home was not a *pensione*. Tucked away from the main thoroughfare, it squatted sideways in a cul-de-sac at the end of an alley. It was a privilege to rent the two rooms on the second floor, and have the use of the new bathroom with the pink bidet that the children considered their own private fountain.

Lucia pocketed the letters. Katherine's humiliation changed to mutiny. She felt a crazy urge to snatch the letters and make off with them. She could certainly outrun Lucia, but where would she run? Upstairs to her rooms where the children were playing? (Were they all right?) Up another flight to the attic where Lucia's old mother lay ingesting American puddings? (Was she really dying?) Or into the empty parlor on the ground floor, daily vacuumed but never used? (Why the disconnected telephone on the rickety table?) Or into the room occupied by Lucia's other boarder, a musician who slept during the day and played the clarinet at night? (Where, in what sinful spot?) Lucia's closet-sized bedroom was near the stairs that led to the spacious kitchen with its two stoves, two huge sinks, and noisy refrigerator. . . .

"I am expecting a letter!" Katherine shouted suddenly.

"*Silenzio!*"

Katherine obeyed. But why this order? What emergency? The children? Or Lucia's mother? Suddenly the silence was broken. The musician was practicing his clarinet. A scale ran up and down two octaves, softly, like a lullaby. It sang to her intimately. Then she heard an earsplitting blast: his warning to both women to stop shouting and let him sleep.

"What's his name?" Katherine whispered. "We've never met."

Lucia spoke in a hissing whisper, her eyes narrowed. The Signor Cardew was *away*; in his absence it was *sinful* for the Signora Cardew to wish introduction to another man; she, Lucia, would not sanction it in her home. Abruptly she thrust two peaches at Katherine. Mutely, with Irish caution, Katherine accepted them, certain in her soul that Lucia had Daniel's letter in her pocket.

"*Grazie, Signora,*" she whispered.

"Hats on, kids!"

Carol and Roo ran to the front gate and hung there like monkeys in blue sunsuits, white hats. Katherine followed, grateful to be out of the house, grateful for her daughters: Carol at six with some newly discovered solemnity and Roo at three, already a rebel. At the end of the alley the tarred highway, blistering and smelling in the noonday sun, boomed with traffic. Here they turned left up the narrow incline that led to the seminary and a small public garden. Turning left again they climbed a steep hill until they reached the cobblestoned market where Lucia shopped and was robbed by thieves. The heat was intense and redolent. Fish stank freshly of the sea; meat hung from hooks, dripping blood, gorged upon by flies; potatoes, heaped high upon pushcarts, smelled of earthy fields; and purple onions hung in ropes. Here, stepping over cobbles that glistened with fish scales, small puddles of blood, shallow pans of entrails, Katherine spoke her limited Italian. Here, too, she was admired and knew it. Perhaps these vendors were thieves, ready to rob her by hidden and practiced methods, and mock her afterward. But they were also Italians with a famous tradition, ready to pay homage to her foreign beauty, her long blond hair, her pretty children. Today she bought salad greens that Lucia might share with them. They were both women without men. Shouldn't they be friends, enjoy a certain tranquility together?

"Look at the pregnant lady!" Carol cried, pointing.

"Roo! Where's Roo?"

They found Roo behind a wooden bucket of flowers. Giddy with relief, Katherine bought a huge bouquet. She felt morally slack, extravagant. Was it the heat? Her long hair clung to her neck; her lips tasted of sweat.

"Does the baby have toys?" Carol asked. "In the lady's tummy."

"No, love. The baby sleeps. All curled up."

"But couldn't the pregnant lady swallow something?"

"Swallow what?"
"One tiny toy. For the baby."

Night merely hid the heat in darkness. Katherine sat by the window, gazing at the moon-tinted path and the iron gate, which looked like a spider. Why hadn't Daniel written? Was he still angry at her? They'd argued violently about where to go now that he'd finished his dissertation. No more ancient Roman law! Now what? Stay in Italy, borrowing more money from his family? Or return to America, expatriates in need of a job, a small apartment? The wrangling had left Daniel without a plan but cheerful. He'd take a trip! What about Circe's mountain? Katherine had surrendered, exhausted. She had become listless and strangely chaste, haunted by the suspicion that her mother had been right, the marriage all wrong. Well, she'd agreed to Circe's mountain. And the week's separation. She'd stubbed her cigarette out, and vowed to stop smoking. So off he'd gone to Sabaudia, a Mussolini town of no interest, but the point of departure for Monte Circeo, a tiny village garrisoned against civilization and the angry sea. Daniel's adventure! Leaning on the windowsill, Katherine imagined the sea curling and crashing against the mountain's tumbled rocks, eroding ancient caves with a sucking sound. She felt a twinge of wistfulness, maybe self-pity. She imagined herself there. Oh, to leap upon a rock, stretch her body taut, and dive into the white water! How gloriously cold! But tonight's heat returned her to reason, and she relinquished the caves of Monte Circeo for more personal adventures: Carol and Roo, Lucia, and this foreign heat that drained her of ordinary common sense. Why would Lucia hide a letter from Daniel? She heard the front door open and close, and watched the musician, carrying his clarinet case, walk down the path. At the gate he stopped, as if sensing her presence, then vanished down the alley.

"*Non c'é niente per lei!*" Lucia said. "*Niente lettere!*"
"The post office strike?" Katherine asked. "Or more thieves?"
Italy was full of strikes. Yes, even the cows were on strike. Yet now Lucia's eloquence concerned a much graver governmental failure: the closing of Italy's brothels. Yes, that had been a day of national mourning! Black crepe hung from balconies. For it was

common knowledge that now no marriage was secure from adultery, no husband free from some scheming trollop who worked in an office, no wife safe from scandal. Men accosted virgins and became diseased overnight. Katherine did not know whether this last tidbit concerning Rome's downfall was the result of Lucia's inflamed imagination or her own faulty translation in their polyglot language. Lucia stopped for breath.

"So the Signor Cardew does not write!" she said spitefully.

"Like the Signor Felici!" Katherine said. And she walked upstairs, leaving Lucia to yell at her old mother or tell the young musician about the closing of brothels and the marriage of priests and other horrors. She felt tall and slim and beautiful, as if some Italian vendor was admiring her. Suddenly she regretted her remark about the Signor Felici. At best it was tactless; at worst, wounding. And who was there to forgive her? She felt a punishing headache, and a strange desire to believe, to go to confession as Lucia did every Sunday and have some mysterious male voice forgive her her sins. . . .

Katherine planned the next day out of Lucia's domain.

She treated the children to breakfast at the trattoria on the rumbling highway, and took them to the Borghese Gardens. The trip involved three bus rides, but the gardens blazed with color, and the children played hide-and-seek in the museum. Again Roo disappeared. Finally Katherine found her curled up at the base of an equestrian statue, asleep on the cool marble. After lunch they rested in the seminary garden. Few people came to this small patch of baked earth, oddly lacking in sundial, fountain, or statue. But there were some flower beds, and a stone bench canopied by a huge gnarled tree. In this season the tree was the one flourishing growth; its exposed roots tilted the bench and spread out in lumps and loops beyond its shade, strangling all other vegetation. The children took off to watch an old gardener dig up one of the flower beds. Katherine rested against a root, but she felt nagged by suspicions: that Lucia was hiding Daniel's letter, that Lucia was a little paranoid, crazy, and that's why her rooms were cheap. Yet who had picked these cheap rooms with the rowdy, persecuted Lucia? Mrs. Cardew, speaking her fractured Italian. Katherine blinked against the sun, and told herself to take one day at a time.

Tomorrow was Sunday. Lucia would go to Mass. Katherine looked forward to a day of peace.

Every Sunday a young priest in a black soutane entered Lucia's home and climbed the stairs to the attic to hear the old lady's confession and give her absolution. Katherine closed her eyes. What could an old woman have to confess? Perhaps she wished for death. Or, suffering her daughter's eternal anger, she might wish for Lucia's death. Was it possible, at her advanced age, that certain memories stirred her to covet the body of a man? Katherine felt the heat pull her consciousness into some fine haze that hung above her body and had to do with God. An unbeliever, she looked upon religion as a mystery that worked in odd ways. Certainly it had inspired St. Peter's dome, the Sistine Chapel ceiling, Bernini's sculpture, art all over Rome. And it inspired banality, too, dreadful trinkets and medals sold everywhere. Arbitrarily, it humbled the proud, took money from the poor, made laws and political alliances, and kept the old gardener turning the brown earth for no apparent reason, sustained by the faith that this was God's will. Perhaps it was. Religion did a lot of odd jobs. It built guilt, made sex a sin, dealt with hysteria in the confessional. The whole concept was terrifying. And she thought of the young men preparing for the priesthood, vowed to celibacy in this climate for love. Yet the young seminarians, walking about with their books, looked a lot healthier than Daniel's friends at the Academy, whose sexual exploits left them haunted and listless. A bell tolled five o'clock. As the last chime fell, a tall brown-clad figure strode toward the tree, his heavy soutane girdled by a tasseled cord, a blue notebook under his arm. At the edge of the shade he stopped and smiled at her as if she were too lovely for words, a painting of this perfect afternoon. She smiled back, returning the compliment. Together they prolonged the moment, held it high above the depths of sex until it reached a silent Amen. Then he strode down the hill. Katherine started breathing again, unaware that she had stopped. And now she felt a peculiar sensation, a cramp that was the sudden pull of the forbidden healthy young man hidden in yards of brown cloth. Why shouldn't priests marry?

"Mummy, why does Daniel have a holiday? And we don't?"

"We're having our holiday. Here in Rome."

"I'm hot," Roo whined.

The children slept as though drugged. Yes, this was her holiday from Daniel and marriage. Something of a blessing. But had he abandoned them forever? Had something happened to Daniel? Had he taken that high dive from Circe's mountain and crashed on the rocks below?

She saw his naked mutilated body being sucked in and out of the caves at each tide . . . my God! What was happening to her? And she wondered whether it was possible to remain sane in this climate that dazed the senses and alerted them without warning, so that she squandered money on flowers and flirted with vendors and smiled wantonly at young priests.

Below her, tones from the clarinet trilled softly like birds strangely awake in the hot night.

"*Grazie, Signora!*"

"*Prego. . . .*"

Their Sabbath decorum was God's job done well. All was forgiven. Huge ripe peaches for the Cardews! Katherine's bouquet of flowers for the Signora Felici's mother! Lucia, wearing pink stockings, sailed off to Mass. Katherine felt a moment's grace, and then envy. Why couldn't *she* sail off to Mass? And she thought of the Chapel of Saint Bartholomew just beyond the seminary. Why not go there today? She would never be able to enter the Kingdom of Heaven, nor receive amnesty for her many sins (sins of thought mostly), but later today she and the children would enter one of God's houses. . . .

She climbed the stairs to the attic, carrying her bouquet.

"*Signora?*" she called softly.

The old lady's room was an oven. Drawn shutters filtered the sun's spectrum to a yellowish light in which Katherine saw a heap of quilts, a wizened brown face, two tiny alert eyes. She put the flowers on a table next to a porcelain bowl and pitcher centered on a crocheted doily. A bedpan stood beneath the table, not yet emptied. Katherine, forever deprived of absolution, felt she should empty it. Reason intervened, and a sense of decorum. Presumably she was Lucia's paying guest, not her servant. She glanced at the mound of quilts. Lucia's mother now seemed asleep behind paper-thin eyelids. She suddenly looked dead. W*as* she dead? And was this asphyxiating heat the climate of old age or a daughter's tyranny? Katherine felt a tomb would be cooler, more comfortable. The eyelids flickered briefly, showing a gleam of senile mischief. Oh, a tomb would be cooler!

They entered the chapel, the children subdued. A small table supported a rack of candles. Katherine knelt, but no prayer came. She selected a burning taper, and feeling a humble fervor, lit one candle after another until they were all burning.

"Oh God, where's Roo?"

"I'm cold," Roo said, hopping. "And I want to . . ."

"Shhhhhhh!"

They sat down on a pew. Katherine shivered, feeling the stone floor through her sandals, and looked about her. A lectern supported an open Bible, and in other dark corners were chalices, statuettes, cloth emblems richly embroidered. High above a flickering oil lamp Christ writhed, glistening with agony on a wooden Cross. Blood dripped in red globules; the beard shone as though drenched with sweat; gold bolts of lightning shot toward the gold frame like fireworks for the glory of raw martyrdom. She heard the chanting from Saint Bartholomew's Church: the priest's incantation, the penitents' answering chorus, and finally the fine thin line of beauty from the boys' choir. She hugged Roo, who was as warm as the outdoors, and glanced down at Carol. She was staring at the Crucifixion, her small face pinched with fear.

"It's only a picture," Katherine whispered. "It isn't real."

"I want to whisper you something," Carol whispered.

"Whisper a little louder."

"Roo's making a tinkle. . . ."

Katherine felt her heart thump strangely, as if it were pumping red paint instead of blood. She lifted Roo to her thigh and ran up the aisle, trying to prevent further desecration of Saint Bartholomew, Jesus, all of Italy, God. She put Roo down on the stone-flagged corridor outside, but Roo had finished.

"*Padre!*"

Young, striding along in his black soutane, the padre turned a ruddy face to her. She grabbed his clothing, a fistful of black serge behind which was the body of a young man who looked, *Gesù Cristo*, kind and intelligent, and understanding. She tried to find the Italian words to explain the wet pew cushion. He removed

her hand gently, and answered in English. Yes, he understood. He
also appreciated her attempts at worship. Thirty-two candles! Two
candles would have been quite proper; one, with devout prayer,
would not have displeased Our Savior. He smiled at her kindly,
and she felt her punishment gather.

Roo had a temperature.

At three in the morning Katherine gave her two more aspirin
and crept downstairs to make her some weak, sweetened tea. She
fumbled for the light switch, which was synchronized to go off
after the few seconds it took to reach the floor below, but she
stumbled, and the light went off, and a long sorrowful moan came
from somewhere. From Lucia's mother? From Lucia, whose tor-
ments would never end? She felt the darkness stir as if gathering
uneasy dreams into this moan of loneliness belonging to the
whole house.

At last Roo slept. Katherine saw the dawn spill thickly through
the shutters like a white soup . . . and felt a sudden piercing hunger. She crept downstairs again. Fatigued beyond the simple action of finding the light switch, she stumbled into Lucia's kitchen
and opened the refrigerator. The food looked sickening: puddings,
congealed fish, spaghetti. A sound made her turn, and she saw the
young musician. He stood by the stove, wearing dark trousers, a
dish towel tucked into his belt as a makeshift apron, his chest
naked except for a small crucifix. He smiled, showing white teeth,
and gestured with a fork toward a plate of sliced green peppers
and a can of American baked beans on the table. Wordlessly she
accepted his hospitality. She attended to the stove, the peppers,
and he emptied the can of beans into the skillet, and she stirred
the mixture, and he opened a bottle of wine and filled two glasses,
and she set the table with plates and Lucia's bent forks. Capable
of speech, they chose silence. Silence was a treasure like love. Together, in a communion of fatigue and hunger, they possessed the
smoky hour between dawn and the milky white morning. Upstairs
a pipe groaned. They put the dishes away, and parted like sleep-
walkers, without a word.

The sun was a silver disc lodged solidly in the floating blue sky.
Katherine lugged her laundry out into the courtyard, a small en-

closure collecting heat behind the thick walls, mottled by stones
that looked like the spots of some disease. After her sleepless
night she felt dreamy and overpowered, and hung the sheets up in
a trance, as if her mind were chloroformed. Death should be as
peaceful as this courtyard. Her father had died noisily, quoting
Descartes. Mom would die one day . . . and so would she. She
saw herself enter this courtyard, a dead soul locked in an eternal
noon, forever hanging up a wash.

Upstairs the children were quarreling.

"Roo did it!" Carol shouted. "*All* over the bathroom!"

Lucia's bidet was indeed a fountain, flooding its pink basin,
spreading gracefully over the mosaic floor, each tile a blue and
white replica of Madonna and Child. She struggled with various
knobs while the tiles mocked her beneath rippling water, and then
kicked savagely at a gleaming handle that looked far too modern
for this old house with its nightly moans and groans. The fountain stopped. Katherine mopped up the flood, praying for Lucia's
forgiveness. . . .

The children played in the courtyard.

Katherine took down her laundry, already spotted with soot,
and brought it indoors. On the kitchen table was a letter
addressed to her in Daniel's thick-nibbed scrawl. She picked it up,
trembling. The envelope had been opened with a knife, and the
paper removed and refolded. Katherine scanned the large, undis-
ciplined handwriting. Apparently the Mediterranean was blue.
Monte Circeo was built entirely within the pastel-shaded walls of
an ancient castle erected centuries ago to protect the mountain
from invasion. They were having a great time. Last night he'd
eaten sparrows for dinner. The birds were trapped alive and cooked
and served whole. The legs crunched between your teeth. This
was real Italy, raw life. He'd sent her some quaint sandals. Had
they arrived?

She turned the page, hoping that the sound of her own voice
would make the words real:

A bunch of us have decided to do our own thing and to
hell with guides! We've rented a boat—re-christened THE
TIN TUB—and are taking off for Sicily and then who

knows where? We'll just keep floating from port to port,
sniffing new smells. This is real life, the real Mediterranean. We sunbathe nude. How are you managing?
And the womb-fruits? I love you . . .

She put the letter down, feeling outrage and a blurry pain, and
saw the slit envelope. It was postmarked Naples, eight days ago,
and the ink was brown. How dare Lucia *fan* herself with Daniel's
letter and then *pocket* it and open it with a *knife?* And how dare
Daniel take off for "who knows where" and float about in something christened THE TIN TUB, "sniffing new smells" and leave her
in Rome with a *mad landlady?* How *dare* he ask if the "quaint
sandals" had arrived, and give no return address? And what right
had he to taste *raw life* at the expense of some little sparrows?
And the "womb-fruits"?

His questions were rhetorical, and so were hers. But she was a
literal person suffering a private chaos, and she had a few answers.
The quaint sandals had not arrived. And how was she managing?
This was how. Chaste and faithful she flirted with priests, and
possessed of some strange religious mania she had taken the children to Saint Bartholomew's Chapel, where Carol had sat in silent terror and Roo had peed on a pew cushion, and where she,
Katherine, had lit *thirty-two candles* when two would have been
quite proper, and one, with devout prayer, would not have displeased Our Savior. She was falling in love with religion. Or maybe
priests, because the young priests looked sexy, and maybe this was
because their bodies were hidden and they weren't spread-eagled
naked on beaches. . . . Oh yes, the bidet had flooded. And she
was spending precious lire on flowers, candles, and the trattoria.
The children were living on spaghetti and peaches, hardly the
Spock diet. But no *baby sparrows,* either! *Raw life?* She'd not
slept for two nights, but she'd had breakfast with a *beautiful*
young man.

She returned to Daniel's letter and felt a new wave of rage. So
he *loved* her, did he? Well, how? In his TIN TUB? Sunbathing
nude? Sniffing new smells? She clutched the table, a quiet soul fer-
menting violence. How *dare* he eat sparrows and talk about *raw
life?* Oh, he loved her, yes! But did she love him? Suddenly she

thought of the cooked sparrows, saw them on a white plate. She
mourned them; she wept for them uncontrollably.

Lucia entered the kitchen, armed with a single word.

"*Polizia!*"

"*Si, si, Lucia . . .*"

Lucia was momentarily silenced. Katherine began folding the
sooty wash. Tears dribbled down her face, and she sniffed un-
ashamedly. "Yes, call the police. The bidet overflowed and I'm
sorry. But I love my children. I love my children and I love real
flowers. And tiny live sparrows. They should not be cooked. And I
approve of brothels. I think they should be free. And I think
priests should marry. And I admire the young musician. I love
him," she added, weeping.

Lucia handed her a piece of paper. It was Daniel's rent check,
and it had bounced.

"I spit on the Signor Cardew!" Lucia cried. "Scum Americano."

Katherine put the children to bed. She promised herself a bath
and twelve hours of sleep, but she found the hot water faucet
locked, the house in darkness, and sleep strangely denied her. In
bed her thoughts bent beneath the drudgery of worry and broke
into fragments. . . . Yes, I approve of brothels. They free husbands from unwilling wives. They free wives. I am a trapped sparrow. I must cable Mom for money, but will she understand? Yes,
only too well! Is Daniel safe in his TIN TUB? And how safe are we
without money? Living with a mad landlady who has every right
to deny me a bath! What is love? Must it be sex? Chaste, I long
to lie with a priest. But Daniel will turn up someday and expect
me to obey him in bed. How can I cable Mom? Easily! Just run
through the night to the trattoria and send a cable, collect. This
marriage is a trap. I am a trapped. . . .

The trattoria was still open. But the telephone operators at this
hour were a quixotic lot. Some appeared ignorant of the alphabet;
others sang their helpfulness in three languages, like opera stars,
and then forgot her with a click. She imagined her mother's
pinched frown when she received the cable.

She spent the rest of the night packing. At dawn she crept
downstairs, hungry for anything edible, green noodles or overripe
peaches. She heard a faint moan. Descending another flight, she

heard another moan, then a whimper. At the kitchen door, her
breathing quickened. She heard her own heart, her own breathing,
and heavier breathing, and suddenly a strangled cry. Two bodies
lay struggling on the kitchen floor. Lucia's bulk heaved beneath a
tangled robe; her bare legs thrashed like trapped cobras. She was
on top of her assailant, but with a sudden movement she lay
pinned beneath the body of a naked man. She flung out her arms
and a gold crucifix lay on his shoulder. Then her arms encircled
his torso, and he rode her. His glistening buttocks rose like moons
above the dawn's horizon and plunged into shadow, and rose
again. Katherine felt an electric current travel her body, like lightning of some voltage that does not kill but paralyzes. She stood
powerless to move. Her mind stood still, insensible. Attuned to
disaster, she possessed the conviction that life was catastrophic,
that Lucia would be left dead or dying on the kitchen floor, that
no woman was safe. She argued with her reason, and it returned.
She was not watching rape. She was watching the tidal wave of an
orgasm being reached by a passionate woman and her young lover.
She took her shocked body upstairs.

"Lucia! My mama sends lire . . ."
"I spit on the Signor Cardew! And on the Signor Felici!"
Lucia was the same. She showed no sign of the night's loving
no sign of respite from her martyrdom. Still robbed and persecuted, she played the angry, unloved woman. Katherine marked
the moment in her own life, and saw its dangers. But what dangers? Life had all sorts of possibilities, such as this trinity of souls
living sinful ecstasies and receiving weekly absolution. She felt her
sanity return, and her humor. And something more: a bit of wisdom that was just around the corner.
"*Molte grazie,*" Katherine said, awed.
Lucia's farewell gift was a wicker basket lined with pink tissue
paper and filled with peaches huge as grapefruit, plums, and tiny
green grapes. This was not all. The fruit was garnished with
artificial flowers made of mauve and yellow crepe paper. Katherine
took the basket in her arms.
"*Grazie, grazie.*"
She knew that the fruit would be surrendered at Customs. But

she would keep Lucia's flowers: crepe paper taped to bits of wire in patience and fury and love.

Lucia lowered her voice to a whisper. Yes, she knew about godless men who took off for Naples and other sinful places; she knew about men like the Signor Cardew and the Signor Felici; and she knew about women left to live with their mothers who . . . *st, st!* And she thrust two plums at the children and sent them outdoors to watch for the taxi.

Carol and Roo hung on the gate.

"Poor Lucia," Roo said. "She shouts and shouts."

"It's because she wants toys in her tummy. For her baby. She has that baby there and all that room for toys in her tummy. And no one understands."

"*My* mummy understand everything!" Roo said.

The taxi arrived with a great rattle; the luggage was piled inside.

The two women embraced. Lucia yelled directions to the driver, wiping her tears with her gaudy apron. Katherine put on her dark glasses, her disguise behind which she might glimpse the last of real Italy, raw life. And hide her own tears. Yes, she would stay with her mother, but not forever. She'd settle in New York, find a job, get her divorce. Mom lived in Pennsylvania and was a vegetarian. She was a tiny energetic woman who worked as a lab technician, analyzing blood.

"*Arrivederci, Lucia!*"

"*Arrivederci!*"

THE MEN'S CLUB

LEONARD MICHAELS

Leonard Michaels usually writes about New York City, where he was born. For the past twenty years, he has moved farther and farther west. Mr. Michaels has published two collections of stories: *Going Places* (1969) and *I Would Have Saved Them If I Could* (1975).

Women wanted to talk about anger, identity, politics, etc. I saw posters in Berkeley urging them to join groups. I saw their leaders on TV. Strong, articulate faces. So when Cavanaugh phoned and invited me to join a men's club, I laughed. Slowly, not laughing, he repeated himself. He was six foot nine. The size and weight entered his voice. He and some friends wanted a club. "A regular social possibility outside our jobs and marriages. Nothing to do with women's groups." One man was a tax accountant, another was a lawyer. There was also a college teacher like me and two psychotherapists. Solid types. I supposed there could be virtues in a men's club, a regular social possibility. I should have said yes immediately, but something in me resisted. The prospect of leaving my house after dinner. Blood is heavy then. Brain is slow. Besides, wasn't this club idea corny? Like trying to recapture high school days. Locker room fun. Wet naked boys snapping towels at each other's genitals. It didn't feel exactly right. To be wretchedly truthful, any social possibility unrelated to wife, kids, house, and work felt like a form of adultery. Not criminal. Not legitimate.

"Cavanaugh, I don't even go to the movies anymore."

"I'm talking about a men's club. Good company. You talk about women's groups. Movies. Can't you hear me?"

"When the phone rings it's like an attack on my life. I get confused. Say it again."

"Look, you're one of my best friends. You live less than a mile away. Do we see each other three times a year?"

"I lose over a month every year just working to pay property taxes. Friendship is a luxury. Unless you're so poor it makes no difference how you spend your time."

"A men's club. Good company."

"I hear you."

But I was thinking about good company. Some of my married colleagues had love affairs, usually with students. You could call it a regular social possibility. It included emotional chaos. Gonorrhea. Even guilt. They would have been better off in a men's club.

"What do you say? Can we expect you?"

"I'll go to the first meeting. I can't promise more. I'm very busy."

"Yeah, yeah," said Cavanaugh and gave me an address in the Berkeley flats.

The night of the meeting I told my wife I'd be home before midnight. She said, "Take out the garbage." Big sticky bag felt unpropitious and my hands soon smelled of tuna fish. After driving five minutes I found the place. The front of the house, vine covered, seemed to brood in lunatic privacy. Nobody answered when I knocked, but I heard voices, took hold of a wrought iron handle and pushed, discovering a large Berkeley living room and six men inside. I saw dark wood paneling and potted ferns dangling from exposed beams. Other plants along the window ledges. A potted tree in a far corner, skinny, spinsterish looking. Nervous yellow leaves filled its head. Various ceramics, bowls on tabletops and plates on the walls beside huge acrylic paintings, abstractions like glistening viscera splashed off a butcher block. There was an amazing rug, but I couldn't take it in. A man was rising from a pillow on the floor, coming toward me, smiling.

"I knocked," I said.

"Come in, man. I'm Harry Kramer."

"I'm Cavanaugh's friend."

"Who isn't?"

"Really," I said, giving it the L.A. inflection to suggest sympathetic understanding, not wonder. Kramer registered the nuance and glanced at me as at a potential brother. His heavy black hair was controlled by a style, parted in the middle, shaped to cup his ears with a feeling that once belonged to little girls and now was common among TV actors and rock musicians. It was contradicted by black force in his eyes, handshake like a bite, and tattooed forearms. Blue winged snake. Blue dagger amid roses. They spoke for an earlier life, I supposed, but Kramer wore his sleeves rolled to the elbow. It was impossible to connect him with his rug, which I began to appreciate as spongy and sensuous. Orange. I felt myself wading through it as Kramer led me toward the men.

Shaking hands, nodding hello, saying my name, each man was a complex flash—eyes, hand, names—but one had definition. Solly Berliner. Tall. Wearing a suit. Dead white hair and big greenish light in his eyes. The face of an infant surprised by senility. His suit was gray polyester, conservative and sleazy. Kramer left me with Berliner beside the potted tree, a beer in my hand. A man about five foot six with an eager face came right up to us. "Care for a taste?" In his palm lay two brown marijuanas, slick with spittle. I declined. Berliner said, "Thanks, thanks," with frightening gratitude and took both cigarettes. We laughed as he dropped one back into the man's palm. The little face turned toward the other men. "Anybody care for a taste?"

The sound of Berliner's voice lingered after the joke. Maybe he felt uneasy. Out of his natural environment. I couldn't guess where that might be. He was a confusion of clues. The suit wasn't Berkeley. The eyes were worlds of feeling. His speedy voice flew from nerves. Maybe the living room affected him. A men's club would have been more authentic, more properly convened, elsewhere. What did I have in mind? A cold ditch? I supposed Kramer's wife, exiled for the evening, had cultivated the plants and picked the orange rug and the luscious fabrics on the couches and chairs. Ideas of happiness. Berliner and I remained standing as if the fabrics—heavy velvets, beige tones—were nothing to violate with our behinds. It was a woman's room, but the point of the club was to be with men, not to escape from women, so I turned to Berliner and asked what he did for a living.

"Real estate," he said, grinning ferociously, as if extreme types were into that. Wild fellows. "I drove in from San Jose." He spoke with rapid little shrugs, as if readjusting his vertebrae. His eyes were full of green distance after two drags on the cigarette. He was already driving back to San Jose, I figured, but then he said, "Forgive me for saying this, but, a minute ago when Kramer introduced us, I had a weird thought." His eyes returned.

"You did?"

I'd seen the look before. It signalled the California plunge into truth, a conversational style developed in encounter groups where sensitivity training occurs.

"I hope this doesn't bother you. But I thought you had a withered leg."

"You did?"

"I see you don't. Weird?" He giggled. His mouth was tense.

"Weird that I don't have a withered leg?"

"I thought your leg was all screwed up. Like withered."

I wiggled my legs. For my sake, not his. He stared as if into unusual depths, waiting for a truth to rise, perhaps leap into the air like a fish. I said nothing. He said, "I'm forty-seven."

"You look much younger." This was true. But, with the white hair, he also looked older.

"I stay in shape," he answered, marijuana smoke leaking from his nostrils. "Nobody," he said, sucking the leak back with crackling sheets of snot, "nobody else in the room is forty-seven. I'm oldest. I asked the guys."

He gagged a little, then released the smoke, knifing it through compressed lips. "Kramer is thirty-eight." I wondered if conversation had ever been more like medical experience, so rich in gas and mucus. "I'm always the oldest. Ever since I was a kid I was the oldest." He giggled and intensified his stare. I giggled, too, in a social way. Then the door opened and Cavanaugh walked in.

"Excuse me," I said, intimating regret but moving quickly away to greet Cavanaugh.

Cavanaugh, big and good looking, had heroic charisma. He'd once been a professional basketball player. Now he worked at the university in special undergraduate programs, matters of policy and funding. Nine to five, jacket and tie. To remember his former work—the great naked shoulders and legs flying through the air—was saddening. In restaurants and airports people still asked for his autograph.

Things felt better, more natural, healthier, with the big man in the room. Kramer reached him before I did. They slapped each other's arms, laughing, pleased at how they felt to each other. Solid. Real. I watched, thinking I'd often watched Cavanaugh. Ever since college, in fact, when he'd become famous. To see him burn his opponent and score was like a miracle of justice. Now, in civilian clothes, he was faintly disorienting. Especially his wristwatch, a golden, complicated band. A symbolic manacle. Cavanaugh's submission to ordinary life. He'd once said, "I don't want my kids to grow up like me, necks thick as their heads." He wanted his kids in jackets and wristwatches.

He'd stopped slapping Kramer's arms, but Kramer continued touching him. Kramer looked as though he might soon pee in his pants. People love athletics. Where else these days do they see such mythic drama? Images of unimpeachable excellence. I was infected by Kramer's enthusiasm. When Kramer left to get Cavanaugh a beer, we shook hands. He said, "I didn't think I'd see you tonight." There was mockery in his smile.

"It's not so easy getting out of the house. Nobody but you could have dragged me to this."

"You open the door, you're out."

"Tell me about it."

"I'm glad you're here. Anything happen yet? I'm late because Sarah thinks the club idea is wrong. I'm wrong to be here. We argued a little at dinner." He whispered then, "Maybe it isn't easy," and looked at his wristwatch, frowning, as if it were his mind. Kramer returned with the beer just as a phone started ringing.

"I'll be right back," said Kramer, turning toward the ringing.

Sarah's word "wrong" made me wonder. If something was wrong with Cavanaugh, it was wrong with the universe. Men could understand that. When Cavanaugh needed a loan to buy his house, the bank gave him no problem. You could see his credit was good; he was six foot nine and could run a hundred yards in ten seconds. The loan officer, a man, recognized Cavanaugh and felt privileged to help him with financial negotiations. He didn't ask about Cavanaugh's recent divorce, his alimony payments.

Men's clubs. Women's groups. They suggest incurable disorders. I remembered Socrates—how the boys, not his wife, adored him. And Karl Marx running around with Engels while Jenny stayed home with the kids. Maybe men played more than women. A men's club, compared to women's groups, was play. Frivolous; virtually insulting. It excluded women. But I was thinking in cir- cles. A men's club didn't exclude women. It also didn't exclude kangaroos. It included only men. I tried to imagine explaining this to Sarah. "You see, men love to play." It didn't feel convincing. She had strong opinions and a bad temper. When Cavanaugh de- cided to quit basketball, it was his decision, but I blamed her any- way. She wanted him home. The king became the dean.

Kramer shouted from another room, "Is anybody here named Terry? His wife is on the phone. She's crying." Shouting again, more loudly, as if to make sure the woman on the phone would hear him, Kramer said, "Is anybody in this house named Terry?"

Nobody admitted to being named Terry. I heard Kramer, still shouting, say, "Terry isn't here. If Terry shows up, I'll tell him to phone you right away. No, I won't forget. I'll tell Terry to phone you right away."

When Kramer returned he said, "You guys sure none of you is named Terry?"

Cavanaugh muttered, "We're all named Terry."

We made a circle, some men sitting on the rug. Kramer settled into his pillow, legs folded and crossed. He began talking to us in a slow rational voice. The black eyes darkened his face. His words became darker, heavier, because of them.

"What is the purpose of this club?"

To make women cry, I thought. Kramer's beginning was not very brilliant, but he looked so deep that I resisted judgment.

"Some of us—Solly Berliner, Paul, Cavanaugh—had a discus- sion a few weeks ago. We agreed it would be a good idea . . ." Paul was the short, marijuana man with the eager face. Kramer nodded to him when he said his name. He went on about the good idea, but I wasn't listening.

I thought again about the women. Anger, identity, politics, rights, wrongs. I envied them. It seemed attractive to be deprived in our society. Deprivation gives you something to fight for, it makes you morally superior, it makes you serious. What was left for men these days? They already had everything. Did they need clubs? The mere sight of two men together suggests a club. Consider Damon and Pythias, Huck and Jim, Hamlet and Horatio. The list is familiar. Even the Lone Ranger wasn't lonely. He had Tonto. There is Gertrude Stein and Alice B. Toklas, but, generally, two women suggest gossip and a kiss good-bye. Kramer, talking, meandered in a sea of nonexistent purpose. I said, "Why are you talking about our purpose? We're all here. Let's just say what we want to do." I'd stopped him mid-meander. He looked relieved —a little surprised, not offended. "Can you offer a suggestion?" he asked.

I glanced at the other faces, particularly Cavanaugh's. I didn't want to embarrass him. I was his guest and I'd been too aggressive maybe. He said, "Go on."

"I suggest each of us tell the story of his life."

The instant I said it I laughed, as if I'd intended a joke. What else could it be? I didn't tell the story of my life to strangers. Maybe I'd lived too long in California, or I'd given too many lectures at the university. Perhaps I'd been influenced by Berliner, becoming like him, a confessional person. Nobody else laughed. Cavanaugh looked at me with approval. Berliner grinned, his rigid ferocity. He loved the suggestion. He could hardly wait to begin. Kramer, however, said, "I'll go first."

"You want to? You do like the idea?"

"One of us can talk at each meeting. I have listened in this room to numerous life-stories." Kramer, apparently, was a psychotherapist.

"It will be good for me," he said, "to tell the story of my life, especially in a nonprofessional context. It will be a challenge. I'm going to put it on tape. I will tape each of us."

Suddenly I imagined him sitting among his plants listening to life-stories, his tape recorder going, his dark face and tattoos presiding over everything.

"Oh, come on. Let's talk to one another, Kramer. No machines."

To my dismay, Kramer yelled, "Why the hell not? I have so much talk on my tapes—friends, clients, lovers—that I don't even know what I have. So much I don't even remember."

Apparently, I'd struck at something he cherished. I didn't know him well enough to do that, but I heard myself yelling back at him, a man who looked angry, even dangerous, "If you didn't put it on tape, you'd remember."

Everyone laughed, including Kramer. He said, "That's good, that's good." No anger at all. I was strangely pleased by this violence. I liked Kramer for laughing.

"That's good," he said. "I'm going to write that down."

"Yeah," said Cavanaugh, "no tape recorder. But I want an idea of what this life-story business is like."

Berliner said, "You know what it's like, Cavanaugh. It's like in the old movies. Lauren Bacall tells Humphrey Bogart about herself. Who she is. Where she's been. Then they screw."

A blond man with plastic-framed glasses and a pastel-blue sweater strained forward in his chair, saying, "I saw that movie on *The Late Show*, right?" He looked youthful, exceptionally clean. He wore cherry-red jogging shoes.

The faces became silent. He retreated. "Maybe it was another movie."

Berliner's face seemed to swell with astonishment, then tighten into eery screeing, tortured noises, screeing, screeing. "Oh, man what is your name?" He pointed at the blond. Kramer, hugging himself, contained his laughter. The blond said, "Harold." Tears, like bits of glass, formed in his eyes as he smiled.

"Oh Harold," shouted Berliner, "the name is the whole story of my life. My mother used to say, 'Solly Berliner, why can't you be like Harold.' Harold Himmel was the smartest, nicest kid in Brooklyn."

"My name is Harold Canterbury."

"Right, man. Forgive me. A minute ago when you were talking, I had a weird thought. I thought—forgive me, man—you had a withered hand."

Harold raised his hands for everyone to see.

Kramer said, "Don't listen to that jackass, Harold. Nothing wrong with your hands. I'm getting more beer."

As he walked toward the kitchen, Cavanaugh followed, saying, "I don't know what this life-story business is about, but it sounds good." Kramer said, "I'll show you what it's about. You get the beers." Cavanaugh returned with the beers and Kramer with a metal footlocker, dragging it into the center of our circle. A padlock banged against the front. Kramer, squatting, tried to fit a

key into the lock. His hands began shaking. Cavanaugh bent beside him. "You need a little help?" Kramer handed him the key,
saying, "Do it."

Cavanaugh inserted the key and the lock snapped open as if
shocked by love.

Kramer removed the lock, heaved back the lid of the footlocker,
then withdrew to his pillow, quickly lighting a cigarette, his hands
still shaking. "This is it, my life-story." His voice, slower than before, labored against feeling. "You guys can see my junk, my trinkets. Photos, diaries, papers of every kind." Had Kramer left the
room it would have been easier to look, but he remained on his
pillow, a dark pasha, urging us to look. Paul suddenly scrambled
on hands and knees to the footlocker, looked, then plucked out a
handful of bleary, cracked snapshots and fanned them across the
rug. We could see inscriptions. Paul read aloud, "Coney Island,
1953, Tina. Party at Josephine's, New Year's, 1965. Holiday Inn,
New Orleans, 1975, Gwen." He looked from the photos to
Kramer, smiling. "All these pictures in your box of women?"

Kramer, in the difficult voice, answered, "I have many photos. I
have my Navy discharge papers, my high school diploma, my first
driver's license. I have all my elementary school notebooks, even
spelling exams from the third grade. I have maybe twenty-five
fountain pens. All my old passports; everything is in that box."

Paul, nodding, smiling, said, "But these photos, Kramer. All
these photos women?"

"I have had six hundred and twenty-two women."

"Right on," shouted Berliner, his soul projecting toward
Kramer through the big green eyes, doglike, waiting for a signal.
Paul took out more photos and dropped them among the others
on the rug. Over a hundred now, women in bathing suits, in winter coats, in fifties styles, sixties styles, seventies styles. Spirits of
the decades. If men make history, women wear its look; even in
their faces and figures. But, to me, Kramer's women looked fundamentally the same. One poor sweetie between twenty and thirty
years old forever. On a beach, leaning against a railing, a tree, a
brick wall, with sun in her eyes, squinting at the camera. A hundred fragments, each of them complete if you cared to scrutinize.
A whole person who could say her name. Maybe love Kramer.
That she squinted touched me.

Kramer, with his meticulously sculpted hair, cigarette trembling in his fingers, waited. Nobody spoke, not even Berliner. Looking at the pictures, I was reminded of flashers. See this. It is my entire crotch. Have a scream.

Berliner suddenly blurted, "Great. Great. Let's all do it. Let's all talk about our sexual experience." His face jerked in every direction, seeking encouragement.

As if he'd heard nothing, Kramer said, "I was born in Trenton, New Jersey. My father was a union organizer. In those days it was dangerous work. He was a Communist, he lived for an idea. My mother believed in everything he said, but she was always depressed and she sat in the bedroom, in her robe, smoking cigarettes. She never cleaned the house. When I was six years old I was shopping and cooking, like my mother's mother. I cannot remember one minute which I can call my childhood. I was my mother's mother. I had a life with no beginning, no childhood."

"Right," said Berliner. "You had your childhood later. Six hundred and twenty-two mothers. Right?"

"The women were women. Eventually I'll have another six hundred. I don't know where my father is, but when I hear the word 'workers' or the word 'struggle,' I think of him. If I see a hardhat carrying a lunch pail, I think he's struggling. My mother now lives in New York. Twice a year I phone New York and get migraine headaches. Blindness and nausea. Just say the area code, 212, and I feel pain in my eyes."

I'd been looking at Kramer all evening, but now, to my surprise, I noticed that his eyes didn't focus steadily. The right eye was slightly askew. He blinked hard and brought it into line with the other eye. After a while it drifted away. He'd let it go for a moment, then blink hard again. His voice was trancelike, compulsive, as if he'd been trying to tell us something before he would be overwhelmed by doubt and confusion.

Cavanaugh said, "What about Nancy?"

"What about her?" Kramer sounded surprised, as if unsure who Nancy was.

"Nancy Kramer. These are her plants, aren't they?" Cavanaugh was looking at the photos on the rug, not the plants.

"You mean the women? What does Nancy think about my women?"

"That's right."

"We have a good understanding. Nancy goes out, too. It's cool. The plants are mine."

"Yours?" I said.

"Yes. I love them. I've even got them on my tape recorder. I could play you the fig tree in the corner." Kramer said this to me with a sly, dopey look, as if trying to change the mood, trying to make a joke.

"Too much. Too much, Kramer," said Berliner. "My wife and me are exactly the same. I mean we also have an understanding."

I said, "Let Kramer talk."

Kramer shook his head and bent toward Berliner, saying, "That's all right. Do you want to say more, Solly?"

Berliner looked down at his knees. "No. You go on, Kramer. I'm sorry I interrupted."

Cavanaugh, imitating Kramer, bent toward Berliner. "Solly, aren't you jealous when your wife is making it with another guy?"

Berliner raised his face toward Cavanaugh. "Jealous?"

"Yeah, jealous."

"No, man. I'm liberated."

"What the hell does that mean?" I said.

Looking at me now, Berliner said, as if it were obvious, "I don't feel anything."

"Liberated means you don't feel anything?"

"Yeah," said Berliner. "I'm liberated."

Harold, with a huge stare of pleasure, began repeating, "You don't feel anything. You don't feel anything."

Berliner shrugged. "Once, I felt something."

Writhing in his creamy slacks, Harold said, "Tell us about that, please." The little tears were in his eyes again. "Tell us about the time you felt something."

"Does everyone want to hear?" said Berliner, looking at me.

I said, "Yes."

He smiled. His voice was full of accommodation. "We had a weekend in the mountains with another couple. A ski cabin near Lake Tahoe. The first night we became a little drunk after dinner and somebody—maybe me—yeah, yeah, me—I said let's trade partners. It was my own idea, right? So we traded. It was OK. It wasn't the first time we did it. But then I heard my wife moaning. I couldn't help hearing her. A small cabin. And that was OK. But she was not just moaning, you know what I mean. You know? It was love."

"Love?" said Kramer.

"Yeah, I didn't like it. She was moaning with love. Moaning is OK. But she was going too far, you know what I mean. She was doing love. I wanted to kill her."

Cavanaugh reached over and squeezed Berliner's elbow. Berliner was still smiling, the big green eyes searching our faces for the meaning of what he'd said. "Is that what you wanted to know, Harold?"

"Did it ruin your weekend?"

"It was horrible, man. I lost my erection."

Berliner began screeing again and I heard myself doing it, too, just like him, making that creepy sound.

"It was horrible, horrible. I was ashamed. I ran out of the cabin and sat on a rock. My wife started calling through the door, 'Solly, Solly, Solly Berliner.' Then she came outside, laughing, and found me. I showed her what she had done to me. She said it wasn't her fault. She said it was my idea. I hit her and said that was my idea, too. She started crying. Soon as she started crying, my erection came back."

Kramer said, "What happened next?"

"But you were talking, Kramer," I said. "You know what happened next. Next she hit him and then they made it together. It's a cliché. You should finish telling your story. You should have a full turn." I wanted things done according to my idea, one man at a time.

Berliner, incoherent with excitement, shouted at me, "How the hell do you know? I'm telling what happened to me. Me. Me."

"All right, all right. What happened next?"

"Next she hit me and we made it together."

Cavanaugh, with two fists, began hammering the rug until everyone quieted. Then he said, "Look at Kramer." Kramer was slumped in his pillow, elbows on his knees, the dark face hanging, glancing vaguely back at Cavanaugh.

"Let's let him alone," said Cavanaugh. "Maybe he'll want to go

on later. I want to hear about the childhood he didn't have. But
we're talking about love tonight. I'll tell you guys a love story.
OK?"

I said, "Kramer tells us he made it with six hundred women.
Berliner says he traded his wife, then beat her up and had an erection. You call that love?"

Cavanaugh gave me a flat look, as if I'd become strange to him.
"Yeah, why not?"

"Oh God."

"Hey, man, what do you want to hear about? Toothpaste and
deodorants?"

"You're right, Cavanaugh. I give up. I'll bet your story's about
how you made it with ten thousand high school cheerleaders."

Cavanaugh stared at the place in the rug he had just ham-
mered. The big body and big face were immobilized, getting
things in order, remembering his story, and then his voice was
simply there.

"About three months after we got married my second wife and I
started having arguments. Bad scenes. We would go to bed every
night hating each other. There were months with no sex. I didn't
know who was more miserable. I was making a lot of money playing ball and I was playing good. It should have been good for us
altogether. The marriage should have been fine. In the middle of
a game with the crowd screaming, I'd think this was no fantastic
deal, because I had no love at home. Soon there was nothing in
my body but anger. I got into fights with my own teammates. I
couldn't take a shave without slicing my face. I was smoking cigarettes. I had something against my body and wanted to hurt it.
When I told my wife I was moving out, she said, 'Great.' She
wanted to live alone. I moved out and stayed with a friend until I
found an apartment. One day in the grocery store, I was throwing
every kind of thing into my shopping cart. I was making sure
nothing I needed would show up later as being not there. And
this woman, I notice, is pushing her cart behind me, up and down
the aisles, giggling. I knew she was giggling at me. When I got to
the cashier she is behind me in line, still giggling, and then she
says, very sweet and tickled, 'You must have a station wagon waiting for you.' I said, 'I have a pickup truck. Do you want a ride?' A

man buying so much food, she figured, has a family. Safe to ask
for a ride. She didn't have a car. I gave her a ride and carried her
groceries up to her apartment. A little boy was sitting on the floor
watching TV. She introduced us and offered me a drink and we
sat in another room talking. The boy took care of himself. Just
like in Kramer's story. He cooked dinner for himself. He gave
himself a bath. Then went to bed. But his mother wasn't depressed
like Kramer's. She laughed and teased me and asked a lot of questions. I talked about myself for five or six hours. We ate dinner
around midnight, and then, at four in the morning, I woke up in
her bed, thinking about my ton of groceries rotting in the pickup.
But that wasn't what woke me. What woke me was the feeling I
wanted to go home. Back to my apartment, my own bed. I hadn't
left one woman to sleep with another. I didn't know what I was
doing in this woman's bed. I got up and dressed and left. As I was
about to drive away she comes running to the window of my
pickup, naked. 'Where are you going?' she says. I told her she had
nothing on. She says, 'Where are you going at this hour?' I said I
wanted to go home. She says, 'Oh, OK, I'll come with you.' I told
her no and said I would phone her. She said OK and smiled and
said good-night. She was like that little boy. Or he was like her.
Easy. OK. OK good-night. I didn't think I would phone her. Now
this is my story. I woke up the next afternoon. I liked it, waking
up alone. I liked it very much, but I felt something strange. I
wanted something. Then I remembered the woman and I knew
what I wanted. I wanted to phone her. So I went to the phone
and I realized I didn't know her number. I didn't even know her
name. Well, I showered and got dressed and stopped thinking
about her. I went out for something. I didn't know what. I had
everything I needed in the apartment. But I started driving and
right away I was driving back to the grocery store, as if the car had
a mind of its own. I was just holding the wheel. I didn't get further than the grocery store, because I didn't remember where she
lived. I remembered leaving the store with her, driving toward the
bay and that's all. She said, 'Turn right, turn left, and go straight,'
but I never noticed street names or anything. Now I wanted to
see that woman more and more. The next day I went back to the
grocery store and hung around the parking lot. I did that every
day for a week, at different times. I thought I remembered how

she looked talking to me through the window of my pickup, how she smiled and said OK. I wanted to see her again badly. But I wasn't sure that I could recognize her in the street, looking normal. She was wearing gold loop earrings, jeans, and sandals. What if she came along in a skirt and heels? Anyhow, I never saw her again."

Cavanaugh stopped. It was obvious he had no more to say, but Kramer said, "Is that your story?"

"Yes." Cavanaugh smiled, leaning back, watching us.

"That's your love story?" I asked.

"Right," he answered, nodding. "I fell in love with a woman I couldn't find the next day. She might live around the corner, man."

"You still love her?" asked Paul, tremendous delicacy in his voice, the slight small body poised, full of tenderness and tension.

Cavanaugh smiled at him with melancholy eyes, the whole expression of his great face and body suggested that he'd been humbled by fate.

Paul said, "That can't be it, that can't be the end."

"The end."

"Cavanaugh," Paul said, pleading, "I've known you for years. How come you never told me that story?"

"I never told anyone. Maybe I'm not sure it happened."

"You did go back to the grocery?"

"So what?"

I said, "Paul means, if you looked for her, it happened."

"I still look. When Sarah sends me out to do the shopping, she doesn't know the risk she's taking."

"Cavanaugh," I said, "do you think you ever passed her in the street and she recognized you, but you didn't recognize her?"

Immediately, Kramer said, "Not recognize Cavanaugh? I'd recognize him even if I never saw him before."

"How would you recognize me?"

"From your picture in the papers."

"She didn't read the sports pages."

"Hey," said Berliner, "I have an idea. We can all look for her. What do you say?"

Paul said, "Shut up."

"Why is everyone telling me to shut up? I drove here from San

Jose and everyone tells me to shut up." Berliner was sighing in a
philosophical way. He'd just seen into the nature of life. "Looking
for Cavanaugh's woman. To me it's a good idea. Hey, man, I have
a better idea. Cavanaugh, take a quick look through Kramer's
snapshots."

Cavanaugh smirked. "She wasn't one of them. She was a
queen."

"Queen what?" shouted Kramer. "My women have names.
What did you call her? You call her Queen? Berliner, get me my
telephone directory. I'll find her. How many women in Berkeley
can be named Queen?"

"I'm sorry, Kramer. Take it easy. I didn't intend to crap on your
six hundred women. He thinks I crapped on his harem."

I said, "Let me talk. I want to tell a love story."

"Great," said Berliner. "Everybody shut up. Go, man. Sing the
blues."

"You don't want to hear my story? I listened to yours, Berliner."

"Yes he does," said Kramer. "Let him talk, Solly."

"I didn't try to stop him."

Cavanaugh said, "Just begin."

"Yeah," said Berliner, grinning in an animal way, brilliant, stiff
with teeth.

"So far," I said, "I've heard three stories about one thing. Cavanaugh calls it love. I call it stories about the other woman. By
which I mean the one who is not the wife. To you guys only the
other woman is interesting. If there wasn't first a wife, there
couldn't be the other woman. Especially you, Berliner; especially
in your case. Moaning, just moaning in the other room, your wife
is only your wife. Moaning with love, she's the other woman. And
Kramer with the snapshots. Look at them. Kramer spent most of
his life trying to photograph the other woman, not knowing that
every time he snapped a picture it was like getting married. Like
permanently eliminating another woman from the possibility of
being the other woman. As for Cavanaugh, why can't he find his
woman? Because he doesn't want to. If he finds her, she won't be
the other woman anymore. This way he can protect his marriage.
Every time he goes to the grocery store and doesn't see the other
woman, which is every single time, his marriage is stronger."

Cavanaugh, frowning at me, said, "What are you trying to tell

us? What's all this business about the other woman? Why don't
you just say it, man?"

Kramer then said, "You're trying to tell us you love your wife.
You think I don't love mine? You think Solly doesn't love his
wife?"

Berliner cried, "If that's all you think, you're right. I hate my
wife."

"Tell your story," said Cavanaugh. "Enough philosophy."

"I don't know if I can tell it. I never told it before. It's about a
woman who was my friend in high school and college. Her name
is Marilyn. We practically grew up together. She lives in Chicago
now. She's a violinist in a symphony orchestra. I spent more time
with her than with any other woman except maybe my mother.
She wasn't like a sister. She was like a friend, a very close friend. I
couldn't have had such a friendship with a man. We'd go out together a lot and if I brought her home late, I'd stay over at her
place, in the same bed. Nothing sexual. Between us it would have
been a crime. We would fight plenty, say terrible things to each
other, but we were close. She phoned me every day. We stayed on
the phone for an hour. We went to parties together when neither
of us had a date. I liked showing up with her because she was attractive. Showing up with her increased my chances of meeting
some girl. It gave me a kind of power, walking in with Marilyn,
feeling free to pick up somebody else. She had the same power.
Anyhow, we never analyzed our relationship, but we joked about
what other people thought. My mother would sometimes answer
the phone and, if she heard Marilyn's voice, she would say, 'It's
your future wife.' She used to worry about us. She used to warn
me that any woman I was serious about would object to Marilyn.
Or she'd say it wasn't nice, me and Marilyn being so thick with
each other, because I was ruining her chances of meeting a man.
That wasn't true. Marilyn had plenty of affairs. All of them ended
badly, but I had nothing to do with it. One of her men scissored
her dresses into rags. Another flung her Siamese cat out the window. She would manage to find some man who was well educated,
had pleasant manners, and turned out to be a brute. She suffered,
but nothing destroyed her. She had her violin. She also had me.
When I was out of a job and not going to school, she loaned me

money and let me stay at her place for weeks. I didn't have to ask. I just showed up one day with my suitcase. One weekend, while I was staying at her place, she came home with a friend, a girl who looked something like her. Lean, with curly brown hair, with beautiful skin faintly olive colored, like Marilyn's. Before dinner was over, Marilyn remembered something important she had to do. She excused herself and went to a movie. Her friend and I were alone in the apartment. It was glorious. Two weeks later, when I was talking to Marilyn about this and that, I mentioned her friend. Marilyn said she didn't want to hear about her. She said that friendship was over and it was something she couldn't discuss. Furthermore, she said I had acted badly that night at dinner, driving her out of her own apartment. I said, 'I thought you left as a favor to me. I thought you did it deliberately.' She said she did do it deliberately, but only because I made it extremely obvious that I was hot for her friend and I acted like a slob. Now I began to feel angry. I told her she didn't have to leave her apartment for my sake and it was rotten of her to make me feel guilty about it two weeks after I'd started having very strong feelings about her friend, so strong in fact we had been talking about marriage. I thought this would change everything. Marilyn would laugh and give me a hug. Instead she lights a cigarette and begins smoking with quick, half-drags, flicking ashes all over her couch. Then she says, 'Why don't you just say that you consider me physically disgusting and you always have.' This was my old friend Marilyn speaking, but it seemed like science fiction. It looked like her. It sounded like her. It was her, but it wasn't. Some weird mongoose had seized her soul. Then she starts telling me about what is inside my head, things she has always known though I tried to hide them from her. Her voice is getting bitter and nasty. She says she knows I can't stand her breasts and the birthmark on her neck sickens me. I said, 'What birthmark?' She says, 'Who are you trying to kid? I've seen you looking at it a thousand times when you thought I didn't notice.' I sat down beside her on the couch. She says 'Get away from me, you pig.' I felt confused. Ashamed and frightened at the same time. Then she jumps off the couch and strides out of the room. I hear her slamming around in the toilet, bottles toppling out of her medicine cabinet into the sink. Smashing. I said, 'Marilyn, are you all right?' No answer. She finally comes out, wearing a bathrobe with nothing underneath and the robe is open. But she's standing there as if nothing has changed since she left the room, and she talks to me again in the same nasty voice. She sneers and accuses me of things I couldn't have imagined, let alone thought about her, as she says I did, every day, all the time, pretending I was her friend. Suddenly, I'm full of a new feeling. Feeling I've never had before. Not what a normal person would call sexual feeling, but what does a penis know? It isn't a connoisseur of normal feeling. Besides, I was a lot younger, still mystified by life, especially my own chemicals. I leap off the couch and grab her. No, I find myself leaping, grabbing her, and she's twisting, trying to hit me, really fighting. I feel she's seriously trying to hurt me, but there's no screaming or cursing, there's nothing but the two of us breathing and sweating and then she begins to collapse, to slide toward the floor. Next thing I'm on top of her. I'm wearing my clothes, she's lying on her open robe. It's supernaturally exciting. Both of us are shivering and wild. We fell asleep like that and we slept at least an hour. I woke when I felt her moving. The lights were on. We were looking at each other. She says, "This is very discouraging." Then she went to her bedroom and shut the door. I got up and followed her and knocked at the door. She opens it and lets me kiss her. Then she shut the door again. I went home. Six months later she phoned me from Chicago to tell me about her new job and to give me her address. After a while she asked about her friend. I told her it was finished between her friend and me. I was seeing somebody else. She changed the subject. Now every few months I get a letter. I write to her also. Someday, if I happen to be in Chicago, I'll visit her."

In the silence following my story, I began to regret having told it. Then a man who had said nothing all evening asked, "Did you make it that night with Marilyn?"

"No. Nothing changed. I don't think it ever will. I could show up tomorrow in Chicago with my suitcase and move into her place."

The man shook his head softly and started to say something, then stopped.

"Go on," I said. "Do you have a question?"

He smiled.

We waited. It was clear that he was a shy man. Then he said, "Was it a true story?"

"Yes."

He shrugged and smiled and said, "I liked Marilyn."

I said, "I like her, too. Maybe I can fix you up with her. What's your name?"

"Terry."

"Terry?" shrieked Berliner. "Terry, you're supposed to phone your wife."

Grinning at Berliner, Terry seemed less a shy man than a man surprised. "It's not my wife," he said, intimating complexities. Old confusions. As if to forbid himself another word, he shook his head. Long and bald. Sandy tufts of hair beside the ears, like baby feathers. His eyes were light brown. His nose was a straight, thick pull. "I mustn't bore you fellows with my situation." He nodded at me as if we had a special understanding. "We're enjoying ourselves, telling melancholy stories about love." He continued nodding. For no reason, I nodded back.

Cavanaugh said, "Talk about anything you like, Terry. You say the woman who phoned isn't your wife?"

He grinned. "I'm a haunted house. For me, yesterday is today. The woman who phoned is my former wife. A strange expression, but what else can I call her? Ex-wife?"

"Call her by her name," I said.

"Her name is Nicki."

"How long have you been divorced?" asked Cavanaugh.

"Usually one asks how long you've been married. Nicki and I have been divorced ten years. Nicki . . ."

"It's better," said Berliner, "if you say former wife. Nicki, Nicki —you sound like a Ping-Pong game."

"All right. After ten years of divorce we're closer than during our marriage. If you don't remarry, this is natural. She phones me two or three times a week. Listen to how personal I'm becoming. Why is everything personal so funny?"

"Who is laughing?" said Berliner. "Do you sleep together? To sleep with your former wife, I think—I mean just to me—it is immoral. I couldn't do it."

"You couldn't do it," I said. "Who asked you to?"

"He's right. I'm sorry, Terry. Go on."

"It doesn't happen often. Nicki has a boyfriend. His name is Harrison. But they don't live together. Nicki can't get along with kids. She doesn't like kids. More complicated yet, Harrison's daughter, eleven years old, is a very sad fat girl. His boy, six years old, has learning problems. Harrison phones me, too. I meet him now and then to talk about his kids."

"He wants to talk to you?" I said.

"I'm a doctor. Even at parties people come up to me for an opinion. 'Terry, I shouldn't discuss professional matters in these circumstances, but my aged aunt Sophie has a black wart on her buttock. She wants you to know. She says to tell you it is beginning to grow hair.'"

"So what about Nicki? She was crying on the phone," Kramer says.

"She always does. Your Marilyn story reminded me of a fight we had when I was in medical school in Montreal. We lived in a two room flat above a grocery store. It was a Saturday morning. I was studying at the kitchen table. Can I tell this story?"

Berliner said, "Only if it's miserable."

"Anyhow, a blizzard had been building for days. I watched it through the kitchen window as it attacked the city. The sky disappeared. The streets were dead. Nothing moved but wind and snow. In this deadly blizzard, Nicki decided to go out. She had been saving money for a particular pair of boots. Fine soft leather. Tight. Knee high. They had a red brown tone, like dried blood, but slightly glossy. Totally impractical and too elegant. The wind would tear them off her legs. Nobody in our crowd owned such boots. Our friends in Montreal were like us—students, poor, always working, always worried about money. Nicki had worked as a secretary all that year and she never bought presents for herself. Her salary paid for our rent and food. I had a tiny scholarship that covered books and incidental tuition fees. We were badly in debt, but she wanted these boots. I don't know how she saved a penny for them. I pleaded with her not to go out in the blizzard. Something in my voice, maybe, suggested more anxiety about the price of the boots than her safety. The more I pleaded the more determined she became."

"Why didn't you go with her?" I asked.

"I wanted to. But the idea of the boots—so trivial, such a lux-

ury—and her wanting to go get them that morning—made me furious. I could sympathize with her desire for beautiful boots. She
deserved a reward. But why that minute did she have to go get
them? I was trying to study. My papers and books were on the
kitchen table. Also a box of slides and a microscope I carried
home from the laboratory. Today, though I own a house with ten
rooms, I still use the kitchen table when I read medical journals
or write an article. Anyhow, I was trying to study. I needed the
time. It's difficult for me to memorize things, but I can do it if
there is peace and quiet and no bad feelings in the air. You don't
have to be a genius to be a doctor. But now I was furious. I yelled,
'Go on, do what you like. Buy the stupid boots. Just leave me
alone.' She slammed the door.

"For a while I sat with my papers and books. Outside the blizzard was hysterical. Inside it was warm and quiet. I worried about
her, but my fury cancelled the worry. Soon I began really to study
and I forgot about Nicki. Maybe three hours passed and, suddenly, she's home. Pale and burning and happy. I didn't say hello.
My fury returned. She had a big shoe box under her arm. She had
returned with her boots. While she put them on, I continued trying to study. I didn't watch her, but I could tell she needed help.
The boots were tight. After a while she managed to get them on
by herself, then she walked up to my table and stood there, in
blood colored legs, waiting for me to notice. I could feel her excitement. She was trembling with pleasure. I knew what expression was in her face. Every muscle working not to smile. She
waited for me to look up, collapse with approval, to admit she was
magnificent in those boots. But the blizzard was in my heart. I refused to look. Suddenly, my papers, books, slides, microscope—
everything on the table was all over the kitchen floor. Nicki is
strong. She plays tennis like a man. I jumped up. I felt I had been
killed, wiped out of the world.

"She still claims I hit her. I don't remember. I remember rushing out into the blizzard with no coat or hat. Why? To buy a gun.
I didn't really know what I wanted until I happened to pass a
pawnshop. I saw guns in the window. I had a pocket watch that
my father gave me when I left for medical school. A Waltham
Premier worth about two hundred dollars. Gold case. Gothic nu-
merals. A classic watch. Also a heavy gold chain. In exchange for

that watch I got a rifle. Then I asked the man for a bullet. I couldn't pay for it, but I told him the deal was off unless he gave me a bullet. He said, 'One bullet?' I screamed, 'Give me a bullet.' He gave it to me. If I'd asked for a ton of bullets, he would have thought nothing. But ask for one bullet and there's trouble."

"The police were waiting for you," said Berliner, "when you got home."

"I noticed the police car in front of the house, its light blinking through the storm. So I entered an alley behind the house and went up to the roof and loaded the rifle. I intended to go to the flat and blow my brains out in front of Nicki."

"I thought you were going to shoot her," I said.

"Her? I'd never shoot her. I'm her slave. I wanted to make a point about our relationship. But the police were in the flat. I was on the roof with a loaded rifle, freezing in a storm. I aimed into the storm, toward the medical school, and fired. How could I shoot myself? I'd have been on that roof with a bullet in my head, covered by snow, and nobody would have found me until spring. What comes to mind when you commit suicide is amazing. Listen, I have a question. My story made me hungry. Is there anything to eat?"

Kramer rose from his pillow with a brooding face. "Men," he said, "Terry is hungry. I believe him because I too am hungry. I suppose all of us could use a little bite. Any other night I would suggest we send out for pizza. Or I myself would make us an omelet. But not tonight. You are lucky tonight. Very lucky. Tomorrow, in this room, Nancy is having a meeting of her women's group. So the refrigerator happens to be packed with good things. Let me itemize. In the refrigerator there is three different kinds of salad. There is big plates of chicken, turkey, and salmon. There is also a pecan pie. I love pecan pie. There is two pecan pies and there is two lemon pies. There is a chocolate cake which, even as I speak of it, sucks at me. I am offering all this to you men. Wait, Berliner. I have one more thing to say, Berliner. In the alcove behind the kitchen, rests a case of zinfandel. It is good, good California. Men, I offer to you this zinfandel."

Berliner was already in the kitchen. The rest of us stayed to cheer Kramer. Even I cheered. Despite his tattooed arms, which reminded me of snakes, I cheered. His magnanimity was un-

qualified. No smallest doubt or reluctance troubled his voice.
Every face in the room became like his, an animal touched by
glee. We were "lucky," said Kramer. Lucky, maybe, to be men.
Life is unfair business. Whoever said otherwise? It is a billion bad
shows, low blows, and number one has more fun. Nancy's prepara-
tions for her women's group would feed our club. The idea of delicious food, taken this way was thrilling. Had it been there for us,
it would have been pleasant. But this was evil, like eating the
other woman. We discovered Berliner on his knees before the refrigerator, door open, his head inside. We cheered again, crowding
up behind him as he passed things out to us, first a long plate of
salmon, the whole pink fish intact, then the chicken, then a salad
bowl sealed with a plastic sheet through which we saw dazzling
green life. It would be a major feast, a huge eating. To Cavanaugh, standing beside me, I said, "I thought you had to leave
early." He didn't reply. He pulled his watch off, slipped it into his
pocket, and shouted, "I see pâté in there. I want that, too." The
cheers came again. Some of the men had already started on the
salmon, snatching pieces of it with their fingers. Kramer, who had
gone to the alcove, reappeared with black bottles of zinfandel, two
under his arms, two in his hands. He stopped, contemplated the
scene in his kitchen, and his dark eyes glowed. His voice was all
pleasure. "This is a wonderful club. This is a wonderful club."

GHOSTS LIKE THEM

"Ghosts Like Them" is Shirley Ann Taggart's first published
story. Ms. Taggart lives in Lexington, Massachusetts; she
studied creative writing at Harvard University under the direction of Cynthia Rich.

I. AUNT AMANDA JANE

Dear Amanda Jane, she writes. But she is too ashamed and guilty
to continue. Ashamed of her contempt and fear of Amanda Jane,
of the name Amanda Jane itself, the way it makes her think of
black women in white kitchens, of Aunt Jemima. Although, she
herself had loved Aunt Jemima once; as a little girl. A little girl
dreaming on her aunt's front porch. Dreamed Aunt Jemima into
the kitchen to bake special cakes for Angela Powers. But Aunt
Jemima always turned in those dreams and viciously locked the
oven door, so that she, Angela, would have to watch all the cakes
turn black and burn to ashes. But when she woke up crying, Aunt
Amanda Jane, sitting on that porch with her, would take Angela
into her big arms and tell her sternly that bad dreams was God's
reminder to sinners to make their peace with the Lord, and you
was never too young to make your peace, to drive off the devil.

So how can she write Miss Amanda Jane Powers, Natchez, Mississippi, without feeling her soul burning and going to hell, without seeing her Aunt Amanda Jane with her straw hat and the
Bible she couldn't read, rocking on an old weathered rocking chair
on her front porch. Her Aunt Amanda Jane with her old black
eyes fumbling in their yellow sockets, grabbing at Angela's face,
her thin body, saying, "Amen, girl, Amen. I been there and back.

Reprinted by permission from *The Hudson Review*, Vol. XXXI, No. 3
(Autumn 1978). Copyright © 1978 by Shirley Ann Taggart.

Yes, Lawd, I been there and back." An old heavy black woman who is neither particularly impatient nor particularly peaceful with all her flesh, just a little tired of it, a little bored with it. "But it jes a house, Angela Ann, jes a house, honey, and the Lawd seen fit to give me a big one and if He seen fit to do it, then I seen fit to keep it."

Yesterday from Philadelphia, Pennsylvania, Angela Powers said, "How is she?" Her mother in Mississippi said, "She's an old woman, Angela." Her mother sighed into the telephone not in sympathy or resignation, but just as a habit. "But you don't think she'll die, do you Mama?" And she imagined her mother shaking her head, sad and intense and tired herself, before she said, "Honey, that old woman's been dead a long time now, her body just ain't believed it yet."

Ten years ago, she, Angela Powers, had sat on that old rotting front porch with her. A skinny nineteen-year-old from a poor Mississippi family of eleven children, all younger than her, yet home from college in those summers not to teach the children, but the aunt (who even then was well into her eighties, well into dying). A promising young woman on a full scholarship to a northern university, mysteriously compelled home into that fiercely hot summer sun in Natchez, to teach her aunt that the Lord didn't give her a fat body, a tired body; that, she, herself, made her body fat, made it tired.

Going off every day to her aunt's porch until her mother had said, "Lawd, child, what do you want with that old woman?"

And she would shrug her awkwardly tall and thin body and say, "I don't know, Mama."

But she had refused dates to sit on that porch with her, refused offers to drive into town with the tall predatory young men and sometimes older men, that hovered around her aunt's front gate, its broken-down condition, its peeling paint.

"I ain't never read me no books," was all her aunt had said, "and girl I ain't about to now." And then she sang, "Ain't about to leave you, Lawd. Ain't about to."

But Angela, always patient and polite, would continue sitting there reading out loud; sitting with her hair pulled painfully and neatly straight back from her high-cheekboned face, her continually washed and creamed face. Whose aunt had even said she

could smell the mothballs and cleaning liquids still on Angela's
sweaters and skirts. An old aunt whose voice would come on with
a sudden power like a radio left on high, violently plugged in, and
would sink into Angela's ears, anchor in her heart. "You stink,
chile. You stink like a new bicycle and you gonna rust, chile. I
knows, chile. I knows."

So sometimes she had hated her, her Aunt Amanda Jane; rocking there on that front porch that looked out over nothing now
but broken rhubarb stems and ghosts of cotton plants. Hated that
old woman singing and rocking there; picking at her decayed
teeth between songs, and tapping on her chair a different beat
from whatever songs she sang; as if there was such a multitude of
songs, such an urgency to sing them, that they had had to appear
in pairs, multiples. And how that had confused Angela, tangled
up her words, until her aunt, alert to sounds, their patterns in
space, had said, "Don't mumble, girl."

Yes, and hated her aunt's laziness too, her preaching from a
rocking chair she never left to know one way or another what she
was preaching about. Angela's mother had told her that Amanda
Jane had been a flirt, a tease, but that men sensed that stubborn
density of her soul, its competence and independence too; the
Amanda Jane Powers who could go out in a heavy storm, her hair
all done up for a date and a new dress just sewed; could go out
and direct all her brothers and sisters to getting the animals inside
and who brought in the last pig herself. So she had plenty of pro-
posals, although one sweetheart was killed, but she said she wasn't
about to marry him anyway, so who knows. But she never did get
married, never did anything past 25, when her father died and left
her in the house; had brothers and cousins and then nephews and
then great-nephews to look after her. Took right to the porch,
sewing in the beginning, and talking about opening a sewing
place, selling her quilts and dresses, but then after a while, just
rocking and remembering. So, of course, Angela couldn't help pitying her, pitying the way her life slipped into the wood she rocked
in; but pitying her from far away exactly like she thought some
white northerners with a brand new color TV might, tuning in to
a documentary on the south, taking time to sigh and shake their
heads before turning the channel. But then she would feel
ashamed. Because, really, she loved her aunt.

But couldn't write to her. Even said she didn't have time to visit her the last time she was home. Said she didn't have time to see an old woman rock and sing and not even know you're there; an old woman who might even die right there, right in front of Angela herself. Although her mother had laughed that same mournful trying to be joyful sound of her aunt's songs, and said, "No, honey, you ain't about to see that." But when her mother had turned back to washing down the kitchen floor, she had said, "Then you wouldn't have to worry about death no more, child. You'd have to worry about the resurrection."

No, wasn't going over to see her aunt six months ago when she was home, until her mother had leaned her own deep, dark face into Angela's and said, "You my daughter, girl, my flesh and blood; but girl, you as cold as the north you live in." So it was fear that got her over those three-hundred yards to her aunt's porch; guilty and ashamed in that hot stagnant Mississippi air.

Was it fear of her aunt dying, she had thought, or fear of an aunt who at ninety-five, wouldn't die?

Yet she loved her.

And was afraid of her. Of the way she sang, so loud and uncontrolled. Afraid of the wrinkles in her aunt's face, the wrinkles even in her faded white socks pulled down below her heavy black ankles. And Angela would become a little dizzy at this loss of moisture and life in her aunt's skin, even mirrored in her aunt's clothes, as if the woman herself had already left them, routinely and unsentimentally abandoned them, moved inward. Her Aunt Amanda Jane turning inward upon herself like a dead star in space.

In the last summer before she graduated from college, she had gone over to see her aunt and her aunt had said, "A woman's got to be saved, chile. She was His second thought and He wasn't yet done with her when the world got started. So she need a man, honey."

But she hadn't needed those men in Mississippi, men who hung around on a broken gate, smelling of chewing tobacco and a boisterous camaraderie. "Good afternoon, Mizz Angela. Ain't it a good afternoon, Miss Angela. Now ain't it just a real fine afternoon?" Dragging out the word fine with their wide mocking toothy grins.

Her aunt said, "If a woman not saved by love and childruns, her soul jes dries up and dies, chile. Dries up and dies. Oh Lawdy, you can hear it crack. Yes, Lawd. Happened to women I knows. Women, I knows, chile."

So in the late summer afternoons of 1967 Angela dreamed she saw images in the haze off her aunt's front porch. Of her savior who would be the strongest, blackest man she had ever seen. One day washing dishes with her sisters she thought she saw him coming through the field in the back. But up close, she recognized him as a preacher and saw him put his arms around their mother who had run out the back door drying her hands on her dress. Angela stood stiff and still when her mother came back inside. "Was it . . . ?" And she was surprised at her panic, her fear, and her coldness. "Why honey, no," her mother had said startled, guessing her question. "It was Grandma Powers who went with the Lord." And she wondered how she could have forgotten her Grandmother Powers deathly sick in her bed and still reciting her tales of Mississippi that Angela's brother Latent, at 16, convinced of his pending importance and superiority, had generously vowed to write and publish. So that later, the preacher had said she had died slightly frantic, angry at the Lord for taking her too soon, right in the middle of that final story. The end lost forever in ordinary Mississippi dirt and rock.

But her brother, Latent, believed in ghosts, in his grandmother reappearing, in the ending being revealed to him. He believed in ghosts, more than in her, his sister, who he admitted was exceptionally bright, but who he was convinced would get lost, become anonymous and harmless in marriage and fertility, like so many other sisters, all the sisters he had ever known. Impotent with their big bellies and their big breasts, he had said. But it was all right. Acceptable for women. Only men needed to commit suicide.

In the late summer evenings her savior committed murder and theft. In the movies downtown. Breaking up rocks on a chain gang with Sidney Poitier. Or maybe even Sidney Poitier himself. A man so strong she imagined she could smell his sweat, like hot burnt rubber, all the way through the paper movie screen in the concrete church basement on Farm Street. Heard his cry through the giggling and whistles, when he finally broke the rock, when he said in that fierce amplified whisper, his black face blazing with sweat, "God, I can't stay here. These men are dead. And I'm still alive." And when he was sentenced to die she dreamed that she was the woman he saw in that movie, the woman who turned his soul to love and repentence; and mystically, magically this saved her. She was saved.

II. ENRIQUE JONES

In real life she was also finally saved. His name was Enrique Jones, a tall, exotic looking black man who wore hand embroidered Swedish shirts and vests sent to him by a sister in Scandinavia, so that he almost looked like a shepherd, lost in the wrong land, the wrong contour of the earth, in the mountainless, flat, sea-level city of Philadelphia. Enrique Jones, her savior. His mother was Spanish and his father was black and the combination of strange bloods never quite jelled, so that Enrique never quite understood Spanish and never quite identified with blacks, with any of their rallies, their tears, their rage. He only understood rage in a purer, more impersonal sense and when he broke Angela's nose with his fist, he had cried. Gently and lovingly he tried to persuade her that it wasn't personal, that it wasn't even because he hated his job, hated collecting people's trash, because, he joked, even those rich, smart-assed politicians had to do that, all that wealth and power and they still had to take people's trash every day! And they couldn't even punch out at 4:00 either. Enslaved forever with other people's trash! And he would laugh heavily, heartily, at this irony until he had had too much beer or until his friends left or until he felt sick. And then he might hit her again, punch her in the stomach. But it wasn't personal, he would tell her; he loved her, god how he loved her. And then he would watch television, watch people in new clothes wander into ski lodges and unwrap fancy bottles of booze in front of a fireplace, and over their heads, wooden rafters, that someone could have rubbed their skin, their goddamn soul out polishing. And through those big glass windows was new snow; all white and clean like those faces, all those contented, uncluttered white faces smiling at him. And on another channel, doctors staring seriously, thoughtfully at patients; prescribing perfect treatments, exercises, love.

White male doctors. Over 40. Fatherly and respected. And then suddenly they were younger. And then women. And now black. But all with the same smiles, all pointing fearlessly, confidently, to the remedy, the cure. But he could never quite focus on the cure, never quite concentrate on those prescriptions because he would be trying to remember when it started. When he first saw them. Those doctors. And it gives him a headache, a pounding and throbbing in his head trying to remember all those puffy, broken-up streets in his old neighborhood; his youth in those pot-holes, those bars, so cloudy and noisy with the same people, the same dudes, the same friendly slaps, the same angry punches. But the TV was always going, he remembers that, remembers the exact day they got color TV's downtown, has a good memory; but there were never black doctors, never, he would have noticed. And he can't imagine who snuck out, Jesus Christ, who would even think of sneaking out and masquerading as a doctor?

So he broke her nose, and her glass Christmas tree ornaments, and their daughter's wrist. When she left, he said it was personal, it was personal now. Very personal. He said, "Woman, I'll kill you if you leave." He said, "You hear? You hear that woman?" And his rage had finally taken shape, crystallized. But when she was out the door he ran after her, yelled from the sidewalk to her, "Get your fucking little ass out of here, woman. And don't you come running back. Don't you ever come running back."

And she could feel him behind her, watching her, trying to hyp-notize her with his eyes, trying to pull her back to him. So she didn't turn around once. Not once. And then what? And then nothing.

III. ANGELA POWERS JONES

She just walked straight ahead and didn't look back. Walked into this apartment with Mandy, her nine-year-old daughter, and signed the lease, signed him out of her life, and she didn't cry once. Since then she hasn't seen him, doesn't want to, but hasn't bothered with a divorce the way the people in this neighborhood don't always bother with marriage, with written laws; the power-ful inertia of all those words and papers that drive educated men to horror movies and roller coasters, to get going again, to get their blood moving again.

But she still lives in Philadelphia, a city with historic landmarks, the Liberty Bell. The cracks in the bell for when freedom starts to break apart, break down into slavery again. But when she married Enrique and had a child, there were things she had to do, meals she had to cook, love she had to give to a man who was her husband. And she didn't cry when he hit her, hardly moved at all. He said she was so good, even her body was so good, not crazy and out of control like his body; and then he would start to cry and she would comfort him. Other times he caressed her and said, "How do you live with me? How are you so brave?"

Didn't whimper or scream like her sisters did, five sisters still in that shack at home on that burned-out farmland in Mississippi with a hundred kids and animals and lovers running over them, keeping their faces down so close to the dried-up useless soil that they wouldn't leave because it wouldn't feel right, because that was their home. But with no way out for them anyway; no scholarships and no beauty. Their mother had said Angela was the only one about to get anywhere. And if she didn't get anywhere, her mother had said, no one she knew in the whole world would.

But once when he slapped her, slapped her hard, and then looked right into her face, into how hard she tried not to change that face, not to remember that slap, he had gotten angry and said, "Je-sus, woman. Are you human?" But she was always in love with him. She doesn't remember a time when she wasn't in love with him, just a time when she had to go away and not look back. Like going away to college had been. And now she dreams of walking in tunnels. Of doors being slammed shut. And this bothers her. Because wasn't leaving home, going to college, leaving a husband who beat her, weren't these good decisions? Wise decisions? Wouldn't psychiatrists agree with this, applaud her; so many people couldn't do that well. Couldn't just walk out of a life like that. Like she did.

But she still lives in the same kind of neighborhood, a neighborhood that is a little worn-out and neglected. A neighborhood starting to shrivel, crack, like old photographs kept too long, kept in too much light; as if the light from the city was too powerful for neighborhoods so close and unprotected. A neighborhood that could burn and turn to ashes, like something in a childhood nightmare that she can almost taste, that makes her uneasy.

So she sits on guard at her window on the fourth floor. Looking out for whole days while Mandy's in school. At the holes in the streets. The broken bottles and old tires in yards, wherever there are yards. At the collapsed buildings. The condemned buildings. At the collapsing wooden fence around a vacant lot across the street with "Jarcy and Jimmy '77" in big awkward red letters, and in a corner on that same fence, in piercing angular black print: "You die, man."

In the afternoons she watches the adolescent boys stand around and pass out plastic bags of drugs and put them in their jackets. Watches them push each other against the fence and laugh, imitating violence, but not violent yet, not ready in the daylight to try and blast the souls out of their own or each other's bodies yet; but excited, desperate to get out, to take off, to get away finally from so many people so close screaming into each other's hearts, or on hot nights, all vegetating in crowds outside on their steps like colonies of seals. She thinks that's what it looks like from up here, from her window.

And in the mornings she watches the prostitutes come home in their flashy clothes and heavy make-up. And the old men and old women asleep or drunk on someone's front steps. The most harmless people in this neighborhood and yet these are the ones that panic her, like dead fish washed up on beaches always do, as if there was some disaster just out of the corners of her eyes that could suddenly move in and destroy her. But she knows these old people are not dead, not even very dramatic, just lonely and tired. But she would like to take their pulses, listen to their hearts; shake their old bony shoulders right out of their skins just to make sure they are still there.

But most of the time she watches the strangers, well-dressed strangers not from this neighborhood, who walk quickly from block to block, absorbed and entranced by their destinations, seeing nothing.

Her destination today was the supermarket, the welfare office. But she tells herself it's all right, the welfare, the food stamps, won't always be like this, things will change, get better, after all she has a college degree, a diploma, something magic, the first in her family. So she has to remember that. "But in history?" An employment counsellor had said, astonished, but a very familiar, routine astonishment. He had said, "Well, you know you can't do anything with that." And then he asked her what machines she could operate, was she familiar with any of the machines on this list?

But one of the employment counsellors was friendly, sympathetic. She was a little older than Angela, a white woman, pretty, but a woman who wore a little more make-up, a little more force in her smile than Angela. She studied her a minute and then said, "Your boyfriend made a bad husband and you got a couple kids, right? And you don't know what to do. Oh, honey, I know." She took her hand. "I know. And look at this, you graduated from college. But honey, I got a kid in here today with a master's degree in something you couldn't even pronounce, and I don't want to discourage you, but she was useless, good lord, didn't know anything you need to know to live, to keep alive."

And good grades. Angela always had good grades, and good grades must mean something. She was convinced of it. She must be able to do something. Her mother said she could come home, that's what she could do. She said Latent was working in a plant in Birmingham part-time, "but he still thinking about his ghosts, still waiting for Grandma's ghost to finish that book of his. Amanda Jane has a touch of the flu, been in bed all week, nothing serious, but wants to hear from you. Keeps asking if there's a letter from Angela Ann. Keep the Lord in your heart and come home. Love, Mama."

She tears up the letter. She didn't believe in ghosts, she didn't even believe in her fear of ghosts, only Aunt Amanda Jane believed in that. She would tell Angela's stiff little body, "Now don' you worry bout them ghosts Latent tell you bout, he ain't gonna conjure up no ghosts. Even if he could, oh, Lawdy, help us, they never hurt you honey, cause ghosts is the soul. Theys not the body that does, theys the soul that is. Ghosts like them, they might wanna scream up the grass in the winna, and oh, Lawdy, they in pain, yes, Lawd; but ghosts like them, chile, they jes can't do nuthin. They jes can't."

She throws the pieces of the letter into a wastebasket in her living room.

Her living room is a greenish-brown, with a little blue. A couple of worn blue tweed chairs and the wallpaper is light green with brown dancing women who have cried the whole way down one wall, the wall that faces that street, the rain and the snow. She asked the landlord about the leaks, said he was letting his own apartment depreciate, it wasn't her wallpaper after all. He had smiled, the kind of smile babies smile by accident, with a burp. He had said, "Yes." Just yes. So she let them cry, all those women who lost their limbs, their faces. Good, she thought that they should be mutilated by nature and not by men. But how did it happen? How did her husband break her nose? And how could she know when even Sidney Poitier on a chain gang, a convicted murderer, gave her such a gentle, loving look? Her mother agreed with Enrique's gentle soul; she had said, "You treat this man good, honey." Of course Angela had known Enrique had gotten into fights, knifed someone once. A long time ago. But his life with her would be different. Saved by their love. Protected. Yes, she admitted she was tired and needed protecting. But wasn't that her privilege, after all, as a woman? No, those were someone else's words. She, Angela Powers Jones, advocated equality. And in their marriage they both had had an equal chance to escape, to die gracefully.

Dear Amanda Jane, she writes from an old round kitchen table with a formica top. Writing Dear Amanda eternally, she believes, into her one hundredth year of life. One hundred sheets of her daughter's tablet paper crumpled up and stuffed under the exposed pipes of her kitchen sink, although later she would dig them out and count them and find that, really, there were only 15. Dear Amanda Jane, she writes, but a friend of hers from college, whom she hasn't seen since college, comes over and interrupts her with her good clothes, her good job, her advanced degrees; she takes her hand and says, "Oh, Angela." Her friend's face is disappointed, compassionate, going out of control. But Angela's face, her perfect smile, her perfect bone structure and perfect teeth are convincing, persuasive. She says, "It's not so bad, really. It's just the wallpaper. It's such an awful color." Later, her friend, brave in her expensive dress, her neatly sculptured afro, her solid gold hoop earrings, asks, "But a man like that, Angela? A man who would physically abuse you?"

Angela shrugs. She looks out the window at the buildings. Buildings like her building. Old and dirty with small cement yards. And she thinks that some place else in Philadelphia things must be growing, coming alive. She thinks of trees and grass and flowers, and she feels suddenly deserted, angry.

Her friend makes an effort to sit neatly in one of Angela's sagging chairs, not to get stuffing on her dress. She says, "Angela Powers. Our social conscience. That Angela Powers shrugs?" She makes another effort to laugh, to joke about this. Then enthusiastically she says, "Angela, remember that paper you read in sociology? About our people struggling to get up north where the cold air will revive them, but with the cotton still caught under their fingernails. Remember? And about their new life in the north, how ironically it wasn't new at all, but the same. The same rats and the same weariness to be white, so that they felt cheated, as if they had been purposefully distracted at that moment when things were going to change. Remember that? God, Angela, we couldn't believe it was you . . . you were always so quiet. And remember our professor, Miss Dover, a white conservative woman, a little sickly, and how we swore she turned even whiter, embalmed right there at her own familiar worn desk she had written a poem about. Do you remember that? A poem about a *desk!* But anyway, your paper and Miss Dover, god, I've remembered that all these years!" Angela says nothing and after a minute her friend leans out of her chair and reaches over and touches Angela's hand again. She says, "If you ever want to talk about it. . . ." Angela doesn't move, she thinks only how hot it is. As hot as Mississippi. And it's only April. Only spring and still expected to be pleasant, comfortable.

She gets up and opens the window, feeling a little dizzy, a little tired. But in her mind she sees that her sociology professor does turn a little whiter, paler, behind that solid mahogany desk. A little shocked on such a routinely drowsy late May afternoon. And Angela feels that this, this must be something.

Her friend says, "Angela . . . ?" She says other things also, but Angela is only aware of the beat of that other black woman's voice, aware of the beat of the tires, the horns outside, a faster, more demanding beat that continually assaults and wears down the streets and eardrums of her neighborhood. And she wonders what the beat is like in Africa in 1978, the Africa she sees on the news, and whether the beat of a thousand guns and bodies being pounded into the ground will destroy their forests; their jungles. But secretly, she wonders how really this has anything to do with her.

Her friend says, "Angela, can I help you? Is there any way I can help?"

"You help them," a skinny, angry young college woman of the 1960's says in her mind. "You help them set up programs. You give them food. And yet they deceive you, they cheat you and your government. They take your money and watch your televisions, your dreams. Because their dreams aren't so visible, so concrete. Surely you know that. And your dreams are too expensive, too impossible for them. And they know this, they smell this like they smelled those sweet suffocating lilacs, that wet cotton and oily sweat that permanently opened, widened their nostrils."

Words rehearsed over and over in a life she can hardly remember so it is a surprise they are still there, still in perfect order. She looks out the window and the bricks in the building across the street make her feel dizzy and confused, the way she felt dizzy for two months before her freshman year in college, alarming her parents. What was she just thinking about? Suddenly she can't remember. But who was that vicious accusing college girl with all those white faces staring at her, and four black ones too, all staring blankly at her. And who was this woman now who stared out her window all day, rocking on a rocking chair. No, that at least, wasn't true, she didn't have a rocking chair. And she did do something, she did take care of her daughter, of course, and she does have a college degree. . . .

Her friend comes over to her, concerned with her silence, her appearance of nausea and sickness, concerned also with the dust that makes her cough, blown in from somewhere she can't see. But she manages to ask Angela if she is all right. Is she all right? Angela, her mind blank now, not dizzy anymore, assures her she is fine, fine in her strong thin, handsome black body, she is just tired. Saw her lover last night, not a violent man either, not very violent at all. And her daughter will be home from school soon. And the dishes have to be washed, and the roaches chased off the counters; her daughter is very fussy, squeamish; not good at all in the role of a poor minority child. Her friend says, "God, Angela, look at me. You can do better, girl. Girl, you can do so much better." Angela says of course, she plans on it. She smiles and says, "Don't worry about me, Rennie." She stares at her hands, so long and thin and graceful. "I think I'll become a doctor. Enrique hated doctors. Was scornful of them. Scornful of healing itself." She says, but today she is just so tired. Her friend nods, and they walk together to the door. Her friend hugs and kisses her goodbye. She says, "But you still look good Angela. Fantastic. Remember that. You still have a chance."

When her friend leaves, she falls asleep and dreams she is in a jungle in Africa and a tribal chief whom she knows is a murderer, insists she is his wife. She is attracted to him and thinks maybe this is true, but she somehow feels she is married to someone else, although she can't remember him, can't picture him at all. And then she thinks of her Aunt Amanda Jane and she can't remember if she is dead or alive, but surely if she were dead, surely she would remember the funeral? So she comes to the conclusion in the dream that she must have amnesia. And in her amnesia married the tribal chief. A handsome man who treats her gently. So why should she strain to remember a life she's already forgotten? And she can't think of a reason why. And yet she feels uncomfortable. And is glad to wake up.

Since it is 1:00 in the afternoon she fixes herself a light lunch. Some lettuce and tuna fish. She thinks about her dream and laughs because the tribal chief looked like Sidney Poitier, although she is a little ashamed to have dreamed herself so easily married to a murderer.

Sitting in a light cotton dress at her kitchen table, having finished eating now, and absent-mindedly peeling the formica off the top of the table. White and black formica, although the white has yellowed a little. Has given up writing to an old inert woman furiously trying to rock away her life on a porch in Mississippi that won't quite collapse and give up like that fence across the street; and not even Angela, Angela's elevation and rise into the mystical white forests of the north could save her. And of course Angela's marriage didn't work out, couldn't save anyone.

She cuts her thumb peeling the formica, but stubbornly she keeps peeling it, breaking it off in her fingers. And yes, it's true, she is ashamed of her aunt, an old ignorant woman who won't move and won't listen and won't die. Yes, so ashamed of her aunt, that she can't even write to her when she is sick in bed, a ninety-five-year-old woman of her own blood sick in bed, waiting to hear from her and she can't even tolerate her name, Amanda Jane, and yet she named her own daughter Amanda. Ashamed of her shame.

At 2:00 she gets up and goes over to the window and looks out, vaguely daydreaming, vaguely watching for her daughter to come home from school. She has been waiting, watching at this window for such a long time, so many months, and nothing has happened. A "dangerous, high risk" neighborhood where, after all, there is no danger, no risk. A disappointment. Disappointing that the women on this wall cry, suffer, for only bad weather, too much spring rain. So she is surprised when there is an accident outside in front of her building, and her heart is pounding. A man hit by a car! A black man in a gold suit, hit and thrown to the sidewalk. Two men run away, quickly, deftly, and other people gather, press against each other, greedy for a better view. Kids run over and circle the area, kicking aimlessly at the garbage and then pushing and jostling each other to see the man.

Angela watches this from her window. She watches the people move slowly closer to that man lying on the ground not quite twisted out of shape, out of their reach. And she thinks of insects. Insects around a light. Swarms. Swarming. But the movement, the whispers, are choked off suddenly by sirens, police cars, an ambulance. And then someone yells. A thick, heavy voice, heavy with rage, pain, yelling, "He's dead so get the fuck out of here."

But they come anyway, the police, the ambulance. Two men bring out a stretcher. They cover the man on the ground with a white sheet. And Angela dreams of ghosts rising from the sidewalk, of white socks on black legs. And she wonders where this dream comes from and where it goes from here, wonders if she is going crazy finally, when there has never been any sign of it, no hint at all. They put the stretcher in the ambulance. They close the doors and drive away. She is shaking. Violently cold on such a warm spring day. Ashamed. Guilty. Almost sick. But she can't quite cry. She can't quite cry with the hundred other women in this apartment. A hundred brown women crying. And one who isn't. But after all she didn't even know him. "I didn't even know him," she says to no one of them in particular.

THE OLD FOREST

PETER TAYLOR

Peter Taylor was born in Trenton, Tennessee, in 1917. He
has spent most of his life there and in Virginia. He is married to the poet Eleanor Ross Taylor and has two grown
children—both of whom are writers. The Taylors live in
Charlottesville, Virginia, where Mr. Taylor teaches in the
English Department of the University of Virginia. Mr. Taylor is the recipient of numerous awards, including a Guggenheim Fellowship, a Fulbright Fellowship to France, and
several previous O. Henry Awards. He is the author of a
novel, A *Woman Of Means* (1950), several plays, and
many short stories.

I was already formally engaged, as we used to say, to the girl I was
going to marry. But still I sometimes went out on the town with
girls of a different sort. And during the very week before the date
set for the wedding, in December, I was in an automobile accident at a time when one of those girls was with me. It was a ca-
lamitous thing to have happen—not the accident itself, which
caused no serious injury to anyone, but the accident plus the presence of that girl.

As a matter of fact, it was not unusual in those days—forty
years ago and a little more—for a well brought up young man like
me to keep up his acquaintance, until the very eve of his wedding,
with some member of what we facetiously and somewhat ar-
rogantly referred to as the Memphis demimonde. (That was
merely to say with a girl who was not in the Memphis débutante
set.) I am not even sure how many of us knew what the word
"demimonde" meant or implied. But once it had been applied to

such girls it was hard for us to give it up. We even learned to speak of them individually as demimondaines—and later corrupted that to demimondames. The girls were of course a considerably less sophisticated lot than any of this sounds, though they were bright girls certainly and some of them even highly intelligent. They read books, they looked at pictures, and they were apt to attend any concert or play that came to Memphis. When the old San Carlo Opera Company turned up in town, you could count on certain girls of the demimonde being present in their block of seats, and often with a score of the opera in hand. From that you will understand that they certainly weren't the innocent, untutored types that we generally took to dances at the Memphis Country Club and whom we eventually looked forward to marrying.

These girls I refer to would, in fact, very frequently and very frankly say to us that the M.C.C. (that's how we always spoke of the Club) was the last place they wanted to be taken. There was one girl in particular, not so smart as some of the others perhaps and certainly less restrained in the humor she sometimes poked at the world we boys lived in, an outspoken girl, who was the most vociferous of all in her disdain for the Country Club. I remember one night, in one of those beer gardens that became popular in Memphis in the late thirties, when this girl suddenly announced to a group of us, "I haven't lost anything at the M.C.C. That's something you boys can bet your daddy's bottom dollar on." We were gathered—four or five couples—about one of the big wooden beer-garden tables with an umbrella in its center, and when she said that, all the other girls in the party went into a fit of laughter. It was a kind of giggling that was unusual for them. The boys in the party laughed, too, of course, but we were surprised by the way the girls continued to giggle among themselves for such a long time. We were out of college by then and thought we knew the world pretty well; most of us had been working for two or three years in our fathers' business firms. But we didn't see why this joke was so very funny. I suppose it was too broad for us in its reference. There is no way of knowing, after all these years, if it was too broad for our sheltered minds or if the rest of the girls were laughing at the vulgar tone of the girl who had spoken. She was, you see, a little bit coarser than the rest, and I suspect they were laughing at the way she had phrased what she said. For us boys, anyhow, it was pleasant that the demimondaines took the lighthearted view they did about not going to the M.C.C., because it was the last place most of us would have wished to take them. Our *other* girls would have known too readily who they were and would not willingly or gracefully have endured their presence. To have brought one of those girls to the Club would have required, at any rate, a boy who was a much bolder and freer spirit than I was at twenty-three.

To the liberated young people of today all this may seem a corrupting factor in our old way of life—not our snobbery so much as our continuing to see those demimonde girls right up until the time of marriage. And yet I suspect that in the Memphis of today customs concerning serious courtship and customs concerning unacknowledged love affairs have not been entirely altered. Automobile accidents occur there still, for instance, the reports of which in the newspaper do not mention the name of the driver's "female companion," just as the report of my accident did not. If the driver is a "scion of a prominent local family" with his engagement to be married already announced at an M.C.C. party, as well as in the Sunday newspaper, then the account of his automobile collision is likely to refer to the girl in the car with him only as his "female companion." Some newspaper readers might, I know, assume this to be a reference to the young man's fiancée. That is what is intended, I suppose for the general reader. But it would almost certainly not have been the case—not in the Memphis, Tennessee, of 1937.

The girl with me in my accident was a girl whose origins nobody knew anything about. But she was a perfectly decent sort of girl, living independently in a respectable rooming house and working at a respectable job. That was the sort of girl about whom the Memphis newspapers felt obliged to exercise the greatest care when making any reference to her in their columns. It was as though she were their special ward. Such a girl must be protected from any blaze of publicity. Such a girl must not suffer from the misconduct of any Memphis man or group of men— even newspaper publishers. That was fine for the girl, of course, and who could possibly resent it? It was splendid for her, but I, the driver of the car, had to suffer considerable anguish just because of such a girl's presence in the car and suffer still more because of her behavior afterward. Moreover, the response of certain older men in town to her subsequent behavior would cause me still further anguish and prolong my suffering by several days. Those men were the editors of the city's two newspapers, along with the lawyers called in by my father to represent me if I should be taken into court. There was also my father himself, and the father of my fiancée, *his* lawyer (for some reason or other), and, finally, no less a person than the mayor of Memphis, all of whom one would ordinarily have supposed to be indifferent to the caprices of such a girl. They were the civic leaders and merchant princes of the city. They had great matters on their minds. They were, to say the least, an imposing group in the eyes of a young man who had just the previous year entered his father's cotton-brokerage firm, a young man who was still learning how to operate under the pecking order of Memphis's male establishment.

The girl in question was named Lee Ann Deehart. She was a quite beautiful, fair-haired, hazel-eyed girl with a lively manner, and surely she was far from stupid. The thing she did which drew attention from the city fathers came very near, also, to changing the course of my entire life. I had known Lee Ann for perhaps two years at the time, and knew her to be more levelheaded and more reserved and self-possessed than most of her friends among the demimondaines. It would have been impossible for me to predict the behavior she was guilty of that winter afternoon. Immediately after the collision, she threw open the door on her side of the car, stepped out onto the roadside, and fled into the woods of Overton Park, which is where the accident took place. And from that time, and during the next four days, she was unheard from by people who wished to question her and protect her. During that endless-seeming period of four days no one could be certain of Lee Ann Deehart's whereabouts.

The circumstances of the accident were rather complicated. The collision occurred just after three o'clock on a very cold Saturday afternoon—the fourth of December. Although at that time in my life I was already a member of my father's cotton firm, I was nevertheless—and strange as it may seem—enrolled in a Latin class out at Southwestern College, which is on the north side of

Overton Park. (We were reading Horace's Odes!) The class was not held on Saturday afternoon, but I was on my way out to the college to study for a test that had been scheduled for Monday. My interest in Latin was regarded by my father and mother as one of my "anomalies"—a remnant of many "anomalies" I had annoyed them with when I was in my teens and was showing some signs of "not turning out well." It seemed now of course that I had "turned out well" after all, except that nobody in the family and nobody among my friends could understand why I went on showing this interest in Latin. I was not able to explain to them why. Any more than I was able to explain why to myself. It clearly had nothing to do with anything else in my life at that period. Furthermore, in the classroom and under the strict eye of our classics professor, a rotund, mustachioed little man hardly four feet in height (he had to sit on a large Latin dictionary in order to be comfortable at his desk), I didn't excel. I was often embarrassed by having to own up to Professor Bartlett's accusation that I had not so much as glanced at the assigned odes before coming to class. Sometimes other members of the class would be caught helping me with the translation, out in the hallway, when Professor Bartlett opened his classroom door to us. My real excuse for neglecting the assignments made by that earnest and admirable little scholar was that too many hours of my life were consumed by my job, by my courtship of the society girl I was going to marry, and by my old, bad habits of knocking about town with my boyhood cronies and keeping company with girls like Lee Ann Deehart.

Yet I had persisted with my Horace class throughout that fall (against the advice of nearly everyone, including Professor Bartlett). On that frigid December afternoon I had resolved to mend my ways as a student. I decided I would take my Horace and go out to Professor Bartlett's classroom at the college and make use of his big dictionary in preparing for Monday's test. It was something we had all been urged to do, with the promise that we would always find the door unlocked. As it turned out, of course, I was destined not to take the test on Monday and never to enter Professor Bartlett's classroom again.

It happened that just before I was setting out from home that afternoon I was filled suddenly with a dread of the silence and the

peculiar isolation of a college classroom building on a weekend afternoon. I telephoned my fiancée and asked her to go along with
me. At the other end of the telephone line, Caroline Braxley
broke into laughter. She said that I clearly had no conception of
all the things she had to do within the next seven days, before we
were to be married. I said I supposed I ought to be helping in
some way, though until now she had not asked me so much as to
help address invitations to the wedding. "No indeed," said my
bride-to-be, "I want to do everything myself. I wouldn't have it
any other way."

Caroline Braxley, this capable and handsome bride-to-be of
mine, was a very remarkable girl, just as today, as my wife, she
seems to me a very remarkable woman of sixty. She and I have
been married for forty-one years now, and her good judgment in
all matters relating to our marriage has never failed her—or us.
She had already said to me before that Saturday afternoon that a
successful marriage depended in part on the two persons' develop-
ing and maintaining a certain number of separate interests in life.
She was all for my keeping up my golf, my hunting, my fishing.
And, unlike my own family, she saw no reason that I shouldn't
keep up my peculiar interest in Latin, though she had to confess
that she thought it almost the funniest thing she had ever heard
of a man of my sort going in for.

Caroline liked any sort of individualism in men. But I already
knew her ways sufficiently well to understand that there was no
use trying to persuade her to come along with me to the college. I
wished she would come with me, or maybe I wished even more
she would try to persuade me to come over to her house and help
her with something in preparation for the wedding. After I had
put down the telephone, it even occurred to me that I might simply drive over to her house and present myself at her front door.
But I knew what the expression on her face would be, and I could
even imagine the sort of thing she would say: "No man is going
to set foot in my house this afternoon, Nat Ramsey! *I'm* getting
married next Saturday, in case the fact has slipped your mind. Besides, you're coming here for dinner tonight, aren't you? And
there are parties every night next week!"

This Caroline Braxley of mine was a very tall girl. (Actually
taller than she is nowadays. We have recently measured ourselves

and found that each of us is an inch shorter than we used to be.)
One often had the feeling that one was looking up at her, though
of course she wasn't really so tall as that. Caroline's height and
the splendid way she carried herself was one of her first attractions
for me. It seems to me now that I was ever attracted to tall girls—
that is, when there was the possibility of falling in love. And I
think this was due in part to the fact that even as a boy I was half
in love with my father's two spinster sisters, who were nearly six
feet in height and were always more attentive to me than to the
other children in the family.

Anyhow, only moments after I had put down the telephone
that Saturday, when I still sat with my hand on the instrument
and was thinking vaguely of rushing over to Caroline's house, the
telephone underneath my hand began ringing. Perhaps, I thought,
it was Caroline calling back to say that she had changed her
mind. Instead, it was Lee Ann Deehart. As soon as she heard my
voice, she began telling me that she was bored to death. Couldn't
I think of something fun she and I could do on this dreary winter
afternoon? I laughed aloud at her. "What a shameless wench you
are, Lee Ann!" I said.

"Shameless? How so?" she said with pretended innocence.

"As if you weren't fully aware," I lectured her, "that I'm getting married a week from today!"

"What's that got to do with the price of eggs in Arkansas?" She
laughed. "Do you think, old Nat, I want to marry you?"

"Well," I explained, "I happen to be going out to the college
to cram for a Latin test on Monday."

I could hear her laughter at the other end. "Is your daddy going
to let you off work long enough to take your Latin test?" she
asked with heavy irony in her voice. It was the usual way those
girls had of making fun of our dependence on our fathers.

"Ah, yes," I said tolerantly.

"And is he going to let you off next Saturday, too," she went
on, "long enough to get married?"

"Listen," I said, "I've just had an idea. Why don't you ride out
to the college with me, and fool around some while I do my
Latin?" I suppose I didn't really imagine she would go, but suddenly I had thought again of the lonely isolation of Dr. Bartlett's
classroom on a Saturday afternoon. I honestly wanted to go ahead

out there. It was something I somehow felt I had to do. My preoccupation with the study of Latin poetry, ineffectual student
though I was, may have represented a perverse wish to experience
the isolation I was at the same time dreading or may have represented a taste for morbidity left over from my adolescence. I can
allow myself to speculate on all that now, though it would not
have occurred to me to do so at the time.

"Well," said Lee Ann Deehart presently, to my surprise and
delight, "it couldn't be more boring out there than sitting here in
my room is."

"I'll pick you up in fifteen minutes," I said quickly. And I hung
up the telephone before she could possibly change her mind.

Thirty minutes later, we were driving through Overton Park on
our way to the college. We had passed the Art Gallery and were
headed down the hill toward the low ground where the Park Pond
is. Ahead of us, on the left, were the gates to the Zoo. And on beyond was the point where the road crossed the streetcar tracks and
entered a densely wooded area which is actually the last surviving
bit of the primeval forest that once grew right up to the bluffs
above the Mississippi River. Here are giant oak and yellow-poplar
trees older than the memory of the earliest white settler. Some of
them surely may have been mature trees when Hernando de Soto
passed this way, and were very old trees indeed when General
Jackson, General Winchester, and Judge John Overton purchased
this land and laid out the city of Memphis. Between the Art Gallery and the Pond there used to be, in my day, a little spinney of
woods which ran nearly all the way back to what was left of the
old forest. It was just when I reached this spinney, with Lee Ann
beside me, that I saw a truck approaching us on the wrong side of
the icy road. There was a moderately deep snow on the ground,
and the Park roads had, to say the least, been imperfectly cleared.
On the ice and the packed snow, the driver of the truck had
clearly lost control of his vehicle. When he was within about
seventy-five feet of us, Lee Ann said, "Pull off the road, Nat!"

Lee Ann Deehart's beauty was of the most feminine sort. She
was a tiny, delicate-looking girl, and I had noticed, when I went to
fetch her that day, in her fur-collared coat and knitted cap and
gutta-percha boots she somehow seemed smaller than usual. And I
was now struck by the tone of authority coming from this small

person whose diminutive size and whose role in my life were such that it wouldn't have occurred to me to heed her advice about driving a car—or about anything else, I suppose. I remember feeling something like: This is an ordeal that I must and that I want to face in my own way. It was as though Professor Bartlett himself were in the approaching truck. It seemed my duty not to admit any weakness in my own position. At least I *thought* that was what I felt.

"Pull off the road, Nat!" Lee Ann urged again. And my incredible reply to her was "He's on *my* side of the road! Besides, trucks are not allowed in the Park!" And in reply to this Lee Ann gave only a loud snicker.

I believe I did, in the last seconds, try to swing the car off onto the shoulder of the road. But the next thing I really remember is the fierce impact of the two vehicles' meeting.

It was a relatively minor sort of collision, or seemed so at the moment. Since the driver of the truck, which was actually a converted Oldsmobile sedan—and a rather ancient one at that—had the good sense not to put on his brakes and to turn off his motor, the crash was less severe than it might have been. Moreover, since I *had* pulled a little to the right it was not a head-on meeting. It is worth mentioning, though, that it was sufficiently bad to put permanently out of commission the car I was driving, which was not my own car (my car was in the shop, being refurbished for the honeymoon trip) but an aging Packard limousine of my mother's, which I knew she would actually be happy to see retired. I don't remember getting out of the car at all and I don't remember Lee Ann's getting out. The police were told by the driver of the truck, however, that within a second after the impact Lee Ann had thrown open her door, leaped out onto the snow-covered shoulder, jumped the ditch beyond, and run up the incline and into the spinney. The truck driver's account was corroborated by two ice skaters on the Pond, who also saw her run through the leafless trees of the spinney and on across a narrow stretch of the public golf course which divides the spinney from the old forest. They agreed that, considering there was a deep snow on the ground and that she was wearing those gutta-percha boots, she travelled at a remarkable speed.

I didn't even know she was out of the car until I got around on the other side and saw the door there standing open and saw her tracks in the snow, going down the bank. I suppose I was too dazed even to follow the tracks with my eyes down the bank and up the other side of the ditch. I must have stood there for several seconds, looking down blankly at the tracks she had left just outside the car door. Presently I looked up at the truck driver, who was standing before me. I know now his eyes must have been following Lee Ann's progress. Finally he turned his eyes to me, and I could tell from his expression that I wasn't a pleasant sight. "Is your head hurt bad?" he asked. I put my hand up to my forehead and when I brought it down it was covered with blood. That was when I passed out. When I came to, they wouldn't let me get up. Besides the truck driver, there were two policemen and the two ice skaters standing over me. They told me that an ambulance was on the way.

At the hospital, the doctor took four stitches in my forehead; and that was it. I went home and lay down for a couple of hours, as I had been told to do. My parents and my two brothers and my little sister and even the servants were very much concerned about me. They hovered around in a way I had never before seen them do—not even when somebody was desperately sick. I suppose it was because a piece of violence like this accident was a very extraordinary thing in our quiet Memphis life in those years. They were disturbed, too, I soon realized, by my silence as I lay there on the daybed in the upstairs sitting room and particularly by my being reticent to talk about the collision. I had other things on my mind. Every so often I would remember Lee Ann's boot tracks in the snow. And I would begin to wonder where she was now. Since I had not found an opportunity to telephone her, I could only surmise that she had somehow managed to get back to the rooming house where she lived. I had not told anyone about her presence in the car with me. And as I lay there on the daybed, with the family and servants coming and going and making inquiries about how I felt, I would find myself wondering sometimes how and whether or not I could tell Caroline Braxley about Lee Ann's being with me that afternoon. It turned out the next day—or, rather, on Monday morning—that the truck driver had told the two policemen and then, later, repeated to someone who called from one of the newspapers that there had been a girl with

me in the car. As a matter of fact, I learned that this was the case
on the night of the accident, but as I lay there in the upstairs sitting room during the afternoon I didn't yet know it.

Shortly before five o'clock Caroline Braxley arrived at our
house, making a proper sick call but also with the intention of
taking me back to dinner with her parents and her two younger
sisters. Immediately after she entered the upstairs sitting room,
and almost before she and I had greeted each other, my mother's
houseboy and sometime chauffeur came in, bringing my volume
of Horace. Because Mother had thought it might raise my spirits,
she had sent him down to the service garage where the wrecked
car had been taken to fetch it for me. Smiling sympathetically, he
placed it on a table near the daybed and left the room. Looking at
the book, Caroline said to me with a smile that expressed a mixture of sympathy and reproach, "I hope you see now what folly
your pursuit of Latin poetry is." And suddenly, then, the book on
the table appeared to me as an alien object. In retrospect it seems
to me that I really knew then that I would never open it again.

I went to dinner that night at Caroline's house, my head still in
bandages. The Braxley family treated me with a tenderness equal
to that I had received at home. At table, the serving man offered
to help my plate for me, as though I were a sick child. I could
have enjoyed all this immensely, I think, since I have always been
one to relish loving, domestic care, if only I had not been worrying and speculating all the while about Lee Ann. As I talked ge-
nially with Caroline's family during the meal and immediately afterward before the briskly burning fire at the end of the Braxleys'
long living room, I kept seeing Lee Ann's boot tracks in the snow.
And then I would see my own bloody hand as I took it down
from my face before I fainted. I remember still having the distinct
feeling, as I sat there in the bosom of the Braxley family, that it
had not been merely my bloody hand that had made me faint but
my bloody hand plus the tracks in the deep snow. In a way, it is
strange that I remember all these impressions so vividly after forty
years, because it is not as though I have lived an uneventful life
during the years since. My Second World War experiences are
what I perhaps ought to remember best—those, along with the
deaths of my two younger brothers in the Korean War. Even
worse, really, were the deaths of my two parents in a terrible fire

that destroyed our house on Central Avenue when they had got to
be quite old, my mother leaping from a second-story window, my
father asphyxiated inside the house. And I can hardly mention
without being overcome with emotion the accidental deaths that
took two of my and Caroline's children when they were in their
early teens. It would seem that with all these disasters to remember, along with the various business and professional crises I
have had, I might hardly be able to recall that earlier episode. But
I think that, besides its coming at that impressionable period of
my life and the fact that one just does remember things better
from one's youth, there is the undeniable fact that life *was*
different in those times. What I mean to say is that all these later,
terrible events took place in a world where acts of terror are, so to
speak, all around us—everyday occurrences—and are brought
home to us audibly and pictorially on radio and television almost
every hour. I am not saying that some of these ugly acts of terror
did not need to take place or were not brought on by what our
world was like in those days. But I am saying that the context was
different. Our tranquil, upper-middle-class world of 1937 did not
have the rest of the world crowding in on it so much. And thus
when something only a little ugly did crowd in or when we, often
unconsciously, reached out for it the contrasts seemed sharper. It
was not just in the Braxleys' household or in my own family's that
everything seemed quiet and well ordered and unchanging. The
households were in a context like themselves. Suffice it to say that
though the Braxleys' house in Memphis was situated on East
Parkway and our house on Central Avenue, at least two miles
across town from each other, I could in those days feel perfectly
safe, and *was* relatively safe, in walking home many a night from
Caroline's house to our house at two in the morning. It was when
we young men in Memphis ventured out with the more adventurous girls of the demimonde that we touched on the unsafe
zones of Memphis. And there were girls still more adventurous, of
course, with whom some of my contemporaries found their way
into the very most dangerous zones. But we did think of it that
way, you see, thought of it in terms of the girls' being the adventurous ones, whom we followed or didn't follow.

Anyhow, while we were sitting there before the fire, with the
portrait of Caroline's paternal grandfather peering down at us

from above the mantel and with her father in his broad-lapelled, double-breasted suit standing on the marble hearth, occasionally poking at the logs with the brass poker or sometimes kicking a log with the toe of his wing-tipped shoes, suddenly I was called to the telephone by the Negro serving man who had wanted to help my plate for me. As he preceded me the length of the living room and then gently guided me across the hall to the telephone in the library, I believe he would have put his hand under my elbow to help me—as if a real invalid—if I had allowed him to. As we passed through the hall, I glanced through one of the broad, etched sidelights beside the front door and caught a glimpse of the snow on the ground outside. The weather had turned even colder. There had been no additional snowfall, but even at a glance you could tell how crisply frozen the old snow was on its surface. The serving man at my elbow was saying, "It's your daddy on the phone. I'd suppose he just wants to know how you'd be feeling by now."

But I knew in my heart it wasn't that. It was as if that glimpse of the crisp snow through the front door sidelight had told me what it was. When I took up the telephone and heard my father's voice pronouncing my name, I knew almost exactly what he was going to say. He said that his friend the editor of the morning paper had called him and reported that there had been a girl in the car with me, and though they didn't of course plan to use her name, probably wouldn't even run the story until Monday, they would have to *know* her name. And would have to assure themselves she wasn't hurt in the crash. And that she was unharmed after leaving the scene. Without hesitation I gave my father Lee Ann Deehart's name, as well as her address and telephone number. But I made no further explanation to Father, and he asked me for none. The only other thing I said was that I'd be home in a little while. Father was silent a moment after that. Then he said, "Are you all right?"

I said, "I'm fine."

And he said, "Good. I'll be waiting up for you."

I hung up the telephone, and my first thought was that before I left Caroline tonight I'd have to tell her that Lee Ann had been in the car with me. Then, without thinking almost, I dialled Lee Ann's rooming-house number. It felt very strange to be doing this

in the Braxleys' library. The woman who ran the rooming house
said that Lee Ann had not been in since she left with me in the
afternoon.

As I passed back across the wide hallway and caught another
glimpse of the snow outside, the question arose in my mind for
the first time: *Had* Lee Ann come to some harm in those woods?
More than the density of the underbrush, more than its proximity
to the Zoo, where certain unsavory characters often hung out, it
was the great size and antiquity of the forest trees somehow and
the old rumors that white settlers had once been ambushed there
by Chickasaw Indians that made me feel that if anything had
happened to the girl it had happened there. And on the heels of
such thoughts I found myself wondering for the first time if all
this might actually lead to my beautiful, willowy Caroline Braxley's breaking off our engagement. I returned to the living room,
and at the sight of Caroline's tall figure at the far end of the
room, placed between that of her mother and that of her father,
the conviction became firm in me that I would have to tell her
about Lee Ann before she and I parted that night. And as I drew
nearer to her, still wondering if something ghastly had happened
to Lee Ann there in the old forest, I saw the perplexed and even
suspicious expression on Caroline's face and presently observed
similar expressions on the faces of her two parents. And from that
moment began the gnawing wonder which would be with me for
several days ahead: What precisely would Caroline consider
sufficient provocation for breaking off our engagement to be married? I had no idea, really. Would it be sufficient that I had had
one of those unnamed "female companions" in the car with me at
the time of the accident? I knew of engagements like ours which
had been broken with apparently less provocation. Or would it be
the suspicious-seeming circumstance of Lee Ann's leaping out of
the car and running off through the snow? Or might it be the
final, worst possibility—that of delicate little Lee Ann Deehart's
having actually met with foul play in that infrequently entered
area of underbrush and towering forest trees?

Broken engagements were a subject of common and considerable interest to girls like Caroline Braxley. Whereas a generation
earlier a broken engagement had been somewhat of a scandal—an

engagement that had been formally announced at a party and in the newspaper, that is—it did not necessarily represent that in our day. Even in our day, you see, it meant something quite different from what it had once meant. There was, after all, no written contract and it was in no sense so unalterably binding as it had been in our parents' day. For us it was not considered absolutely dishonorable for either party to break off the plans merely because he or she had had a change of heart. Since the boy was no longer expected literally to ask the father for the girl's hand (though he would probably be expected to go through the form, as I had done with Mr. Braxley), it was no longer a breach of contract between families. There was certainly nothing like a dowry any longer—not in Memphis—and there was only rarely any kind of property settlement involved, except in cases where both families were extraordinarily rich. The thought pleased me—that is, the ease with which an engagement might be ended. I suppose in part I was simply preparing myself for such an eventuality. And there in the Braxleys' long living room in the very presence of Caroline and Mr. and Mrs. Braxley themselves I found myself indulging in a perverse fantasy, a fantasy in which Caroline had broken off our engagement and I was standing up pretty well, was even seeking consolation in the arms, so to speak, of a safely returned Lee Ann Deehart.

But all at once I felt so guilty for my private indiscretion that actually for the first time in the presence of my prospective in-laws I put my arm about Caroline Braxley's waist. And I told her that I felt so fatigued by events of the afternoon that probably I ought now to go ahead home. She and her parents agreed at once. And they agreed among themselves that they each had just now been reflecting privately that I looked exhausted. Mrs. Braxley suggested that under the circumstances she ought to ask Robert to drive me home. I accepted. No other suggestion could have seemed so welcome. Robert was the same serving man who had offered to help my plate at dinner and who had so gently guided me to the telephone when my father called. Almost at once, after I got into the front seat of the car beside him—in his dark chauffeur's uniform and cap—I fell asleep. He had to wake me when we pulled up to the side door of my father's house. I remember how warmly I thanked him for bringing me home, even shaking his hand, which was a rather unusual thing to do in those days. I felt greatly refreshed and restored and personally grateful to Robert for it. There was not, in those days in Memphis, any time or occasion when one felt more secure and relaxed than when one had given oneself over completely to the care and protection of the black servants who surrounded us and who created and sustained for the most part the luxury which distinguished the lives we lived then from the lives we live now. They did so for us, whatever their motives and however degrading our demands and our accept-ance of their attentions may have been to them.

At any rate, after my slumber in the front seat beside Robert I felt sufficiently restored to face my father (and his awareness of Lee Ann's having been in the car) with some degree of equa-nimity. And before leaving the Braxleys' house I had found a mo-ment in the hallway to break the news to Caroline that I had not been alone in the car that afternoon. To my considerable surprise she revealed, after a moment's hesitation, that she already knew that that had been the case. Her father, like my father, had learned it from one of the newspaper editors—only he had learned it several hours earlier than my father had. I was obliged to realize as we were saying good night to each other that she, along with her two parents, had known all evening that Lee Ann had been with me and had fled into the woods of Overton Park—that she, Caroline, had as a matter of fact known the full story when she came to my house to fetch me back to her house to dinner. "Where is Lee Ann now?" she asked me presently, holding my two hands in her own and looking me directly in the eye. "I don't know," I said. Knowing how much she knew, I decided I must tell her the rest of it, holding nothing back. I felt that I was seeing a new side to my fiancée and that unless I told her the whole truth there might be something of this other side of her that wouldn't be revealed to me. "I tried to telephone her after I answered my father's call tonight. But she was not in her room and had not been in since I picked her up at two o'clock." And I told Caroline about Lee Ann's telephoning me (after Caroline and I had talked in the early afternoon) and about my inviting her to go out to the college with me. Then I gave her my uncensored version of the ac-cident, including the sight of Lee Ann's footprints in the snow.

"How did she sound on the telephone?" she asked.

"What do you mean by that?" I said impatiently. "I just told you she wasn't home when I called."

"I mean earlier—when she called you."

"But why do you want to know that? It doesn't matter, does it?"

"I mean, did she sound depressed? But it doesn't matter for the moment." She still held my hands in hers. "You do know, don't you," she went on after a moment, "that you are going to have to find Lee Ann? And you probably are going to need help."

Suddenly I had the feeling that Caroline Braxley was someone twenty years older than I; but, rather than sounding like my parents or her parents, she sounded like one or another of the college teachers I had had—even like Dr. Bartlett, who once had told me that I was going to need outside help if I was going to keep up with the class. To reassure myself, I suppose, I put my arm about Caroline's waist again and drew her to me. But in our good-night kiss there was a reticence on her part, or a quality that I could only define as conditional or possibly probational. Still, I knew now that she knew everything, and I suppose that was why I was able to catch such a good nap in the car on the way home.

Girls who had been brought up the way Caroline had, in the Memphis of forty years ago, knew not only what was going to be expected of them in making a marriage and bringing up a family there in Memphis—a marriage and a family of the kind their parents had had—they knew also from a fairly early time that they would have to contend with girls and women of certain sorts before and frequently after they were married: with girls, that is, who had no conception of what it was to have a certain type of performance expected of them, or girls of another kind (and more like themselves) who came visiting in Memphis from Mississippi or Arkansas—pretty little plantation girls, my mother called them —or from Nashville or from the old towns of West Tennessee. Oftentimes these other girls were their cousins, but that made them no less dangerous. Not being on their home ground—in their own country, so to speak—these Nashville or Mississippi or West Tennessee or Arkansas girls did not bother to abide by the usual rules of civilized warfare. They carried on guerrilla warfare. They were marauders. But girls like Lee Ann Deehart were something else again. They were the Trojan horse, more or less, es-

tablished in the very citadel. They were the fifth column, and
were perhaps the most dangerous of all. At the end of a brilliant
débutante season, sometimes the most eligible bachelor of all
those on the list would still remain uncommitted, or even secretly
committed to someone who had never seen the inside of the
Memphis Country Club. This kind of thing, girls like Caroline
Braxley understood, was not to be tolerated—not if the power of
mortal woman included the power to divine the nature of any
man's commitment and the power to test the strength and nature
of another kind of woman's power. Young people today may say
that that old-fashioned behavior on the part of girls doesn't matter today, that girls don't have those problems anymore. But I suspect that in Memphis, if not everywhere, there must be something
equivalent even nowadays in the struggle of women for power
among themselves.

Perhaps, though, to the present generation these distinctions I
am making won't seem significant, after all, or worth my bothering so much about—especially the present generation outside of
Memphis and the Deep South. Even in Memphis the great majority of people might say, Why is this little band of spoiled rich
girls who lived here forty years ago so important as to deserve our
attention? In fact, during the very period I am writing about it is
likely that the majority of people in Memphis felt that way. I
think the significant point is that those girls took themselves
seriously—girls like Caroline—and took seriously the forms of the
life they lived. They imagined they knew quite well who they
were and they imagined that that was important. They were what,
at any rate, those girls like Lee Ann were not. Or they claimed to
be what those girls like Lee Ann didn't claim to be and what very
few people nowadays claim to be. They considered themselves the
heirs to something, though most likely they could not have said
what: something their forebears had brought to Memphis with
them from somewhere else—from the country around Memphis
and from other places, from the country towns of West Tennessee, from Middle Tennessee and East Tennessee, from the Valley
of Virginia, from the Piedmont, even from the Tidewater. Girls
like Caroline thought they were the heirs to something, and that's
what the other girls didn't think about themselves, though probably they were, and probably the present generation, in and out of

Memphis—even the sad generation of the sixties and seventies—is heir to more than it thinks it is, in the matter of manners, I mean to say, and of general behavior. And it is of course because these girls like Caroline are regarded as mere old-fashioned society girls that the present generation tends to dismiss them, whereas if it were their fathers we were writing about the story would, shocking though it is to say, be taken more seriously by everyone. Everyone would recognize now that the fathers and grandfathers of these girls were the sons of the old plantation South come to town and converted or half converted into modern Memphis businessmen, only with a certain something held over from the old order that made them both better and worse than businessmen elsewhere. They are the authors of much good and much bad in modern Memphis—and modern Nashville and modern Birmingham and modern Atlanta, too. The good they mostly brought with them from the old order; the bad they mostly adopted from life in cities elsewhere in the nation, the thing they were imitating when they constructed the new life in Memphis. And why not judge their daughters and wives in much the same way? Isn't there a need to know what they were like, too? One thing those girls did know they were heirs to was the old, country manners and the insistence upon old, country connections. The first evidence of this that comes to mind is the fact that they often spoke of girls like Lee Ann as "city girls," by which they meant that such girls didn't usually have the old family connections back in the country on the cotton farms in West Tennessee, in Mississippi, in Arkansas, or back in Nashville or in Jonesboro or in Virginia.

When Robert had let me out at our sidedoor that night and I came into the house, my father and mother both were downstairs. It was still early of course, but I had the sense of their having waited up for me to come in. They greeted me as though I were returning from some dangerous mission. Each of them asked me how the Braxleys "seemed." Finally Mother insisted upon examining the stitches underneath the bandage on my forehead. After that, I said that I thought I would hit the hay. They responded to that with the same enthusiasm that Mr. and Mrs. Braxley had evidenced when I told them I thought I should go ahead home. Nothing would do me more good than a good night's sleep, my parents agreed. It was a day everybody was glad to have come to an end.

After I got upstairs and in my room, it occurred to me that my parents both suddenly looked very old. That seems laughable to me now almost, because my parents were then ten or fifteen years younger than I am today. I look back on them now as a youngish couple in their early middle age, whose first son was about to be married and about whose possible infidelity they were concerned. But indeed what an old-fashioned pair they seem to me in the present day, waiting up for their children to come in. Because actually they stayed downstairs a long while after I went up to bed, waiting there for my younger brothers and my little sister to come in, all of whom were out on their separate dates. In my mind's eye I can see them there, waiting as parents had waited for hundreds of years for their grown-up children to come home at night. They would seem now to be violating the rights of young individuals and even interfering with the maturing process. But in those times it seemed only natural for parents to be watchful and concerned about their children's first flight away from the nest. I am referring mainly to my parents' waiting up for my brothers and my sister, who were in their middle teens, but also as I lay in my bed I felt, myself, more relaxed, knowing that they were downstairs in the front room, speculating upon what Lee Ann's disappearance meant and alert to whatever new development there might be. After a while, my father came up and opened the door to my room. I don't know how much later it was. I don't think I had been to sleep, but I could not tell for sure even at the time—my waking and sleeping thoughts were so much alike that night. At any rate, Father stepped inside the room and came over to my bed.

"I have just called down to the police station," he said, "and they say they have checked and that Lee Ann has still not come back to her rooming house. She seems to have gone into some sort of hiding." He said this with wonderment and with just the slightest trace of irritation in his voice. "Have you any notion, Nat, why she *might* want to go into hiding?"

The next day was Sunday, December 5th. During the night it had turned bitterly cold. The snow had frozen into a crisp sheet that covered most of the ground. At about nine o'clock in the morning, another snow began falling. I had breakfast with the family, still wearing the bandage on my forehead. I sat around in my bathrobe all morning, pretending to read the newspaper. I didn't see any report of my accident, and my father said it wouldn't appear till Monday. At ten o'clock, I dialled Lee Ann's telephone number. One of the other girls who roomed in the house answered. She said she thought Lee Ann hadn't come in last night and she giggled. I asked her if she would make sure about it. She left the phone and came back presently to say in a whisper that there was no doubt about it: Lee Ann had not slept in her bed. I knew she was whispering so that the landlady wouldn't hear. . . . And then I had a call from Caroline, who wanted to know how my head was this morning and whether or not there had been any word about Lee Ann. After I told her what I had just learned, we were both silent for a time. Finally she said she had intended to come over and see how I was feeling but her father had decreed that nobody should go out in such bad weather. It would just be inviting another automobile wreck, he said. She reported that her parents were not going to church, and I said that mine weren't either. We agreed to talk later and to see each other after lunch if the weather improved. Then I could hear her father's voice in the background, and she said that he wanted to use the telephone.

At noon the snow was still falling. My father stood at a front window in the living room, wearing his dark smoking jacket. He predicted that it might be the deepest snowfall we had ever had in Memphis. He said that people in other parts of the country didn't realize how much cold weather came all the way down the Mississippi Valley from Minneapolis to Memphis. I had never heard him pay so much attention to the weather and talk so much about it. I wondered if, like me, he was really thinking about the old forest out in Overton Park and wishing he were free to go out there and make sure there was no sign of Lee Ann Deehart's having come to grief in those ancient woods. I wonder now if there weren't others besides us who were thinking of the old forest all day that day. I knew that my father, too, had been on the telephone that morning—and he was on it again during a good part of the afternoon. In retrospect, I am certain that all day that day

he was in touch with a whole circle of friends and colleagues who
were concerned about Lee Ann's safety. It was not only the heavy
snow that checked his freedom—and mine, too, of course—to go
out and search those woods and put his mind at rest on that possibility at least. It was more than just this snow, which the radio reported as snarling up and halting all traffic. What prevented him
was his own unwillingness to admit fully to himself and to others
that this particular danger was really there; what prevented him
and perhaps all the rest of us was the fear that the answer to the
gnawing question of Lee Ann's whereabouts might really be out
there within that immemorial grove of snow-laden oaks and yellow poplars and hickory trees. It is a grove, I believe, that men in
Memphis have feared and wanted to destroy for a long time and
whose destruction they are still working at even in this latter day.
It has only recently been saved by a very narrow margin from a
great highway that men wished to put through there—saved by
groups of women determined to save this last bit of the old forest
from the axes of modern men. Perhaps in old pioneer days, before
the plantation and the neo-classic towns were made, the great forests seemed woman's last refuge from the brute she lived alone
with in the wilderness. Perhaps all men in Memphis who had any
sense of their past felt this, though they felt more keenly (or perhaps it amounts to the same feeling) that the forest was woman's
greatest danger. Men remembered mad pioneer women, driven
mad by their loneliness and isolation, who ran off into the forest,
never to be seen again, or incautious women who allowed themselves to be captured by Indians and returned at last so mutilated
that they were unrecognizable to their husbands or who at their
own wish lived out their lives among their savage captors. I think
that if I had said to my father (or to myself), "What is it that's
so scary about the old forest?" he (or I) would have answered,
"There's nothing at all scary about it. But we can't do anything
today because of the snow. It's the worst snow in history!" I think
that all day long my father—like me—was busily not letting himself believe that anything awful had happened to Lee Ann Deehart or that if it had it certainly hadn't happened in those woods.
Not just my father and me, though. Caroline's father, too, and all
their friends—their peers. And the newspapermen and the police.
If they waited long enough, it would come out all right and there

would be no need to search the woods even. And it turned out, in
the most literal sense, that they—we—were right. Yet what guilty
feelings must not everyone have lived with—lived with in silence—
all that snowbound day.

At two o'clock, Caroline called again to say that because of the
snow her aunt was cancelling the dinner party she had planned
that night in honor of the bride and groom. I remember as well as
anything else that terrible day how my mother and father looked
at each other when they received this news. Surely they were wondering, as I had to also, if this was but the first gesture of with-
drawal. There was no knowing what their behavior or the behavior of any of us that day meant. The day simply dragged on until
the hour when we could decently go to bed. It was December, and
we were near the shortest day of the year, but that day had
seemed the longest day of my life.

On Monday morning, two uniformed policemen were at our
house before I had finished my breakfast. When I learned they
were waiting in the living room to see me, I got up from the table
at once. I wouldn't let my father go in with me to see them.
Mother tried to make me finish my eggs before going in, but I
only laughed at her and kissed her on the top of the head as I left
the breakfast room. The two policemen were sitting in the very
chairs my parents had sat in the night before. This somehow
made the interview easier from the outset. I felt initially that they
were there to help me, not to harass me in any way. They had already, at the break of dawn, been out to Overton Park. (The
whole case—if case it was—had of course been allowed to rest on
Sunday.) And along with four other policemen they had con-
ducted a full scale search of the old forest. There was no trace of
Lee Ann Deehart there. They had also been to her rooming house
on Tutwiler Avenue and questioned Mrs. Troxler, whose house it
was, about all of Lee Ann's friends and acquaintances and about
the habits of her daily life. They said that they were sure the girl
would turn up but that the newspapers were putting pressure on
them to explain her disappearance and—more particularly—to explain her precipitate flight from the scene of the accident.

I spent that day with the police, leaving them only for an hour
at lunchtime, when they dropped me off at my father's office on

Front Street, where I worked. There I made a small pretense of
attending to some business for the firm while I consumed a club
sandwich and milkshake that my father or one of my uncles in the
firm had had sent up for me. At the end of the hour, I jogged
down the two flights of steep wooden stairs and found the police
car waiting for me at the curb, just outside the entrance. At some
time during the morning, one of the policemen had suggested
that they might have a bulldozer or some other piece of machinery brought in to crack the ice on the Overton Park Pond and
then drag the Pond for Lee Ann's body. But I had pointed out
that the two skaters had returned to the Pond after the accident
and skated there until dark. There was no hole in the ice anywhere. Moreover, the skaters had reported that when the girl left
the scene she did not go by way of the Pond but went up the rise
and into the wooded area. There was every indication that she
had gone that way, and so the suggestion that the Pond be
dragged was dismissed. And we continued during the rest of the
morning to make the rounds of the rooming houses and apartments of Lee Ann's friends and acquaintances, as well as the
houses of the parents with whom some of them lived. In the afternoon we planned to go to the shops and offices in which some of
the girls worked and to interview them there concerning Lee
Ann's whereabouts and where it was they last had seen her. It
seemed a futile procedure to me. But while I was eating my club
sandwich alone in our third-floor walkup office I received a shocking telephone call.

Our office, like most of the other cotton factors' offices, was in
one of the plain-faced, three- and four-story buildings put up on
Front Street during the middle years of the last century, just before the Civil War. Cotton men were very fond of those offices,
and the offices did possess a certain rough beauty that anyone
could see. Apparently there had been few, if any, improvements or
alterations since the time they were built. All the electrical wiring
and all the plumbing, such as it was, was "exposed." The wooden
stairsteps and the floors were rough and splintery and extremely
worn down. The walls were whitewashed and the ceilings were
twelve or fourteen feet in height. But the chief charm of the
rooms was the tall windows across the front of the buildings—
wide sash windows with small window lights, windows looking

down onto Front Street and from which you could catch glimpses of the brown Mississippi River at the foot of the bluff, and even of the Arkansas shoreline on the other side. I was sitting on a cotton trough beside one of those windows, eating my club sandwich, when I heard the telephone ring back in the inner office. I remember that when it rang my eyes were on a little stretch of the Arkansas shoreline roughly delineated by its scrubby trees and my thoughts were on the Arkansas roadhouses where we often went with the demimonde girls on a Saturday night. At first I thought I wouldn't answer the phone. I let it ring for a minute or two. It went on ringing—persistently. Suddenly I realized that a normal business call would have stopped ringing before now. I jumped down from my perch by the window and ran back between the cotton troughs to the office. When I picked up the receiver, a girl's voice called my name before I spoke.

"Yes," I said. The voice had sounded familiar, but I knew it wasn't Caroline's. And it wasn't Lee Ann's. I couldn't identify it exactly, though I did say to myself right away that it was one of the city girls.

"Nat," the voice said, "Lee Ann wants you to stop trying to trail her."

"Who is this?" I said. "Where is Lee Ann?"

"Never mind," the girl on the other end of the line said. "We're not going to let you find her, and you're making her very uncomfortable with your going around with the police after her and all that."

"The police aren't 'after her,'" I said. "They just want to be sure she's all right."

"She'll be all right," the voice said, "if you'll lay off and stop chasing her. Don't you have any decency at all? Don't you have a brain in your head? Don't you know what this is like for Lee Ann? We all thought you were her friend."

"I am," I said. "Just let me speak to Lee Ann."

But there was a click in the telephone, and no one was there any longer.

I turned back into the room where the cotton troughs were. When I saw my milkshake carton and the sandwich paper up by the window, and remembered how the girl had called my name as soon as I picked up the telephone, I felt sure that someone had been watching me from down in the street or from a window across the way. Without going back to my lunch, I turned quickly and started down the stairs toward the street. But when I looked at my watch, I realized it was time for the policemen to pick me up again. And there they were, of course, waiting at the entrance to our building. When I got into the police car, I didn't tell them about my call. And we began our rounds again, going to the addresses where some of Lee Ann's friends worked.

Lee Ann Deehart and other girls like her that we went about with, as I have already indicated, were not literally ladies of any Memphis demimonde. Possibly they got called that first by the only member of our generation in Memphis who had read Marcel Proust, a literary boy who later became a college professor and who wanted to make his own life in Memphis—and ours—seem more interesting than it was. Actually, they were girls who had gone to the public high schools, and more often than not to some school other than Central High, which during those Depression years had a degree of acceptance in Memphis society. As anyone could have observed on that morning when I rode about town with the policemen, those girls came from a variety of backgrounds. We went to the houses of some of their parents, some of whom were day laborers who spoke in accents of the old Memphis Irish, descendants of the Irish who were imported to build the railroads to Texas. Today some of the girls would inevitably have been black. But they were the daughters also of bank clerks and salesmen and of professional men, too, because they made no distinction among themselves. The parents of some of them had moved to Memphis from cities in other sections of the country or even from Southern small towns. The girls were not interested in such distinctions of origin, were not conscious of them, had not been made aware of them by their parents. They would have been highly approved of by the present generation of young people. Like the present generation in general, these girls—Lee Ann included—tended to be bookish and artistic in a middlebrow sort of way, and some of them had real intellectual aspirations. They did not care who each other's families were or where they had gone to school. They met and got to know each other in roadhouses, on double dates, and in the offices and stores where they worked. As I have said, they tended to be bookish and artistic. If they had found themselves in Proust's Paris, instead of in our Memphis of the nineteen-thirties, possibly they would have played some role in the intellectual life of the place. But of course this is only my ignorant speculation. It is always impossible to know what changes might have been wrought in people under circumstances of the greatest or slightest degree of difference from the actual.

The girls we saw that afternoon at their places of work were generally more responsive to the policemen's questions than to my own. And I became aware that the two policemen—youngish men in their late thirties, for whom this special assignment was somehow distasteful—were more interested in protecting these girls from any embarrassment than in obtaining information about Lee Ann. With all but one of the half-dozen girls we sought out, the policemen sent me in to see the girl first, to ask her if she would rather be questioned by them in her place of business or in the police car. In each case the girl treated my question concerning this as an affront, but always she finally sent word back to the policemen to come inside. And in each case I found myself admiring the girl not only for her boldness in dealing with the situation (they seemed fearless in their talk with the police and refused absolutely to acknowledge close friendship with Lee Ann, insisting—all of them—that they saw her only occasionally at night spots, sometimes with me, sometimes with other young men, that they had no idea who her parents were or where she came to Memphis from) but also for a personal, feminine beauty that I had never before been fully aware of. Perhaps I saw or sensed it now for the first time because I had not before seen them threatened or in danger. It is true, I know, that the effect of all this questioning seemed somehow to put them in jeopardy. Perhaps I saw now how much more vulnerable they were than were the girls in the set my parents more or less intended me to travel in. There was a delicacy about them, a frailty even, that didn't seem to exist in other girls I knew and that contrasted strangely—and disturbingly—with the rough surroundings of the roadhouses they frequented at night and the harsh, businesslike atmosphere of the places where they worked. Within each of them, moreover, there seemed a contrast between the delicate beauty of their bodies, their prettily formed arms and legs, their breasts and hips, their small feet and hands, their soft natural hair—hair worn so becomingly,

groomed, in each case, on their pretty little heads to direct one's
eyes first of all to the fair or olive complexion and the nicely proportioned features of the face—a contrast, that is to say, between
this physical beauty and a bookishness and a certain toughness of
mind and a boldness of spirit which were unmistakable in all of
them.

The last girl we paid a call on that afternoon was one Nancy
Minnifee, who happened to be the girl who was always frankest
and crudest in making jokes about families like my own and who
had made the crack that the other girls had laughed at so irrepres-
sibly in the beer garden: "I haven't lost anything at the M.C.C."
Or it may not have been that she just happened to be the last we
called on. Perhaps out of dread of her jokes I guided the police
last of all to the farm-implement warehouse where Nancy was a
secretary. Or perhaps it wasn't so much because of her personality
as because I knew she was Lee Ann's closest friend and I somehow dreaded facing her for that reason. Anyway, at the warehouse
she was out on the loading platform with a clipboard and pencil
in her hands when we drove up.

"That's Nancy Minnifee up there," I said to the two policemen
in the front seat. I was sitting in the back seat alone. I saw them
shake their heads. I knew that it was with a certain sadness and a
personal admiration that they did so. Nancy was a very pretty girl,
and they hated the thought of bothering this lovely creature with
the kind of questions they were going to ask. They hated it without even knowing she was Lee Ann's closest friend. Suddenly I
began seeing all those girls through the policemen's eyes, just as
next day, when I would make a similar expedition in the company
of my father and the newspaper editor, I'd see the girls through
their eyes. The worst of it, somehow, for the policemen, was that
the investigation wasn't really an official investigation but was
something the newspapers had forced upon the police in case
something had happened which they hadn't reported. The girl
hadn't been missing long enough for anyone to declare her
"officially" missing. Yet the police, along with the mayor's office
and the newspaper editor, didn't want to risk something's having
happened to a girl like Lee Ann. They—all of them—thought of
such girls, in a sense, as their special wards. It would be hard to
say why they did. At any rate, before the police car had fully

stopped I saw Nancy Minnifee up there on the platform. She was wearing a fur-collared overcoat but no hat or gloves. Immediately she began moving along the loading platform toward us, holding the clipboard up to shield her eyes from the late-afternoon winter sun. She came down the steps to the gravelled area where we were stopped, and when the policeman at the wheel of the car ran down his window she bent forward and put her arm on his door. The casual way she did it seemed almost familiar—indeed, almost provocative. I found myself resenting her manner, because I was afraid she would give the wrong impression. The way she leaned on the door reminded me of the prostitutes down on Pontotoc Street when we, as teen-age boys, used to stop in front of their houses and leave the motor running because we were afraid of them.

"I've been expecting you two gentlemen," Nancy said, smiling amiably at the two policemen and pointedly ignoring my presence in the back seat. The policemen broke into laughter.

"I suppose your friends have been calling ahead," the driver said. Then Nancy laughed as though he had said something very funny.

"I could draw you a map of the route you've taken this afternoon," she said. She was awfully polite in her tone, and the two policemen were awfully polite, too. But before they could really begin asking her their questions she began giving them her answers. She hadn't seen Lee Ann since several days before the accident. She didn't know anything about where she might be. She didn't know anything about her family. She had always understood that Lee Ann came from Texas.

"That's a big state," the policeman who wasn't driving said.

"Well, I've never been there," she said, "but I'm told it's a mighty big state."

The three of them burst into laughter again. Then the driver said quite seriously, "But we understand you're her best friend."

"I don't know her any better than most of the other girls do," she said. "I can't imagine who told you that." Now for the first time she looked at me in the back seat. "Hello, Nat," she said. I nodded to her. I couldn't imagine why she was lying to them. But I didn't tell her, as I hadn't told the other girls or the police, about the call I had had in the cotton office. I knew that she must know all about it, but I said nothing.

When we had pulled away, the policeman who was driving the car said, "This Lee Ann must be all right or these girls wouldn't be closing ranks so. They've got too much sense for that. They're smart girls."

Presently the other policeman turned his head halfway around, though not looking directly at me, and asked, "She wouldn't be pregnant by any chance, would she?"

"Uh-uh," I said. It was all the answer it seemed to me he deserved. But then I couldn't resist echoing what he had said. "They've got too much sense for that. They're smart girls." He looked all the way around at me now and gave me what I am sure he thought was a straight look.

"Damn right they are," said the driver, glancing at his colleague with a frown on his forehead and speaking with a curled lip. "Get your mind out of the gutter, Fred. After all, they're just kids, all of them."

We rode on in silence after that. For the first time in several hours, I thought of Caroline Braxley, and I wondered again whether or not she would break our engagement.

When the policemen let me off at my office at five o'clock, I went to my car and drove straight to the apartment house at Crosstown where Nancy Minnifee lived. I was waiting for Nancy in the parking lot when she got home. She invited me inside, but without a smile.

"I want to know where Lee Ann is," I said as soon as she had closed the door.

"Do you imagine I'd tell you if I knew?" she said.

I sat myself down in an upholstered chair as if I were going to stay there till she told me. "I want to know what the hell's going on," I said with what I thought was considerable force, "and why you told such lies to those policemen."

"If you don't know that now, Nat," she said, sitting down opposite me, "you probably won't ever know."

"She wouldn't be pregnant by any chance, would she?" I said, without really having known I was going to say it.

Nancy's mouth dropped open. Then she laughed aloud. Presently she said, "Well, one thing's certain, Nat. It wouldn't be any concern of yours if she were."

I pulled myself up out of the big chair and left without another word's passing between us.

Lee Ann Deehart and Nancy Minnifee and that whole band of girls that we liked to refer to as the girls of the Memphis demimonde were of course no more like the ladies of the demimonde as they appear in French literature than they were like some band of angels. And I hardly need say—though it does somehow occur to me to say—their manners and morals bore no resemblance whatsoever to those of the mercenary, filthy-mouthed whores on Pontotoc Street. I might even say that their manners were practically indistinguishable from those of the girls we knew who had attended Miss Hutchison's School and St. Mary's and Lausanne and were now members of the débutante set. The fact is that some of them—only a few perhaps—were from families who were related by blood, and rather closely related, to the families of the débutante set, but families who, for one reason or another, now found themselves economically in another class from their relatives. At any rate, they were all freed from old restraints put upon them by family and community, liberated in each case, so it seems to me, by sheer strength of character, liberated in many respects, but above all else—and I cannot say how it came about—liberated sexually. The most precise thing I can say about them is that they, in their little band, were like hordes of young girls today. It seems to me that in their attitude toward sex they were at least forty years ahead of their time. But I cannot say how it came about. Perhaps it was an individual thing with each of them—or partly so. Perhaps it was because they were the second or third generation of women in Memphis who were working in offices. They were not promiscuous—not most of them—but they slept with the men they were in love with and they did not conceal the fact. The men they were in love with were usually older than we were. Generally speaking, the girls merely amused themselves with us, just as we amused ourselves with them. There was a wonderful freedom in our relations which I have never known anything else quite like. And though I may not have had the most realistic sense of

what their lives were, I came to know what I did know through
my friendship with Lee Ann Deehart.

She and I first met, I think, at one of those dives where we
all hung out. Or it may have been at some girl's apartment.
I suspect we both would have been hard put to it to say where
it was or exactly when. She was simply one of the good-looking
girls we ran around with. I remember dancing with her on several occasions before I had any idea what her name was. We
drifted into our special kind of friendship because, as a matter of fact, she was the good friend of Nancy Minnifee, whom
my own close friend Bob Childress got very serious about for a
time. Bob and Nancy may even have been living together for a
while in Nancy's apartment. I think Bob, who was one of six or
eight boys of approximately my background who used to go about
with these girls, would have married Nancy if she'd consented to
have him. Possibly it was at Nancy's apartment that I met Lee
Ann. Anyway, we did a lot of double-dating, the four of us, and
had some wonderful times going to the sort of rough night spots
that we all liked and found sufficiently exciting to return to again
and again. We would be dancing and drinking at one of those
places until about two in the morning, when most of them closed.
At that hour most of us would take our girls home, because we
nearly all of us had jobs—the girls and the boys, too—which we
had to report to by eight or nine in the morning.

Between Lee Ann and me, as between most of the boys and
their girls, I think, there was never a serious affair. That is, we
never actually—as the young people today say—"had sex." But in
the car on the way home or in the car parked outside her rooming
house or even outside the night spot, as soon as we came out, we
would regularly indulge in what used to be known as "heavy neck-
ing." Our stopping at that I must attribute first of all to Lee
Ann's resistance, though also, in part, to a hesitation I felt about
insisting with such a girl. You see, she was in all respects like the
girls we called "nice girls," by which I suppose we really meant society girls. And most of us accepted the restriction that we were
not to "go to bed" with society girls. They were the girls we were
going to marry. These girls were not what those society girls
would have termed shopgirls. They had much better taste in their
clothes and in their general demeanor. And, as I have said, in the

particular group I speak of there was at least an intellectual strain. Some of them had been to college for as much as a year or two, whereas others seemed hardly to have finished high school. Nearly all of them read magazines and books that most of us had never heard of. And they found my odd addiction to Latin poetry the most interesting thing about me. Most of them belonged to a national book club, from which they received a new book each month, and they nearly all bought records and listened to classical music. You would see them sometimes in groups at the Art Gallery. Or whenever there was an opera or a good play at the city auditorium they were all likely to be there in a group—almost never with dates. If you hadn't known who they were, you might easily have mistaken them for some committee from the Junior League or for an exceptionally pretty group of schoolteachers—from some fashionable girls' school probably.

But mostly, of course, one saw them with their dates at one of the roadhouses, over in Arkansas or down in Mississippi or out east on the Bristol Highway, or yet again at one of the places we called the "town joints." They preferred going to those roadhouses and town joints to going to the Peabody Hotel Roof or the Claridge—as I suppose nearly everyone else did, really, including society girls like Caroline. You would, as a matter of fact, frequently see girls like Caroline at such places. At her request, I had more than once taken Caroline to a town joint down on Adams Street called The Cellar and once to a roadhouse called The Jungle, over in Arkansas. She had met some of the city girls there and said she found them "dead attractive." And she once recognized them at a play I took her to see and afterward expressed interest in them and asked me to tell her what they were like.

The fact may be that neither the roadhouses nor the town joints were quite as tough as they seemed. Or they weren't as tough for the demimonde girls, anyway. Because the proprietors clearly had protective feelings about them. At The Jungle, for instance, the middle-aged couple who operated the place, an extremely obese couple who were forever grinning in our direction and who were usually barefoot (we called them Ma and Pa), would often come and stand by our table—one or the other of them—and sing the words to whatever was playing on the jukebox. Often as not, one of them would be standing there during the entire evening. Sometimes Ma would talk to us about her two little daughters, whom she kept in a private school in Memphis, and Pa, who was a practicing taxidermist, would talk to us about the dogs whose mounted heads adorned the walls on every side of the dimly lit room. All this afforded us great privacy and safety. No drunk or roughneck would come near our table while either Ma or Pa was close by. We had similar protection at other places. At The Cellar, for instance, old Mrs. Power was the sole proprietor. She had a huge goitre on her neck and was never known to smile. Not even in our direction. But it was easy to see that she watched our table like a hawk, and if any other patron lingered near us even momentarily she would begin moving slowly toward us. And whoever it was would catch one glimpse of her and move on. We went to these places quite regularly, though some of the girls had their favorites and dislikes among them. Lee Ann would never be taken to The Cellar. She would say only that the place depressed her. And Caroline, when I took her there, felt an instant dislike for The Jungle. She would shake her head afterward and say she would never go back and have those dogs' eyes staring down through the darkness at her.

On the day after I made the rounds with the two policemen, I found myself following almost the same routine in the company of my father and the editor of the morning paper, and, as a matter of fact, the mayor of Memphis himself. The investigation or search was, you see, still entirely unofficial. And men like my father and the mayor and the editor wanted to keep it so. That's why after that routine and off-the-record series of questionings by the police they preferred to do a bit of investigation themselves rather than entrust the matter to someone else. As I have said, that generation of men in Memphis evidenced feelings of responsibility for such girls—for "working girls of a superior kind," as they phrased it—which I find somewhat difficult to explain. For it wasn't just the men I drove about town with that day. Or the dozen or so men who gathered for conference in our driveway before we set out—that is, Caroline's father, his lawyer, the driver of the other vehicle, his lawyer, my father's lawyer, ministers from three church denominations, the editor of the afternoon newspaper, and still others. That day, when I rode about town with my father and the two other men in our car, I came as near as I ever had or ever would to receiving a satisfactory explanation of the phenomenon. They were of a generation of American men who were perhaps the last to grow up in a world where women were absolutely subjected and under the absolute protection of men. While my father wheeled his big Cadillac through the side streets on which some of the girls lived and then along the wide boulevards of Memphis, they spoke of the changes they had seen. In referring to the character of the life girls like Lee Ann led—of which they showed a far greater awareness than I would have supposed they possessed—they agreed that this was the second or third generation there of women who had lived as independently, as freely as these girls did. I felt that what they said was in no sense as derogatory or critical as it would have been in the presence of their wives or daughters. They spoke almost affectionately and with a certain sadness of such girls. They spoke as if these were daughters of dead brothers of their own or of dead companions-in-arms during the First World War. And it seemed to me that they thought of these girls as the daughters of men who had abdicated their authority and responsibility as fathers, men who were not strangers or foreign to them, though they were perhaps of a different economic class. The family names of the girls were familiar to them. The fathers of these girls were Americans of the great hinterland like themselves, even Southerners like themselves. I felt that they were actually cousins of ours who had failed as fathers somehow, had been destined to fail, even required to do so in a changing world. And so these men of position and power had to act as surrogate fathers during a transitional period. It was a sort of communal fatherhood they were acting out. Eventually, they seemed to say, fathers might not be required. I actually heard my father saying, "That's what the whole world is going to be like someday." He meant like the life such girls as Lee Ann were making for themselves. I often think nowadays of Father's saying that whenever I see his prediction being fulfilled by the students in the university where I have been teaching for twenty years now, and I wonder if Father did really believe his prediction would come true.

Yet while he and the other two men talked their rather sanguine talk that day, I was thinking of a call I had had the night before after I came back from seeing Nancy Minnifee. One of the servants answered the telephone downstairs in the back part of the house, and she must have guessed it was something special. Because instead of buzzing the buzzer three times, which was the signal when a call was for me, the maid came up the back stairs and tapped gently on my door. "It's for you, Nat," she said softly. "Do you want to take it downstairs?"

There was nothing peculiar about her doing this, really. Since I didn't have an extension phone in my room, I had a tacit understanding with the servants that I preferred to take what I considered my private calls down in that quarter of the house. And so I followed the maid down the back stairway and shut myself in the little servants' dining room that was behind the great white-tiled kitchen. I answered the call on the wall phone there.

A girl's voice, which wasn't the same voice I had heard on the office telephone at noon, said, "Lee Ann doesn't want another day like this one, Nat."

"Who is this?" I said, lowering my voice to be sure even the servants didn't hear me. "What the hell is going on?" I asked. "Where is Lee Ann?"

"She's been keeping just one apartment or one rooming house ahead of you all day."

"But why? Why is she hiding this way?"

"All I want to say is she's had about enough. You let up on pursuing her so."

"It's not me," I protested. "There's nothing I can do to stop them."

Over the phone there came a contemptuous laugh. "No. And you can't get married till they find her, can you?" Momentarily I thought I heard Lee Ann's voice in the background. "Anyhow," the same voice continued, "Lee Ann's had about as much as she can take of all this. She was depressed as it was, when she called you in the first place. Why else do you think she would call you, Nat? She was desperate for some comic relief."

"Relief from what?"

"Relief from her depression, you idiot."

"But what's she depressed about?" I was listening carefully to the voice, thinking it was that of first one girl and then another.

"Nat, we don't always have to have something to be depressed about. But Lee Ann will be all right, if you'll let her alone."

"But what is she depressed about?" I persisted. I had begun to think maybe it was Lee Ann herself on the phone, disguising her voice.

"About life in general, you bastard! Isn't that enough?" Then I knew it wasn't Lee Ann, after all.

"Listen," I said, "let me speak to Lee Ann. I want to speak to Lee Ann."

And then I heard whoever it was I was talking with break off the connection. I quietly replaced the receiver and went upstairs again.

In those days I didn't know what it was to be depressed—not, anyway, about "life in general." Later on, you see, I did know. Later on, after years of being married and having three children, and going to grownup Memphis dinner parties three or four times a week and working in the cotton office six days a week, I got so depressed about life in general that I sold my interest in the cotton firm to a cousin of mine (my father and uncles were dead by then) and managed to make Caroline understand that what I needed was to go back to school for a while so that we could start our life all over. I took degrees at three universities, which made it possible for me to become a college professor. That may be an awful revelation about myself—I mean to say, awful that what decided me to become a teacher was that I was so depressed about life in general. But I reasoned that being an English professor— even if I was relegated to teaching composition and simpleminded survey courses—would be something useful and would throw us in with a different kind of people. (Caroline tried to persuade me to go into the sciences, but I told her she was just lucky that I didn't take up classics again.) Anyway, teaching has made me see a lot of young people over the years, in addition to my own children, and I think it is why, in retrospect, those Memphis girls I'm writing about still seem interesting to me after all these many years.

But the fact is, I was still so uneasy about the significance of both those calls from Lee Ann's friends that I was unwilling to mention them to Caroline that night. At first I thought I would tell her, but as soon as I saw her tall and graceful figure in her white, pleated evening dress and wearing the white corsage I had sent, I began worrying again about whether or not she might still break off the engagement. Besides, we had plenty of other matters to discuss, including the rounds I had made with the two policemen that day and her various activities in preparation for the wedding. We went to a dinner that one of my aunts gave for us at the Memphis Country Club that night. We came home early and spent twenty minutes or so in her living room, telling each other how much we loved each other and how we would let nothing on earth interfere with our getting married. I felt reassured, or I tried to feel so. It seemed to me, though, that Caroline still had not really made up her mind. It worried me that she didn't have more to say about Lee Ann. After I got home, I kept waking all night and wondering what if that had not been Lee Ann's voice I had heard in the background and what if she never surfaced again. The circumstances of her disappearance would have to be made public, and that would certainly be too embarrassing for Caroline and her parents to ignore.

Next day, I didn't tell my father and his two friends, the editor and the mayor, about either of the two telephone calls. I don't know why I didn't, unless it was because I feared they might begin monitoring all my calls. I could not tolerate the thought of having them hear the things that girl said to me.

In preference to interviewing the girls whose addresses I could give them, those three middle-aged men seemed much more interested in talking to the girls' rooming-house landladies, or their apartment landlords, or their mothers. They did talk to some of the girls themselves, though, and I observed that the girls were so impressed by having these older men want to talk to them that they could hardly look at them directly. What I think is that the girls were *afraid* they would tell them the truth. They would reply to their questions respectfully, if evasively, but they were apt to keep their eyes on me. This was not the case, however, with the mothers and the landlords and the landladies. There was an immediate rapport between these persons and the three men. There hardly needed to be any explanation required of the unofficial nature of the investigation or of the concern of these particular men about such a girl as Lee Ann. One woman who told them that Lee Ann had roomed with her for a time described her as being always a moody sort of girl. "But lots of these girls living on their own are moody," she said.

"Where did Miss Deehart come from?" my father asked. "Who were her people?"

"She always claimed she came from Texas," the woman said. "But she could never make it clear to me where it was in Texas."

Later the mayor asked Lee Ann's current landlady, Mrs. Troxler, where she supposed Lee Ann might have gone. "Well," Mrs. Troxler said, "a girl, a decent girl, even among these modern girls, generally goes to her mother when there's trouble. Women turn to women," she said, "when there's real trouble."

The three men found no trace of Lee Ann, got no real clue to where she might have gone. When finally we were leaving the editor at his newspaper office on Union Avenue, he hesitated a moment before opening the car door. "Well," he began, but he sat for a moment beating his leg thoughtfully with a newspaper he had rolled up in his hand. "I don't know," he said. "It's going to be a matter for the police, after all, if we can't do any better than this." I still didn't say anything about my telephone calls. But the calls were worrying me a good deal, and that night I told Caroline.

And when I had told her about the calls and told her how the police and my father and his friends had failed to get any information from the girls, Caroline, who was then sitting beside me on the couch in her living room, suddenly took my hand in hers and, putting her face close to mine and looking me directly in the eye, said, "Nat, I don't want you to go to work at all tomorrow. Don't make any explanation to your father or to anybody. Just get up early and come over here and get me. I want you to take me to meet some of those girls." Then she asked me which of the girls she might possibly have met on the rare occasions when I had taken her dancing at The Jungle or at The Cellar. And before I left that night she got me to tell her all I knew about "that whole tribe of city girls." I told her everything, including an account of my innocent friendship with Lee Ann Deehart, as well as an account of my earlier relations, which were not innocent, with a girl named Fern Morris. When, next morning, I came to fetch Caroline for our expedition, there were only three girls that she wanted to be taken to see. One of the three was of course Fern Morris.

There was something that had happened to me the day before,
when I was going about Memphis with my father and his two
friends, that I could not tell Caroline about. You see, I had been
imagining, each place we went, how as we came in the front door
Lee Ann was hurriedly, quietly going out the back. This mental
picture of her in flight I found not merely appealing but strangely
exciting. And it seemed to me I was discovering what my true
feelings toward Lee Ann had been during the past two years. I
had never dared insist upon the occasional advances I had naturally made to her, because she had always seemed too delicate, too
vulnerable, for me to think of suggesting a casual sexual relationship with her. She had seemed too clever and too intelligent
for me to deceive her about my intentions or my worth as a person. And I imagined I relished the kind of restraint there was between us because it was so altogether personal and not one placed
upon us by any element or segment of society, or by any outside
circumstances whatever. It kept coming to my mind as we stood
waiting for an answer to the pressure on each doorbell that she
was the girl I ought and wanted to be marrying. I realized the absolute folly of such thoughts and the utter impossibility of any
such conclusion to present events. But still such feelings and
thoughts had kept swimming in and out of my head all that day. I
kept seeing Lee Ann in my mind's eye and hearing her soft, somewhat husky voice. I kept imagining how her figure would appear
in the doorway before us. I saw her slender ankles, her small
breasts, her head of ash-blond hair, which had a way of seeming to
fall about her face when she talked but which with one shake of
her head she could throw back into perfect place. But of course
when the door opened there was the inevitable landlady or
mother or friend. And when the next day came and I saw Caroline rolling up her sleeves, so to speak, to pitch in and settle this
matter once and for all, then my thoughts and fantasies of the day
before seemed literally like something out of a dream that I might
have had.

The first two girls Caroline had wanted to see were the two that
she very definitely remembered having met when I had taken her
—"on a lark"—to my favorite night spots. She caught them both
before they went to work that morning, and I was asked to wait in
the car. I felt like an idiot waiting out there in the car, because I

knew I'd been seen from some window as I gingerly hopped out
and opened the door for Caroline when she got out—and opened
it again when she returned. But there was no way around it. I
waited out there, playing the car radio even at the risk of running
down the battery.

When she came back from seeing the first girl, whose name was
Lucy Phelan, Caroline was very angry. She reported that Lucy
Phelan had pretended not to remember ever having met her.
Moreover, Lucy had pretended that she knew Lee Ann Deehart
only slightly and had no idea where she could be or what her disappearance meant. As Caroline fumed and I started up the car, I
was picturing Lee Ann quietly tiptoeing out the back door of
Lucy's rooming house just as Lucy was telling Caroline she
scarcely knew the girl or while she was insisting that she didn't
remember Caroline. As Caroline came back down the walk from
the big Victorian house to the car, Lucy, who had stepped out
onto the narrow porch that ran across the front of the house and
around one corner of it, squatted down on her haunches at the
top of the wooden porch steps and waved to me from behind
Caroline's back. Though I knew it was no good, I pretended not
to see her there. As I put the car into second gear and we sped
away down the block, I took a quick glance back at the house.
Lucy was still standing on the porch and waving to me the way
one waves to a little child. She knew I had seen her stooping and
waving moments before. And knew I would be stealing a glance
now.

For a short time Caroline seemed undecided about calling on
the second girl. But she decided finally to press on. Lucy Phelan
she remembered meeting at The Cellar. The next girl, Betsy
Morehouse, she had met at The Jungle and at a considerably
more recent time. Caroline was a dog fancier in those days and
she recalled a conversation with Betsy about the mounted dogs'
heads that adorned the walls of The Jungle. They both had been
outraged. When she mentioned this to me there in the car, I realized for the first time that by trying to make these girls acknowledge an acquaintance with her she had hoped to make them feel
she was almost one of them and that they would thus be more
likely to confide in her. But she failed with Betsy Morehouse, too.
Betsy lived in an apartment house—an old residence, that is, con-

verted into apartments—and when Caroline got inside the en-
trance-hall door she met Betsy, who was just then coming down
the stairs. Betsy carried a purse and was wearing a fur coat and
overshoes. When Caroline got back to the car and told me about
it, I could not help feeling that Betsy had had a call from Lucy
Phelan and even perhaps that Lee Ann was hiding in her apartment, having just arrived there from Lucy's. Because Betsy didn't
offer to take Caroline back upstairs to her apartment for a talk.
Instead, they sat down on two straight-backed chairs in the entrance hall and exchanged their few words there. Betsy at once denied the possibility of Caroline's ever having met her before. She
denied that she had, herself, ever been to The Jungle. I knew this
to be a lie, of course, but I didn't insist upon it to Caroline. I said
that perhaps both she and I were mistaken about Betsy's being
there on the night I had taken Caroline. As soon as Caroline saw
she would learn nothing from Betsy, she got up and began to
make motions of leaving. Betsy followed her to the door. But
upon seeing my car out at the curb—so Caroline believed—she
turned back, saying that she had remembered a telephone call she
had to make. Caroline suspected that the girl didn't want to have
to face me with her lie. That possibly was true. But my thought
was that Betsy just might, also, have a telephone call she wanted
to make.

There was now no question about Caroline's wanting to pro-
ceed to the third girl's house. This was the girl I had told her
about having had a real affair with—the one I had gone with before Lee Ann and I had become friends. Caroline knew that she
and Fern Morris had never met, but she counted on a different
psychology with Fern. Most probably she had hoped it wouldn't
be necessary for her to go to see Fern. She had been sure that one
of those two other girls would give her the lead she needed. But as
a last resort she was fully prepared to call on Fern Morris and to
take me into the house with her.

Fern was a girl who still lived at home with her mother. She was
in no sense a mama's girl or even a home-loving girl, since she was
unhappy unless she went out on a date every night of her life. Perhaps she was not so clever and not so intellectual as most of her
friends—if reading books, that is, on psychology and on China
and every new volume of André Maurois indicated intellectuality.

And though she was not home-loving, I suppose you would have to say she was more domestic than the other girls were. She had never "held down" a job. Rather, she stayed at home in the daytime and kept house for her mother, who was said to "hold down" a high-powered job under Boss Crump down at City Hall. Mrs. Morris was a very sensible woman, who put no restrictions on her grown-up daughter and was glad to have her as a housekeeper. She used to tell me what a good cook and housekeeper Fern was and how well fixed she would leave her when she died. I really believe Mrs. Morris hoped our romance might end in matrimony, and, as a matter of fact, it was when I began to suspect that Fern, too, was entertaining such notions that I stopped seeing her and turned my attentions to Lee Ann Dechart.

Mrs. Morris still seemed glad to see me when I arrived at their bungalow that morning with Caroline and when I proceeded to introduce Caroline to her as my fiancée. Fern herself greeted me warmly. In fact, when I told her that Caroline and I were going to be married (though she must certainly have already read about it in the newspaper) she threw her arms about my neck and kissed me. "Oh, Natty," she said, "I'm so happy for you. Really I am. But poor Lee Ann." And in later life, especially in recent years, whenever Caroline has thought I was being silly about some other woman, usually a woman she considers her mental and social inferior, she has delighted in addressing me as "Natty." On more than one such occasion I have even had her say to me, "I am so happy for you, Natty. Really I am."

The fact is, Mrs. Morris was just leaving the house for work when we arrived. And so there was no delay in Caroline's interview with Fern. "I assume you know about Lee Ann's disappearance?" Caroline began as soon as we had seated ourselves in the little front parlor, with which I was very familiar.

"Of course I do," said Fern, looking at me and laughing gleefully.

"You think it's a laughing matter, then?" Caroline asked.

"I do indeed. It's all a big joke," Fern said at once. It was as though she had her answers all prepared. "And a very successful joke it is."

"Successful?" both Caroline and I asked. We looked at each other in dismay.

"It's only my opinion, of course. But I think she only wants to make you two suffer."

"Suffer?" I said. This time Caroline was silent.

Fern was now addressing me directly. "Everybody knows Caroline is not going to marry you until Lee Ann turns up safe."

"Everybody?" Both of us again.

"Everybody in the world practically," said Fern.

Caroline's face showed no expression. Neither, I believe, did mine.

"Fern, do you know where Lee Ann is?" Caroline asked gently.

Fern Morris, her eyes on me, shook her head, smiling.

"Do you know where her people are?" Caroline asked. "And whether she's with them or hiding with her friends?"

Fern shook her head again, but now she gazed directly at Caroline. "I'm not going to tell you anything!" she asserted. But after a moment she took a deep breath and said, still looking at Caroline, "You're a smart girl. I think you'll likely be going to Lee Ann's room in that place where she lives. If you do go there, and if you are a smart girl, you'll look in the left-hand drawer of Lee Ann's dressing table." Fern had an uneasy smile on her face after she had spoken, as if Caroline had got her to say something she hadn't really meant to say, as if she felt guilty for what she had just done.

Caroline had us out of there in only a minute or so and on our way to Lee Ann's rooming house.

It was a red brick bungalow up in north Memphis. It looked very much like the one that Fern lived in but was used as a rooming house. When Mrs. Troxler opened the front door to us, Caroline said, "We're friends of Lee Ann's, and she wants us to pack a suitcase and bring it to her."

"You know where she is, then?" Mrs. Troxler asked. "Hello, Nat," she said, looking at me over Caroline's shoulder.

"Hello, Mrs. Troxler," I said. I was so stunned by what I had just heard Caroline say that I spoke in a whisper.

"She's with her mother—or with her family, at least," Caroline said. By now she had slipped into the hallway, and I had followed without Mrs. Troxler's really inviting us in.

"Where are her family?" Mrs. Troxler asked, giving way to

Caroline's forward thrust. "She never volunteered to tell me anything about them. And I never think it's my business to ask."

Caroline nodded her head at me, indicating that I should lead
the way to Lee Ann's room. I knew that her room was toward the
back of the house and I headed in that direction.

"I'll have to unlock the room for you," said Mrs. Troxler.
"There have been a number of people coming here and wanting
to look about her room. And so I keep it locked."

"A number of people?" asked Caroline casually.

"Yes. Nat knows. There were the police. And then there were
some other gentlemen. Nat knows about it, though he didn't
come in. And there were two other girls. The girls just seemed idly
curious, and so I've taken to locking the door. Where do her people live?"

"I don't know," said Caroline. "She's going to meet us downtown at the bus station and take a bus."

When Mrs. Troxler had unlocked the door she asked, "Is Lee
Ann all right? Do you think she will be coming back here?"

"She's fine," Caroline said, "and I'm sure she'll be coming back.
She just wants a few things."

"Yes, I've wondered how she's been getting along without a
change of clothes. I'll fetch her suitcase. I keep my roomers' luggage in my storage closet down the hall." We waited till she came
back with a piece of plaid luggage and then we went into the
room and closed the door. Caroline went to the oak dresser and
began pulling things out and stuffing them in the bag. I stood by,
watching, hardly able to believe what I saw Caroline doing.
When she had closed the bag, she looked up at me as if to say,
"What are you waiting for?" She had not gone near the little mahogany dressing table, and I had not realized that was going to be
my part. I went over and opened the left-hand drawer. The only
thing in the drawer was a small snapshot. I took it up and examined it carefully. I said nothing to Caroline, just handed her
the picture. Finally I said, "Do you know who that is? And where
the picture was taken?" She recognized the woman in the picture
at once. It was the old woman with the goitre who ran The Cellar. The picture had been taken with Mrs. Power standing in one
of the flower beds against the side of the house. The big cut stones
of the house were unmistakable. After bringing the snapshot up

close to her face and peering into it for ten seconds or so, Caroline looked at me and said, "That's her family."

By the time we had stopped the car in front of The Cellar, I had told Caroline all that I knew about Lee Ann's schooling and about how it was that, though she had a "family" in Memphis, no one had known her when she was growing up. She had been to one boarding school in Shreveport, Louisiana, to one in East Texas, and to still another in St. Charles, Missouri. I had heard her make references to all of those schools. "They kept her away from home," Caroline speculated. "And so when she had finished school she wasn't prepared for the kind of 'family' she had. That's why she moved out on them and lived in a rooming house."

She reached that conclusion while I was parking the car at the curb, near the front entrance to the house. Meanwhile, I was preparing myself mentally to accompany Caroline to the door of the old woman's living quarters, which were on the main floor and above The Cellar. But Caroline rested her hand on the steering wheel beside mine and said, "This is something I have to do without you."

"But I'd like to see Lee Ann if she's here," I said.

"I know you would," said Caroline. "Of course you would."

"But, Caroline," I said, "I've made it clear that ours was an innocent—"

"I know," she said. "That's why I don't want you to see her again." Then she took Lee Ann's bag and went up to the front entrance of the house.

The main entrance to The Cellar was to the side of and underneath the high front stoop of the old house. Caroline had to climb a flight of ten or twelve stone steps to reach the door to the residence. From the car I saw a vague figure appear at one of the long first-floor windows. I was relatively certain that it was Lee Ann I saw. I could barely restrain myself from jumping from the car and running up that flight of steps and forcing myself past Caroline and into the house. During the hundred hours or so since she had fled into the woods of Overton Park, Lee Ann Deehart had come to represent feelings of mine that I didn't try to comprehend. The notion I had had yesterday that I was in love with her and wanted to marry her didn't really adequately express the emotions that her disappearance had stirred in me.

I felt that I had never looked at her really or had any conception of what sort of person she was or what her experience in life was like. Now it seemed I would never know. I suddenly realized—at that early age—that there was experience to be had in life that I might never know anything about except through hearsay and through books. I felt that this was my last moment to reach out and understand something of the world that was other than my own narrow circumstances and my own narrow nature. When, nearly fifteen years later, I came into a comfortable amount of money—after my father's death—I made my extraordinary decision to go back to the university and prepare myself to become a teacher. But I knew then, at thirty-seven, that I was only going to try to comprehend intellectually the world about me and beyond me and that I had failed somehow at some time to reach out and grasp direct experience of a larger life which no amount of intellectualizing could compensate for. It may be that the moment of my great failure was when I continued to sit there in the car and did not force my way into the house where the old woman with the goitre lived and where it now seemed Lee Ann had been hiding for four days.

I was scarcely aware of the moment when the big front door opened and Caroline was admitted to the house. She was in there for nearly an hour. During that time I don't know what thoughts I had. It was as though I ceased to exist for the time that Lee Ann Dechart and Caroline Braxley were closeted together. When Caroline reappeared on the high stone stoop of the house, I was surprised to see she was still carrying Lee Ann's suitcase. But she would soon make it all clear. It *was* Lee Ann who received her at the door. No doubt she had seen that Caroline was carrying her own piece of luggage. And no doubt Caroline had counted on just that mystification and its efficacy, because Caroline is an extremely clever psychologist when she sets her mind to it. At any rate, in that relatively brief interview between them Caroline learned that all she had surmised about Lee Ann was true. Moreover, she learned that Lee Ann had fled the scene of the accident because she feared that the publicity would reveal to everyone who her grandmother was.

Lee Ann had crossed the little strip of snow-covered golf course and had entered the part of the woods where the old-forest trees

were. And something had made her want to remain there for a
while. She didn't know what it was. She had leaned against one of
the trees, feeling quite content. It had seemed to her that she was
not alone in the woods. And whatever the other presences were,
instead of interfering with her reflections they seemed to wish to
help her clear her thoughts. She stood there for a long time—
perhaps for an hour or more. At any rate, she remained there until
all at once she realized how cold she had grown and realized that
she had no choice but to go back to the real world. Yet she wasn't
going back to her room or to her pretty possessions there. That
wasn't the kind of freedom she wanted any longer. She was going
back to her grandmother. But still she hoped to avoid the publicity that the accident might bring. She decided to go, first of all,
and stay with some of her friends, so that her grandmother would
not suppose she was only turning to her because she was in trouble. And while making this important change in her life she felt
she must be protected by her friends. She wanted to have an inter-
val of time to herself and she wanted, above all, not to be bothered during that time by the silly society boy in whose car she had
been riding.

During the first days she had gone from one girl's house to another. Finally she went to her grandmother. In the beginning she
had, it was true, been mightily depressed. That was why she had
telephoned me to start with, and had wanted someone to cheer
her up. But during these four days she had much time for thinking and had overcome all her depression and had no other
thought but to follow through with the decision to go and live
openly with her old grandmother in her quarters above The
Cellar.

Caroline also, in that single interview, learned other things
about Lee Ann which had been unknown to me. She learned that
Lee Ann's own mother had abandoned her in infancy to her
grandmother but had always through the years sent money back
for her education. She had had—the mother—an extremely successful career as a buyer for a women's-clothing store in Lincoln,
Nebraska. But she had never tried to see her daughter and had
never expressed a wish to see her. The only word she ever sent was
that children were not her dish, but that she didn't want it on her
conscience that, because of her, some little girl in Memphis, Ten-

nessee, had got no education and was therefore the domestic slave of some man. When Caroline told me all of this about the mother's not caring to see the daughter, it brought from her her first emotional outburst with regard to the whole business. But that was at a later time. The first thing she had told me when she returned to the car was that once Lee Ann realized that her place of hiding could no longer be concealed, she was quickly and easily persuaded to speak to the newspaper editor on the telephone and to tell him that she was safe and well. But she did this only after Caroline had first spoken to the editor herself, and obtained a promise from him that there would be no embarrassing publicity for Lee Ann's grandmother.

The reason Caroline had returned with Lee Ann's suitcase was that Lee Ann had emptied it there in her grandmother's front parlor and had asked that we return to her rooming house and bring all of her possessions to her at her grandmother's. We obliged her in this, making appropriate, truthless explanations to her landlady, whom Lee Ann had meanwhile telephoned and given whatever little authority Mrs. Troxler required in order to let us remove her things. It seemed to me that that poor woman scarcely listened to the explanations we gave. Another girl was already moving into the room before we had well got Lee Ann's things out. When we returned to the grandmother's house with these possessions in the car, Caroline insisted upon making an endless number of trips into the house, carrying everything herself. She was firm in her stipulation that Lee Ann and I not see each other again.

The incident was closed then. I could be certain that there would be no broken engagement—not on Caroline's initiative. But from that point—from that afternoon—my real effort and my real concern would be to try to understand why Caroline had not been so terribly enraged or so sorely wounded upon first discovering that there had been another girl with me in the car at the time of the accident, and by the realization that I had not immediately disclosed her presence, that she had not at least once threatened to end the engagement. What her mental processes had been during the past four days, knowing now as I did that she was the person with whom I was going to spend the rest of my life, became of paramount interest to me.

But at that age I was so unquestioning of human behavior in general and so accepting of events as they came, and so without perception or reflection regarding the binding and molding effect upon people of the circumstances in which they are born, that I actually might not have found Caroline's thoughts of such profound interest and so vitally important to be understood had not Caroline, as soon as we were riding down Adams Street and were out of sight of The Cellar and of Mrs. Power's great stone house above it, suddenly requested that I drive her out to the Bristol Highway, and once we were on the Bristol Highway asked me to drive as fast and as far out of town as I could or would, to drive and drive until she should beg me to turn around and take her home; and had she not, as soon as we were out of town and beyond city speed limits, where I could press down on the accelerator and send us flying along the three-lane strip of concrete which cut through the endless expanse of cotton fields and swamps on either side, had she not then at last, after talking quietly about Lee Ann's mother's sending back the money for her education, burst into weeping that began with a kind of wailing and grinding of teeth that one ordinarily associates more with a very old person in very great physical pain, a wailing that became mixed almost immediately with a sort of hollow laughter in which there was no mirth. I commenced slowing the car at once. I was searching for a place where I could pull off to the side of the road. But through her tears and her harsh, dry laughter she hissed at me, "Don't stop! Don't stop! Go on. Go on. Go as far and as fast as you can, so that I can forget this day and put it forever behind me!" I obeyed her and sped on, reaching out my right hand to hold her two hands that were resting in her lap and were making no effort to wipe away her tears. I was not looking at her—only thinking thoughts of a kind I had never before had. It was the first time I had ever witnessed a victim of genuine hysteria. Indeed, I wasn't to hear such noises again until six or seven years later, during the Second World War. I heard them from men during days after a battle, men who had stood with great bravery against the enemy—particularly, as I remember now, men who had been brought back from the first onslaught of the Normandy invasion, physically whole but shaken in their souls. I think that during the stress of the four previous days Caroline Braxley had shed not a tear of self-pity or of shame and had not allowed herself a moment of genuine grief for my possible faithlessness to her. She had been far too busy with thinking—with thinking her thoughts of how to cope with Lee Ann's unexplained disappearance, with, that is, its possible effect upon her own life. But now the time had come when her checked emotions could be checked no longer.

The Bristol Highway, along which we were speeding as she wept hysterically, was a very straight and a very wide roadway for those days. It went northeast from Memphis. As its name implied, it was the old road that shot more or less diagonally across the long hinterland that is the state of Tennessee. It was the road along which many of our ancestors had first made their way from Virginia and the Carolinas to Memphis, to settle in the forest wilderness along the bluffs above the Mississippi River. And it occurred to me now that when Caroline said go as fast and as far as you can she really meant to take us all the way back into our past and begin the journey all over again, not merely from a point of four days ago or from the days of our childhood but from a point in our identity that would require a much deeper delving and a more radical return.

When we had got scarcely beyond the outskirts of Memphis, the most obvious signs of her hysteria had abated. Instead, however, she began to speak with a rapidity and in tones I was not accustomed to in her speech. This began after I had seen her give one long look over her shoulder and out the rear window of the car. Sensing some significance in that look and sensing some connection between it and the monologue she had now launched upon, I myself gave one glance into the rearview mirror. What met my eye was the skyline of modern Memphis beyond the snow-covered suburban rooftops—the modern Memphis of 1937, with its two or three high-rise office buildings. It was not clear to me immediately what there was in that skyline to inspire all that followed. She was speaking to me openly about Lee Ann and about her own feelings of jealousy and resentment of the girl—of *that* girl and of all those other girls, too, whose names and personalities and way of life had occupied our thoughts and had seemed to

threaten our future during the four-day crisis that had followed
my accident in the Park.

"It isn't only Lee Ann that disturbs me," she said. "It began
with her, of course. It began not with what she might be to you
but with her freedom to jump out of your car, her freedom *from*
you, her freedom to run off into the woods—with her capacity,
which her special way of living provided her, simply to vanish, to
remove herself from the eyes of the world, literally to disappear
from the glaring light of day while the whole world, so to speak,
looked on."

"*You* would like to be able to do that?" I interrupted. It
seemed so unlike her role as I understood it.

"*Any*body would, wouldn't they?" she said, not looking at me
but at the endless stretch of concrete that lay straight ahead.
"*Men* have always been able to do it," she said. "In my own family, for as many generations back as our family stories go, there
have been men who seemed to disappear from the face of the
earth just because they wanted to. They used to write 'Gone to
Texas' on the front door and leave the house and the farm to be
sold for taxes. They walked out on dependent old parents and on
sweethearts or even on wives and little children. And though they
were considered black sheep for doing so, they were something of
heroes, too. It seemed romantic to the rest of us that they had
gone Out West somewhere and got a new start or had begun life
over. But there was never a woman in our family who did that!
There was no way it could happen. Or perhaps in some rare instance it did happen and the story hasn't come down to us. Her
name simply isn't recorded in our family annals or reported in stories told around the fire. The assumption of course is that she is a
streetwalker in Chicago or she resides in a red-plush whorehouse
in Cheyenne. But with girls like Lee Ann and Lucy and Betsy it's
all different. They have made their break with the past. Each of
them has had the strength and intelligence to make the break for
herself. But now they have formed a sort of league for their own
protection. How I do admire and envy them! And how little you
understand them, Nat. How little you understand Lee Ann's loneliness and depression and bravery. She and all the others are wonderful—even Fern. They occupy the real city of Memphis as none
of the rest of us do. They treat men just as they please. And not

the way men are treated in *our* circles. And men like them better
for it. Those girls have learned to enjoy life together and to be
mutually protective, but they enjoy a protection also, I hope you
have observed, a kind of communal protection, from men who admire their very independence, from a league of men, mind you,
not from individual men, from the police and from men like my
father and your father, from men who would never say openly
how much they admire them. Naturally we fear them. Those of us
who are not like them in temperament—or in intelligence, because there is no use in denying it—we must fear them and find a
means to give delaying action. And of course the only way we
know is the age-old way!"

She became silent for a time now. But I knew I was going to
hear what I had been waiting to hear. If I had been the least bit
impatient with her explanation of Lee Ann and her friends, it was
due in part to my impatience to see if she would explain *herself* to
me. We were now speeding along the Bristol Highway at the very
top speed the car would go. Except when we were passing through
some crossroad or village I consciously kept the speed above
ninety. In those days there was no speed limit in Tennessee. There
were merely signs placed every so often along the roadside saying
"Speed Limit: Please Drive Carefully." I felt somehow that, considering Caroline's emotional state and my own tension, it would
be altogether unreasonable, it would constitute careless and unsafe driving, for me to reduce our speed to anything below the
maximum capability of the car. And when we did of necessity
slow down for some village or small town it was precisely as
though we had arrived at some at once familiar and strange point
in the past. And on each occasion I think we both experienced a
sense of danger and disappointment. It was as though we expected
to experience a satisfaction in having gone so far. But the satisfaction was not to be had. When we had passed that point, I felt
only the need to press on at an even greater speed. And so we
drove on and on, at first north and east through the wintry cotton
land and corn land, past the old Orgill Plantation, the mansion
house in plain view, its round brick columns on which the plaster
was mostly gone, and now and then another white man's an-
tebellum house, and always at the roadside or on the horizon,
atop some distant ridge, a variety of black men's shacks and

cabins, each with a little streamer of smoke rising from an impro-
vised tin stovepipe or from an ill-made brick chimney bent away
from the cabin at a precarious angle.

We went through the old villages of Arlington and Mason and
the town of Brownsville—down streets of houses with columned
porticoes and double galleries—and then we turned south to Bolivar, whose very name told you when it was built, and headed
back to Memphis through Grand Junction and La Grange. (Mississippi towns really, though north of the Tennessee line.) I
had slowed our speed after Bolivar, because that was where Caroline began her second monologue. The tone and pace of her
speech were very different now. Her speech was slow and deliberate, her emotions more under control than usual, as she described
what she had felt and thought in the time since the accident and
explained how she came to reach the decision to take the action
she had—that is, action toward searching out and finding Lee Ann
Deehart. Though I had said nothing on the subject of what she
had done about Lee Ann and not done about our engagement, expressed no request or demand for any explanation unless it was by
my silence, when she spoke now it was almost as though Caroline
were making a courtroom defense of accusations hurled at her by
me. "I finally saw there was only one thing for me to do and saw
why I had to do it. I saw that the only power in the world I had
for saving myself lay in my saving you. And I saw that I could
only save you by 'saving' Lee Ann Deehart. At first, of course, I
thought I would have to break our engagement, or at least postpone the wedding for a year. That's what everybody thought, of
course—everybody in the family."

"Even your father and mother?" I could not help interjecting.
It had seemed to me that Caroline's parents had—of all people—
been most sympathetic to me.

"Yes, even my mother and father," she went on, rather serenely
now. "They could not have been more sympathetic to you personally. Mother said that, after all, you were a mere man. Father said
that, after all, you were only human. But circumstances were circumstances, and if some disaster had befallen Lee Ann, if she was
murdered or if she was pregnant or if she was a suicide or whatever other horror you can conjure up, and it all came out, say, on
our wedding day or came out afterward, for that matter—well,

what then? *They* and *I* had to think of that. On the other hand, as I kept thinking, what if the wedding *was* called off? What then for me? The only power I had to save myself was to save you, and to save you by rescuing Lee Ann Deehart. It always came to that, and comes to that still. Don't you see, it was a question of how very much I had to lose and how little power I had to save myself. Because *I* had not set *myself* free the way those other girls have. One makes that choice at a much earlier age than this, I'm afraid. And so I knew already, Nat, and I know now what the only kind of power I can ever have must be."

She hesitated then. She was capable of phrasing what she said much more precisely. But it would have been indelicate, somehow, for her to have done so. And so I said it for her in my crude way: "You mean the power of a woman in a man's world."

She nodded and continued, "I had to protest *that*. Even if it had been *I* that broke our engagement, Nat, or even if you and I had been married before some second scandal broke, still I would have been a jilted, a rejected girl. And some part of my power to protect myself would be gone forever. Power, or strength, is what everybody must have some of if he—if she—is to survive in any kind of world. I have to protect and use whatever strength I have."

Caroline went on in that voice until we were back in Memphis and at her father's house on East Parkway. She kissed me before we got out of the car there, kissed me for my silence, I believe. I had said almost nothing during the whole of the long ride. And I think she has ever since been grateful to me for the silence I kept. Perhaps she mistook it for more understanding than I was capable of at the time. At any rate, I cannot help believing that it has much to do with the support and understanding—rather silent though it was—which she gave me when I made the great break in my life in my late thirties. Though it clearly meant that we must live on a somewhat more modest scale and live among people of a sort she was not used to, and even meant leaving Memphis forever behind us, the firmness with which she supported my decision, and the look in her eyes whenever I spoke of feeling I must make the change, seemed to say to me that she would dedicate her pride of power to the power of freedom I sought.

LOOKING FOR MOTHER

MARILYN KRYSL

Marilyn Krysl was born in Kansas. She is the author of a book of stories, *Honey, You've Been Dealt a Winning Hand* (Capra Press, 1980), and two volumes of poetry, *Saying Things* (1975) and *The Brain Has A Secret Desire* (The Cleveland State Poetry Series, 1980). Ms. Krysl has published poetry in numerous periodicals, such as *The Atlantic*, *The Nation*, and *The New Republic*. She is the recipient of several awards, including a National Endowment for the Arts Fellowship. Ms. Krysl currently teaches at the University of Colorado at Boulder.

January. My mother dies. I inherit her diary. It arrives on the sixteenth, Wednesday, but when the postman knocks I am not at home. I am at the supermarket, between the meat counter and the frozen fowl case, wiping Ann's nose and choosing a ham. I shiver, weighing the merits of butt and shank, and the postman leaves the package propped against the aluminum screen door. Later the neighbors' collie, Buff, drags the package onto the lawn, snarling and worrying the twine with his teeth. At 2:30 Ann and I still have not returned, and an eighth-grader on his way home from school lifts the package, hurries to his vacant-lot hideout and peels away the tight brown wrapping. Crouching, glancing furtively over his shoulder, he opens the little book, hoping for excitement—a treasure map, dirty pictures. But there are no maps, no pictures, and he cannot read the fine scrawl. Disappointed, he drops the diary into the gutter where—

No. January. My mother dies. I inherit her diary. It arrives on the sixteenth, Wednesday, by special delivery mail. Certified. Return receipt requested. A knock at the door, a brisk, insistent rapping. A glass figurine on a small shelf near the door totters—

No, wait. I can't see the doorway. I'm kneeling on the bathroom floor, sorting laundry, the automatic washer thudding two feet from my right ear. It's Wednesday, and John, my husband, is where he always is on Wednesday, at his glass-topped desk on the seventh floor of the Malibar Building, making checkmarks in the margin beside a column of base prices. I am alone with the baby, Ann. As she crawls toward me, whining, through the scattered sheets and shirts, as she reaches for the top button of my blouse, I hear a knock at the front door, the resonance of bone on wood which tells me the caller has opened the screen and put his knuckles to the pine.

I begin to tremble. I am ordinary, a woman, twenty-nine, with breasts and long hair, married and living in a house. There is no reason to expect anything unusual. Maybe it's my next-door neighbor or the milkman or a Girl Scout selling cookies—

But the truth is that the knocking terrifies me. I crouch on the bathroom tile and cling to my baby, and there are tears in my eyes, as though I fear she will be taken from me, as though I'm afraid this is only the beginning of some frightful end. I hold her and I stay very quiet, hoping the knocking will stop. The caller knocks once, twice, and that is all. I don't answer the door—

Of course I answer the door. My hair is cut short and I am responsible and steady and cheerful. I answer the door politely while the automatic washer vibrates, while Ann cuts teeth on buttons and zippers of my dresses and her father's flies. The figurine on its tiny shelf does not quiver but simply stands, still and erect. The postman and I exchange remarks on the weather and I sign his yellow receipt. Then he hands me the package. He presses the small, brown parcel into my trembling hands—

No. I sign the receipt, take the package and close the door. The washer flicks off at the end of its cycle and the momentum of its spin slows, stops. Silence—

No. No silence. In fact, while the washer continues to whir I simply go to the kitchen and cut the twine with a knife. I cut my thumb. I cut—

No. None of this happens except my mother's dying. When Mother dies in Chicago it is 7:00 a.m. in San Francisco, the ordinary morning of an ordinary day. At 7:00 the sun is up, streaming across the kitchen table toward the base of a cracked tumbler filled with water and daffodils. Ann bangs the aluminum tray of her high chair with a spoon, I am stirring scrambled eggs, and just before the phone rings, John, who is watching me from behind, raises his eyebrows and remarks, playfully and affectionately, "Some legs, yours!"

Then the phone. It is Aunt Kay in Wyoming. Calling to tell me of Mother's death. While John shaves I have to make a list for him and put on a suit and stockings. I have to kiss John and Ann and board a DC-8, fly east across North America's time zones to Chicago, that cold, impersonal city where Mother is dead. To Mother's tiny apartment, a microscopic point inside the vast mesh of that city. I have to go because my sister, Ellen, married to a structural engineer, has four children under age seven and can't leave Tallahassee without elaborate advance arrangements. Because my brother, Frank, a junior in political science at UCLA, is taking final exams. Because Mother has no other relatives except Aunt Kay, their three brothers already dead from cancer, from heart attack—

Wait. One of them is a lawyer, very much alive, but I don't know much about him. (This is the truth!) I've heard Ellen say "a lawyer, in Duluth," but I have no Christmas cards, no snapshots of his children, nothing. Does he have children? Does he have a dog, maybe a golden retriever? Mistresses? Debts? For five minutes I stare at this paper and try to imagine his life. For five minutes the paper remains blank. I can't get together any credible details, nothing but a glimpse of a man's figure entering a revolving glass door—and that he regrets that business commitments preclude a trip to Chicago.

So Aunt Kay meets me at the airport in Chicago, kisses me on the cheek. And in that sprawling city in the stale, pink apartment where Aunt Kay and I sort Mother's things, I come upon the diary in the middle desk drawer. Beside books of blank checks, loose paperclips, Kleenex. Aunt Kay flips the pages hastily, as though only something quite unusual, a photograph or an illustration, could interest her. Then she says, "Here. You take it, dear . . ."

No. I never let Aunt Kay see the diary. The diary may tell me
something about Mother, Mother who has never been present.
And if there is information, I want to hoard it. I need all the information I can get about Mother, and I don't want to take the
chance that Aunt Kay might want the diary. Because I despise
Aunt Kay. All through those long years of childhood I resented
her trying to take Mother's place, and all through those long years
of childhood I gave her nothing, not one atom of myself. I kept
myself back from her, I refused to use the potty, I hid food in my
bed. My whole life was a capital NO to Aunty Kay. And even
now that I am grown and understand why I couldn't love her,
even now I won't share the diary, that document of Mother.

In Mother's apartment I stand in front of an open drawer, dipping my hands aimlessly into her lingerie, fingering a smooth satin
slip, wondering what to do with this ownerless underwear, these
intimate articles of clothing that belonged to someone now dead—

And my hand finds the diary.

When I hear Aunt Kay walking toward the bedroom I toss the
diary into my suitcase and close the lid.

1939. A small town in Wyoming. Mother and Father working in a bakery that belongs to Father's Uncle Nate, living with
Nate and Aunt Martha in rooms (sunny?) above the bakery.
Mother leaning over a counter, spreading white icing, the smell of
yeast rising to the flat above. At night Nate and Father drink beer
while Father plays the accordion. An accordion singing in Wyoming's summer dark, and Martha—or Mother?—no, both Mother
and Martha, bending and lifting as though winnowing grain, lifting a starched, white sheet above their heads, letting it fall and settle like snow on my bed . . .

And then my father becomes an Army private in a funny hat
like a boat, leaves for the Japanese war and never returns. In 1945
I am four, sobbing in Mother's lap—

No. Why would I sob? At four I don't care about the dead, not
even Father. I don't remember him. At four I care only about the
bugles glittering against the blue sky, the bugles playing taps. The
music is sad, sad and beautiful, and Mother's lap is warm and
ample, and I savor the notes as I savor the licorice in my mouth.

The licorice in my mouth is the present, the licorice in my pocket is the future. Why should I care about the past?

And Mother is a widow. She is bereft and beautiful. She is bereft, briefly, and particularly beautiful, and then she leaves the huge quiet of Wyoming and plunges into the huge noise of Chicago. Because Father's death leaves a silence she has to keep filling with noise—music, chatter, doors slamming, neighbors' radios blaring, traffic. And she can't sleep because the silence she has filled with noise might empty, leaving a blank hole into which she would then fall. She is deaf with this noise, deaf from the blast of the Japanese rifle aimed at Father's head. And her eyes cannot bear to look at Wyoming's flat, empty space because it is like the sound of the gaping hole in Father's head, the empty hole in Mother's lap—

So my childhood is not a continuous sunny morning. Instead I lust endlessly after all Aunt Kay prohibits—candy, mud, certain ragged, dirty children. I am defiant, talking back and plotting how to stay out after dark, and I live in fear of the consequences—sharp words, smacks, paddlings, penances to be performed. I hang in this balance between desire and fear, sitting on the floor beside an electrical socket, nervously plugging and unplugging the kitchen clock's double-pronged cord, breathing noisily, jamming the plug in, ripping it out again, until the sound of footsteps wakes me and I startle guiltily. I can't wait to grow up and get married, to escape Aunt Kay—

And it's true, I do marry. In a white satin gown I marry John, who loves me and cherishes me daily in an ordinary American way, who will change a diaper on request, who takes us out for pizza, who carries Ann in the backpack when we wander the zoo hand in hand in July. And in 1970 in the midst of the life secure in its flatness, surrounded by beloved, familiar circumstances, the breakfast dishes shimmering in the drainer like a still life, sunlight beginning to slide across the table toward a handful of daffodils—in 1970 I kiss my husband and child good-bye. I kiss them casually, as though I am only going around the block, as though without question I shall be back for dinner—I kiss them and set off. I set off in search of Mother, with only a few clues—a city where she died, some limp lingerie which no longer holds the warm imprint of her body, and, if I am lucky, one or two photographs—

Yes. Let me find a photograph. Let me see you in a park in Chicago, a lush summer park. The branches of trees hang heavy with sprays of leaves, leaves flickering in black and white sunlight, and in the background, blurred, a white fountain, its water lifting, arching and falling—

And Mother, you are lovely as you walk briskly through this summer park. You have just come from your lover—or maybe you are going to meet him. Does it really matter? But wait—Yes. You re-tie the sash of your dress, he puts his lips lightly on your forehead, and now you walk briskly toward us, toward Ellen, Frank and me—

And I am the one squinting through the camera's lens. Inside this small black frame you are beautifully alive and shining. I can see your shoulders rise and fall with your breathing, your feet in pretty shoes are tapping on the walk, coming closer and closer, and now your eyes see me, finally recognize Ellen and Frank and me, and you begin to smile—

No. This never happened. I would have given anything to leave Wyoming, to leave dull, strident, well-meaning, authoritarian Aunt Kay, and to go with Mother, to have walked across that park toward Mother, to see her face to face as now I see Frank, Ellen, John, Ann—

But it didn't happen. I had a brownie camera, I took a lot of pictures of Frank, of Ellen, of the dog, of the peonies in the garden, but this photograph of Mother is a lie. I made this up.

What happens is that: a month after Father's funeral the family assembles in the parlor, in those rooms above the bakery. Aunt Kay is there and Martha and Nate, in their seventies now, and the three brothers and, I suppose, their wives. In the garden Ellen and I play follow-the-leader with our cousins, the cousins we see only on special holidays or the momentous occasions of wedding and death. Panting and shouting, we weave in and out among the peonies, sweat wilting our starched, uncomfortable clothes.

Mother is in the parlor with the family, and she is the occasion for this reunion. Beneath her black wool dress she is finally calm, and she is beautiful, I think, in a still, suspended way, like a glassy lake unruffled by wind. Tears in full measure have fallen from her swollen eyes, like a penance exacted, and now her eyes are clear. She sits with her hands folded in her lap, waiting. And then she says:

"I have asked you to come here to talk about the children. I can't keep them. Someone must take them, and I would like them to stay together. I'd like it to be you, Kay, if you want to."

Aunt Kay nods. Perhaps the uncles nod. Perhaps the hydrangeas in their vase on the sill nod. The aunts and uncles stand up. Even Nate, supported by Martha, leans on his cane. Then Mother walks out of the parlor, out of the bakery, out of Wyoming. This is what Aunt Kay told me, "It had to be."

So I am not to have a Mother. I am to have Aunt Kay. And Frank and Ellen and John and Ann. December 24th, Christmas Eve, our first Christmas with our first child, Ann. Ellen phones from Tallahassee to wish us Merry Christmas. Ellen can't come, but Aunt Kay is coming, is on a plane that has already left Chicago. And Frank is coming, is in L.A. now boarding a bus that will reach San Francisco tonight. Handsome Frank, a junior in political science, leaning over the desk in his library carrel, taking notes from the *Journal of Foreign Affairs*. Frank, who calls me "Legs," who lies all morning under the Chevy grunting and sweating, who slouches on the deck and smokes as John drops lines overboard enticing bass, while Ann plays in the shade of the cabin, and I close my eyes and float on the hot surface of sleep—

I am twenty-nine and I believe my life is nearly perfect. There is a seventeen-pound turkey in the refrigerator, and in the living room a tinseled spruce tree with its base of presents. While Frank and Aunt Kay are on their way toward us, Ann crawls to the tree and tugs at a red bow, trying to get it into her mouth; and as I watch her John comes toward me, his hand extended like a gift, offering a glass of Christmas sherry.

My life is nearly perfect, and at 4:00 p.m. it begins to snow, a perfect Christmas snow. At 7:00 when John drives us to the airport to meet Aunt Kay it is still snowing, great wet clumps of flakes that plunge past the headlights and disappear into the black pavement. I cover Ann's head with the corner of her blanket as we hurry into the terminal and through the milling crowd to Gate 7 of Concourse B.

The jet lands, and the passengers begin one at a time to file down the ramp. When Aunt Kay appears in the doorway and begins to descend she seems smaller than I remember, and I have the impression that at fifty-five she is delicate, perhaps even frail. I have the impression that she can scarcely manage the stack of packages she is balancing, and I give Ann to John and begin to push through the crowd toward her.

I wind among the people waiting here in clusters, people like me loving other people, watching the perfect snow while they wait for those others to arrive. And now Aunt Kay walks quickly across the black pavement, a tiny figure swirled in snow. I hurry toward her and amidst the glitter and flash of foil paper and silver ribbon I try to see her face, her eyes . . .

Ellen doesn't phone from her kitchen in Tallahassee to wish us Merry Christmas. And Frank—Frank never arrives on that bus from L.A. A sister and a brother—luxuries I want but will never have. Stylistic decorations of this grim afternoon in Chicago where I pace, aching and waiting. A sister and a brother, etchings. Black ink on white paper. A lie.

I lie on the bed and stare at the pink ceiling. My body is hungry for John's body, far to the west of Chicago, and for the sight and sound and feel of Ann.

In our house in San Francisco Ann sits in a pile of white sugar, picking it up in handfuls, letting it run through her fingers like sand. And John in the Malibar Building sits at his desk, running a blue pencil down a column of prices, making little checkmarks in the margin, yawning inside the minor boredom of elevators and wire baskets. Ben, one of John's co-workers, stops at John's desk, leans over and begins to whisper. In the story a woman's car has run out of gas on the freeway . . . They snicker, John replies with a story of his own, and then the secretary comes in with coffee, two black and three with cream. Ben goes back to his adding machine, John makes more checkmarks in more margins, and in a still, sleep-edged room of his mind I sit at the kitchen table feeding the baby soft, tan cereal with a tiny silver spoon. John imagines this, an ordinary scene from our ordinary life, a serenity in which the three of us belong, and to which it will later occur to him to add a bouquet of flowers. After which he will decide whether or not to repeat to me a story about a woman whose car runs out of gas—

I continue to lie and stare at the ceiling until—until certain obligations are fulfilled, certain objects disposed of—cooking utensils, clothing, old magazines, blankets, rugs, bars of soap—and I settle into the seat of another DC-8. I fasten the seat belt and pick up a magazine, read this magazine over Minneapolis, St. Louis, Denver, Salt Lake—

I don't have an Aunt Kay. I've never had one. I have only the family I myself have made. I have a husband who loves me simply and straight out, sometimes yawning, who drives us into the country, through grassy hills, who carries the picnic basket as we stroll under the slender, new branches of oaks—I have a husband, a daughter, a house, a life, and I have a diary. I have a diary and February 10, 1969, the page of my daughter's birth, is black with writing. Would you like to read it?

And now I am restless, impatient to fly down to them, to my John and my Ann. Enough reading, enough tedious chatter with the mutual funds salesman beside me, enough. I want to go home, forget this.

They will meet me. Maybe Ann will be perched on John's shoulders, maybe a wind will lift her fine hair, John's hug will lift me, and then we will walk down the concourse, laughing and talking. And now in my thoughts I rush ahead up the steps to our porch, our living room and, inside, our chairs, pillows, mirrors, the texture of curtains, certain prints on certain walls, Ann's crib—

And it occurs to me to look for October sixth, the day of my birth. I sit up, swing my legs over the edge of the bed, and I hurry toward October sixth as toward an important rendezvous. And while October sixth is still several pages away I am already leaning forward, eagerly, a lock of my hair falls forward—

She will write that my father is aboard a cruiser in the Pacific and she is alone. How outside in the dark it is snowing, a thin, dry snow, how in the field behind the water tower pronghorns graze undisturbed. How she finds, horrified, that she cannot control her mouth, how when it is finally over both of us are exhausted and bloody, and a pronghorn lifts its head for five, eight, eleven seconds, and then continues grazing—

I find October sixth. 1941. Nothing. A blank page.
Strange, I think.
Then angrily I snap the pages back and forth across October
sixth. There is nothing here about me! Nothing!

With the other passengers I file into the aisle and out into California's brisk January air. As I descend I do not see John immediately, I do not immediately see Ann's tiny head bobbing above
the crowd. I hesitate, scanning the close faces, the faces further
away. I hurry into the concourse, push through the crowd, the
men, women and children waiting for other men, women and
children—
But John and Ann are not in the concourse. I do not meet
them anywhere in the concourse. And now fear, like a fist,
tightens my body. I hold still inside this tightness and make myself walk slowly to the baggage claim counter. But they are not at
the baggage claim counter. They are not—
Of course. Of course. They are not here.

My father was killed by the Japanese. He was killed before I
was born, in a military hospital, in Tacoma, Washington. I was
born in February, I weighed seven pounds, six ounces. My mother
died in childbirth. I don't know if it was quick, like a flame going
out, or longer and bloody. If anyone was with her, a cousin, an
uncle, I have never seen them.
Very likely it was raining. In February, in Tacoma. Possibly a
steady rain, falling all day, as though quite ordinary things were
happening. Or there might have been a thin snow, followed by a
sharp freeze. Or a lush, thick snow, big clusters of flakes, unusual
for Tacoma, bringing people out into the streets. I don't know.
All this is speculation.
On the table a cracked tumbler, filled with water and
daffodils. I picked the daffodils myself, I filled the tumbler and set
the whole on the table.
This is true. Why would I lie about a bouquet of daffodils.

ELIZABETH

WALTER SULLIVAN

Walter Sullivan was born in Nashville, Tennessee, where he
now resides, and is director of the creative writing program
at Vanderbilt University. Mr. Sullivan was educated at Vanderbilt and the University of Iowa. He is the author of two
novels, two volumes of criticism, stories, and essays.

The first thing she saw when she awakened was a relic out of her
past, a carved figure of the Virgin Mother of God on a sconce
above the chair in her bedroom. The statue had belonged to
Elizabeth's mother, and even in those better times when the family had been together in the little house on Powers Street, the
figure had looked out of place, too elegant for their shabby living
room. Now Elizabeth's living room was also her bedroom. She had
the chair, a couch that made a bed, a dresser, a table, a radio. She
had a bathroom, a small kitchen where the brown linoleum was
peeling away from the floor, and a closet quite adequate for the
few clothes, which, like the statue, she had been able to salvage
when she had escaped from Lucky.

She worked till late at night waiting tables in a bar, and after
she got home, she would sit for a while in the bathtub, the hot
water covering her tired legs. Sometimes she would read one of
the books she got from the drugstore stories about girls who had
had almost as hard a time as she had, but whose fortunes in the
end always took a glorious turn for the better. She was not de-
ceived. She knew that no rich man, no prince from another country, would ever find his way to Bernie's and fall in love with her
and ask her to marry him. She knew that even if such an impossi-

ble thing could happen, she would probably answer the polite pro-
posal with the same grim face and tight lips with which almost
nightly she fended off less advantageous propositions. "Listen,
Lizzie," Bernie Greenspan would occasionally say, "you got good
legs. Your face ain't bad. Smile at the customers. We'll both make
more moola."

"Be happy," Bernie would say. He would tell her jokes. He
would show her cartoons in magazines. At slow times he would
point out funny things on the television. "Ain't no cloud," he
would say, "ain't got no silver lining."

She tried, God knows she did, because she did need to get
bigger tips and because she liked Bernie. Standing near the beer
taps, listening to some clown on the tube crack wise, she would
make her mouth open, force the sound to come out, a series of
broken cackles as harsh as winter. "You like that one, huh?" Bernie would ask, but he knew she was faking. His eyebrows would
give an almost imperceptible lift, and he would gaze at the bottles
on the backbar.

Her smile was no better. She would catch herself in the dim
wall mirrors, a strong figure whom she hardly recognized. She had
no full-length mirror where she lived, and she could not remember
how thin she had grown, nor how pale her face had become. Her
long straight hair was sable against the whiteness of her skin, her
brown eyes were deepened into black by the contrast. Strongest of
all was her mouth, the lips parted, the corners turned up, the
teeth, not perfect, but by no means bad, exposed in what should
have been a smile but distinctly was not. What she showed the
world—and herself when she caught herself off guard—was a stiff
grin, a parody of mirth, her whole expression as rigid and severe as
the face of a pumpkin. O God, O God, she would think. I've got
to do better than that. He'll fire me. Bernie would give her the
axe, and what could she say? She had worked here for three
months. She kept the orders straight and did not slosh the drinks;
she answered when she was spoken to and smiled her awful smile.
But she knew that she moved among the tables like a zombie, a
fugitive from the city of the dead. She would, she thought ironically, be a big hit on Hallowe'en if she could make it that long.

"Get a good night's sleep," Bernie said. "Get yourself all rested up. Some of these rich guys will slip you ten bucks just to make sure you catch their table next time."

But that was the trouble: she could not sleep. That was her problem. Downers were too expensive and booze made her sick and grass was unreliable. She often thought of how funny it was, how when she had first started dating Lucky, he was always after her to turn on, to take a hit, a pill, a drink. A few times when he came to pick her up, he was tripping. She had spent evenings holding his head in her lap, trying to calm him with her touch, her kiss, trying with her straight mind to enter the world into which he had traveled, to see the expanding shapes, the flashing colors that only he could discern. She had learned to drive on his old Chevrolet, sprung like a racing car with the gearshift on the column and decals of flames and devils and naked girls that made it a rolling invitation to a bust. She had no license. But when Lucky was out cold or giggling softly with his eyes closed or mumbling words she could not understand, or bleeding and groggy from a fight he had started—at such times she had had no option. She would take them bouncing, jerking home, saying Hail Marys all the way, and park a couple of blocks beyond her house so the neighbors would not see him still laid out in his car, in case he were still there when they left for work the next morning.

Knowing all this and a lot more—how he had cheated in school and lifted parts for his car and got in trouble once for breaking a girl's nose—knowing all this, why had she married him? Sometimes in the dark of early morning, she lay on her folded-out couch and thought of this question. Was it because both of her sisters were married and moved away, one to L.A., one to Louisville? Or because her mother was sick and dying and then dead? Or because in spite of his faults and ways she was truly in love with him? How could she know what she had felt then when now the memory of him, the image of his face, simply tightened further the rigidity that she always felt and further increased her heart's emptiness? At the best of times, when she had herself under control and could bear to recall moments that she had once considered good, he remained for her lifeless and cold, a wax figure.

She had met him at Archbishop Moore, a big smoke-stained high school in the center of town, recently made coed. Like her older sisters, Elizabeth had been to grade school under the nuns at St. Philip Neri. Madeleine and Nora had gone on to St. Brigid, but by the time Elizabeth got to the ninth grade, her father was dead and money was scarce and her only choices were Moore, where she could go almost free, or a public school which her mother would not hear of. She saw him within the first hour that she spent in Archbishop Moore, and what drew her to him was his friendliness and his apparent self-confidence. On the first day she had risen before six, ridden two buses, and walked through autumn fog to the wide steps leading up to the yellow brick building. At the bottom of the steps she paused to gather her courage. For a moment it seemed to Elizabeth that she had spent most of her life getting herself ready for encounters that she would prefer to avoid. She did not pause long to pity herself. In a way she was in luck. This school did not require uniforms. Torn sneakers and threadbare jeans were the style. She glanced at her own ripped shoes, climbed the stairs, and went through the door into a corridor filled with students.

After her experience at St. Philip Neri, where order prevailed, Elizabeth was struck by the choas of all that surrounded her. Boys and girls, most of them older and larger than she, moved about, scuffled, slammed lockers, hugged each other, walked arm in arm. As she came to find out, the principal was a priest, and there was a nun who taught Latin, but most of the faculty were lay. Their pupils came from everywhere: some had transferred from the better Catholic schools, unable or unwilling to do the work or abide by the regulations; others were Protestants who liked the athletic program at Moore; and there were the Catholics such as Elizabeth who could afford nothing better. All of this she was to learn later. On that first morning she edged back against the wall, her stomach tight, her hands perspiring. It seemed to her that only she was alone and confused. Others knew what to do and where to go and had friends to go with them. In her helplessness she let her gaze wander among the crowd, and after a while her eyes came to rest on Lucky.

What she saw was a small boy, not much taller than she; he was strong, probably, in his wiry way. He stood in the middle of the corridor, and he was telling a story to half a dozen boys and girls, who laughed over and over again and wiped their mirthful eyes and held their stomachs. A girl leaned over to whisper in the small boy's ear, her faded jeans stretching tight across her slim backside, and the boy nodded, his wavy brown hair swinging around his collar. Then he said something—Elizabeth could not hear him for the noise—and the girl took a step back, her lips parted in apparent surprise. The others turned, still laughing, and looked at her; another boy pointed at her breast. She blushed and shook her head as if in denial.

Elizabeth did not meet Lucky that day, and she did not have her first date with him until she was a senior. She learned very quickly that his name was Herman Baker, that everybody called him Lucky, and that he played football and basketball and ran track. He was little, but he was quick and fast, and through autumn after autumn she watched him from afar, a darting midget fleeing from giants, finding strength somehow to rise again after the giants had tackled him. When he broke for a touchdown, scampering through a hole that future college players made for him, the stands would roar and call his name. *Lucky! Lucky! Lucky!* they would shout, and the cheerleaders would turn cartwheels, the girls' short white skirts flipping up to show their crimson tights. Elizabeth passed him in the corridors; she was in his class in American history; and whenever he saw her, he always spoke, but it was clear that he did not know her name. "Hi, sweetie," he would say, or "Hello, babe," and once he stopped and gave her skin. "Like that," he said, showing her how, and she carried her hand through the dingy hall, reverently, palm up until the flesh ceased to tingle.

She had been flattered when he first asked her out. He had had a dozen other girls, most of them better looking, all of them more popular than she: girls with closets full of clothes and enough rings for all their fingers and money to spend for cigarettes and family cars they could borrow. They lived in a world that Elizabeth could only imagine, and it did not occur to her until too late that it had been they who had dropped him and not Lucky who had flitted, careless as a bird, from one of them to another. Why had she not been warned by his crazy disposition, by the way he would turn from gentleness to anger, usually for no reason that she could discover? He would be standing talking to another boy, or a group of boys, his friends, people with whom he had been on teams and out on dates, and all of a sudden he would be flailing away, usually before anybody else had thought of fighting.

Why had she not paid attention to the things he had said and done to her before they were married? He had called her a nerd, a bitch, a whore. Once, when they were walking in the park, he had shoved her so hard that she fell and cut her hand, and he had stood over her with his fists clenched telling her she was crazy, dumb, stupid. When he was calm again, after times like this, he would put his arm around her and say he was sorry, and because he was Lucky and she was in love with him, she would forgive him.

He was graduated with what looked like a whole column of type beneath his picture in the yearbook. He had played everything, done everything, been elected to everything: he had won honors in whatever he had tried except for his studies. He told Elizabeth later that his graduation from Moore had been one of the great disappointments of his life. He got honorable mention as the league's most valuable football player in his senior year, and all through the winter and spring he kept listening for the phone and watching the mailbox, waiting for some college to make him an offer. At first he had thought of Notre Dame, then of Oklahoma and Ohio State, then of the lesser state universities, then of anywhere. He told her this not long after their marriage, during the time when he was still working steadily and content to stay home at night to make love and to drink and talk afterwards. On this night he was sitting in their Naugahyde chair, sipping tequila and flexing his muscles, watching as the hard ropy sinews leaped beneath his skin.

When his teammates began to sign letters of intent, Lucky began to panic. One morning the newspaper ran a picture of Moore's starting offensive line, every one of whom had got a scholarship. Lucky did not say to Elizabeth—and she was certain that he had never admitted to himself—that these six agile giants were the reason he had gained over a thousand yards and broken free for twenty touchdowns. It was *his* name that the cheerleaders had shrieked, *his* name that the responding stands had chanted. He was convinced that a mistake had been made—the letter meant for him had been lost in the mail, so he wrote some letters himself and even took a few short bus rides. The answers, when they came, were always the same: at under 140 pounds he was too small to play college football.

"It was those linemen," he said on the night that he talked about it to Elizabeth. "Those bastards wanted to hog all the glory. They talked about me. Ran me down to recruiters."

The tequila made his eyes water, and his face with its narrow nose and thin lips seemed small and pinched and sad. Elizabeth, sitting opposite him, leaned forward and put her hand on top of his. "But you could go to college," she said. "You could take some night classes now. We could save up our money."

"College," he said softly. Then loudly, shouting, "Who's talking about a goddamned college?"

The blast of his breath was strong on her face. His wet green eyes were close to hers. She was frightened of him as she had been frightened before when he yelled; his voice left a silence that she did not know how to fill, and the quietness between them seemed to threaten her. She wanted to say that she meant to try to help him, that she loved him, that he was the only dear thing that she possessed, but her tongue was paralyzed. Wordlessly she stared back at him until he rose quickly and hit her with his open hand.

"Bitch!" he screamed. "You goddamned bitch!"

He hit her again, and she and the chair in which she was sitting fell. She landed on her shoulder and slid along the bare floor.

"Lucky," she said. "My God! Lucky!"

Quick as he was, she saw the kick coming and shifted her body in time to take it on the thigh. Pain shot through her knee, her hip; it ranged downward to her feet and up toward her shoulder.

"No, no," she wailed, her voice a scream, a sob.

She saw him lift his foot once more and tried to roll away, but she was helpless, tangled in the legs of the chair.

"Yeah," he said, holding the heavy work shoe just above her head, the stained sole of it an inch from her nose. "Yeah. You move and I'll mash your damned head like you was a black widow."

Later he helped her treat her wounds. He washed out the cut on her head; he brought her ice to hold on her leg; he gave her aspirin.

"You feeling all right now?" Lucky asked.

Except when her mother died, she had never felt worse. She lowered her head and let the tears run down her cheeks. Her body felt hollow as if pain had eaten out her bones. She was betrayed, alone, abandoned.

He stood over her and let his hand rest tentatively on her shoulder. "Listen," he said, "you ought to be careful. I never meant for that to happen."

Without looking up, she shook her head. Her body trembled and he moved his hand.

"College," he said scornfully, an edge of anger returning to his voice. "Jesus Christ, it wasn't college I wanted. It was football. To play football. To be somebody."

She heard him pace across the floor, felt her body tense when he stood once more beside her.

"You see, I got a bad temper. I get mad when you say something stupid. You don't say nothing stupid, you won't get hurt."

Still she wept and did not show her face.

"Goddamn it!" he said, his voice rising. "I'm trying to tell you something. I can't help getting mad. You want me to change the way I am?"

"Oh, stop," she said. "Stop. Stop."

Crying helplessly, she struggled to her feet and dragged herself toward the darkness of the bedroom.

In the days and weeks that followed, he hit her whenever she or anything else displeased him. Any slight that he felt, no matter from whom, any dark memory that surfaced in his brain, might be enough to make him turn on her with his quick hands, his hard fists, his green eyes glittering with hatred. She bought makeup to disguise the bruises on her face, sunglasses to hide her blackened eyes, dark stockings and long-sleeved shirts to hide her limbs' discoloration. She learned to stay out of his way, to be across the room from him when his rage struck, to be on watch and give herself time to duck and to cover her face when he started swinging. He hated questions: she asked him nothing. He wanted money: she gave it to him. He demanded to know what she did with her time: she told him. She tried with fair success to read his moods, to know when he wanted to talk and when he wanted to make love and when he wanted her to rub his back or let him lie with his head in her lap while she stroked his forehead.

And as she had been taught by her mother and the nuns who had trained her, she prayed for assistance. She worked carefully around whatever humor Lucky might be in to make a Saturday or Sunday mass. On her way home from the Shoney's where she waited tables on the early shift, she would stop by St. Vincent's and pray. If her tips had been good, she would light a candle. She would kneel in front of the Virgin's statue in the cold and shadowy church and wait for the tightness in her breast to recede, for her mind to empty. The votive lights made a shifting pattern on the carved marble figure. Sometimes a board in the floor would creak. Traffic moved beyond the stained-glass windows. Elizabeth prayed her rosary, but for exactly what she could not say. For peace, for strength to endure, for relief of some sort. She knew that her devotions could not make Lucky change. For him to stop beating her would be a miracle like that of the loaves and fishes. She counted out her prayers bead by bead. She finished her mysteries and crossed herself. She genuflected and moved back into the world, to the bed she had made and now must surely lie on.

Would she have married Lucky, she sometimes wondered, if her mother had lived or if one of her sisters had been at home to share the agony of her mother's illness with her? There were moments during her prayers when she felt that the Virgin owed her some answers. Why was it that she had no aunts and uncles around, no cousins? Why did she, a Catholic of all things, have no family to turn to? Oh, it was fate, she knew that: early deaths and far removals. But no explanation, however clear, eased the burden of her being virtually alone through the last weeks of her mother's sickness. And why, back then, had Lucky been so good to her—between the outbursts of his fury—anxious for the way she felt, eager to take her in his arms when she cried, if after they were married he was going to scream at her and beat her? Oh, why, God? she would occasionally ask as she knelt in the dim and drafty church. O Jesus, Mary, and Joseph, why? And though her prayers softened the pain in her heart, she heard no response, she learned nothing.

And why, dear God, had he married her if he did not love her? Certainly he knew that he was getting only a wife: she came to

him with only the clothes on her back: what little her mother had
had went to pay for her illness. He had driven Elizabeth to and
from the hospital; he had held her while she wept; he had seemed
to understand the desolation that she felt when she emerged after
long hours at her mother's bedside. "I know, baby," he said. "I
understand. It don't matter." When the end came, he met Nora
at the airport, he entertained Madeleine's children, taking them
to ride in his ridiculous car. He bought a suit for the funeral—
perhaps the only one he had ever had—and she was proud of him
and comforted by him. Elizabeth leaned heavily on his arm as she
followed her mother's casket out of the church; in the limousine
he held her hand and commented on the beauty of the day and
the spring flowers that were blooming in the cemetery.

She had loved him and married him, and now he beat her and
she did not love him any more. Or so she put the matter to herself, knowing always that such ordinary words as love and hate did
not cover her case. What she felt was a deep loneliness, an es-
trangement so profound that it separated her somehow from every
other person and thing in God's creation. She saw herself changing, growing cold and hard: she turned a brazen mask to the
world while in her heart there was only turmoil and sorrow. Her
letters to her sisters grew infrequent and short. She could not tell
them what Lucky was doing to her, and what else was there for
her to say? What he was doing to her was everything: her whole
existence could be summed up in less than half a dozen words:
her husband beat her. Her manner toward her customers changed
from easy friendliness to formal courtesy. She did not talk much
to the other waitresses. And she began to look for another job.

The decision was made as if by instinct. She had not been to
confession since the first time Lucky had hit her. The old priest
who had buried her mother was himself now dead, though Elizabeth was by no means sure that she would have gone to him for
counseling if he remained among the living. Priests, the very
saints themselves, were included in the otherness, the outside
world from which she more and more withdrew. Her only alternative was to advise herself, and she could bring to the task only
habits and shards of intuition. It did not occur to her that she
might divorce Lucky; she did not really think of leaving him, of
living beyond his reach, but she did not think of continuing with

him either. This was one definition of her problem. She had no future: there was no way for her to visualize next month or next year: there was only today to be got through with as little pain as possible. But she knew beyond the need for logic or plan that she ought to have some money.

Lucky drifted from job to job; he worked mostly in service stations, though he was a good enough mechanic to be with an agency. He could not stay anywhere long without getting mad and mouthing off at the boss or starting a fight with a fellow worker. When he lost a job, he would beat Elizabeth and tell her she blamed him for the way he was and accuse her, not untruthfully now, of wanting to change him. "Women," he would say, "God-damned women. Don't want a man to be a man." She of course did not answer him. She ducked and took what she had to take, dried her tears and patched herself up and went off to wait her tables the next morning. He had learned how much money she made, even what her tips were likely to be. He left her just enough to get to and from work: she had to negotiate for permission to get a pair of panty hose from Walgreen's. She began to watch the want ads in the hope that she might better her situation.

Elizabeth found a new job in a hotel downtown: she was given the luncheon shift on a trial basis. She knew all too well that she was courting disaster. If she did not make good on this job, she would have no job at all and Lucky would kill her. It would be the same if she kept the job, and he learned she was deceiving him. And what if he beat her before she proved she could do the work and was hired permanently? Would they let her go on the floor with her face made up or her bruises showing? The first day of her new job, she left home early as usual and went to the church and lit a candle and prayed her rosary. *For today*, she said, *and tomorrow. That I don't spill anything. That I don't get the orders wrong*. Was this too much for her to ask? *Oh, help me, help me*, Elizabeth said. She had plenty of time to spare. She remained kneeling until her knees ached. She did all the mysteries.

Most of the people who came to the restaurant were men who wore coats and ties and shined shoes and gold watches. They were very sure of what they were doing, easy with each other and with her. They asked her how the various dishes were and laughed

when she said this was her first day. They read her nametag and
called her Elizabeth and said they would have to choose for themselves and take their chances. The food was expensive, and many
of her customers had drinks. Some of the men lingered at their
tables, talking seriously, smoking. She remembered to fill their
cups and glasses and to take away their dirty plates. She made almost thirty dollars in tips. So much! she thought in a burst of ela-
tion that was immediately tempered by her old fear. What if
Lucky found out? How was she going to keep him from getting
her money?

Elizabeth was able to solve this too, for by now she was
schooled in the ways of craftiness. She hid her money in her
locker at work until she had a hundred dollars. Then she had her
fives and tens changed into one bill and sewed it in the lining of
her coat, which Lucky never touched. She had five one-hundred-
dollar bills when she discovered she was pregnant. Elizabeth had
learned the symptoms from Nora before she moved away: the
missed period, the slightly swollen and sore breasts, the spasms of
nausea in the mornings. She took some of her money and went to
see a doctor and called his office the next day. She phoned from a
booth at the hotel, and after she hung up, she sat for a moment
looking beyond the fountain toward the crowded escalators and
the cocktail lounge on the mezzanine; she rested her hand on her
stomach, half believing that she might feel the wonder of what
was happening inside her. A child, she thought, a gift from God.
Her soul celebrated this event, rejoiced without regard to practical
considerations. The joy of creation declared itself with the beating
of her heart. A baby, a baby, she repeated to herself, remembering
tiny hands and feet, minute mouths and bald heads and blue eyes
that could not focus. Surely this was what she had saved her
money for.

But what would Lucky say when she told him?

He would be glad, she insisted to herself, proud that he was
going to be a father. Still, for five of the six months she had lived
with him, he had pounded almost every inch of her flesh, and
even the excitement of having a baby would not make her abandon all caution. She would watch for an opportunity: she would
try to catch him on a day when nobody had made him angry and
when he hadn't been drinking or smoking pot, and she would

smile and she would tell him. She waited for almost a week. Then on Thursday, when he had not been to work, but had spent the afternoon playing pool and had won some money, she decided that the time had come. Faced with the moment, she felt not so much afraid as timid before him. He sat on the end of the couch looking at a magazine about automobiles. His eyes peered intently from his small tight face. A reddish-brown stubble softened his sharp chin. He licked his finger, turned a page. She drew breath to speak, then lost her nerve and retreated to the bedroom.

She went to the window and looked out at the narrow yard. Near the sidewalk daffodils were in bloom; the grass showed a tinge of green. It was spring again. Elizabeth's mother had been dead for almost a year. Elizabeth thought of how life and death went on. She was struck with her own piquant discovery of the movement of time, the passing of generations. Perhaps if the baby were a girl, Lucky would let her call it Monica after her mother. She moved back toward the living room, but paused once more in front of the dresser. She searched her own eyes in the mirror. They were wide and dark and they caught the last deep light of day. My hair is getting dull, she thought, but it too reflected the dying afternoon; her white flesh, unbruised for once, lay smooth around her mouth and eyes and on her forehead. She looked closely to see if her baby showed, but she saw no bulge beneath her jeans. Her glorious secret was still hers, but she must share it with Lucky.

She returned to the living room, and out of old habit she stood across from him, beyond his reach. Then she thought that this would not do. She must trust him now: when she told him he was going to be a father, she should be beside him. She sat on the couch next to him and rested her hand on his leg.

"Lucky?"

"Yeah," he replied without looking up from the magazine.

"Lucky. Listen. I've got something to tell you."

He turned to face her. "All right, I'm listening."

She took a deep breath. "I—" she began and paused. "We—I'm pregnant, Lucky. We're going to have a baby."

He was silent for what seemed like a long time, his eyes narrowed, his lips pressed together. Then, in a voice that was quiet and cold and thin, he said, "What the hell do you mean? What the goddamned hell do you mean, you're pregnant?"

At first she could not reply. She felt numb, cold as if her blood had ceased to flow, though she felt her heart pounding.

"Lucky," she said finally, "it's ours, yours and mine. I'm pregnant with our baby."

"Get this straight. I don't want no damned baby. I don't want to pay for one or put up with one or listen to the little bastard cry. What the hell you mean doing this? Who the hell you think you are, getting pregnant?"

"No," Elizabeth said. "Don't talk like that."

She moved away from him, crossed the room, and stood by the door to the kitchen. "It's your baby too. How can you say those things? How can you call our baby a bastard?"

"There ain't no baby," he replied in his thin dangerous voice. "Not now, not ever. Whatever you got, you're going to get rid of. But there ain't no baby."

"You're crazy!" Even as a part of her brain warned her to be careful, not to make things any worse than they were, her voice rose in outrage. "I'm pregnant. It's done. I'm going to have my baby."

"I'll kill you!" he shouted. "You goddamned whore!"

He jumped up and threw the magazine at her. She saw it fluttering toward her face and turned away and tried to escape into the kitchen. She lunged toward the table, thinking she might hide beneath it, but the chairs were in her way. She was on her hands and knees holding to a chair rung, a table leg. He grabbed the waistband of her jeans, and as the pressure around her stomach tightened, she released her grip for fear of hurting her baby. Lucky lifted her to her feet.

"I'll kill you!" he said again.

She knew that he would swing first with his right hand. She turned away from the lick, moved her head, and caught his fist behind her left ear. The jolt upset her balance, made her vision blur. Then she felt two quick blows to her stomach that brought her pain sharper than any she had ever felt, and she was falling, plunging into profound darkness.

When she came to, the pain was still there, throbbing through the lower part of her body as if Lucky were still pounding on her. But Lucky had gone. The kitchen and the living room beyond it were empty. The apartment was quiet. And she was bleeding. She

saw the dark stain at her crotch: she touched it, and its dullness
turned bright red on the white tips of her fingers.

She began to cry. "O God," she said. "O God, please, no."

"O God," she kept saying as she pulled herself to her feet. She
staggered into the bedroom, found her purse and the coat with
her money sewn inside. "O God, O God," she repeated as she
eased her way down the stairs. Her knees were buckling beneath
her; she was half blinded by her tears. She got through the door
and across the sidewalk. She held to a lamp post; then she felt
herself moving slowly toward the pavement, her legs giving way,
her arms sliding down the smooth metal, and once more she lost
consciousness.

She awakened alone in a room with four beds in it. She knew
immediately where she was. She had visited her mother too often
in the hospital to mistake the furniture, the smell, the noises in
the corridor. O God, she said again, but she could not name the
terror that she felt: she could not yet face what her heart knew.
She concentrated on what had happened to her after she left the
apartment, on the snatches of memory that were available to her.
A face glimpsed in half darkness, a stretcher, a bright light in a
white room, voices in the distance. She fought against knowledge,
but truth impinged. She moved and found that she was sore inside; there was a sanitary pad between her legs; she had lost her
baby.

Her body felt heavy against the bed as if it were being pressed
down by her grief. Her baby whom she had never seen, who had
lived but had never been born, was dead now, and she would
never know what it might have looked like. If only she could have
seen it. If only she could have a picture of it. If only somebody
could tell her whether it would have been a boy or a girl. She
made one last attempt to hope. Maybe, oh, maybe, oh, please,
God, let there be a chance that the doctors had saved it. She
looked around the strange room for some clue, some evidence of
joy; she peered at the white walls, the empty beds, the strips of
early sunlight that came through the slanted blinds. Finding no
comfort, she closed her eyes and tried to make truth out of her
wishes. It's all right, it's all right, she thought, but the emptiness
of her body testified against her. She felt deep inside an enormous

vacancy. She was herself again; she was alone. She felt rigid, stiff, as if all grace had left her with the baby. She turned her face to the pillow, but her eyes remained dry.

Later a doctor came, a tall young man with red hair and a neatly trimmed red beard. He sat down by her bed and smiled at her as if they were old friends.

"You all right?" he asked. "You feel okay this morning?"

She gazed back at him, unable to answer.

He picked up her hand and held it between his. "I know," he said gently. "I know. But you're in good shape. You'll be out of here in a day or two. You're going to do just fine."

There was a silence. Then the doctor smiled again and said, "You know something? You didn't have any identification when the police found you. We don't know your name."

My purse, Elizabeth thought. My coat. But against her larger loss these hardly mattered.

"Can you tell me?" the doctor said. "I need to know who you are."

She searched for strength in the realms of her own emptiness. Whoever she was, she was not the same as she had been yesterday. Whatever happened in the future, she would never be the same again. I am Elizabeth Baker, she thought, and would have said so, but she could not force the words past her lips.

"What's your name?" the doctor asked softly.

"Elizabeth Noland." Her voice to her own ears sounded strange and lifeless.

"Are you married?"

She shook her head.

"Do you have an address here in the city?"

"No," she replied. "I don't live anywhere."

Two days later, when she was ready to leave the hospital, the doctor with the red beard came to tell her goodby. She was dressed in the jeans which had been washed, but which still bore the stain of her blood. Her coat with her money still intact was over her arm. She sat stiffly on the side of the bed, waiting for a nurse to return with the forms she would have to sign, the wheelchair she would have to ride to the hospital entrance.

"Well," the doctor said, "you're going to leave us. We didn't do so badly by you, did we?"

"No," she replied in the dull voice that she had come to recognize as her own.

"No, indeed," the doctor said. "We take good care of pretty girls."

She tried to return his smile, but she was not up to it. She felt the muscles in her cheeks work, felt her lips draw into a line, but she could get no further.

"Elizabeth," the doctor said, "don't grieve about this. You're young. You're in good health. If you want to, you can have a dozen children."

But not this one, she thought. Never again the one that she had lost, the one in whom she had placed her hope—for comfort, for the salvation of her marriage.

"Thank you," she said. Then, "I ought to go. If the nurse is ready for me to sign those papers, I ought to leave."

"Where?"

"I need to go," Elizabeth replied.

The doctor gave her five dollars, to get home on, he said; and she was conscious of him standing in the doorway of the room watching as the nurse wheeled her away down the corridor. Outside the sun was bright, the air warm and still. Beds of tulips bloomed on the hospital lawn. People came and went. An ambulance rolled up the drive, then turned away toward the back of the building. To Elizabeth everything was the same, no flower more beautiful than another, no face more interesting. She felt the sun on her skin, but it did not warm her. She heard her heels on the pavement; noises came to her from the street; a few clouds moved in the sky. She noticed only the soreness in her womb; she was conscious only of the agony of her emptiness.

I should have died too, she said to herself, as she had said a thousand times since Lucky had killed her baby. But she had not died. If feeling the way she felt, if vacancy and numbness, could be called living, then she had lived. But she would never be happy again or clean again or able even to feel sorrow or disappointment or pain. Every possibility of emotion had left her with her baby. She knew what she had to do. She found a cab and rode to within a block of the apartment she had shared with Lucky. She stayed in the shadows, walked close to the walls of buildings, and peeked carefully around the corner. Lucky's car was not in sight. She crossed the street, and in spite of her numbness, or through it, beyond it, she was conscious of fear which struck like a chill and caused her to tremble. She forced herself forward. She entered the building, climbed the stairs, and put her ear against the apartment door. She heard nothing. She waited a moment longer, started to reach for the knob: then she remembered that her key had been stolen with her purse. She hesitated again and tried the door and it opened.

She delayed for a few seconds. Lucky might have forgotten the door, or he might not have bothered to lock it, having only gone for beer or cigarettes. Or maybe by some accident she had overlooked his car: maybe he was here. Holding her breath, she let the door swing slowly inward. She saw no one. There were dirty plates on the couch and the television set, beer cans and a glass on the floor; the ash trays were full; she could see two pans on the stove and dried grease on the linoleum. Now, closer than the fear and for the moment almost filling her emptiness, she felt regret: three days ago this had been her home; three nights ago—no, she told herself, no; do what you came for. She found the old suitcase that had belonged to her mother. She stuffed it with all the clothes it would hold. She got her old missal—no good any more—from the drawer, took the carving of the Virgin, then paused in the living room and looked around once again, at the scarred table, a hole in the arm of the couch, a plant on the window sill wilting for lack of water. She breathed deeply, and the stale air sat like a weight on her lungs. Then she walked through the door, down the steps, and out of the building to the bus stop.

Elizabeth found a new place to live, as far away from Lucky as she could conveniently get, and a new job because she was afraid he had found out about her old one. She would have taken back her maiden name as she had in the hospital, except that her social security card said Baker. But considering what had happened to her, the name did not matter all that much. She was Mrs. Baker, and she developed her new routine of waiting the tables at Bernie's and coming home to her bath and then lying rigid in the dark, letting her mind wander around the edges of the vacuum that was her existence, thinking of the past, of her mother and sisters and the baby she had lost; and sometimes, unbidden, Lucky's face would appear in her mind quick as an apparition and equally unwelcome, and she would think immediately of something else. She would try, almost successfully, to deny that he had ever lived to do what he had done and bring her through deep misery into her present nothingness.

I ought to write Nora, she would think; I ought to write Madeleine. Neither of them knew where she was, which was wrong, for families should stick together. Occasionally she would compose letters in her mind, but she never put a word on paper. She let the birthdays of her nieces and nephews come and go without so much as a card from her, and so the weeks passed and she felt no better. Every morning she awakened to the sight of the figure of the Blessed Virgin, and she thought of her mother who had owned the figure and prayed before it in that time that seemed a thousand years in the past.

One day, because she was remembering her mother and knew what her mother would want her to do, she left for work early and stopped by St. Vincent's, where in the time before she left Lucky she would go to mass and stop in the mornings to pray. Instead of going to the front of the church and kneeling before the statue of the Virgin, she sat down at the back and waited. She noticed how the light of the afternoon was different from the light of the morning, brighter—or was this because the seasons had changed and the days were longer? The church with its creaking boards was the same. The same noises came from outside—the groan of a truck in low gear, a long angry bleat of a horn, a shout—muffled by the heavy walls. Above the altar Christ still hung on his cross; the baby Jesus nestled in Joseph's arms; above the slow and patiently burning candles the Mother of God gazed serenely off into the distance. Elizabeth sat and waited. She had lost her rosary when her purse was stolen, but she felt no desire to say prayers: she knew that if she had beads in her hand, she would remain as she was now—mute in the presence of the statues and candles and the Host in the tabernacle. She saw a bulletin from the past Sunday and she glanced over its chronicle of masses said for the souls of the dead and the aspirations of the living.

Speak to me, she wanted to say to the Virgin's statue. Help me.

Comfort me. What have I done that my heart should be broken
past all mending? There was no response, no miracle, in Elizabeth's soul, no warmth of healing. The cool emptiness of the
church answered the emptiness that she felt inside. She waited
without moving, as lifeless as the marble figures. Certain now
that she could not pray, she wondered if she even believed: was
everything that her mother and the nuns had taught her false?
Were her years of devotion all a joke? Had the words whispered
through the grill, the penance done, the wafer on the tongue
meant nothing? She could not answer this: the question was too
large for her, too far beyond the ambience of her own experience.
She knew only that her soul had been crushed, and that whoever
and wherever God and His Mother were, she, Elizabeth, had been
abandoned. She looked once more around the church, at the statues and stations and empty pews. Then she rose and went out
into the city's fading afternoon.

Three days later, about ten o'clock on a Sunday night when the
crowd had begun to thin, Bernie asked Elizabeth to come into his
office. This is it, she thought. Bernie was fed up with her smile
that never grew to mirth, her thin voice devoid of all emotion. He
was going to fire her, and where could she go then? Would the
hotel give her another chance? Would they take her back at
Shoney's? She followed him into the office, a small paneled room
with a glass-topped desk, a filing cabinet, a few chairs, and found
there another man waiting.

"Lizzie," Bernie said, peering at her with more than the usual
sadness in his deep brown eyes, "this is Sergeant Butler. He's
from police headquarters. A cop."

Sergeant Butler was smaller than Bernie, of medium height and
thin with thick gray hair and a dark rough complexion. "Are you
Mrs. Baker?" he asked.

No, she wanted to say. Not any more. But she knew that she
was. She nodded.

"Mrs. Baker," the sergeant said, "you haven't seen your husband
recently, have you?"

She looked at Bernie, his great shining bald head, his big nose,
his profound eyes. He took Elizabeth's hand and guided her to-

ward a chair. "Sit down, sweetheart," he said. "I got to talk to you."

He sat too and licked his lips and looked down at his hand which still held hers. Then he said, "I never pried, you know that. You do the work, I never ask you about your own business."

Bernie glanced back at Sergeant Butler, but when the sergeant opened his mouth to speak, Bernie shook his head.

"Lizzie," Bernie went on, "I don't know how you got along with the guy you were married to. I didn't even know you had a husband." Once more he looked down. Then he said, "But, baby, they got a man they think is him, and he's dead."

Only the knowledge, the fact of what Bernie had said, penetrated her consciousness. She felt nothing—no joy, no bereavement, not even relief that she would never see him again, never turn a corner and come upon him with his eyes glittering in anger and his fists poised to strike.

"You all right?" Bernie asked. "You want a drink? A brandy, maybe?"

"No." I ought to say I'm sorry, she thought. They probably think something's wrong with me that I don't cry. Softly she said again, "No, thank you, Bernie."

"Look, Mrs. Baker," the sergeant said. "We're not absolutely sure who we got. He's a little guy, smaller than I am, green eyes, reddish-brown hair, a two-inch scar on his right leg, no significant dental work."

Elizabeth remembered the scar. He was proud of it. He had got it playing football. "Lucky," she said softly.

"Ma'am?"

"That was his nickname. We called him Lucky."

"We got him as Herman Jerome Baker."

"Yes," Elizabeth replied, "that's who he was."

"Mrs. Baker, I'm sorry, but you'll have to come down and identify him. I hate to ask you, but there's not anybody else."

"He has a father."

"No," Sergeant Butler replied. "His father died three weeks ago."

So he had been alone at the end too, Elizabeth thought. Like her. But not like her in the loss she had suffered, the emptiness.

"Listen," Bernie said, "she's got to have somebody to go with her." He asked her if there was anyone she wanted to call.

"No," she said in the same flat voice which had been hers since the morning she had awakened in the hospital. "My sisters don't live here. No."

Bernie's eyes seemed to grow deeper still. He moved quickly to his desk. "Leah," he said. "I'll get Mrs. Greenspan."

Bernie talked to his wife. When he had hung up, the sergeant took out a cigarette, tapped it down, lit it. Smoke drifted toward the light.

Bernie said, "You ought not to use them things. Coffin nails, my father used to call them." He glanced quickly at Elizabeth, and she would have smiled to show that she was all right except that she knew no smile of hers would work.

"You ought to see them out there," Bernie said, jerking his head toward the lounge. "Smoking away. Young and old. Cancer don't seem to matter to them. We throw away ten thousand butts an hour."

There was another silence.

"How did he die?" Elizabeth asked.

"A fight in a bar. He was stabbed. I'm sorry, Mrs. Baker."

Of course, Elizabeth thought. He got himself killed proving he was a man. Immediately she regretted her bitterness. Even through her numbness, what she had been taught as a girl came back: he was dead and you ought to forgive the dead. All right, she thought, I do forgive. But she felt nothing.

They waited a few minutes longer, and then Mrs. Greenspan arrived and walked directly to Elizabeth. She was a large woman, a little plump, and almost as tall as Bernie. The detective followed her with his eyes. She was wearing a green dress and carrying a beige purse, and she knelt by Elizabeth's chair.

"I'm Leah," she said. "I'm Bernie's wife. Honey, I'm so sorry." She lifted her hand in a gentle tentative motion and lightly stroked the back of Elizabeth's head.

Elizabeth smelled Mrs. Greenspan's perfume. She felt Mrs. Greenspan's warm breath on the side of her face and the touch on her head, the large soft hand that sought to comfort her. "Honey," Mrs. Greenspan said, "what can I do for you? Is there anything that would make you feel better?"

Elizabeth caught her breath as if she had been struck by a sharp and unexpected pain. Mrs. Greenspan's solicitude made something twist inside Elizabeth.

"No, I'm all right, Mrs. Greenspan."

"Leah, honey. It's Leah. Do you feel like doing what this man wants you to do? You don't have to go tonight. We'll make him wait."

"Mrs. Greenspan—" the sergeant began.

"Hush!" Mrs. Greenspan said, putting her arm around Elizabeth's shoulder. "You don't have to go till you're good and ready. We'll call Bernie's lawyer if we have to."

"Please, Mrs. Greenspan," Sergeant Butler said.

"It's all right. I can do it now."

"If you're sure." Leah Greenspan rose and stood for a moment, looking down from her majestic height at the slender sergeant. "She'll ride with me. You lead the way."

They drove in Leah's white car past the courthouse to the safety building and walked down corridors to the morgue where an attendant waited for them.

"Mrs. Greenspan—" Sergeant Butler began once more.

"Not on your life," Leah Greenspan replied. "Where this girl goes, I go. Don't speak to me about rules and regulations."

They moved into a brightly lighted room. Elizabeth saw enameled tables, cabinets filled with instruments and bottles, rows of steel doors against one wall. There was a chemical smell, as raw and harsh as the reflected light from the tile walls. Was this the true precinct of death? Elizabeth wondered. She thought of the dead that she had seen: her father when she was very young, her mother, other relatives and friends. All of them had lain primly in their caskets, rosaries in their folded hands, their shrouds neatly arranged, their neckties firmly knotted. In home and funeral parlor, lights shed a soft glow and the smell was of flowers. The attendant, wearing a white coat and squinting through glasses, read the nametags on the doors. "Baker, Baker . . . Right." Out came the sheeted figure and back came the sheet.

Suddenly Elizabeth knew that she did not want to see. She wanted to turn away, to run, to escape from this last confrontation with the man who had been her husband, whom she had loved as she had loved her own life, and who had beaten her and given her a baby and destroyed it before it could grow its time in her womb. Oh, she could not bear to see him! Whatever defined and enforced the vacancy inside her threatened to give way, to disintegrate against this thrust of old and new emotions. She felt as if she were on the verge of destruction, and she was helpless against what might come. She averted her eyes, but she managed to move toward the body. With Leah Greenspan's arm around her waist, she put one reluctant foot in front of the other until an edge of sheet came into her view. Now, she told herself. I must look now. And with all the strength that was left to her, she lifted her head.

She let her eyes fall on the pale face of her dead husband. Momentarily her vision blurred: her head felt light, her body weak: she would have fallen had Leah not been supporting her. She breathed deeply and saw the reddish-brown hair that lay tangled around the face and dark against the white slab. His eyes were closed, but not as if in sleep. She had never seen him look so still. There was a crust of something white at the corner of his mouth and the usual stubble around his chin. His neck riding out of his bare shoulders was longer than she remembered. She saw her hand reach out. She knew that she was going to touch his face, though a part of her brain cringed at the notion of such an encounter. The flesh was colder than she could have believed, and as hard as marble. Like a statue, she thought, like the figures which kept their perpetual vigil at St. Vincent's.

She was overwhelmed by images out of her past, by memories of joy and sorrow and pain and loss and comfort: her mother and her sisters and others she had loved; the plain face of a nun bending over her desk; a dog she had owned; the boy who had taken her to the graduation dance her last year at St. Philip Neri. She thought of the times Lucky had beaten her and of how he had killed her baby and in doing so had taken her life and soul, leaving her dead and empty. But she had loved him once, and somewhere along the way he must have loved her. She recalled their apartment in the early months of their marriage. They had been proud to have it for their own—their bed, their couch, their stove, their table, no matter if everything was secondhand. Then she would wait in happiness for him to come home so they could have supper together and lie in bed together, husband and wife. What private agonies had lurked in his heart? What pains had he suffered, she wondered now, and never mentioned to her? If only he had shared whatever he had felt, if only he had let her try to help him. But perhaps, like her in the months just past, he had been locked in his own kind of emptiness.

"O Lucky," she said, hearing the voice that used to be hers before the vacancy had engulfed her. "O Lucky."

She sobbed loudly and turned away and put her face against Mrs. Greenspan's breast. Her body shook from the force of her weeping. The room echoed with the sound of it. Leah Greenspan's arms held her firmly. "There, there, honey. It's all right. Go on and cry."

She wept until the front of Mrs. Greenspan's dress was wet, and still the tears came. Leah's gentle hands patted her shaking back. Elizabeth clung to the warmth of Leah Greenspan's breast, to the softness of her voice, to the comfort of the firm arms which enfolded her. While she leaned against Leah and continued to cry, old memories continued to invade her consciousness. Out of the disintegrating center of her emptiness they thrust upward like a wind. O God, she said, thinking of Lucky. O God, she said, thinking of herself. Images continued to sweep through her mind: Lucky with his eyes open, his lips smiling, his face filled with happiness; a shadowy figure whose features she could not make out, but whom she knew to be her baby. Elizabeth saw her mother and father, and she wanted to tell them to pray for her baby, to pray for Lucky, but they were gone too quickly. In their place was a scene out of the distant past.

Elizabeth was a child not yet in school, and she had gone with her mother and other ladies to the cemetery to pray for the poor souls in purgatory. It was a gorgeous day, October she would guess, the sky blue, the sun warm, the air bright with autumn. On maple trees leaves glowed yellow and red; nearby on a new grave lilies and roses and chrysanthemums held unwithered and beautiful. Above Elizabeth the prayers of the ladies droned on. Two bees circled around the flowers. The old stones softened in the light; crosses and angels and saints stood guard; many of them were beginning to decay and seemed unlikely to endure till the day of judgment. That was all long ago. Now she leaned against Leah Greenspan, who tried to comfort her.

"Baby, baby," Leah said. "I know it hurts. But everything's going to be all right. I promise."

Elizabeth knew that she ought to try to answer. She should pull herself together so they could all get out of the tiled room with its bright lights and gleaming walls and porcelain tables. I'm fine, she wanted to say, I can go now. But no words came. She was too weak to do anything but rest in Leah Greenspan's arms and cry and feel her thoughts drift—back to the cemetery, the autumn sky, the praying voices of the women. And she remembered how on that other day she had turned and seen, almost close enough for her to touch, a statue of the Mother of God rising above her.

THE GOODBYE PRESENT

DANIEL ASA ROSE

Daniel Asa Rose was born thirty years ago in New York City and grew up in Rowayton, Connecticut. Other stories of his have appeared in *The New Yorker*, *The North American Review*, and *The Southern Review*. He lives with his wife and two sons in a small Massachusetts village, where he is working on his first novel, an "anti-Western."

1. *How did Roy's wife react when Roy said: "This? This here's an elk tree," and slapped the bark authoritatively?*

Roy's wife did not say a word or change her expression. But she felt victorious. Rita invariably felt victorious when her husband faltered, or made a mistake, or made a fool of himself. She was always prepared for victory of this type, and so she wore an expression of patient, queenly sufferance whenever she listened to him. Behind this frozen expression she waited passionately for her husband to stumble. Even if he were telling a funny story which happened to amuse her, Rita would project the pleasant, bored air of having endured the story a hundred times before. It was as if she were saying to everyone else: "You think he's charming, but put up with it as long as I have. . . ." And then when he made a mistake she'd be proven right—all she had to do was hold the expression, it was proof.

2. *Surely this was not a funny story he was telling?*

Correct. He was answering a question about a tree's identity.

3. *In what way was his answer a mistake?*

There is no such thing as an elk tree. There are elms and there are oaks.

4. Did Rita always feel better after this sort of victory?

Always. Rita was not a ham like her husband, so this was how she competed: counting minutes before he stumbled, waiting, waiting; and gloating sweetly once he did. Hearing him say "elk tree" was particularly gratifying. Silently, and without batting an eyelash, she cherished the moment he said it, and wished deeply that the moment would freeze, that everyone could stay as they were for eternity; she would love them all then, even Roy. Please freeze!

5. Did God answer her prayer?

There is no God. Rita was just a bad winner.

6. Was she born that way?

She was not born that way. She was not even married that way. Rita began to exult in each of her husband's mistakes, and secretly to rejoice every time something unfortunate happened to them as a couple, only when it became evident they were getting more than their share of bad luck. Her early hysterectomy. Adopted son turning out poorly. Roy's career as a songwriter washed up prematurely. All this would have been spooky had Rita allowed herself to be surprised each time. Instead she grew to accept misfortune, to anticipate and to welcome it.

7. She was bitter?

Not in the ordinary sense. She specialized in misfortune and derived satisfaction from it. There is a popular expression for this strategy.

8. If you can't lick 'em, join 'em?

Precisely. She joined 'em with glee. It was almost a game, it became her way of winning. It was like those card games where certain cards were bad, they counted against you . . . unless you got all of them. Then they were very valuable.

9. Then Rita was ugly as a witch?

On the contrary. She was bewitchingly beautiful. The more bad things she collected—husband mistakes, family tragedies, and so on—the more beautiful she became. On the day in question she wore a yellow ribbon in her black hair. She glowed with a negative electricity.

10. *What kind of day was it?*

The second day of the hottest weekend in years. The day before, Saturday, had been so bad that factories and offices up and down the Eastern seaboard were forced to close, suburban families to spend the weekend sitting in glacial shopping malls. Saturday night was even worse because of a black-out in New York City. All night thousands of half-delirious New Yorkers flocked to the Staten Island ferry for a ride through moving air, and by dawn Sunday mad schemes of escape had been concocted. One young couple on Manhattan's Riverside Drive awoke so faint that they hastily made arrangements to show up at Roy's place in Westhampton. As well as to catch an ocean breeze, they came to say goodbye.

11. *How did Roy like that?*

Roy loved his niece Henrietta; he could do without Henry. He did not like that they were moving the next day to Cambridge, England. He did not like that they were to pursue their doctorates. He thought they were overschooled already. They were. But their appearance in Westhampton was convenient because Roy had a goodbye present for Henrietta.

12. *How did they react to Roy's identification of the elk tree?*

They were sticky with embarrassment. However they were often and easily embarrassed these days. Partly it was because Henrietta had recently learned that she was carrying their first child; they felt particularly impressionable, as if outside events could not only have an unnatural effect on themselves but could jinx the embryo, as well. Consequently they were often and easily bullied. Just the evening before, for instance, they had been bullied by a (hot and harried) barmaid on Bleeker Street. "Don't you have any food?" asked Henry when no menu had arrived with their second drinks. "How was I supposed to know you wanted to eat?" parried the barmaid effectively, giving them an order form to fill out. "Two spring chickens," Henrietta wrote. They laughed and blushed at the meaning.

"Three spring chickens" would have summed it up, for there was no doubt the progeny of such a gentle couple would be of the same cast: plump, pale, scholastic.

13. How do you know? There's no God. . . .

I'm playing, playing. The progeny tried to kill himself over his first girlfriend nineteen years later. He tried to kill himself over his divorce thirty years later. He let a tour bus strike his wife dead in Piccadilly Circus fifty years later. He was brought up British.

14. Is it fun playing?

Eh.

15. Why didn't Henrietta correct her uncle about the elk tree?

She had no right to contradict him. She lost that right when she allowed him to love a heightened image of herself, a Henrietta far more merry, adorable, witty and surprising than the one she happened to be. She couldn't help it. Roy made her feel phony when she was most her true self. "I didn't mean it as a pun," she'd protest half-heartedly after he'd misconstrue one of her sentences; Roy would look at her sideways, see no livelier way the sentence could have been intended, think her all the more clever for protesting, and laugh with renewed appreciation. She would acquiesce, but it cost her her rights. If she couldn't stick up for her true self, she had no right to stick up for the rest of reality, including trees. An elk tree was just as real as the Henrietta she allowed to exist.

Henrietta guessed that Roy had heightened images, queenly but disturbed images, of all his women friends. It was his way of flirting with women and ultimately of ruling them. Henrietta always ended up feeling haggard and dull in the shadow of what he supposed her to be.

16. Why didn't Henry correct Roy?

Physical cowardice.

Roy ruled men by sheer might and it was apparent that he would relish an excuse to make mincemeat of Henry. He was always wanting to lock horns with Henry. He would interrupt the younger man, closing in with his colossal chest and saying: "Ah ha! You mean . . ." and twisting what Henry had said. Then he'd ruffle Henry's hair or playfully take a swing at him and the argument would be over. And soon the next argument would begin. Henry sensed that Roy did not keep male friendships very long, that sooner or later he would have to prove himself mightiest, that he'd have to start pushing. He wouldn't be able to stop until he made his friend feel like a fairy.

17. *Was Henry losing his hair?*
And how. It wasn't to be ruffled.
So if Roy wanted to think there was such a thing as an elk tree, that was alright by Henry.

18. *To sum up, Roy's identification of the elm or oak as an elk tree was received in silence?*
Wrong! But to see where you made your mistake, it may be useful to rewind our tale to the wee hours of the morning.
Roy awoke with a familiar but ghastly pain in his chest. Carefully he took himself out of the bedroom, out of the house, and across the dark yard. He slumped in the middle seat of the family station wagon and groaned in privacy for an hour until the sun came up and the pain subsided. Thereupon he walked into the house and put on the kitchen radio softly. When Rita came downstairs he was fixing an omelette with chopped ham, green peas and red pepper. Rita activated the oven fan and removed herself to the living room, where twelve pillows were lying in wait for their Sunday fluffing. She went around the room giving each pillow four wallops, little by little loosening her yellow blouse from her black short-shorts. By her fourth pillow she had worked up a sweat above her lip, and by her sixth pillow she had worked up a rage. Physical activity first thing in the morning, when what she really wanted to do was lounge in bed, could always be counted upon to rouse some rage. She did it to herself deliberately, as if she were two people, one a sleepy-headed camper and the other a bugle-mouthed counselor on a campaign to make life miserable for all spoiled slugabeds. Rise and shine, you pampered bitch! Eight, nine, ten—each pillow was socked harder than the last—and the twelfth was carried furiously into the kitchen. "Will you please wake our darling young son!" she demanded over the racket of the fan.
Roy took the skillet with its bubbling omelette up to Ricky's room. "Oh Ricky boy . . ." he sang to the tune of "Danny Boy," waving the dish, filling the dark, draped bedroom with an adventurous odor, ". . . your parents want you dowhown stairs." "Ugh," said Ricky. "Oh yes they do . . ." began the father again,

". . . or they will fry your fa-an-ny," humorously touching the
skillet to the appointed mound in the blankets. "Leave me
alone!" snarled the boy, turning his head to the wall, "I'll be
down in a minute." Roy started to leave as there came, from
under the pillow, an exclamation like a defiant "Good night!"—
but lewd.

His chest seized up and Roy hurried out of the room.

The morning heated; telephone arrangements were made to receive refugees from Riverside Drive; at around eleven the not-
quite-sporty Datsun crunched up the driveway with Henrietta at
the wheel and Henry looking nervous; Bloody Marys and sardine
finger-sandwiches were served under the leaves on the patio.
"You're turning into a regular boozer," Roy told Henry sarcas-
tically at 11:30. "It's quite spicy," gasped Henry. At 11:45
Henrietta commented favorably on the patio's absence of mosqui-
toes. "That may be true," answered Rita, smacking her fingertips,
"but there are enough spiders to make up for them." At noon Roy
stood up. "Give your baby a good first name," he told his guests
sonorously, "and then give it a better middle one." (The statement was not supposed to mean anything, necessarily, it was just
supposed to sound sonorous.) Roy and Henrietta left the shade to
play horseshoes. The percussive sounds from the sunny, close-
cropped lawn continued for half an hour while Rita and Henry
made political chit-chat marked by a near perfect shortage of facts
and mutually agreeable conclusions. By 12:30 their conversation
had turned personal. Rita asked him—clang! a howl and a squeal
told her a rematch was to begin—how his doctoral program was
set up, if he looked forward to the baby, did he feel sad about
leaving the States, why he kept his shirt on in such weather. In
reply to the last, Henry lowered his shirt and showed her the painful heat blisters on his shoulders; Rita shuddered, gaped, dared to
touch . . . finally her breath trembled so strangely at the sight of
the injury that she went inside to make another batch of Bloodys.
A leaf floated down onto Henry's head. Rita returned with nail
polish on the tray and began to apply it to one hand, then the
other. "Roy always lets me win," wailed Henrietta from the horseshoe pit. "Nonsense!" bellowed Roy, reaching the patio suddenly
and dropping himself onto his stool, "I let no one win! Ever!"
They nibbled and drank. They perspired, all four: Roy steamed,

shaking his massive head and sprinkling everyone; Rita seemed cool but, oppressed by her husband's reappearance, occasionally sighed at an oversized drop of sweat that tumbled down from the yellow ribbon at her hairline; Henrietta took Henry's soggy hand in her soggy hand. Peace and balance reigned for a quarter hour until, toward one o'clock, a second leaf landed on Henry's head. Looking up, Henry managed to spill the leaf and to study the branch whence it came. "Is this a hickory?" he mused. "This?" said Roy, slapping the bark authoritatively, "this here's an elk tree."

There was no "silence."

Ricky boy had arisen.

Question carefully.

19. *What was Ricky wearing?*

A purple bathrobe and purple slippers. Black frame glasses over his orange bangs. A scowl. In his position on the upstairs deck he looked like a figurehead on the prow of a haunted ship.

20. *Ricky slept until one?*

Even at one he was not happy about rising. Experts say this is rare for twelve year old boys, but it was typical of Ricky, who suffered nightmares in the dark and frequently could not get to sleep until two, three, even four a.m. The night before he had stayed up extra late, pacing, reading, and finally passing off at about the time Roy was getting up.

21. *Reading?*

Monster paperbacks. And drawing monster pictures, gluing monster models, chewing monster bubblegum. It was Ricky's way of working out his nightmares. During the day he didn't have to be so quiet and was able to create imaginative monster sounds on his father's quadriphonic tape recorder. Remember that Roy was a songwriter and you will see what a distortion, what an affront, Roy considered this last practice to be.

22. *Sounds like little Ricky needed help, yes?*

But where was he to get it? He was pretty certain his parents were monsters, and he was convinced, after one session, that the school psychologist was one of them too—else how could the guy know so much about them? Ricky protected his secrets from these dissemblers. If they asked about his preoccupation, he'd explain that he loved monsters, that monsters were his friends—a sensible lie, one curries favor where one can. If they asked him to name his favorite color, he'd say lime green, his least favorite. If they asked him to make his bed, he'd tuck the quilt in crossways. Ricky was safer when he kept others off balance in these ways but he blanched if they managed to throw him off balance. His world was perilous enough without people playing games, tampering with words, merging concepts, and saying things like "elk tree." Thus his scowling appearance on the upstairs deck, thus his pronouncement that his father was an "old drunk."

23. *That's what happened?*
Excuse me?

24. *That's what happened when Roy identified the tree?*
Yes.
"You old drunk!" said Ricky.
Rita looked up from her nail polish and turned to the two guests to reveal her wondrously mild expression: "Isn't this pleasant," it seemed to say, "wouldn't it be excellent to hear this day in and day out, as I do?"
Henrietta squeezed Henry's hand.
Roy said: "What. Did. You. Say?"
"You heard me," said Ricky, tittering a bit with excitement.
"WHAT?"
"An elk tree," said Ricky derisively, trying to expand the dialogue.
"Did you call me what I think you did?" asked Roy.
Ricky got the upper hand. "Probably," he said. "Hi Cousin Henrietta, hi Cousin Henry."
The cousins looked to Rita for directions on how to reply. Her face was wondrously mild and blank. "G'morning," they said.
"It's not morning," thundered Roy, "it's one o'clock in the afternoon. That's what time this big man gets up to take his breakfast!"
"Did you have a nice ride out here, Cousin Henry?" asked Ricky.
"Leave them out of it!"
Ricky's expression slowly changed from one of concern to one

of grief. "I'm just trying to talk to my 'relatives,' " he told his father mournfully. "Goodbye Henry and Henrietta," he said, turning to shuffle into the house.

"Ricky!" said Roy. "I would like an apology this minute."

"Don't you even want me to get dressed?" cried Ricky, vexed at every turn.

"I'm only going to say it two more times," warned Roy quietly.

"Alright, I'm going," Ricky sighed.

"Apologize."

Ricky opened the door to the house.

"Apologize!" Roy burst to his feet.

Ricky let go of the door and watched it pump shut. With his head down and his hands in the pockets of his bathrobe, he shuffled back to his podium. "I'm sorry I told everyone that you were an old drunk, Daddy," he sniffed.

But that's what his daddy was turning into.

25. Roy was turning into an old drunk?

So I have said.

With all due respect I must warn you not to waste questions.

26. Don't I get as many questions as I like?

This may come as a surprise. You get fifty questions altogether. Theoretically, we could go on and on, but fifty should give you an ample chance to get the complete story provided you don't waste any more of them.

27. How did I know to ask the first question about something called an elk tree and someone named Roy?

That question was given to you free, compliments of the house. Since then you've been on your own—and done magnificently.

28. Was the way in which Roy and Rita met prophetic?

The way every husband and wife meet is prophetic.

Roy and Rita met through a fun-loving, warm-hearted anatomy professor named Professor Abel. Roy took Professor Abel's introductory course as a requirement for freshmen. It met at eight a.m. One day Roy came to class with a hangover. Professor Abel asked Roy to stand and to recite all the bones in a human being's lower body. Roy included the penis. The professor thought this was hilarious and he went out of his way to befriend Roy. Six years later

Rita, a coed without a hangover, made the same error. The professor couldn't get over it. He traced Roy through the alumni office and urged his two pupils to meet. Being young they were good sports about it. They met, they laughed at how outlandish it was, they laughed some more, they romanced, they eloped and moved to Hollywood where Roy was beginning a decade of prominence in the music field.

29. *Did this beginning portend of things happy or sad?*

Sad. The fact that the penis is boneless was crucial to the decay of their relationship.

30. *Are you saying Roy became impotent?*

Let's say he did not feel good about himself once his songs began to dry up. Rita became more beautiful every year, like a flame that blazes most brightly on its last bit of fuel, if you will.

31. *Whom did long-time friends consider to be at fault in the marriage, Roy or Rita?*

Nearly everyone believed that Rita was emerging as the good soul in the marriage, that Roy—with his drinking, his bad-natured outbursts, his overly large mannerisms—was showing his true colors. Even people who liked Roy best were surprising themselves by coming to this conclusion.

One of the only persons to know better was the anatomy professor. He was no longer a "friend" because Roy had taken offense at something or other long ago, but from what reports he could get the good professor surmised that Rita was the villain. In his view Rita took Roy's penis-bone, she took his backbone, she took his ribs—she filleted him. And all because life wasn't working out perfectly, beginning with the hysterectomy and then the other setbacks, and she had to make bad worse. She wanted a clean sweep of badness. The professor thought Rita to be a powerful and dangerous woman. He was correct. The wondrous mildness she displayed in times of stress, the inner calm, the patience, was not that of someone who was bearing up under terrible odds, but of a sated despoiler. She had collected nearly all the bad cards and now she could afford to relax.

32. *What did Roy do after Ricky apologized?*

He muttered "Ricky, Ricky, Ricky," and then he addressed his

pregnant niece and said: "It's still worth it—with all the heartache, and with all the . . . crap! . . . it's still worth it," and then
to Henry: "You remember that," and then looking up at the tree
he hummed the melody of "Try To Remember," and then he
faced Rita with new energy and sang: "Try to remember that this,
is an elk tree, it is, just that, because, I—say—so," and then he
switched to bourbon. This entailed his walking into the house.

33. *Did anything transpire in his absence?*

You bet. While Roy was getting the bourbon Rita quietly told
the two youngsters that Roy had lung cancer.

They said. "What!" and Henrietta added: "Can anything be
done?"

"Since he found out about it he refuses to see any doctors,"
Rita said, screwing closed the sky-scraper cap of the nail polish
with fingers that needed to dry. She was plainly wearied of the
way Roy handled real-life situations. "Your uncle thinks that
would be giving in to it, you see."

The door opened and Ricky, who knew nothing of this matter,
approached with the bourbon tray. He still wore his bathrobe and
slippers. Rita said: "Oh, I thought you were your father."

"No," said Ricky, "my father's on the potty." As he leaned to
set down the tray he grunted emphatically, by way of rounding
out the picture.

"So that's the latest," Rita concluded, taking a sip from Roy's
glass.

"I can't believe it," said Henrietta.

"Neither can I," said Henry.

"Why not?" interrupted Ricky. "Everybody's got to go sometime. Sometimes when he has to go number one he does it right
out here."

Rita sputtered into her husband's drink, a short laugh. "That's
disgusting," she said lightly, wiping the side of the glass and rele-
gating it to the arm of Roy's chair.

"I just think it's horrible," reaffirmed Henrietta.

"Same here," said Henry. "Cut it out," he told Ricky, who had
taken a seat at his feet and was harmlessly tossing patio pebbles
up onto his lap.

"No, but this is really, really horrible," said Henrietta. "Do you think," she asked Rita, "I could be of any help if I talked to him?"

"He'll most likely tell you it's nothing, a virus," she answered. "An elk virus."

"I know what you mean," interrupted Ricky. They turned to him with alarm. "He's crazy. He really thinks this is an elk tree, just because he wants it to be. Somebody," he said, tossing up three larger pebbles, "should really call his bluff sometime."

The grown-ups thought about that for a couple of minutes. Finally Rita said: "Oh go away Ricky."

34. *What was taking Roy so long?*

Sad to report, Roy was feeling sorry for himself on the john. It began when he noticed the guest towels beside him, lovely towels with blue and brown Peruvian designs. He recalled that he had bought them for Rita long ago in Hollywood. In the store the towels had been stiff and coarse, but Roy figured they would soften with a few washings. It had seemed to him that the towels were too expensive to remain stiff and impractical. Young, newly rich, in love, the songwriter believed money was like that: it would automatically buy you things that were both lovely to look at and practical, too. But the towels never softened. They remained completely useless, scratchy. Roy's life seemed to him a folly.

Roy drew three sheets of toilet paper from the spool. He held the first one, the furthest one, in his hand.

"Damn it already, Ricky!" he heard. It was Henry yelling. Henry had jumped up and brushed the pebbles from his lap onto Ricky's face. "Enough already!"

Roy pulled on the furthest sheet. It ripped inadequately. Instead of getting all three sheets, he only got part of one. A sob of outrage, at things both great and small, came out of Roy. Immediately he snapped back, he regained control—but this was a very frustrated man.

35. *Isn't it unusual for a successful man to act like that?*

I'm afraid not very. You should have seen him earlier in the middle seat of the station wagon.

36. *Was Roy now a better gift-buyer than he had been in Holly-wood?*

Not in Henrietta's view. All the gifts she had ever received from Roy, from the shocking Arabic perfume he gave her in first grade, to the Danish handmirror of last Christmas, were inappropriate; they managed to make Henrietta feel insufficient. The handmirror was royal but Henrietta was not; it was a fantasy she could not live up to. The sight of her chubby, unproud face reflected in the Danish oval, framed by silver swan figurines, revolted Henrietta, it made her feel homely by contrast, a fat duck. She felt odd when she used it, as if she were part of a frightening fairy tale—worshipped by a blind suitor or captured by a 200 year old prince.

Actually it was Roy who had captured her. He had forced the gift upon her, as he forced all his gifts, and she hadn't had the nerve to reject it. She couldn't bring herself to say: "Here, take it back. You've got me all wrong. I don't like seeing myself this way." Dutifully she took the mirror and dutifully she kept it on her dresser. And every time she looked in it she was his prisoner, she was his princess, as surely as if he had molded a silver crown around her head.

37. *Did Roy ever buy things for himself?*

From time to time. He didn't scrimp on himself except when important matters were at stake, such as his health.

38. *Why wouldn't Roy see a doctor for his cancer?*

A. He preferred to think of it not as cancer but as a cigarette pain. He had quit smoking already; what more could a doctor prescribe?

B. He had a superstition that he'd be a goner if he underwent an operation. He knew it was irrational but he feared that the open air would "stimulate" the cancer.

39. *Two excuses?*

But of course. Every bad move Roy made was supported by at least two excuses so that if something should happen to one, he would be held steady to his error by the other. He refrained from locking the bathroom door, for instance, on the grounds that: (A) he might find himself lacking some item and have to call out for it, and (B—in which he was very much a child of his time) he considered locking the bathroom door a sign of paranoia.

40. In what way was this a bad move?
People generally do not like their niece's husbands to surprise them in the bathroom.

41. Was Henry embarrassed about barging in?
"Oops, sorry!" he exclaimed. "I just came in to wash my face! It's so humid! Boy! I'll let you finish!"

"That would be good of you, Henry," said Roy.

Naturally he was embarrassed, but worse was to come a minute later when Roy passed him in the kitchen. "Sorry about that," he said, rinsing his face with a moist paper napkin.

"About what?" said Roy, "I've already forgotten it." He began to pour himself a scotch.

"Oh I think," ventured Henry, dabbing around his neck, "I think your bourbon is waiting for you on the patio."

"Lucky me," said Roy. "Well, I guess I can handle the both of them."

"'Lucky Me,'" repeated eager, wire-brained Henry. "Wasn't that the name of your first hit song?"

Roy was well pleased. But he looked as if he were going to hit Henry.

"You big boozer," he said threateningly, putting down the drink. "You little rummy. Since when do you know about my past, you lush? Think you caught me being sentimental, making private jokes?" He came towards Henry with the wide, circling arms of a performing wrestler. "You have not lived until you have been in one of my famous four-hour headlocks."

"Wait wait," gabbled Henry, uttering a laugh. "Ow, ow," he yelped just before Roy grabbed him by the neck and the waist and bent him like a fluffy pipe cleaner. "My blisters!"

Gently, manfully, Roy turned his advantage into a paternal hug. With one hand he buried Henry's head in his big shoulder, patting and rubbing. "I'd never hurt you," he told Henry in a voice thick with emotion, "you know I'd never hurt you. Henry," he said, rocking them both, "you're a good man, Henry. You're going to be a good father. And Henrietta," he inhaled sharply, "she's going to be a wonderful mother . . . loving and kind and . . . beautiful as a queen. I want you to believe that. You believe that, don't you, Henry?"

"Sure," came the muffled, mortified voice of Henry, who was quickly formulating a cancer superstition of his own, namely, that cancer might be contagious at certain proximities.

Embarrassed? Yes, but Henry was used to that; far worse was feeling infected.

42. *How did Henry deal with this new feeling?*

By proceeding, directly upon his return to the patio, to get smashed.

43. *Did this help?*

It might have helped had Henry chosen an appropriate chair from which to do it, but he mistakenly chose a low-slung canvas chair situated below the level of the table. Henry was too inexperienced a drinker to know the connection between posture and mood, so he sprawled, he stewed, he half-snoozed as the heat collected, as the chatter peaked and peaked again, as Ricky ate monster bubble gum at his ear. Cheese muffins were passed down to him. Brown apple slices were passed down to him. Conversation strayed into his space and was trapped. Henrietta offered to spray his feet with a hose; Henry waved off the treat; she sprayed elsewhere. Ricky created a ghoulishly green bubble nearby. Suddenly Henry took one drop past his limit. The stupor clutched him before he'd even had time to set his glass back down on the pebbles. The bubble grew closer, paler, larger; it filled his vision. Rita was enveloped; the elk tree squeezed in; Roy entered laughing, telling a serious Henrietta: "Not to worry about me, not to worry." Henry saw with dismay that the not-quite-sporty Datsun parked beyond the patio had also been swallowed up; it looked not-quite-capable of driving him out and away. For one long second Henry believed he was sitting in a cold tub, at his home on Riverside Drive . . . sweating, he came to and pinpointed the handkerchief in his breast pocket.

"Are you alright?" asked the black and yellow lady.

"He looks unsocial," advised the purple boy.

"Henry," panted the wife.

Roy had an idea. "Alright, everyone give him room," he instructed. "Henry, just relax and breathe normally. Ricky," he said evenly, "get that out of his face."

"It's just a bubble," explained Ricky. Nevertheless, it withdrew.

"Is he going to be alright?" Henrietta asked.

Roy chuckled. There was a wet, echoing chuckle from Henry.

The relief was too fast for Rita. She stared out to the horseshoe pit, then blinked back to her fingernails. "I must be quite a hostess," she sighed.

There was the sound of an airplane, invisible.

Roy stood Henry on his feet and proceeded to walk him around the premises. They stopped briefly at the bird bath, where Henry consented to douse his head, they spent a few minutes at the tomato patch, and then continued through the back door of the house.

44. Were they going any place in particular?

Roy led Henry to his music den. It looked like the fix-it area of a rich man's radio shop. The thick white broadloom was strewn with tape reels, breakable television components; the shelves were loaded with electronic machinery, tiny screwdrivers . . . and a small cardboard box that Roy took down. It was sealed with masking tape.

45. The goodbye present!

"This here is for Henrietta," he said. "Think you're steady enough to carry it?"

"In a minute," said Henry, lowering himself to the piano bench.

"I was going to scrub it with ammonia, but I decided that was the husband's job," Roy said. "It'll be priceless when you get the crime out."

"The what?"

"The cobwebs and grime," said Roy. "Whatever."

Henry struck middle C on the keyboard. "I feel somewhat better," he said.

Roy supported Henry by the elbow back to the patio. As they approached he whispered: "It's from one of Westhampton's great big mansions. I picked it up at a garage sale. Give it to her with a little build-up, you know?"

Obligingly, Henry placed the box on the table before his wife. "This is from Roy," he said. "It may be a little dirty but it's supposed to be quite valuable."

"Oh Roy," said Henrietta, delicately unpeeling the masking tape. "An antique?"

"Well, kind of," said Roy happily.

"That means junk," warned Ricky.

Before anyone could respond Henrietta pulled out a tall crystal baby bottle. Her heart skidded. She could find nothing to say. One side of the interior was caked with fruity white cocoons. The nipple was cracked and moldy.

"I was just telling Henry that a little ammonia will clean it right up," chirped Roy. "Of course, you might want to replace the nipple. That's easy enough."

"Yes," said Henrietta slowly, "yes."

"You're unfocusing again," Roy told Henry.

There was a sweaty silence . . .

. . . But Rita, for once, was not inclined to cherish it. "Maybe Henrietta wanted to breast-feed, Roy."

Roy didn't like that. "I don't give a damn what she wants to do," he shouted. "She can use it for a juice bottle. Or what if the baby is a biter?" He was angry at his wife. "You've got to have a little imagination, damn it all!"

Henrietta had lost her color. She looked up at Roy.

"That's real crystal," he pointed out. "You'll have to be careful if you want to boil it. Now I know a lot of women like to have all new things for their first baby, and that's fine: I don't mind if you go out and get a hundred new bottles. I just thought it was important for you to have this, too."

"It's from an ancient kingdom," Henrietta breathed.

"There, you see!" crowed Roy. "Someone here's got a head on her shoulders."

Henrietta looked pleadingly at Rita. "But it's horrible!" she said. "It's for a queen that's dead and buried! Can't you tell him that?"

"What in the hell is going on here?" said Roy. "Everybody's jinxed on account of a few little spiders have gotten in. Give it back if you don't like it. I'll trade it for a couple of art books or something. Jesus Christ, I'm telling you." He looked around for someone to tell.

"Why did you make me carry it out?" stammered Henry.

"Oh shit," said Roy.

"Can I see it?" asked Ricky. Henrietta handed him the bottle.

"Dead, my foot," said Roy. "Who's got a cigarette?"

Ricky put the bottle to the light and studied it with detachment. "Daddy," he said reasonably, "it's second hand."

"Well so are you buddy!"

Ricky continued studying the bottle.

"Forget that," said Roy very quietly. "It didn't mean anything. Please stop," he said. "Everyone stop thinking."

"It was a mistake," said Rita. "It didn't mean anything."

"That's right," Roy said. "People say things that are stupid and cruel and meaningless sometimes. And I'm no exception."

"It's alright," said Henrietta. "Sometimes things pop out of my mouth that don't mean anything. It happens to everybody."

"Silly, dumb things," said Roy. "The trouble is that people don't think before they speak."

"It's nothing to remember," said Henry. "It's easily forgotten."

"I think so, too," said Roy. "We'll forget it here and now. No need to spoil the afternoon. Whom can I help with another drink? Rita, some bourbon? Ricky," he said, turning to his son for the first time, "can I get you a glass of something?"

Thoughtfully Rick smashed the bottle down so that the crystal shards flew up and about like a shower of ice in the sunlight, turning red and blue and green. No one moved. No one spoke.

The end.

46. The end?

The end.

47. They just sat there, frozen?

Frozen. Some more than others.

48. Did time stand still?

Yes. No. It seemed to, but slowly, gracefully, it reasserted itself. The afternoon had nearly passed.

49. And Henry and Henrietta?

After a while they began to talk about going. The heat was breaking up. The sun was going down. Still they sat amid the bits of broken crystal. The sunset was seen through the leaves of the elk tree. You might think the sunset after that infernal weekend was ghoulish, green, like a monster bubble. But it was radiant, pink. . . .

It was their last sunset in the States. Next day they would leave for England forever.

50. *The sky radiant, ablaze with death, with new life, a hex broken, a baby on its way, arrival and departure! Isn't the world rich?*

The farewells took place in semi-darkness. Rick did not trouble to come out of his father's den where he was engrossed in watching baseball on his father's large, and rather loud, television. Rita and Roy quietly walked their guests to the car. There was much solemn hugging, kissing and waving. A mile down the road Henrietta discovered she had left her purse behind. They drove back to the house and Henrietta walked inside. No one was around. She located her purse. She stood around a moment and then called: "Goodbye again!" Roy came out of the den with a drink in his hand and a finger to his lips. "Shh," he said, "Rita's taking a rest." Then he hugged Henrietta once more, saying: "It'll be good. Don't worry. Even after everything. . . ." Quietly he walked her to the front door and pressed their foreheads together under the lamplight. His eyes welled up. "I wish the world were dead," he told her.

SNOW

JAYNE ANNE PHILLIPS

Jayne Anne Phillips was born in 1952 in West Virginia. Her work has appeared in *Fiction, Ploughshares, Redbook, Fiction International, Iowa Review, The North American Review, The Paris Review,* and *Best American Short Stories, 1979. Black Tickets,* her book of short stories (Delacorte/ Seymour Lawrence) will appear soon in German, Italian, Swedish, and British editions. Two previous collections, *Sweethearts* (Truck Press, 1976, 1978), and *Counting* (Vehicle Editions, 1978), were published in limited edition. Miss Phillips is the recipient of a Fells Award, a National Endowment for the Arts Fellowship, two Pushcart Prizes (1977 and 1979), and a St. Lawrence Award for Fiction. She has worked at a variety of jobs, and more recently taught at the University of Iowa as a Teaching-Writing Fellow.

The school opened iron gates to show its clowns and jugglers. Crowds came to watch the mutes, the senseless ones. Those lawns and high walls were not so fearsome in summer, and the flags rippled from posts striped in crepe paper by the deaf. Molly watched her mother, and the crowd pressed up. Her father stood beside her holding Callie. Laura was her mother. Laura danced, with her light hair blowing wild about her face and the filmy dress moving to show her legs. The focus of her blind eyes didn't change even in leaping; in those controlled jumps which could not keep her arms from rising, as though the feeling of air made her want to enter it. Afterward she stood very still. A silence. The dress blew about her thighs. Her moonish breasts were heaving.

Men in the back of the crowd began to hoot. But the rain came on. A wind blew up and knocked over one of the stands. Two hundred balloons were let fly when the flimsy stand broke; people scrambled and fell on each other to catch them. Molly saw the colors twisting. Her father stood beside her but he could not see, ever. Laura stood there listening. And the balloons went up.

The town slept and remembered wars. Especially in heat, it slept. The river shrunk in its deep bed; clay along the dried banks grew giant cracks. Every day was very long and it was 1948. Molly thought it would always be this way. Spenser, South Carolina, had two factories, a lumber mill, and a training parlor for beauticians. There were three grade schools, a grammar school, a high school, and a business college. And there was the School for the Deaf, Dumb and Blind where Molly's father taught. Everywhere there were heavy trees hung with ivy that threw their long shadows out even on the hottest days. Molly and her mother took Callie to the park. In summer they bought Sno Cones from a man with one eye and a red striped coat. His name was Barney, and Molly asked him where his eye was. She had never seen a deformed person; only her mother and father and their friends at the school with their calm hands and lost sense. Expressions passed so slowly and totally over their features that the coarsest face looked delicate. Only them, and now Barney with his one eyelid pulled down harsh, and grown together with the skin of his cheek.

My eye? he said. Wouldn't surprise me none if somebody had my eye in a box this minute.

He laughed loudly. Molly knew he could see. His one eye wasn't still like Mama's, but darted back and forth like the head of a quirky bird. Molly was only glad nobody had her mama's eyes in a box, but was suddenly afraid and clutched at her.

Mr. Parsons, said Laura, you've frightened her.

But he had seen it already with his one eye and was bending over Molly. Why, honey, he said, don't you worry. Ain't nobody gonna touch them jewels of your mama's. Why, they got close, their hands surely turn to ice like this here.

And Molly watched him dip the crushed white into paper cones with painted clowns and balloons on them like at the fair. Then he poured blue syrup over for blueberry and red for strawberry. Callie was sitting in his stroller watching with his big eyes that caught and held but were focused far away like Mama's. He watched Barney hold the long colored bottle up high and squirt the bright blue far down as it faded into the ice. Molly watched the color go. Her mother's eyes were pale like ice, that cool blue smoke of hard ice. Barney would give them the cones and they'd go over on the grass and eat them, Callie falling and pushing his fat hands. The paper cones got melty and the balloons would bleed.

Molly asked her mother, These clowns can't hear what we say, can they.

She said, Molly, all clowns aren't deaf.

They'd walk back later, having stayed by the duck pond for hours because Callie loved them. Laura would walk down to the edge of the water. She made a sound so much like the low murmurings of the ducks that they'd get confused and swim close. Callie would sit absolutely still. They'd put him in the stroller to leave and he'd turn his head around to hear the ducks until they were over the hill. Molly told him the ducks were still there, they were always there. Her mother's stick reached out in front, thin whisk back and forth. Laura felt for the curbs and stones and she pushed the stroller one-handed. Molly walked holding to the other side, pushing at Callie. Always, any light tapping sound would make her smell trees. Near dusk; how the heavy dark-leaved trees hung over them and the stroller's wheels creaked uneven on brick sidewalks up Spenser Hill. They would talk, walking till they got to the house. Molly knew her father had lemonade in the tall glass pitcher on the blue table. Her mother would say, Randal, you're home so soon? And he'd answer, No, my Laura, you're late. Oh Randal, not again, and she would touch him like she did, her pale hands behind his head.

Once when they were downtown, Laura spoke to Molly and she didn't answer. Standing by the stroller as always, Molly didn't answer and waited to see what would happen. Laura felt with her hand but Molly knelt below it, hearing the edge in her mother's voice and ashamed now but afraid. She said Molly? in different directions and screamed finally, *Molly!* Albers from the bookstore was behind them.

He said to her quietly, Mrs. Collier, here's Molly.

Molly, don't joke with me, she said. And as soon as he had passed, But it wasn't a joke, was it.

At night Molly's father came to talk to her. Callie was asleep in the other bed, his thumb jammed in his mouth. Muted light from the street lamp swam through the windows. She could see the tiny frenzied swarming of insects in ellipses around the yellow globe. Light fell blue on Callie's face; his cheeks had shadows dark as holes. That night all her father said to her was Molly, no one can always take care of you.

Then he told the story of the dancing princess who lifted up her bed at night to go down the silver steps.

But what did she do down there?

She danced, he said, like your mother at the fair. And wore out all her slippers.

Up and down the block they heard footsteps alone on the sidewalks. Still it was not night. Doors shut their private sounds. Cars purred a muffled chugging as they slowed for the turn, then growled deep as they picked up speed. Her father told the story all the way through, and by the end Molly wasn't listening any more; only watched his big shape and his hands in the air that fell and stayed in her hair. His lips moved in his still face, and the dark came.

Molly, Molly, he thought as she sank in her rocking sleep. He was himself a light sleeper, waking from dreams several times a night to hear the house settle around him. It made him wonder that his daughter should draw shut like Lazarus, and no sound would wake her until she swam up alone from where she had been. He wondered how she dreamed. He sat on her bed with his hand in her hair trying to hear her dreams.

When Randal first began teaching braille, the young wife of one of his students asked him how a blind person dreams. Randal told her that the sounds and voices have their own shapes and varied thicknesses. Almost like colors, infinite shades of silver. Randal realized then that his sight in dreams was that of his childhood; blurred moving shapes with a light or empty hole behind them. In dreams he could still almost see the fingers on a hand, the beautiful separated films that moved differently and by themselves.

When he was seven he'd had measles and diphtheria. His burning eyes were bandaged. He saw nothing. He practiced remembering how the fingers looked, how they moved in and out and touched shyly and laced their translucence into a ball. When the bandages came away, it was all black. Slowly there was lighter gray, and lighter. In a year he could watch the glimmered blur of bodies running (the violent smacking bat, boys' voices in sweet rising fold *Get him out! Get him out!* feet thudding close and gone) but not again the lovely fingers. The lovely . . .

Randal? Laura's quiet voice was by the door. What are you doing in there so long?

I thought you were asleep, he said. He knew she saw no shapes. Just the black. When they married, her aunt in Washington said now she would never get well (Married to a blind man my God. I did what I could she wants to ruin her life I wash my hands of it).

You know I can't sleep until you come to bed, said Laura. She heard sadness in his voice, more slow distance than pain, as if he struggled patiently in a closet. She never questioned his sadness. She heard his broad hands smooth Molly's bedclothes and then the lifting of his weight as the bed shifted its layers.

He straightened and walked to her. She leaned against him heavily, felt him solid under the robe. Smelling him, she pressed her face where the cloth opened on his chest; touched her mouth to the skin and the fine hair. When she was sixteen he had taught her to read with her fingers and make love. He had given something up to her and she kept it for him gravely.

I've made some tea, it'll help you sleep, she said. Did you talk to Molly?

I didn't, much. I don't think she'll do it again.

Randal felt Laura's small hard shoulders. It seemed to him that she was made of light, that she would float out of his heaviness on the earth, in this town and this house. He felt her pull away.

I forgot the spoons, she said. She went to the kitchen. He heard her long thin feet on the bare floor, the opening drawer, the inanimate silver talking its clatter. In their room the windows were open. The lace curtains dipped in and out, catching on the rose bushes. She had turned down the bed on his side. He knew she had lain there beside the neat triangle of sheet, waiting for him.

Randal, did I tell you they're building a merry-go-round in the park. With a calliope and horses ordered from New York. Mr. Parsons told us about it. Won't Molly love it.

Laura handed him the steaming cup and her hand brushing his was cool next to the heat.

When she was sleeping and he woke at night, there was nothing. There was the house aching. There was the street and the plants moving by the window. At night the magnolias drifted their fleshy scent; he lay and sweat. He felt his son sleep blond and floating in another room that was gone that was oh far gone. He heard Molly weeping into her hands, Molly a grown woman, her heavy black hair in her face. He pulled Laura close to him and her scent washed over him like slow water. He held her sleeping body and was alone until the panic passed.

It was raining. He gradually heard and lay listening (his feet on cold steps and the milk wagon creaking down early morning, wheels groan, hooves on wet stones and yes its musky steaming smell, Randal get back inside you'll catch your death. No you can't touch, but he pulled and ran and the man bundled him, lifted him And the horse big, its long hard velvet head oh). Laura moved breathless and naked to shut the windows.

The curtains are soaked, she said. I didn't hear it raining.

And she stood by the window in the watery air smelling the warm asphalt cool. When she was a child she had seen rain. She remembered it fell in a slanted color. Pearls and ash falling. Rain came from far off to contain everything. You could see it coming. It rained those weeks in the hospital when they operated on her head. They said it was the tail end of a hurricane, named for her because she was the littlest girl on the ward (I'm not little I'm eight and I can read *Ivanhoe*. No one said anything. She knew she couldn't read it any more). Later they asked her to remember. Remember all about it; her mother, the man, the car. Nothing there. For six years, Laura sat in her aunt's house. A sequence of paid widows read aloud to her. Her aunt read the Old Testament.

Your mother, she said, was my sister born in innocence and consumed by her own soul. You are the innocent fruit of her repetitious sin. As we sow, so shall we reap.

Laura sewed; rapidly, constantly, perfectly: long afternoons by a window open even in winter. Unconscious of her fingers' penance on a raised design in linen, she smelled and heard the street. When Laura was fourteen, her aunt became afraid of her. She ordered that Laura's hair be cut; she sent her to the school. In two years, Randal came.

Randal heard Laura's fingers stroke the polished windowsill. Rain continued round. Those years ago her belly was globed and tight with a hollow floating. He remembered the long night of first labor . . . long, long. How she held her breath and spent it, blowing air like an animal adapted to ocean. Then it was over; he heard her fingers on the baby's face. Raining on the sheathed head, first memorizing, then just looking again and again. And he touched her forehead, which always had a peculiar heat to it when she was happy.

When Callie's nose bled, the rocking chairs got blurry. Their shiny arms rippled and ran over themselves. He was five. They bought him glasses and Molly went to school. Molly went to school, putting her face in front of him where she knew he could see, saying, Callie Callie don't untie the string. She had told him about the string no one could see. She said it kept his feet on the ground. She rubbed his back with her hand and took her book away.

You can't read, she said. It's not good for you.

And the door opened. All the cool rained air came in. He heard her feet on the sidewalk; he heard her brown shoes with their neat ties on the criss-crossed brick that was washed now. Fat dark worms writhed on the cool grit. His father said they were trying to find dirt when they rolled like that. He said they were drowning in the air.

Callie heard the cat scratching at the window and dimly saw it beyond the glass. It opened its mouth soundlessly wide and to Callie it looked like a pink hole opening in a steam. Things seemed closer than they were; things were there before he touched them. He pushed his hands through the veil that surrounded them. Then there was a hardness.

They took him to the special doctor's and he read the pictures. There was a boat, and then two boats, and then two cowboys and a boat in the shape of a triangle. He couldn't see the cowboys' faces any more, but he remembered what they looked like from

before. He told how they looked. They were the same one two
times, with their big eyes rolled to the side and their smiles and
their hats. They looked like they were turning and something
pressed them flat. He thought they were afraid of the boat coming. When he squinted he could make the boat roll over them.
Then he pulled it back and they were still turning.

He could read the chart with the letters on it. But Molly said
not to tell, and now she wouldn't let him read her books. With
his glasses he could see the big letters again. He never took the
glasses off. He tried to sleep with them on. Each night his father's
big hand came down and took them in the dark. The hand was
big and dark and his father sang to him when he took the glasses.

I wish I was an apple. A hangin' in a tree.

His father sang it very slowly, trembling his voice. The apple
was in the tree. It was round and red and it had a heart. It was
made of sugar. When he got to the part about the girl, his father's
voice went up and around and in; still slower, like a heavy animal
moving in a snow. Callie had heard about snow.

And ev'ry time my sweetheart passed she'd. Take a bite a me.

Now it was snowing and he and his father walked with the girl
to get along home. Callie led them all home because he could see.
The girl was his mother but she was not his mother. She was
Cindy; Callie knew that, but the song smelled of his mother.

Get along home. Get along. Home.

His father's voice was slower, slow and high. There was cold
honey in the snow.

Get along. Home Cindy Cindy. I'll marry you suh-uhm. Time.

Apples were fallen in the snow and the honey. They went along
home until they were gone.

Callie and his mother went to the movies. Molly went to
school. She saw the movies on Saturdays but not on Wednesdays.
When he and his mother went. They walked down the hill on the
skinny sidewalk. He held her hand and her stick tapped out in
front. It tapped very lightly like the thin finger of a clock. Sometimes he heard it tapping when his mother was asleep, tapping
from the dark corner of the room. He heard all the clocks tapping
in the velvet house. He knew the stick told them when to tap.

As they walked, his mother asked him to look up in the sky and
tell her what creatures were there. A creature was like an animal

but it could be people, or half girl and half horse. Creatures grew in the sky, sliding over each other. Once a cloud came down and covered the town. His mother said it was a creature of a sort, a fog; only he couldn't see its shape because he was inside it. She said she had seen many creatures when she was a girl. The best one was a man with a big pocket in his vest. More creatures kept coming out of the pocket until the man himself came out and then there was nothing left.

There were two movie theaters in town. The finer one was actually closer. But his mother liked the smaller one that was on down Main Street close to the tracks. It was nearly empty in the afternoons except for them and the sweeping man, who moved his big flat broom around and around. The lobby floor was laid with yellow linoleum in diamond shapes. It was coming up in patches where the planked boards showed through black with fuzz. Trains went by and the big mirrors rattled on the walls. In the shadowy closeness their seats shook; he gripped their worn plush delirious with joy.

The screen was a floating square of light. Curtains swung back on rods. His mother cupped his face in the dark. Pouring out of a tiny hole the big lion opened and roared, shuddering its gold weight. With his glasses Callie could almost see the tiny eyes and the fragile underlip quivering its teeth.

On the screen a man danced with a hat rack, holding it like some tender thing and twirling it over his back. He danced his feet around while it circled like a saucer on its side. Tippling its fluted legs, tippling it turned a long brown liquid in his arms in his thin arms. His shiny heels clicked and spun, his mouth a perfect O. He was supple and dapper and his smooth face rippled in the shaking of the trains. Callie was not afraid in the dark because the man was dancing. He danced over the rumble of the blunt-nosed engine and the clack of the boxcar wheels. He danced the tiled cement in front of the old theater and the steamy sidewalk grate. He danced the long cracked Spenser streets under the droop-haired trees, up the hill to the house where Callie's father sat with clinched hands, listening to Chopin in the dark. Callie dreamed them together in the dark house; his mother in the thin hallway, her white dress, her legs clear through the cloth. His father sitting with his music by the rainy window and they were all safe with the dancing man.

It went black and the lights came up. Callie waited for his mother to know, and they walked up the slanted floor to the lobby. It looked smaller to him now, gauzy as a cataract. Night, said the sweeping man. His broom went round and round. They pushed open the double doors and the soft fatal *whish* of his moving followed them away.

She put Callie down to sleep when they got home. Laura wondered why sleep is down. She thought it was like a sinking. Callie was afraid to sleep. She sat by him until he slept and put his glasses where he could reach them.

She pressed herself against the straight back of the wooden chair and touched her face with her hands. She felt the round covered balls of her eyes, the boned sockets, the hard line of her jaw. Her face felt old to her when she touched it; when she was alone and touched it. She hadn't seen her face since she was a child. She remembered seeing it that night in the mirror; the hall light a sudden blindness, her mother laughing, the sweet sick smell as she leaned close to tie a red ribbon too loose in Laura's hair. It fell lopsided in her light hair, in the mirror. She saw her own eyes, then her mother looking at her. And the man laughed holding them both and the car was warm, moving. She crawled into the back and rolled against the seat. They laughed, her mother dangling the discarded ribbon from the rear-view mirror the wrinkled raveled satin and the car lurched and they laughed.

Laura's head was aching. She would not think of it. She would go and lie in the snow. Behind her mother's house the snow was deep. Laura, move your arms up and down like this And your legs, there, like this. . . . Laura would close her eyes under the pines in her warm clothes, feel snow falling on her face . . . all sounds went away. And her mother lifted her laughing, Silly don't fall asleep in the snow. . . .

Laura got up and walked through the quiet house to the bedroom. Clocks ticked. She took off her clothes and folded them neatly across a chair. A car went by. She thought it must be dark by now. She was very tired. She got between the covers feeling the wide empty bed with her legs. It seemed to open, the sheets opening and covering. In the snow they lay down to make women in gowns whose arms had exploded. No Laura, those are angels with wings like the angel in the tree. . . . Snow fell from the trees in clumps, filled the angels up. Laura stamped the exploded arms. Again, in her dreams, she saw the shadow with the open mouth, falling all in fire. It had the sweet sick smell of her mother's words; it crooned, falling the crackling black. Good black and the words said hush. Laura slept. She was sinking and the sounds went away.

On Wednesdays Randal took Molly to the diner. It was a long aluminum room with yellow stools and a red counter. Ralph was a man near fifty whose rubbery face ran with sweat. He shook Molly's hand and called her a lady. Randal and Molly sat up front near the grill. Behind the counter Ralph's flaccid daughter smiled her sideways smile and nodded her head again and again.

Ralph made a bowl of batter for their pancakes. Sylvie shambled blond and big, reaching under the counter for the silverware. How you, she nodded, placing each utensil carefully beside the other. When he heard her turn to get the water glasses, Randal turned the silverware right side up. Molly watched Sylvie put three ice cubes in each glass, one at a time, with her big silver dipper. She put the glasses in front of them and smiled, her mouth twitching. Her father liked the blind man and he told her to wait on him good. Her eyes rolled to the door, swept the wall and the round clock, swept it all to the far end of the red counter. Her hand moved on her thigh as if she held the rag that wiped the formica clean. Her hands smelled like the rag. Its wilted pungence mixed with an oily peanut smell when she lifted her arms.

Her baby Howard was on the floor like always, playing with straws or spoons. He was a fat tow-headed baby who never cried. Sylvie picked him up and held him on her lap while Randal and Molly ate pancakes. Uh huh, huh, Sylvie laughed slow, the baby rocking. Randal thought: She is like a cow burning. He asked her how the week had been, feeling Molly watch her.

Ralph scraped the grill with his iron spatula. Welfare people been to see my girl again, he said . . . But she can count to twenty now. She ain't the first one been taken advantage of—

Look here, Mr. Collier, I got new berries and cream for them pancakes.

The syrup was warm in Randal's mouth. Molly's fingers curled
on his wrist were sticky, her small nails digging in. Her stolid
hands weren't Laura's. Laura's hands (the school that first month,
his quarters a room in the tower; savage thumps of pigeons on the
ledge. The psychologist crossed and recrossed his legs. Laura is a
special case, Her blindness, he said, is to some degree hysterical
. . . thrown free, the car . . . her mother crawled out burning, he
said. We think Laura was, he said, conscious. Gloves at night for
years, he said, to keep from hurting . . . herself in her sleep. I'm
not qualified, he said, to deal with her).

Later, Laura gave Randal the gloves. They were white cotton
gloves like young girls wear to church, but they knotted around
the wrists with string. Her hands, thought Randal. Sylvie went on
with her sounds.

Laura came to his rooms on the grounds. He hadn't been near
her for several weeks. I'm seventeen, she'd said, today I'm seventeen. She came near him, pulling at his hands his chest his hair.
He was afraid her aunt would find out and take her away (She's a
slut like her mother You're not the first or last. I did what I could
now she's your affair). He lived in fear she would be gone or pregnant too soon; still he wanted her so badly he shook. By the time
her pregnancy showed, she was eighteen and they were married.
Randal was thirty-eight, moving in her arms in their empty house.
On the blond wood floors she taught him to waltz. Music loud,
they turned, turning until he was dizzy and he pressed her to him
and they lay down on the floor she—

Take your time, said Ralph, just sweeping up. Randal reached
in his pocket for the money.

Outside, the diner's purple lights made the wet street pink. The
door clicked behind them and did its slow sigh shut. Molly listened. Sylvie pushed her ragged mop and chanted, Nine, ten,
eleven.

Callie heard them come in. His father scuffed his feet and then
they were in the room. They all went out to the kitchen. His
mother had soup for them and the steam came up. His father's

face above him was wide and lost in the steam. Callie reached through and touched him and left his hand there.

When Callie was in the white room, his father's face had been too wide and frightened him. Then he couldn't pull the light on by himself and the women with the cool hands picked him up to put him in the bed. Things were different before he went to the white room; a face sat on top of a face and blurred where they came together. There were angles of light and two prismed doors in the wall. There were two of everything. Nothing was ever by itself because everything faded its edges into something else. Callie was lonely when he saw that his mother had only one face. She had seemed to be all around him. Her arms legs hips breasts hands hair, had been in his sight a milky atmosphere. Now he saw that everyone was separate.

Callie ate his soup. Their separate faces moved around him in the steam. They receded, each one behind a single veil. Their voices shimmered behind the colors and broke.

Callie's mother broke eggs. She held one in the curve of her hand and clicked it against the bowl. She felt for the crack and she pulled it apart; there was a suck of air to break your heart.

No, Callie, she said, that's cracks in the sidewalk, to break your back. But you can say it any way you want to, especially on your birthday.

She gave him an egg to break. It sat in his hand all round and full. No eyes no ears no arms, it was a poor thing. He wanted to keep it.

No, said his mother, it's for your cake. But he ran away with it and put it in a box.

They had a party. They sang the birthday song and it had the same words over and over. They sang it again and again, so slow to the burning candles. Callie blew them to sleep. He walked his fingers around them and made marks in the icing like tiny feet. There was a fire engine in the bag. It screamed when it ran. Callie hated its crying. His father did something to it and then it ran quietly, whispering its wheels. His mother gave him a small gold circle hung with slender pipes. She said they were chimes and they talked in the dark. She hung them in his window and brushed his eyes with her mouth.

Then it was night. They left him alone in his bed. From nowhere there was a sound that flew; the tiny pipes sang when they touched. The fire engine stayed very still. Callie held the egg in his hand. He moved it; he felt something twirl inside the shell.

Molly's father said his own rhymes to Callie and her:

> *Molly Molly Pumpkin Polly*
> *How does your garden growl*
> *With sea horse bells and turtle shells*
> *And midget men all in the aisle*

Somewhere, she thought, little men held sea horses in their arms like dogs; sea horses with bells inside them like the clock on the wall. In that place, the wind left all the hours growling in the grass, soft and scared like Sylvie's repetitive laugh. Molly asked her father where the garden was. He said he would try to remember, but when you try to find some things, there is a snow comes down.

Once it snowed in Spenser. Callie was six but he never went to school. Their father carried him out to see the snow. Molly looked up and the air was falling apart. Callie couldn't see the flakes in the white sky. They melted in his face in his wide eyes Oh he said. Their father took him back into the house.

Callie was so white in bed. Molly read him her arithmetic book and he learned to multiply. He didn't wear his glasses any more. The doctors said he could have them back in a year. When Callie bled, Molly ran and told. Her mother and father held ice wrapped in cloths to his nose. When they tried to lay him out flat, Callie screamed.

Molly, said her mother, Has it stopped?

No, Molly said.

And then they felt it, warm, all over them.

Don't let my head touch down, Callie said. Don't let my head touch down.

The last time they took him to the hospital, it was night. Callie was wrapped tight in a blanket. It was spring it was raining it was the ambulance almost pretty in the dark. A neighbor came and stayed the night. That poor little fella, she said, had no business at the movies with his eyes so weak.

He hasn't been to the movies, said Molly. Not for a long time. He stays in bed. We only talk about the movies.

The neighbor said nothing. She stirred the hot chocolate but it burned. The scalding made a taste like dirt.

Molly's father came back and woke her up. It was almost light. He was by the window, pressing his hands on the glass. He said Callie was mighty sick; something in his head kept bleeding. They were going to the park, then to the hospital to see him.

The park was empty. By the pond, the carousel was already rusting under its pink and yellow roof. There was one black horse with its hooves in the air and its wild tongue slathering out. Her father lifted her up and put a quarter in the box. He sat on the bench. Every time Molly came around, his face was looking where she was. Her hands wouldn't move. She was crying with no sound and finally the music stopped. Her father sat on the bench in the rain with his head tilted, looking with his luminous eyes.

HOPELESS ACTS PERFORMED PROPERLY, WITH GRACE

ROBERT DUNN

Robert Dunn was born in Los Angeles, California, in 1950. He now lives in New York City and is on the editorial staff of *The New Yorker*. His stories and poems have appeared in *The Atlantic*, *Redbook*, *The Nation*, *The Carolina Quarterly*, and *The New Yorker*. A novel, *Negative Space*, will be published by Harper & Row.

When he was young, Peter Dreyer collected baseball cards voraciously but put them away when he was fifteen in a cardboard shoebox, grouped by teams, with a fat rubber band around each group. The box is at his parents' house in Los Angeles, three thousand miles away. Sometimes he gets the urge to riffle a stack, pull out a card and flip it against the wainscoting. When he moved across the country to New York he had his parents ship him a box of his college books, but he doesn't think they would understand why he wants his baseball cards. Peter doesn't understand either. He cares little for organized sports and prides himself on having no idea which team is first in the National Football League or what it means that Doctor J. has left the Nets. He thinks this complete disinterest in sports is one of his attractive features. No woman he ever lives with—Diane? the woman next door, whom he loves—will have to put up with a feet-on-the-sofa, beer-can-in-hand intoxication with TV sports. She'll have him to talk with her, to comment with interest on her *salade niçoise*, to take long walks through the park with her. She won't go to her job and complain about her husband or friend or roommate like the secre-

taries who sit outside his office. Peter is certain he'll always be so-
licitous of this woman when he finds her. At times he aches with
the desire to care for her.

Peter gets some comfort from an article in The New York
Times about changing demographic trends. More and more people are living alone, he reads; people are forsaking marriage, even
ceasing to live together. He reads about a woman in Washington,
a Congressional assistant, who told the reporter she enjoyed living
alone. She had more time to herself, she could do the things she
wanted to do, her life was her own. Peter also has time for himself, he does only the things he wants to do, his life *is* his own.
The Congressional assistant was happy. Peter reads the article
over a pastrami sandwich at a nearby delicatessen. It cheers him
up. Although the streets are icy with frozen snow, he takes a walk
before going home. He passes a long-haired couple with their
hands in each other's coats and it doesn't bother him; he doesn't
think of Diane. Later he reads an article by Mimi Sheraton, the
Times restaurant critic, in which she mentions some criteria to
judge a person's self-respect. They are: (1) having no holes in
your socks, (2) making your bed each morning even if no company is expected and (3) taking the time to prepare good food
even if you are dining alone. Peter's orlon socks look like fishnet
around the toes and are completely bare on the heel. The sleeping
bag and two blankets on his mattress on the floor are tangled and
only half cover the fitted sheet. And even though he hates himself
for doing it, dinner that night is, as usual, a can of chunky-style
soup, a small package of oven-ready buttermilk biscuits, coleslaw
out of a plastic tub and a glass of milk.

Peter's college friend David Halstrom writes from graduate
school at the University of Michigan: "Your letter was good for
me because it made me see that I'm not the only sad and dispos-
sessed man in North America, and because it provided a model
for enduring and getting on with things. What can these women
want? Your Diane has put you through a wringer, yet I think
you're doing all you can. Sometimes you have to wait for events to
reveal themselves. Herrigel says in *Zen in the Art of Archery*: 'You
must learn to wait properly.' It's always going to be like this: people like you and me are going to be waiting all our lives (for the

right woman, the right idea, the right work, the right appreciation). So we should try to perform this hopeless act properly, with grace."

Peter writes back: "Diane and I still aren't talking. I haven't seen her in a week, though I heard her moving around furniture Tuesday. Sometimes I hear her alarm clock go off. That upsets me for the rest of the day. I don't know if she's avoiding me or not. I try not to think of her and sometimes I don't, but trying to forget her usually brings her to mind. You're right, I guess—I'll just have to wait. But it's not easy. I need a vacation, a long boat trip or a sunny stretch of beach in Spain.

"Everything else? The proofreading job is slow. Spring, I'm told, will come. It was never this cold in Los Angeles. How are you in Ann Arbor? . . ."

Peter meets Diane at the trash chute. She's carrying a black plastic bag with an orange twist top. Peter's holding a brown supermarket bag with dark, oily stains. Diane smiles, not at him but past him. Peter doesn't know what to do. She's wearing her Bennington sweat shirt and bell-bottom denim jeans. She's barefoot. Her blond hair is pinned up. Peter looks at her, sees the gentle curve of her nose, remembers running his finger over it and feels a sharp pain in his chest. He turns away. Trying to pretend she's not there, he waits. She says nothing. His hands are shaking and a soup can falls out of the bag. As he picks it up he hears her door shut.

Peter thinks it's both a curse and a blessing that he never slept with Diane. Bad because if he had, there might be more between them now. He might feel he had more of a right to confront her. Good because he mostly misses the idea of her, the possibility of Diane as his lover. If he had slept with her, he'd miss the real person more, and that could only be worse. If she weren't next door, he's sure he'd forget her. As it is, he waits—for her to come to him or for her to move away or back in with her husband.

Peter didn't know Diane was married until after he'd fallen in love with her. Even then he didn't think it mattered. She rarely saw Ralph, and Peter was certain he never spent the night at Diane's apartment. But she wouldn't spend the night with Peter either. The subject had become endlessly tiresome, but it was unavoidable. The last time it had come up was in a Greenwich Village coffeehouse where they had gone after a Truffaut movie at the Bleecker Street Cinema.

"I don't feel right about it," Diane had said. "I'm still confused."

Peter wanted to say, "I love you." He had always thought there was a magic to the words that would disarm resistance. But each time he used the phrase, Diane got nervous. Her fingernails would click against the table. Once she spilled a glass of wine. That was when these discussions took place in her apartment. Weeks ago she stopped letting him come over in the evenings. His beseeching threatened direct action, and she said she'd see him only in a public place. That's when they started going out to movies and coffeehouses.

"You have me coming and going," Peter said. He was smoking cigarettes again, and banged the filter of one against the table. "I don't know what to do."

"Wait," she said. She took his hand and her finger ran over the curve between his thumb and pointer finger. "I have to straighten everything out."

"What do you want?"

"I'm not ready yet. I want you to be close. I want to know that I can count on you, that you're steady, that you'll wait."

Peter was angry. "That's a lot," he said. He took his hand away from hers. He needed a minute alone and got up to go to the toilet. There was a pay meter on the door and he fished through his change for a dime. Finally he broke a dollar with a waiter. When he got back to the table he had a speech set.

"I can't win. I'm damned if I do and now I'm damned if I don't. What you want is unjust. You want me *not* to love you and yet continue to love you. You show me no consideration. I want you—what's wrong with that? You have me feeling guilty for desiring you. That's a terrible thing."

"Don't be angry," Diane said. Peter said nothing. He waited, but she didn't move or say anything else. He stood up and dropped two dollars on the table.

"I'm not angry," he said. "I needed to say some final words and that was it. Can you get home all right by yourself?"

Diane nodded. Peter left.

He decided he'd wait up until two for Diane to return, figuring that she'd come to him or she wouldn't come back at all, that she'd be so upset by his speech that she'd go stay with Ralph. He wanted her to be that upset. So he was surprised when he heard her door open and close five minutes after he got home. He was even more surprised when she passed him in the hall the next day without speaking, and when she didn't acknowledge the African violet plant he left outside her door that evening.

Peter faces another Saturday. It stretches before him like a wide superhighway shooting straight through the desert, with few turnoffs and little of passing interest. There are a few bright spots —one, at eight P.M., when reruns of *The Mary Tyler Moore Show* come on TV. Even this pleasure is compromised, though, by the thought that there are thousands of women, many of whom he'd like, many of whom would like him, watching the same TV show and thinking the same thoughts. At ten thirty Peter goes out for the Times and at eleven thirty watches *Saturday Night Live* while reading the Times Book Review during the commercials. Fortunately his sleep is untroubled.

This Saturday, Peter decides to go out. It's the first warm weekend since November. The winter, everyone says, has been extraordinarily cold. It is his first winter out of southern California, so he has nothing to judge it by. Still, it kept him indoors too much. When he first came to New York, last July, his greatest pleasure was taking long walks. On free days he'd strike out in an arbitrary direction. Always he'd see something of interest—a wind quintet playing Telemann in the park; a building he'd heard of, like the Dakota Apartments, where people said they'd filmed *Rosemary's Baby*. Now he's pleased it's so warm that his breath doesn't mist before him. He walks into the park.

Peter is actively looking for a new girl friend, but he's doing a poor job of it. The affair with Diane has sapped his confidence, which was never too full, and he's much shyer than at other times. It's hard not knowing anyone well here in New York. He waits for someone to invite him to a dinner party and introduce him to an aspiring actress. He expects a dancer will bump into him in the market where he buys his soup, take pity on his lean purchases and invite him home for dinner. So far, nothing like this has happened.

There's a dark-haired woman in a green ski parka throwing a stick to a German shepherd, who, after fetching it, coyly prances around the woman for a minute before she can coax the stick away from him. Peter sits on a wooden bench and watches. He hopes she'll throw the stick by mistake toward him so he can return it and talk with her. Although she's pretty, Peter doesn't really care for the way she looks; yet he does want to meet her. He's become a great and indiscriminate believer in fate. He hardly knows what he wants any more, so he awaits signs that will tell him. Maybe the girl with the stick is the mate destiny has planned for him. Peter supposes that if she lost a little weight, he could get along with her. Probably he could get used to her too-thick eyebrows and weak chin. The dog is slavering onto the wet grass and the woman is retying a calico scarf over her head. She throws the stick again, but the dog is uninterested. "All right, George," she calls to him. "We can go home now." The dog runs up to her and then dashes down the path toward the place where Peter sits. The girl follows. The dog stops before Peter and then leaps up at him. Peter holds him back with two hands. The dog licks Peter. "George, down!" the girl says. "Sorry," she says to Peter. She unrolls a leather leash and clips it onto the dog's collar. "George, come!" she says. It's clear she's not going to stop. Her brown hair flounces beneath her scarf as she walks away.

Peter wakes up and wonders if he should go to work. He has a sore spot way back in his throat. A while back he read an article in *Esquire* about "Lonely Guys." Lonely guys, the article said, have colds all the time. They get strep throat and always have bronchitis. This makes being a lonely guy worse because there is no one to care for him. Peter's throat is definitely raw. He has trouble swallowing. When he was young he could get out of going to school if his father okayed it. He'd take a flashlight and peer into Peter's throat. If he saw an inflammation, Peter could stay home. Peter doesn't have a regular flashlight but he does have a penlight. He stands before the bathroom mirror, twisting his face around so he can see the light shining on the back of his throat. He finally gets everything aligned and his throat does look red, but he's not sure if it's red enough. He goes to work anyway.

Peter hasn't heard a sound from Diane's apartment for four days. At first he was worried that she might have fallen or got sick, or something, but after thinking about it he decides that she is probably just out, and that going to her would be pointless if not inappropriate. He has good reason to stay away from her. The last time they talked it went badly. They were riding up in the elevator together.

"I want to have a talk with you," he said. He couldn't look at her or anything else. "I have to get some things straight."

"I'd be much happier if you didn't bother me," Diane said. She wasn't smiling, but she wasn't not smiling. There was no rancor; she sounded friendly, but without interest in him. The elevator stopped and a woman got in. Peter said nothing. Diane's indifference disarmed him. He was prepared to argue with her, even throw himself before her if she spurned him, but he was not ready for her pleasant, curt response. It had no feeling. He thought she cared something for him, but now it seemed she didn't.

The elevator opened onto their floor. Peter followed Diane out. "Diane—" he said.

She turned; her blond hair flipped. She looked straight at him. "Sorry," she said.

Later Peter decided that her look expressed nothing but deep pity for him. He didn't move until she'd gone into her apartment; then he slunk into his own.

After this Peter knew that approaching her would be humiliating. He was willing to humiliate himself except that he knew it wouldn't do any good and that she'd despise him for it. So he ignores her too. On the fifth day his worry gets the best of him and he knocks on her door. There is no answer. He stops himself before he goes to ask the super to let him in. Two days later he hears her door shut and a Linda Ronstadt record play loudly from her stereo.

Peter likes going to movies alone. He sees what he wants to see; he gives the movie his full attention. He's about to go to a double bill of Robert Altman films when his phone rings. It's Diane; she

asks him if he'd like to go to Avery Fisher Hall to hear the New
York Philharmonic. She says a friend gave her two tickets. Peter is
speechless. Diane's voice is sunny; it's as if there has been no
strain between them. A touch of pride makes him pause and think
to answer that he's busy, but he doesn't. It is Diane on the phone.
"Sure," he tells her. "I'll be over in a minute."

Peter keeps his distance from Diane on the subway and even in
the orchestra seat next to her. It's an all-Mozart performance:
The Masonic Funeral Music, an early divertimento, and the
"Haffner" symphony. Diane is enjoying herself. She is smiling; occasionally her head bobs and her gold, pagoda-shaped earrings jan-
gle. Peter hardly hears the music. Though Diane is not wearing
perfume, something rises off her that Peter is extraordinarly sensitive to. Perhaps it's her body warmth. He tries not to look at her,
but does constantly. She's wearing an apricot-colored blouse with
a Peter Pan collar. Her neck is white and smooth. Peter wipes his
wet hands on his pants leg; then he sets his right hand on the
armrest. Diane's hand falls onto his forearm. He thinks she gives
it a squeeze but he's not sure. She doesn't look at him.

After the symphony Peter can hardly speak. As they wait for
the bus Diane prattles on about a tennis game she played last
weekend. Peter, who couldn't care less about tennis, listens atten-
tively. The bus comes and they find seats. Diane's talking now
about Easter with her family in Larchmont. Her younger brother
said he was going to leave college and her father beat him. Diane
was terribly upset. Peter wonders how she can be so calm now. All
he can do is nod his head and mumble that it's all very interesting.

Diane stops talking when they're in the elevator going up to
their floor. She smiles widely at him, and even winks. Peter
doesn't know what's going on. She's getting ready to do something, though, something unexpected. For a second Peter thinks
she might shoot him. He waits for her hand to go into her purse.
The elevator stops and Peter pulls the handle to open it. They
stand apart, looking at each other.

"Do you mind if I come in?" Diane asks.

Peter waits to answer. He feels his blood course through his
body. Two fingers seem to be pressing against his temples.

"Please," he says.

Inside, Peter apologizes for the mess. Diane says it looks fine to her. She picks up a guitar he bought in Mexico seven years before. It has only five strings and is hopelessly out of tune. She runs a long fingernail down the strings and says, "So, how have you been?"

Peter's decided he's much too nervous to be direct with Diane, and he answers, "Fine, though it's been a cold winter. I've been okay. How have you been?"

"Oh, all right."

"I haven't seen you much lately."

"Oh, I've been busy."

"Doing what?"

"Things . . ."

"I've been busy too," Peter says. He doesn't know why the conversation goes so poorly, and wants to do something about it.

Diane sets the guitar down, tilting it against an end table, and lies back on the couch, propping up her head with two pillows. Her fingers play with a loose curl of hair; her eyelids seem to flutter. This makes Peter jump up and pace across the oval throw rug in front of the couch. He looks at Diane, who seems very comfortable, very much at home there, but also untouchable, like a Chinese vase that's had a place in the family for generations. He's fidgeting with a cigarette and trying to think what to say next when she speaks.

"Peter, do you mind if I stay here with you tonight?"

Peter is startled. He stops moving and looks at her. What can this mean? Does she mean sleep with him?

"Why?" Peter asks, but he swallows the word so it comes out like a cough.

"Excuse me?" Diane says. She's still smiling. Not a line of doubt seems to crease her wide forehead.

"May I ask why?" Peter says.

"I've missed you."

"Why have you been ignoring me, then?"

"I haven't been ignoring you," Diane says. She extends her hand toward Peter. Her fingers wiggle. "I've been busy."

"Diane . . ." he says, but what he meant to say—"Why are you doing this to me? Why are you so capricious?"—is choked off and lost in a quake of uncertainty. "Can I get you something to drink?" he says instead. He shuffles off to the tiny kitchen.

"Please, a glass of white wine."

In the kitchen he pauses. He looks at a wall calendar that Diane gave him for Christmas, with bushels of wheat and ears of corn around the dates, but can't focus on it. He should be happy. But he's just confused. He has an open bottle of Rhine wine in the refrigerator, and he pours two glasses. Back in the other room, Diane beckons him to the couch. He still doesn't know what to expect.

"Why do you want to spend the night here?" he asks. He sits next to her and hands her the teardrop-shaped glass.

Diane gives him a quizzical look, as if he were a dim child. She smiles with the corner of her mouth.

"Do you want to sleep with me?" Peter asks.

"Yes," Diane says. The word comes short and with little breath. Though both of them hold their wineglasses before them, neither thinks to make a toast.

Peter aches with desire. The questions he's been afraid to ask for months come to his mind and mix with the desire: Why *has* Diane ignored him? Does she care at all for him? Does she think of him as he thinks of her? Did she ever? Is she seeing Ralph regularly? Is she going to move back with him? Is she seeing anyone else? And now, why is she here? He sits beside her and tries not to think, to drive these questions away. At points later in the evening, glasses tinkle against each other, pillows are rearranged, the heels of Diane's boots drop with a thud against the floor.

Four days later Diane meets Peter for lunch at a Szechwan Chinese restaurant and tells him she doesn't want to see him any longer. Peter's been expecting something like this. Although they spent two more nights together after the first (though not the night before), Peter was never able to relax or feel certain of Diane's moods. One night they had dinner at Diane's, and then sat talking. Diane went on happily about a veal dish she had learned to make at her French cooking class, and then they talked about a D. H. Lawrence novel she was reading. She left him to do the dishes, and when she got back her mood had changed. She turned on the TV and sat impassively beside him. Peter draped an arm over her shoulders and hugged her to him, but she didn't react and moved like a dead weight. He became nervous, but kept his arm over her shoulder until it started to go dead, and then he was too self-conscious to move it. He didn't know where she had slipped away to, and felt too uncomfortable to ask. After twenty minutes she livened up, and they were able to get through the night.

Now Diane is looking at Peter and asking if their separation is all right with him. The hot-and-sour soup comes and he waits for the waiter to leave. He still wants her and his heart is breaking, but he doesn't know what to say. He knows he can't talk her into loving him, so what good would argument do?

He nods languidly and agrees. Through the meal they make only small talk.

The rest of the day is hell. When he gets home from work there's a letter from David. Peter reads: "I've become involved in a semisecret affair with the wife of a lecturer in Russian. She's pretty and brilliant, twenty-six, bored with her husband but still attached to him. The affair has been marvelous and important to me because it offsets to some degree my theory of my own personality, one that has been growing like a cancer inside me for a long time: viz., that I was a dark, cold and empty person, a human black hole, an eccentric for whom there was no place in normal human relations. Of course, it may be argued that sleeping with the wives of other men hardly describes normal human relations. But still, it's something a dead star couldn't do, and I'm a little encouraged by it. While I don't think there's any danger that I'll ever become a decent and generally acceptable human being, there is now tangible proof that I'm not Caliban either."

Peter waits a week and then writes back: "I'm glad things go well for you. I'm on a teeter-totter here, worse than usual. Last week Diane and I were together for three days. It was very, very good. Then, for no clear reason, we stopped seeing each other and now we avoid each other again. I don't understand it. I think she's seeing her husband. I can hear his key in her door when he comes over late in the evening. Maybe she'll go back to him and get out of my life.

"I need a change. Almost everything seems stale to me, even spring. I'm told I won't get a vacation until September. I've been

trying to go see John Rubinstein in New Haven, but he's involved
with a big project and has no free time. If I simply want to get
out of Manhattan for a day, he says, I can come visit, but he
can't do any more than have dinner with me. I don't see any
point to it, and continue to waste away here. . . ."

In the hallway outside his apartment Peter bumps into Ralph.
Peter's met him before, and they shake hands. Ralph is wearing a
polo shirt and tennis shorts. A blue-and-white-striped headband
rises above his forehead. Ralph is in a good mood—he swings his
right arm back and forth as if he were practicing his forehand
and backhand. Peter has just bought a ten-speed bicycle in honor
of spring, and he asks Ralph to hold it upright while he unlocks
his door. Diane comes into the hallway, carrying a tennis racket
and a can of tennis balls. She greets Peter, who looks back at her
over his shoulder. The situation should be awkward, but Peter
seems to be the only one who thinks it is. He inhales deeply and
then says, "Have a good game."
    "Thanks," Ralph says.
    Peter takes the bicycle from him and wheels it into his vesti-
bule. He hears each link of the bike chain click as it falls into the
sprocket. The elevator opens and closes. He leans the bicycle
against the wall and cringes at the thought of the impossibility of
his situation.

Peter has got a stack of train timetables from Pennsylvania Station. He stretches out on his couch, turns the floor lamp on and
looks through them. A professor of his who once taught a year in
Japan told him that the Japanese regularly pass the time by reading train schedules. It simulates trips they can't take; it carries
them away from their problems. Peter picks at random the flyer
for the Southwest Limited. His eyes run over the list of cities:

> 6 10p New York (Penn. Station)
> 6 25p Newark (Penn. Station)
> 7 05p Trenton
> 7 33p North Philadelphia
> 9 38p Harrisburg
> 3 24a Pittsburgh (Penn. Station)
> 8 05a Columbus . . .

He reaches back and adjusts the pillow behind his head. He imagines the clack of steel wheels roaring over the rails. For quite a while he lies there, absorbed. "This is Santa Fe," he says quietly to himself. "The next stop is Albuquerque."

A week later Peter takes a train from Grand Central to see John Rubinstein in New Haven. John's still too busy to see him but Peter doesn't care; he has to get away. At night he dreams of Diane and hears her moving around next door even when she's not there.

At Grand Central, Peter buys a weekend Post and on the train desultorily leafs through it. Nothing catches his interest. He shoves it under the seat and stares out the window at the parking lots, back yards, glimpses of brackish-looking bay and the backs of factories that surround Bridgeport. The train's half full, and Peter sees the crowns of people's heads pop above the seats in front of him. Fewer people are parting their hair on the left, he notices. Many have no parts at all. Two rows in front of him and across the aisle is a woman with blond hair the shade and cut of Diane's. Could it be she? His fingers beat against the dusty window glass. He tucks his traveling bag out of sight in the seat well, leaves his coat on his seat and walks toward the front of the train. He's too uneasy to turn and look at her, so he goes three cars forward to the club car, buys a soda and heads back. The woman has a fat, blue-covered paperback held up close to her eyes, so Peter can't see her too clearly, but he's sure it's not Diane. The blond woman looks enough like her, though, to attract him. No one's sitting next to her; the seat doesn't even have a book bag or coat on it. Peter slows as he passes her, but she doesn't look up. For a second he wants to stop and talk to her, but doesn't and retakes his seat.

Is he crazy? he wonders. Peter sees her hand—a small, graceful hand with a jade ring on her ring finger—rise above the seat back and stroke her hair. She has beautiful hair. Should he talk to her? Peter recently read the book the woman is reading—a biography of Samuel Johnson—and he could ask her what she thinks of it. Peter continues thinking back and forth about whether he should talk to her until all rational reasons for either case fall away and it's a simple question of whether he has the courage to approach her. A few minutes after the train conductor swings through the car announcing, "Milford, next stop is Milford," he does.

FATAL

HELEN CHASIN

Helen Chasin has written two volumes of poetry, *Casting
Stones* (Little, Brown) and *Coming Close* (Yale University
Press). She has published with *The New Republic* and *The
Paris Review*. She was a winner of the Yale Younger Poets
Award. Her story "Marriage" received honorable mention in
Pushcart Press.

My doctor says I am not contagious. What I have is common:
Vera and Marian have had it, Michelle read about it in *Cosmopolitan*. Most typically it results from heavy sex following a period
of abstinence; my doctor has just in effect described last weekend,
so I do not have cancer. As always I am very relieved to find out.
However, I neglected to ask how long a period of abstinence is.
Vera says the moral is obvious, you have to have regular sex, to be
on the safe side let's say regular heavy sex, don't forget I am a very
sexual person. Also I'm in my late 30s, this is my peak right now.
I'm beginning to feel dangerous.

There are beautiful men everywhere. All kinds. On the street, in
the museum, at the airport, during rock concerts, even poetry
readings, even blonds and they are not my type. So far it is just
aesthetic. Jeans, corduroys, three-piece pinstripes . . . sometimes
our eyes meet and we smile, an acknowledgment, I wonder
whether I could be happy with him, maybe a life together, we
pass. Suppose this is merely the tip of the iceberg, the thin end of
the wedge? I may be insatiable. Maybe I'm going to end up in the
literature.

Vanessa S, later the beautiful Vanessa B, reports experiencing

sexual response at age four; of anything at all prior to that time
she has no memory. What energy! She appears in everyone's auto-
biography: cherished wife and mother, beloved sister, inspiring
colleague, adorable companion of quite a few. And talented; if we
are to believe the accounts of family and friends she never became
the artist she would have been.

My condition is, during onset, so painful that there's no doing
anything else except suffer. The medicine is a miracle—within 12
hours you can get back to the usual, though you have to continue
treatment for a while; the pain is a symptom, it's not the disease.

They always say that.

It turns out that the old argument that chastity can't hurt you
is valid up to a point—that point being the one at which you
abandon it.

Only they don't call it chastity anymore.

When is the last time you heard anyone say, "She sleeps
around," about anyone? And how many constitutes *around*?

Think of beautiful, intense Edna M, literary toast of America,
given to sleeping around and drinking. Maybe a little reefer at an
occasional Saturday night Greenwich Village party. Subsequently
she married a businessman and settled down to life in the country
and a heavy habit; her friends could tell by her eyes. She was a
good example, my mother said, of how you could love a rich man
as easily as a poor one.

I do not find that to be true. I do not find the opposite to be
true either. It's worse, it's more complex.

All three of my lovers live out of town. None is poor, on the
other hand no one's a Rockefeller. All three know each other professionally, and don't know I know the other two. Two are dark,
one is blond. They are all taller and two are older than I am. The
oldest is 26 years older than the youngest. One of them thinks one
of the others is a fuck and the other a cop-out. The cop-out thinks
one of the dark ones has talent but he's immature and there's a
problem about women. My daughter is rooting for the fuck, even
though he is not the one who likes rock and roll. They all think I
am bright, sensitive and interesting; one thinks I am highly eccentric, one says (possibly for effect) he thinks I am crazy. One of
them is very close to being crazy himself. One of the normals
claims to feel alienated from his life. They all think I'm sophis-

ticated. Of the two who arc not married, one never has been. The two who like elegant restaurants are neither the same as the two sports car freaks nor the two who smoke dope. They all have terrific telephone voices. There is a lot of talking.

All of us have gone out to dinner, spent at least one afternoon at a museum, discussed his work in depth. With two I've gone to the Saturday midnight showing of *The Harder They Come*, been to a poetry reading, picnicked in Central Park, made love all night, played pool upstairs at David and Vera's. These are the unique events: a discotheque, the Staten Island Ferry, doing coke, visiting the sister who may be about to have a breakdown and kill herself, body oil. Two of them have met Marian and two Michelle. One of them has seen me not answer the phone, just let it ring and later when it started ringing again not pick it up again. He has concluded that not answering the phone is a practice of mine but he's wrong. I thought it was the fuck and I couldn't handle it. Actually I have no practices.

Here is what has not happened: a fight, one of those long walks in the snow where it's as beautiful as a black-and-white photograph, a pregnancy scare, the scene in which you run into someone it would be better not to or someone who says something and 20 minutes afterward you're still shaking. Another thing that hasn't happened is group sex, and then later you have to deal with it.

On the other hand, this whole situation is a potential situation. Or maybe it is already. Of course it could be worse, they could all live here.

A small, dark, intense, attractive young Englishwoman, Katherine M, was married but kept going away. For her health. She sent letters back: when I come home we will be so happy, my darling, and never be separated again, we will drink tea in the evenings and smoke a cigarette. There are many letters. And a journal, in which a lot of men are referred to obliquely, although this may be a result of editing: a smile, a nationality, a red flower at the train station. These encounters were good for her, they helped her to miss the husband more, and their adorable little house. She died of consumption in a community of Russian mystics. Some of her stories could tear your heart out.

I have never called one of my lovers by another one's name,

even in moments of great passion. That would be absolutely the worst, I couldn't forgive myself. Not that the wrong name doesn't surface sometimes, hover, loom. It does—and from last year too, and before that, maybe a previous life—but I take care, I censor, I maintain a kind of eternal vigilance. Certain names threaten more frequently than others, there's one in particular . . . however my ex-husband's never occurs to me, sometimes even when I'm trying to think of it. Talking with my daughter, for example, I fudge, I stall, I refer to him as "your father." Or "daddy" if I'm feeling friendly. This forgetting is probably emotional. As you might expect there are overlaps: three Michaels, two Jacks, two Maximillians. In such cases I would be the only person to know if I made a mistake.

Five poets, four painters, three lawyers, two photographers, and a partner in a brokerage firm. Actually there have been others but they didn't last long.

All three of my lovers have very unusual names. So unusual that you'd never guess even if they locked you in a tower.

What do they think I'm doing when they aren't around? But they don't ask. What do they think my life is like?

Sometimes I try to picture what the weather is like where they are, the landscape. I imagine them reading, or working or being lonely. One of them is in another time zone. That means it's happening later, or earlier, like light years.

Of course my life is here. I think there are more beautiful men in this town than anywhere except Italy. Michelle says that all of the men in her neighborhood are homosexual. She takes them personally; the walk from her subway stop to her apartment is depressing, going for groceries infuriates her. Either they pay no attention to her at all or they do but it's just aesthetic, so what's the point? Michelle wants results. She wants to impinge: men trembling with desire, falling at her feet, offering the moon. Well everyone likes to be appreciated. The problem is in the fineness of the line between wanting action and looking for trouble. Sometimes you end up reading about it in the newspapers. Or a textbook.

The following ad appeared recently among the Personals in the *Village Voice* Classified:

> *Very attractive single male of 38, professional; highly educated, well traveled & well versed has fatal weakness for fatal women. Would like to hear from those still at large for nocturnal meetings in Manhattan & possibly long term romance.*

Of course your authentic femme fatale doesn't respond to a summons, she just materializes and ruins a person's life. Either Well Versed does not enjoy the pathology he claims or he hasn't encountered the genuine article. How long-term could he expect the affair to be? And "still at large" as opposed to what—imprisonment, death, mandatory retirement? Whatever this man does for a living he can't be a poet or a painter, he's too romantic. And he doesn't have his days free.

My daughter thinks I am irresistible. Not to her, to men. All men: I can have anyone I want, if I like them they like me back, they have no choice. My daughter is bright, sensitive, interesting, sophisticated and she is making a big mistake. She thinks I have these powers . . . She also thinks that sex for anyone past 40 is disgusting, except Paul Newman, which doesn't leave some of us a lot of time. When I pointed out that even if she started in immediately that would give her only 25 years she said, "Okay, past 45."

"Just wait," I said. I always say that. It's my concept of karma.

The three lovers are not the only men in my life. I have a son who lives with his father. I also have an obscene caller. For openers he said, "Hi there." He sounded so cheery, confiding, in fact optimistic . . . whoever it was I felt delighted to hear from him, hopeful even. Then he ruined it.

Actually his voice is a boy's. I wonder what he looks like.

He's been with me for six months now, it's getting to be a long-term relationship. The contacts are intermittent but highly charged. He's gone from talking to breathing to heavy moaning. I guess the carrying-on at the other end is supposed to sound like sex but it's a little off—more like someone doing an impression of sex, or a kind of soliloquy.

My father says the typical picture of these people is around 17, passive, withdrawn and afraid of women but they outgrow it. My daughter says he's not outgrowing it fast enough.

When I referred to him as "my pervert" one of my lovers said I sounded a little possessive.

Well of course, he's in my life, there's this connection, intercourse, *engagement*. Hi There won't let go and I can't, it's not up to me. Whoever he is we're in this together.

Last week a politician on the six o'clock news said about an opponent, "There was no confrontation. If there *was* a confrontation it was unilateral—on his part."

Sometimes I want to answer my pervert back, say it's all talk, I bet he can't get it up, suggest he's no Mick Jagger—but I'm afraid he'll rush over and kill me. With an axe. Impossible, my father says, he can't that's his problem.

Sometimes I picture this creep in his horrible, pathetic little Dickensian furnished room working himself into an obsessive froth. Three-thirty at night, six in the morning, only my actual voice can satisfy those spasmy yearnings. Maybe I'm there in his head all the time and the pressure builds; the froth is only a symptom. Maybe I'm driving him crazy.

The bastard is driving *me* crazy, and my daughter too. I hope he's in pain. My father says of course he's in pain, he's sick, but I mean real pain, not psychology.

When my friend Jeremy telephones he sounds like the pervert, but that's impossible because Jeremy and Barbara were visiting me one night when I got one of those calls. Unless, as my daughter and Barbara pointed out, Jeremy is diabolical. But I can't live like that. About every two or three weeks Jeremy calls and we have long conversations; he tells me the real story behind that stuff you read in the papers: Anjelica H, Elizabeth T, Bianca J, Olivia N-J. The real story often turns out to be in the direction of freaky. People have these predilections, and proclivities. They have these sides to them. Some people even have depths, but I don't know any. The people I know have moods, but that's different.

A long time ago when I was in treatment—never really completed, according to the shrink, there are a few problems we didn't resolve—I thought there were no secrets, just burdens of guilt and questions of definition. But I outgrew that.

I have a secret self. She is afraid she will be found out, and so am I. Encountering the phrase "the woman in me" makes me nervous: when she finally materializes she will ruin my life. She is more real than I because she is inevitable. She is older and fatter and shorter than I am. She has little piggy eyes and her skin is decaying. Over the big moldy housedress she wears a message T-shirt, a vest, sweaters. Her broken-down cotton stockings are rolled just above her knees; she also wears ankle socks and shredded sneakers. She carries around everywhere and at all times three shopping bags full of crap: Gristede's, Bloomingdale's, Astor Wines and Liquors. Talking to herself but right out loud SHE DOES NOT GIVE A FUCK ABOUT THE ROLLING STONES. At the bottom of the Gristede's bag there's a bunch of ratty scraps, smeary pieces of poems.

"Do you think I'm a weirdo?" Janice asks, because she has left the city and is living in a religious community upstate. The landscape is beautiful. They are all women there. Devotion, cooperation, contemplation, celibacy.

When Janice comes in to pick up her unemployment check we have dinner together. Last Wednesday night we witnessed one psychodrama, two heavy street scenes, and a case of hysterical derangement in a bar—gently escorted by police, its exit line was, "And don't call me *dear*, this is the Upper West Side."

Why should Janice be a weirdo? She is relaxed, she doesn't keep getting colds and flu, her work is better than ever. This is why: people keep saying that celibacy comes out of sickness: neurotic, afraid of men, mind/body dichotomy. These women ought to confront their true nature as lesbians, the lesbians said just before they left the group, never mind that social action and spiritual business. Everyone has a diagnosis. In fact the only thing wrong with celibacy is that quitting can make you sick.

Once when I was in college I mentioned to some guy that I liked sweating, the feel of it. He said, "Fenichel calls that skin eroticism."

Jeremy's aunt has a disease—who knows what? There are occasional remissions. The uncle is under continual strain, but hopeful. Every so often he issues bulletins:

We just turned the corner.
Things are looking up.
We just found another doctor and things are gonna be OK.

When I said to my shrink, "I am not afraid of men," he said,
"I know." Thereby managing for once to surprise me.

Here is what I'm afraid of: that I use people up.

About the fires raging in Santa Barbara and threatening LA, a
woman sunning herself into cancer beside a pool in Reno Nevada
remarked, "They've got it out of control."

The three out-of-town lovers, for example, and the pervert are
not the whole story. I have these recurring love dreams: E. L.
Doctorow, Mick Jagger, and Jimmy Cliff. It isn't sex, they take
place in broad daylight, out-of-doors, and he and I are intensely
happy, arm-in-arm, laughing, almost dancing, a regular Coke ad.

The cop-out got upset about Jimmy Cliff. He does not like this
black person's being in my dreams. Because darkness represents
overwhelming, dangerous, forbidden sexuality.

As opposed, say, to Mick Jagger?

What he really means is "that is your illness speaking:" jungle
music, a stud in my bedroom at night, death. What he means is
something about my using him up.

Here is another ad that ran in the *Voice* Personals:

> *Sagittarius. Male inmate. ½ Indian, ½ Black, 6′2″. At-*
> *tending college. Seeking correspondence with woman.*
> *Interested?*
> *#86B1846*
> *Box 17, Comstock, N.Y.*

Sagittarius is taller than one of the lovers and probably darker
than all three of them. Also it could be said that he's more deeply
out-of-town than all of them. Think of the opportunities for contemplation and abstinence. My daughter is interested to know
what he did to land in the slammer.

I am interested in intensity.

A tall blonde attractive American who took up residence
abroad, Sylvia P made much of adoring sex, how healthy it was,
collected newspaper clippings about violent crimes, and killed her-

self shortly before becoming one of the major figures in contemporary writing. One of my former lovers—whose own work is incomprehensible but nonetheless tedious—said of Sylvia P's poetry that ultimately it was disappointing; you couldn't live there.

There is a man who is living with me who is not my lover but he probably will be and it won't work out. He is a tall dark elegant doper. Having a conversation with him is like talking on the phone. He wants peace and I want passion. Neither of us is getting it. He says passion is for literature.

IN CASE OF SURVIVAL

T. GERTLER

T. Gertler lives in New York City.

Late one night, under the sliver of light from his bedside lamp, Harold Stein composed a letter he had long contemplated.

> *Dear Friends,*
>   *An accident is an accident, but what do you call an accident that gives a preview? My wife and I were supposed to take Flight 6 from New York to Miami four months ago. Because I had a premonition of some disaster, I kept us from getting on the plane, and this plane crushed, as you know. Maybe it would have been impossible to convince other people on the basis of the strong sort of nauseous feeling I had, but I think now I should have tried. All that could have happened would be that I would have made a fool of myself or the airline would have sued me for defamation of character. That would be nothing compared to saving twenty-seven lives and other injuries. I'm writing this letter to you to apologize if you lost a loved one or were yourself injured or just upset by being on that plane. It's not much, but it's all I can do.*
>   *Also, I have two shoe stores for ladies, Stein's Footwear in Bal Harbour and one on the Lincoln Road Mall and I would be very happy if you could stop by any time so I could fit you with a complimentary pair of shoes. This may sound foolish, but it would be something I can*

do. Since I am mainly in the Bal Harbour store, it would
be better if you came there.
   Again, I am deeply sorry.

                                          Sincerely yours,

The next morning, his wife, Natalie, complained about a
dream. "I can't remember it," she said. Though he wanted the list
of passengers on the plane, he decided not to ask her where she
kept her newspaper clippings about the crash. He folded the letter
and put it behind his driver's license in his wallet.

There were nights when Harold slept well, nights when he stood
poised on a peak ringed with clouds, then jumped easily, gracefully, into the sea below. He could feel the perfect arch of his
body as he descended, could feel air rushing past him at just the
right speed, in just the right places. This was how it had been for
him years ago at swimming pools and once on a Caribbean island.
He knew that he pierced the water precisely at a ninety-degree
angle and that the surface showed not even a ripple as he passed
beneath it.

There were other nights, nights when he stood on his cloud-
ringed peak and looked down and saw nothing. And jumped
blindly and could feel only terror as he plummeted down. He kept
waking before he landed, dozing off and waking; each time he
checked the shimmering blue-green face of the clock on his night
table and felt the dreaming presence of Natalie beside him.

He would lie in the dark, his eyes open, and imagine the
twenty-seven people who had died on the plane and the people
who had been injured. He remembered faces from among the
crowd at the gate: the black man in priest's clothing, a mono-
chrome figure except for the slash of white collar; the thin, nervous girl of about eighteen with a nose like his older daughter
Edith's original one, his own; the bent woman who for no reason
other than great age reminded him of his mother before she died.
He wondered if these people had survived, or the ones who had
passed him in the boarding corridor as he was already hearing
their screams and feeling his stomach contract with the plane's
shuddering drop. In some equation he could not express, he knew

he owed those passengers something, clearly more than shoes. It was on a night like this that he wrote his letter.

He suffered because his refusal to board the plane had made him, to his wife, a hero. The dread that had assaulted him in the boarding corridor was not heroic. The memory of it sent chills along the backs of his upper arms and calves. He had seen the plane fall. One minute it was gliding through gray sky; then, in unimaginable silence, it dropped, and the screaming inside the plane began. Someone called for God. Ice shot from a plastic glass and struck a window across the aisle. This vision seized him as he and his wife walked toward the plane. It was simple: You did not enter a plane that you knew was going to fall. Natalie said, "Let's go," when he halted. She pulled slightly at him; he pulled slightly back.

"C'mon," she said, and started to walk on. If she had said, "What is it?" or said nothing at all but waited for him to explain, he wouldn't have hit her. Transformed by his vision, in a burst of surrender to the certainty of a crash, he stopped her with a right hook to the jaw that kept her from going forward, that sent her, miraculously, down. His small and at times overpowering wife, whom he had never hurt before and would never hurt again, looked up at him for a moment with the new emotion of pure surprise before she blacked out. Later, telling and retelling the story to friends, she seemed to relish Harold's violence, as if that terrible act, which belied the courtesy of all their years together, proved the force of his love for her. The truth, as he understood it, was baser: He had hit her to keep her from entering the plane because he knew that if she entered the plane, he would have to go, too, and he did not want to go.

Shame and the helplessness of shame confused him; disloyal, he accepted Natalie's ignorance of his feelings as he had after a long-ago weekend with a woman in another city. Still, he felt he must confess something to his wife—if not that truth, then some other horrible truth that linked and yet separated them, like the coupling between train cars. He could not discover it. If, in refusing to board the plane, he had discerned the future, what was preventing him from reading the present?

Sometimes, when he looked at his lathered face in the mirror and saw the approaching razor, he felt he was going to cut himself. The blood mingling with soap and stray whiskers had not been drawn, but he saw it as clearly as if it had. He became lost in the different times, had to remember that the blood was not there, that he was still unshaved. Then he shaved and, no matter how careful he was, cut himself. The sting was doubly painful, carrying as it did the weight of future remembered and present past. And—"Damn, damn," he muttered as he fumbled through medicine cabinet and sent the economy-size unwaxed dental floss flying into the toilet; he could never find a styptic pencil when he needed it.

Dr. Ira Blume, at the university, read about Harold in *The Miami Herald* and telephoned him. "I'd like to evaluate your potential paranormality," Blume's voice said. When Harold said nothing, Blume went on: "That's ESP we're talking about, Mr. Stein."

Harold said, "Forget it."

Blume: "You want to talk about guilt?"

Harold arrived at Blume's lab early, stayed late. Blume dazzled him with cards and patterns. Harold said, "We were going to talk."

Blume shuffled an oversize deck. "Your conception of yourself as having failed in a communal crisis evidences itself as guilt. You show survivor's syndrome. And you're terrified you may have had a psychic episode. Pick a card."

Harold: "It was a coincidence."

Blume: "Sounds reasonable. A hundred times a day in a hundred different airports some bozo is chickening out of a plane ride. Ninety-nine point X percent of those babies don't crash."

"Coincidence."

"Bet your ass. Can you come in next week?"

Blume submitted a paper to a learned journal. "Accuracy in measuring the unknown is essential to the methodology if we are to describe that unknown. Too often in too many statistics the ambiguous is classified and the merely coincidental masquerades as the phenomenal. How do we isolate psychic energy if all we can do is flip coins?" he wrote. Natalie put a copy of *American Parapsychological Review* on the coffee table. Harold had trouble finding *TV Guide*, which had always been on the coffee table before.

Natalie invited Blume to dinner, where he met the Steins' younger daughter, Cheryl.

"I'm minoring in psych," Cheryl told Blume, and for the first time it occurred to Harold that Blume was young and probably handsome.

Blume asked Cheryl if she'd like to undergo tests for ESP.

Harold said no.

Cheryl said yes.

Harold's friend and business partner, Mac Lishinsky, told him, "Relax. So you know you're going to cut yourself before you cut yourself. I'll tell you something, you should know you're not alone. Every night I know I'm gonna hate being home even before I get home. So what do you think about that?"

Mac Lishinsky, Danny Silver, and Frank Merwitz refused to play gin with Harold anymore.

"Can you or can you not tell me what's in my hand?" Danny Silver demanded across the card table one evening in an exhalation of peanut breath.

Harold said, "All you need is the six of clubs."

"I rest my case," Danny Silver said.

"You don't have to be psychic to know about the six of clubs." Harold pointed at the discard pile. "I see what you throw away."

At the women's table, Fredelle Lishinsky, Myra Silver, Diane Merwitz, and Natalie continued their canasta game. It was the last weekly card party that the Steins attended.

Natalie laughed as they were driving home. "I won six dollars, and the girls looked at me suspiciously. At *me!* And I was the one who wanted to get on the plane."

The pebbles in the driveway looked familiar and welcoming as the low beams passed over them. Harold felt the warm plastic grip of the hand brake. He tried to turn off the ignition gently, so that the change from noise to silence would not be abrupt, but it was. The sound of crickets began to fill the silence. "I was with another woman once," he wanted to say to Natalie in that narrow space. He could smell the oversweet hair spray on her freshly done hair, the fading presence of her perfume, the stale cigar aura that Frank Merwitz conferred on them. Beneath or between these odors he caught her scent, clean, modest, still—after all those years—inviting. He did not say "I was with another woman once" because he could not foresee how her face would look when he told her. He decided instead that the next day, in the privacy of his office, he would type his letter to the passengers on the plane and to the families of the victims.

Harold's office occupied a cubicle in the stock room at the back of the store. The top half of the partition walls was glass and afforded Harold a vista of shoe boxes arranged in banks of metal shelves from floor to ceiling. Each bank had a wooden ladder fixed on tracks to the top row and equipped with wheels at its legs. Under the purplish fluorescent lights, the ladders cast shadows on the shelves, on the floor, on the round-backed salesmen walking past them. In places this view was obscured by papers taped to the glass: invoices with small windows punched by computer, an inventory of Italian shoes in a Brazilian shoe factory, yellowing black-and-white snapshots of Natalie and the children. One picture showed Edith and Cheryl standing near a lake at a summer camp on visitor's day, both of them squinting into the sun and waving good-bye. Another picture showed Natalie pointing at a mountain.

In his store Harold noticed the least adjustment of a showcase, the barest shine on a chair's scarlet velour seat. He knew the temperament of each of his salesmen, could register their day-to-day moods and manipulate them without a moment's thought. His customers gave him their frantic loyalty because he remembered them all by name, size, and style preference: "Now, Joe, I want you to take special care of Mrs. Mortimer here. Give her good support in her last and a nice narrow heel, seven with a triple A back there."

At home, though, he lost that certainty; in the wholeness of his family he struggled with details. If asked the color of the bedspread under which he slept—or lay awake—every night, he would have answered, "Yellow. No, wait, maybe orange. A kind of orange-yellow. Sort of gold, I think. A gold-and-green print." He thought that Natalie's bathrobe was white, with eyelets and ruffles, when in fact she had been wearing, under his gaze every morning at breakfast for six months, a blue kimono with yellow piping and frogs. He knew that Cheryl was in college, but in what

year and for what purpose he couldn't say. He knew that Edith
lived in either Denver or Detroit, but he wasn't sure whether she
taught grade school or high school, and he had no idea why she
lived so far away. Her infrequent letters clarified nothing for him:
Though they were filled with descriptions of wonderful friends
and parties, with little anecdotes about her job and apartment, he
felt, when he held her blue stationery and saw her even brown
script, the power of her unhappiness, a wild, unreasoning cry of
"Help me, help me!"

"She really should do something with her talent," Natalie
would say, handing him one of Edith's letters. "When I think of
what they put in magazines . . ." And she would shake her head
and turn to Cheryl. "And you, young lady, I'm expecting things
from you too."

"Oh, Mom."

"I *am*, Cheryl. I most definitely am."

At night, Natalie would whisper into Harold's pajama collar,
"Edith sounds happy, doesn't she?" "I guess," he would answer,
and absently rub his wife's nylon back.

Blume's lab had been designed by a Formica freak. This was
Cheryl's opinion, stated at dinner. She had wandered, barefoot,
into the kitchen for a cup of yogurt and stayed while her parents
ate. She watched the limp slice of pot roast on her father's plate
shiver under the attack of his knife and fork. A slice of carrot slid
away from the meat and traveled through gravy.

"I don't see how you can eat that stuff," Cheryl said.

Natalie murmured something about not imposing one's values
on others. Harold said nothing.

Cheryl dragged the edge of a cracker across a tub of whipped
cream cheese. "Doesn't anybody want to know what happened to
me at Ira's place?"

"Ira?" Natalie asked.

"Blume," Harold said to her.

"Dr. Blume," Natalie said.

Cheryl pushed another cracker through cream cheese. "I went
yesterday, after my Forms of Social Terror class, which, by the
way, stinks."

"Cheryl," Natalie said.

"Sorry, Mom. Anyway, I went over to Ira's lab, Formica Heaven, and he gave me these tests, you know, funny cards and colors."

"Are you all right?" Natalie asked Harold.

Cheryl closed her mouth around a cream cheese-laden cracker. For a moment she didn't chew, but held the cracker in her closed mouth, a habit that Harold remembered from her childhood. He was puzzled by her beauty. She seemed to resemble no one in the family.

Cheryl smiled at her father. "So guess what. Ira says that without a doubt, I am absolutely positively not psychic. I don't have even a little dot of ESP in my whole head."

Natalie began to clear the table. "You have other qualities. Hand me that plate."

Harold did not type his letter at the store. He sat at his cluttered metal desk and tenderly traced each scratch along its surface.

Mac Lishinsky opened a brown paper bag, peeled corned beef from waxed paper. He said over the rustle, "You can't help it if some people died."

"I could have said something, I could have told them," Harold said.

"Oh, sure. A couple a hundred people're getting on a plane, and some nut says, 'Hey, don't go, this plane's gonna crash,' and you think they're all gonna get off the plane?"

"Look, what if it happens again? *Then* I didn't know what . . . what I was feeling. If I was crazy. But if it happens again. . . ."

"So don't fly anywhere."

"I don't mean flying. I mean anything. Anything could happen, and what if I knew about it *before* it happened?"

Mac Lishinsky bit into a loud dill pickle. "Let me tell you something, something very helpful. Don't cross your bridges before you come to them."

Harold banged his desk, and a patent leather pump waving an undone ankle strap fell over. "But that's the problem. What if I *can* cross my bridges before I come to them?"

Mac Lishinsky shrugged. "So what do you want? Don't look a gift horse in the mouth."

Blume said, "On a quantitative basis, your precognitive powers are indeterminable."

Harold asked, "I don't have ESP?"

"We need more tests. Your results are so borderline."

"Borderline ESP?"

"Borderline inconclusive."

"I'm too old for all this."

Blume did his imitation of a hearty chuckle. "A man's never too old to discover a new talent of his."

"A cancer is not a talent."

"Can you come in tomorrow?"

The next morning, while Natalie, her hair wrapped in two layers of gauze and an enormous plastic cap, sang "Strangers in the Night" under the shower, Harold sat at the desk in the living room and opened the bottom drawer. Beneath several blue envelopes from Edith and two gummy sheets of Green Stamps fused to a broken rubber band, he found the newspaper clippings about the crash. They were pasted in a red Woolworth's scrapbook that said My Scrapbook on the cover. They filled ten pages, about a third of the book; Harold wondered if Natalie expected to fill the remaining pages with other instances of his recently erupted ability.

He looked again at the cover and saw faint writing that someone had tried to erase. He held it up to the morning light: "My Poems, by Edith Marcia Stein, 1966." The scrapbook had been Edith's, bought no doubt in one of her fits of organization. In 1966 she had been in high school. Something had happened, or something hadn't happened, and she had never assembled her poems. And Natalie, who hated waste, had saved the red scrapbook even after Edith left home: Someday it would be useful; someday there would be something to paste in it.

Careful not to read anything upsetting, he skimmed through several pages before finding what he wanted.

> *Estrellita Alvarez*
> *Mr. and Mrs. Mark Aronovitz*
> *Jack Bromberg*
> *Father Thomas Dennis*

The colored—the black priest, Harold thought.

> *Jorge Esposito*
> *Dr. William Evans*
> *Sean Goldman*
> *Michelle Goldstein*
> *Mrs. Ronald Goldstein*
> *Mr. and Mrs. Harvey Jacoby*
> *Mr. and Mrs. Daniel Kincaid*

The names brought faces with them, faces he hadn't realized he knew. Particulars of strangers' lives assaulted him. Mr. and Mrs. Mark Aronovitz were honeymooners from Trenton. He was a lawyer. She was already beginning to dislike the red moles on his back. Dr. William Evans, an oncologist, was flying down to Miami to serve as consultant at a rich man's deathbed. Daniel Kincaid, a sandy-haired giant, preferred to be called Dan; his sparrow wife wore dark amethysts because no one had ever given her opals. Estrellita Alvarez was three days pregnant. Michelle Goldstein was in love.

Harold read down the list quickly, hoping that speed would obliterate empathy. "Now I know where Edith gets her imagination," he said out loud.

Natalie said, "Harold?" just as his eyes stopped at

> *Mr. and Mrs. Harold Stein.*

She was standing in a bra and slip at the door to the living room. Talcum powder caked in the creases of her elbows, outlined the fine wrinkles on her neck. In one hand she held an uncapped eyebrow pencil.

"They have our name here," he said.

She came closer. One of her eyebrows had been penciled in; faint hairs described the ghost of the other. "Why are you reading that?" she asked. "It makes you nervous."

"I want to send a letter. I needed the names and addresses. But they have our name here."

"A letter?"

Her missing eyebrow troubled him; the eye beneath it seemed

at once vulnerable and aggressive, introverted and probing, a microscope and a telescope. He had to look away to speak. "A letter. To explain to the people who were on the plane, or to their families."

"To explain what?"

"About me. About why I didn't, why I couldn't save them."

Natalie leaned against the desk and replaced the cap on her eyebrow pencil. She twirled the pencil between two fingers. "Harold, you can't send a letter like that—"

"Why not?"

"It doesn't make any sense. What can you say to those people?"

Reluctantly, he took the folded letter from his wallet and handed it to her. The rims of his ears flushed. "I was going to type it up and get it Xeroxed."

While she read, he closed the scrapbook and put it in the drawer. It crumpled one of Edith's letters, which he extracted and tried to smooth across his knee. His hand seemed clumsy to him as it patted the envelope. The postmark said Denver. That was where Edith was living.

A crackle of paper told him when Natalie turned the page. Her breathing lulled him; for a moment he felt sleepy.

She handed his letter back to him. Though he looked expectantly at her, she said nothing.

"Nat, you think I'm crazy?"

"No," she said automatically. "I love you."

"No, don't answer right away. Sit down, sit on the sofa and really think about it: Am I crazy?"

"Darling, I'm full of powder—"

"Natalie, please."

Powder settled on the sofa with her. She cleared her throat, avoided his eyes, then frowned, as if to show deep thought. The posturing ceased as real thought overtook her. Her face softened, her body assumed a quality of weightlessness on the green sofa.

Time, instead of moving forward, seemed to be spreading, bulging out at the sides, while an overflow streamed irresistibly backward. Harold's mother smiled, a sunburst of lines. Her skin was transparent, like the web of a thumb backlit by a burning candle. Blue veins beneath her skin showed their blurred, delicate network. Behind her wavered Harold's father, shadowed, bent over his sewing machine, singing. He looked up once and nodded before he and his wife disappeared.

Edith, still sleeping in her Denver bedroom, also lay curled up under her childhood quilt on the sofa, her head in Natalie's lap. Natalie stroked her daughter's fine brown hair with one hand and clutched the eyebrow pencil in the other. Edith murmured, "What time is it?" but her eyes stayed closed.

Cheryl, still taking notes in an early class at the university, sat cross-legged on the shag carpeting at Harold's feet. "Hi, Daddy." She wrote something down. "Listen to this." She began to read from her notes. " 'The shoe as an erotic symbol.' Did you ever think of that before?"

"What's neurotic about a shoe?" Harold asked.

" 'Erotic,' not 'neurotic.' Listen: 'The woman's shoe as a symbol of her sexual subservience to man—see the impossibly high shoe down through the ages. The chopines in sixteenth-century Venice. The traditional high clogs of Japanese courtesans.' "

"What course is this?"

"It's called The Self as a Free Entity: End of the Rainbow or Impossible Dream?"

"What's it for?"

"Three credits."

"No, why are you studying it? What do you want to be?"

Cheryl rolled her eyes. "*Uh*-oh. This is getting heavy."

"What time is it, darling?" Edith said in her sleep.

Cheryl said, "And heavier." She raised her voice. "I think you'd better wake up, Edith."

Edith opened her eyes. "Where's Michael?"

"In Denver, I guess," Cheryl said. "Hi."

"Who's Michael?" Harold asked.

Edith yawned, covered her mouth with a thin hand. "Daddy, I'm twenty-six." She stretched under the quilt, and her long pale toes wriggled at the end of the sofa. "I wrote you a letter a couple of days ago." She yawned again, and a tear ran from the corner of her right eye. "Oh, God, I'm talking and I've got morning mouth."

"Who's Michael?" Harold asked.

Natalie said, "Harold, you're shouting," and the girls disap-

peared, though Natalie's hand for a moment stroked the air where
Edith's head had been.

"I'm shouting because no one's telling me who Michael is."

"What on earth makes you bring up Michael?"

"This," Harold shouted, and then he said in a lower voice,
"this." He waved Edith's letter that he had been trying to un-
crumple. "She says, 'Michael may come with me when I come
home to visit.' "

Natalie rolled her eyes. Was she imitating Cheryl, or was
Cheryl imitating her? "That's an old letter, you read it months
ago. You know Michael is her . . . young man."

She stood up and slapped powder from the sofa cushions. Then
she went over to him and kissed his forehead. "I've got to get
dressed. Fight For Sight luncheon."

He was closing the desk drawer when Natalie returned to the
living room, a pink silk dress fluttering over one arm. She had penciled in her missing eyebrow; both brows rose now when she
spoke. "I almost forgot to tell you. No, I don't think you're
crazy." She looked away shyly. "But then," she said as she left,
"what do I know?"

He would have typed his letter at the store that day, but Mac
Lishinsky wanted to calculate the merits of ESP in playing the
market. The singer Eydie Gorme, or someone who looked just like
her, came into the store in search of Guccis. She admired the
travel poster of Florence, then asked directions to Neiman-
Marcus, and laughed when she learned it was a few doors away. It
must have been Eydie Gorme, because she had a very musical
laugh.

After lunch, he climbed one of the wooden ladders in the stock
room and gazed down at his cubicle. He descended to commis-
erate with Fredelle Lishinsky, who came into the store looking for
her husband and left with a consolation prize of chartreuse espa-
drilles.

Later in the afternoon, before closing, Harold drove to the university, where Dr. Blume introduced a machine and a set of electrodes.

"I been waiting a long time for this little mama," Blume said, patting the machine. "This will tell us something, we hope." He began to glue electrodes to Harold's temples.

Harold wrinkled his forehead; an electrode fell into his lap. "You're sure this isn't an electric chair?" he asked.

Blume lowered wounded eyes to Harold. "Mr. Stein, do you believe I feel any hostility toward you?"

Harold said, "It was only a joke."

"Or perhaps, Mr. Stein, you are projecting on me your own hostility."

A yawn pressed Harold's ribs. "I guess I just don't like you very much, Blume, even if you are a scientist. I'm sorry."

Blume finished attaching Harold to the electrodes. Then he said, "It's all right. You don't have to like me."

Expression shaped Harold's face; his forehead had already pleated gently before he stopped it. "So. When is there an end to this?"

"Mr. Stein, there's so much we don't know."

"Do you know how much longer I have to come here?"

Blume held up a tangle of bright wires. "Do you believe the slobs I have to share my equipment with?" He disappeared behind a white Formica construction.

Harold nodded slowly, to avoid disturbing the electrodes.

Blume muttered, "One second, Mr. Stein. I'm trying to get a reading here."

A flute whined at Harold as he opened the front door to his house. An orange reflection of sunset sprang at him from the living room: light deflected from a crystal vase.

"She's been playing that record over and over," Natalie said. "I'd go crazy, but I don't have the strength."

Harold knocked on Cheryl's door. When she didn't answer, he banged on the door. "Can I come in?"

She pushed the automatic-reject button as he entered. The tone arm swung through its maneuvers; the flute stopped in mid-note.

She was lying in bed, wrapped in zebra-striped sheets. Her brown hair spiraled over an arrangement of three large curlers; the scalp showed bloodless between the taut rolls. When she sat up, he noticed the shift of her small breasts beneath her T-shirt. A mystery paperback with a broken spine tumbled over stripes covering her knees. A balled-up paper towel rent by a protruding pear stem balanced in the sheeted valley created by her ankles. Tilting on the stereo near her bed, one of Natalie's good ashtrays held a gnarled yellow cigarette butt. The smell of sweet foreign tobacco clung to the curtains.

"It's off," she said, and he closed the door again.

In the kitchen, Natalie mashed potatoes. Her pink silk dress, unzipped down the back, billowed over her shoulders.

"How'd the luncheon go?" he asked her.

"Madeline Faye and Myra Silver squabbled all afternoon. I'm fed up. And then I come home to your daughter's eternal flute. Plus she 'forgot' to defrost the lamb chops." She rinsed the masher under steaming water at the sink. "We'll have to have eggs."

He lifted a glass of orange juice to her. "Madam Chairman."

"I want to change." She was unfastening the hidden clasp of her gold necklace. "There's a letter from your other daughter on the table," she announced from the living room. She might have been saying something else as she passed through the hall.

He left the letter where it lay, in the center of the kitchen table, a blue sheaf on yellow cloth, and he set two places on either side of it. After he laid a triangular-folded paper napkin under each fork, he sat down to read Edith's letter.

Feb. 8, 1977

Dear Mother & Dad,

I really don't see the point of writing anymore. We never tell each other anything. How many how-are-you-I-am-fine variations are there? Why should I keep writing about the weather in Denver and reading about the weather in Miami Beach? The store is doing well, the new David Evins line is a sellout—is this what you have to tell me?

Harold looked away from the letter, watched a palm tree frond brushing against the kitchen window. Cheryl's flute record started again. He returned to the letter.

*. . . you have to tell me? What are you thinking, what
are you wondering about, what do you want?*

*Here's the truth about teaching. It's a daily battle
against twenty-nine little cretins with the attention span
of a guppy. All they want to know is how to get rich in a
hurry. The school board decrees that I teach them Blake.
When the classroom windows are closed, you could
choke on the lethal fumes of Intimate and Clearasil.
Their pimples are revolting. The idea of their sweaty,
hopeful sex depresses me. The smartest kid in the class
has a glimmering that something's wrong, but he doesn't
know what and goes on quoting Paul Williams songs
when he wants to make a point. Which is more than the
rest of them do.*

*And that's just one of six classes. Try six times twenty-
nine.*

*As for after school: For a while I loved having my own
place. I was happy, you see, because I didn't know any
better. I put a staghorn fern in a very expensive hanging
basket. Then last year, Michael came along—well, as
long as I'm ranting about the truth, Michael moved in
with me.*

Here Harold held his breath. Green spikes of palm frond, their
edges blurred in twilight, scratched at the window. The flutist in
Cheryl's bedroom played on. Harold gasped for air.

*That's when I really loved the apartment. It wasn't a
tastefully underfurnished expression of my soul; it was a
messy, confusing home, with too many books for the
bookshelves, too many shoes on the floor, not enough
room for my makeup in the medicine cabinet, and always the wrong music on the radio.*

*Two months ago, Michael moved out. I hate this
place now. It's still crowded—he hasn't carted away all
his stuff yet, especially the ceremonial spears. And the
boxes of cowrie-shell ornaments. You did know he's an
anthropologist? I think I'm going to move.*

Yesterday, after a profoundly unnerving day (one of

the kids in English 12-2 described *Kafka* as "*a guy who either needed a lay or a can of Raid*"—*this in a test paper*),
*I came home and stood under the shower and cried for
about forty minutes. Then I had a grilled-cheese sandwich, hot dinner of the lonely. Then I climbed into bed
and read two books—sequentially, not simultaneously. I
read until morning, this morning, time to go back to
school. But I didn't go, just stayed in bed and kept reading. I read one favorite, Gulliver's Travels, and then I
read one of Michael's books,* The Secret of the Hittites,
*by C. W. Ceram, which I'd found in the laundry ham-
per last week. The Hittites were a Near Eastern people
who were mentioned maybe three times in the Bible.
The Hittite king had an enormous library and was the
only one in his dominion who could hunt lions. Not exactly fantastic perks by today's standards, but I'm sure
he had the equivalent of stock options too. Anyway,
one day 3,000 years ago, someone wrote a letter to the
Hittite king:*

> So says *Jakim-Addad, your servant: I wrote lately
> to my Lord in the following words: "A lion was
> captured upon the roof-balcony of the house belong-
> ing to Akkara. If this lion should remain on the roof
> until the coming of my Lord, let my Lord write this
> to me." Now the reply of my Lord has been delayed,
> and the lion has remained upon the roof a full five
> days. A dog and a swine have been thrown to him,
> and he also eats bread. I said: "This lion may cause
> a panic among the people." Then I became afraid
> and closed the lion in a wooden cage. I shall load
> this cage upon a barge and have it taken to my
> Lord.*

*Isn't it wonderful? After I read it, I cried. I've been
crying a lot lately. But I know that feeling, the lion up
there on the roof, waiting, and I in my house below him,
listening to his pacing, wondering if he's hungry. And I
ask for help, but no answer ever reaches me. And there's
the solution—just ship the whole damn lion off to the*

only person you know who's allowed to kill lions. But
who is that person? Where's the Hittite king? Do I
check the classifieds under Position Wanted?
I'm all right, really. Even teachers can play hooky. I
told you something. Now what?
Love to Cheryl.

Love,
Edith

P.S. I won't be coming home for Easter vacation. E.
P.P.S. Thank you for the birthday check. E.

Harold placed the letter on his plate. He stood up, noticed it
was dark out. The pot of mashed potatoes on the counter was
cold. He turned off the kitchen light, the darkness outside remained. He turned the light on again.

Bewildered, he wandered to the dining room, looking for Natalie. Then he remembered her hands on her gold necklace, and he
walked down the hall, past Cheryl's closed door, to the bedroom.

Natalie, in the blue kimono, which he noticed for the first time,
sat sewing. The lamp at her side lighted her work and left her face
in shadow. With each rise her needle caught the light.

"What are you doing?" he asked her.

The needle sparkled. He thought he saw her lips press together.

"They're spoiled," she said.

"They're just cold," he answered, thinking that she meant the
potatoes.

"Those girls. They're spoiled."

"Edith's letter?"

She nodded, and he thought he saw her crying. He wanted to
touch her, but something in the way she sat prevented him.

"You're upset," he said.

She sniffled, put her sewing down. From her kimono pocket she
drew a wadded tissue, which she held to her nose. "I'm insulted,"
she said.

"Because of what Edith wrote?"

"Yes. No."

"Then what?"

"Because she wrote it and *sent* it. To us." Natalie blew her nose, a small sad sound. "A thousand times a day I think things—a person thinks things—that you just don't say. You don't tell everything."

Images rushed at Harold, images supplanted one another. Edith, her eyes blue-ringed and swollen, touched a short finger to her bandaged nose. "What if I don't like it?" she asked. Natalie crossed her legs in a rustle of taffeta; one slender bare foot arched and flexed in time to faint music. He smelled roses. He stood at the top rung of a wooden ladder and looked down at himself as he sat working in his cubicle, a purple glow on the balding spot at the back of his head. Cheryl, squinting up at him, waved good-bye. "Save my comic books," she called, "till I get back from arts and crafts." Blume laughed mirthlessly and pointed at the ocean across a paper-strewn beach. An airplane wing floated alone on gray water. "Look into your wife's diamond," Blume said. The wind spun paper over mussel shells, carried paper out to the whitecaps. Natalie offered her familiar cool hand, and Harold bent over it to peer into a diamond. He saw through corridors of stone. Light and the angles of light did not deceive him; at the heart of the diamond he saw the absence of space, the place where light ended. He saw lamb chop bones crusted with gristle and congealed fat as they slid over yellow-and-white porcelain. He saw bones that lay in earth, in the warm brown chaos of roots and insects. He saw bones that rested in weeds and water. He saw a skeleton, his own, standing in his bedroom.

He saw, with relief, that Natalie was whole and alive in her blue kimono. "Why don't you tell everything?" he asked her. He wanted to know the answer.

But she was crying now; even he could see it from where he stood. "Edith," she said, "Edith shouldn't have done that to us."

He went to her, carefully set her sewing on the carpet, then lifted her to his arms. "It's okay, it's okay. Don't."

"It hurts," she sobbed.

"What?" he asked, afraid that he'd injured her.

"Everything." She whispered this to him. A few of her tears trickled down his neck.

They swayed, locked together, in their French provincial bedroom. If he could have told her that everything would be all right, he would have. Comfort was not a vision; he had no access to it. He wondered if it, like his psychic gift, would occur to him one day. He listened to the thumping of his wife's heart.

"Is something wrong?" Cheryl asked, and the two of them looked up, still holding each other.

Their daughter, dressed, made up, and chained in gold, stood in the doorway to their room. Her hair swept over her shoulders, which were thin and narrow. Her mouth seemed an indivisible gleam of red. "I wanted to borrow your ivory hoops, Mom," she said. "Are you crying?"

"I was," Natalie said.

"Why?"

Natalie patted Harold's arms and released him. He felt his hands sliding from her body, felt the sudden absence of her heart-beat.

"I'm overtired," Natalie said to Cheryl. "The earrings are on my dresser."

Cheryl lifted the hoops from their blue velvet box. "I thought you were probably upset because of Edith's letter." She watched herself in the dresser mirror as she slid a gold post through the hole in her left earlobe, then fixed a gold backing in place on the post. "I thought it was a riot. All that stuff about the kids she's teaching and all. Real winners." She repeated the procedure for her right ear, then turned away from the mirror and faced her parents. "You shouldn't take what Edith says personally, you know. How do I look?"

"You look beautiful," Harold said. He sat down on his side of the bed, on a blue bedspread that startled him. "Where are you going?" he asked.

"To Ira's," Cheryl said. She kissed her mother. "Thanks for the earrings."

"To the lab?" Harold asked.

"No." Cheryl kissed her father.

Her lip gloss stuck to his cheek. Her perfume drifted into his eyes. "When will you be home?" he asked. He heard her open the front door. "Drive carefully," he shouted.

"I will," she shouted back. "G'night."

The front door closed.

"Well," Natalie said. In the dresser mirror, Harold could see moist ringlets deserting the upsweep of her hairdo. As if aware of his observation, she touched the back of her neck. "Let's have something to eat," she said.

He followed her, through dark rooms, to the kitchen. She tapped the pot of potatoes, then went to the table and took Edith's letter. She placed it, along with a fifty-cent coupon for instant coffee, in a correspondence folder she kept on the counter.

Harold knew that after he left for work the next morning or the morning after that, she would sit alone at the uncleared breakfast table and open the folder. Sipping warm coffee, she would reread Edith's letter. She would become upset again; distracted, she would burn her hand on the electric percolator when she went to pour a fresh cup.

The butter on her burned hand would glisten in sunlight as she sat writing at the desk in the living room. Her letter to Edith would be loving and almost without reference to Edith's letter. She would write about the family's health, about the stores, about the "really lovely mild winter" they were having. She would mention the Fight For Sight luncheon. She would add, toward the end, "Darling, if you must read two books at one sitting, I hope you are doing so in a proper light. Otherwise you could ruin your eyes."

Against the accustomed evening sounds of the teakettle boiling and water drumming against the stainless steel sink, Harold heard the cycling of his own blood. He watched himself ruffling the eggs that were beginning to solidify in the frypan. Behind him, Natalie stood at the cutting board and carved radish roses for the salad. The thought of her poor burned hand made him careful as he stirred the eggs.

He closed his eyes. In the dark outside the kitchen window, dusk-colored chameleons scuttled over pebbles and hid beneath croton bushes; others, trapped on lamplit whitewashed walls, waited with throbbing throats for danger to pass. The house contracted in the coolness of the evening: The concrete foundation withdrew from the soil, wood beams diminished, paint flaked from the moving walls. On the flat roof, the bleached bones of a dog and a swine trembled.

"What kind of dressing do you want?" she asked.

Helplessness settled on Harold with the steam from reheated potatoes. He opened his eyes and breathed in homely odors. The kitchen offered itself to him: burners, counter, sink, dishwasher, refrigerator, table, chairs, all vibrating against yellow-and-white-and-silver-foil wallpaper. The salt and pepper shakers danced on the tile shelf above the sink. His wife, in a blue kimono, presented him with a bowl of chopped vegetables. He sighed. Questions of guilt and innocence fell away; he contemplated instead his endless, enduring helplessness. The knowledge of it soothed him as the kitchen dipped, shuddered, grew still.

"Whatever you want," he answered.

After dinner, if he took his bath quickly, he would have enough time before the ten o'clock news to make a neat copy of his letter to the air crash survivors and the victims' families. Even if he never sent it to them, it was something, at last, that he could send to Edith.

GROUP SEX

ANN ARENSBERG

Ann Arensberg lives in New York City and Salisbury, Connecticut. "Group Sex" is her second piece of fiction to appear in the O. Henry collection. Her first novel, *Sister Wolf*, will be published this year by Alfred A. Knopf.

Paul Treat and Frances Girard were arguing over the source of Pom Foster's nickname.

"It's from *Winnie-the-Pooh*," said Frances. " 'The more it snows, tiddledy-pom, the more it goes, tiddledy-pom, on snowing.' "

"Not pom, *pum*. Tiddledy-pum."

Paul had decided that Pom was baby-talk for Pamela. Frances was holding out for A. A. Milne. They were two hours southwest of Boston, clearing Hartford on route 91, after the champagne christening of Pom and Toby Foster's baby, Joshua. They had left the party too early because Frances had seen pure evil in Paul's blue eyes. She knew that look. Once, at a hamburger palace called "The Hippo," they had sat waiting twenty minutes for some service. Suddenly Paul had bellowed like the restaurant's wild namesake. The owner, the manager, and two waitresses came running, but that had not made up, to Frances, for the stares and whispers and hasty exits.

"That's Wasp Heaven, up there," said Frances, propping her feet against the glove-compartment. She had taken off her shoes because Paul didn't want the black paint scratched, but left on her socks because bare feet made greasy toe-prints.

"Blonde parents, blonde babies, blonde dogs. Did I ever tell you my favorite thing from *Vogue*? 'Why don't you rinse your blonde children's hair in dead champagne, as the French do?' "

"Why don't you rinse your dead children's hair in blonde champagne?" said Paul, and snorted like a hog.

Paul steered with his left thumb or his right knee. At the moment no part of his person was in contact with the wheel, and they were passing a fuel truck.

"Barney Oldfield," said Frances, instead of grabbing it. Paul ignored her.

"Wasp Heaven is funny, coming from you," he said.

Frances relaxed: he was driving with both thumbs now.

"I have no roots. We moved around too much." She tilted her chin. "Girard isn't Anglo-Saxon anyway; it's Huguenot."

Frances was only a closet pariah, but Paul was the real thing. Nothing attracted Frances like the scorned visionary, the proud pauper, the embattled artist. "I go down for artists," she had been known to say, perfectly aware of the contradiction between her classic profile and her low talk. Paul wrote plays, or rather, he mimeographed sheets of notations for his actors to improvise on, and kept encoded log-books charting the development of the improvisations during rehearsals. Critics and arts-council officers came to these rehearsals, and waited in suspense for the awful moment when work-in-progress would crystallize into work of art. Their suspense was protracted, since Paul's first and current work, based on the incest taboo throughout the ages, had been in progress for two and a half years. Snippy articles began appearing in drama reviews and trade newspapers. Paul answered every one in a serial statement blaming the death of the theatre on the strangle-hold of the written word. Paul was a storm center, and took to carrying himself like the captain of a gale-tossed ship. He had a vast brow, impressive stature, and russet hair, and anonymity ranked very low on his list of fears.

Frances was in love with anonymity. Her myopia was protection on city streets. She could not recognize acquaintances half a block away, and always supposed they did not see her either. If she passed a man she had met the night before at a party, she never tried to stop or greet him, since she assumed he would not remember her name or face. Her profession, as an editor of books, gave her a podium for her views on self-effacement. She disapproved of colleagues who used the phrase "my author" (sometimes she even heard them say "my book"). These glory-boys would grab a writer's coat-tails, and forget they were only toadies and hangers-on. At most an editor was like a teacher whose joy should be in getting the best from the student, who must expect no fame or credit in this life.

Frances didn't bray these notions to the winds: she saved them for her monthly lunch with Toby Foster, who was with the Boston office of the Harwood Press. She might begin the litany: "Editors are service people. . . ." It was useless to scan Toby's round, blank eyes; assent or dissent could be read on his wavy mouth. "Bostonians think Harvard professors are their children's tutors," he might answer in his patient, intimate drawl. After this promising start, they could take on lawyers and stockbrokers, who wouldn't admit to the service rule, and accountants, whose only virtue was that they did. These shared pieties were the basis of their friendship. It mattered also that Toby's mother knew her father; they had grown up together in Cincinnati. Alone in the East, Toby knew who she was, and whom she came from. Frances wondered why Mrs. Manahan risked the struggle to be Grand Duchess Anastasia. How much more satisfying to guard the knowledge in secret, like a lozenge melting on the back of the tongue which prevented coughing during a lecture or chamber concert. Frances left lunches with Toby giddy with high-mindedness; the air was purer around their table, but thin to breathe.

At the Fosters' house the air was thick and charged. Frances stayed there on her business trips to Boston. She and Toby co-administered Harwood's annual prize for college poets. Pom took Frances right over; it was Girls Together. She had to follow Pom as she chugged around the house. "I have an energy problem," Pom had announced, dumping cream cheese onto a plate out of a heart-shaped wicker basket. Pom was modest. Four new projects were an average for her day—making coeur à la crème; tailoring a suit for Toby; building chairs from a photograph in *Good Design*; inventing a new method for teaching Spanish to backward readers. These projects were ranged around the house like the Stations of the Cross. Some would be finished and some would not; the undertaking was all. Frances's head swam and her legs felt like macaroni, symptoms she only got roaming department stores or museums. Shuffling around after Pom she coined herself an axiom: people with private incomes like to live in chaos.

Paul began to growl, a low rasp in the back of his throat. In their private language this sound was called The Natives Are Restless. He looked at Frances as if he would like to bite her.

"You don't share the driving," he said.

It was true. She borrowed no power from being behind the wheel. She didn't like steering shopping-carts at the market, either. She decided to placate him with a little malice.

"Pom has fits," she said. "She just falls to the floor. Toby stands over her and won't even pick her up."

"She's a hysteric," said Paul, "and he's a faggot."

"She does dream in technicolor," agreed Frances. "She also sees animals in the back of the car."

"Bullshit," said Paul, but his ears were pricking up. "What kind of animals?"

"I don't know, but she was driving to Needham, where she teaches, and she could see them in the rear-view mirror. They followed her into the ladies' room at school."

"I hope they ate her," said Paul. "I'd like to eat her."

"You're an outrage," laughed Frances, who had not quite come to terms with this kind of talk.

Frances was a sponge for technical language. Osmotically she had picked up the jargons of surfers, fly-fishermen, truckers, and sound-studio engineers. Before Paul, her profanity had been grade-school level. Half the time she didn't know what the odd words meant. She tried a few of Paul's choice ones out on Toby, who told her never to use expressions ending in "job" or "off." Bad language was a part of Paul's self-made image; some of it was theatre-talk, and some of it he had lifted from *Ulysses*. Frances copied it because it lined her up with artists and outcasts.

Then why did Paul's lewd remarks still stir her fears? She treasured his impish nature and his choice obscenities. But language was never just fancy-dress or borrowed feathers; it might reflect the inner imp, and his real desires. Perhaps he really wanted to perform vile acts with Pom. Pom was small and taut, like a well-made pony, with strong legs, and a perfect, rounded crupper. Her streaky hair looked chopped, not trimmed, and some piece of her clothing was always unpressed or unbuttoned. She arched her chest up when she was talking to men, or women. She also stroked her neck and scratched her knees. Every gesture she made was jerky and urgent. Frances had swallowed an image taken from fashion journals, that sexual signals can only be transmitted by the graceful and well-groomed. She did not like being wary of Pom; but now that she'd started, she remembered Pom bragging about attentions from the Wards and the De Lessières. On the other hand, Pom was known for her tabloid mind.

Paul was tailgating a Lincoln, and honking hard.

"It's a blue-hair," said Frances, leaning forward. "Don't honk. You'll scare her. She'll slow way down."

He forced the Lincoln over to the right and sped ahead.

"Seventy-five?" she asked. "There's a lot of traffic."

He flung his hands off the wheel and Frances shrieked. Then he eased down to sixty, laughing like a fiend from hell. Frances was phobic on the road, and Paul was a tease. She pushed her fists into her lap, and prayed she wouldn't comment next time. They stopped for dinner at a *Hoof 'n' Claw* outside of Bridgeport. They ordered little rock lobster tails, which tasted of iodine. Paul had finished two dinners, five beers, and a cup of coffee. Frances was spooning damp frozen chives on a baked potato. She could tell his mind was wandering; he was taking his pulse.

"You inhale your food," she said, dipping into the sour cream substitute.

He looked hurt. "Slow eaters are passive-aggressive."

Without unclasping his fingers from his wrist, he pushed his back against the side partition and slung his legs up on the leather banquette. His feet stuck way out into the aisle.

"This booth is too small," he grumbled.

Frances felt her stomach knot up and little veins began to drum in her temples. Just once it would be nice to relax and linger at the table. She liked to sip and ruminate; he liked to bolt and wolf. If she wanted to finish her meal, she would have to distract him.

"You are aware," she said, dressing her salad, "that Pom Foster was molested by her choirmaster."

"No," breathed Paul. He was enraptured.

"On two separate occasions," said Frances cagily. "She got him unfrocked."

"Where?" asked Paul.

"In Vermont, where she comes from," answered Frances.

"No, where on her?"

"I didn't ask, for lord's sake!"

"You never get the good stuff," growled Paul, unjustly.

"I do so. I tell you everything!"

"Skittish broads like that are all talk," said Paul. "Put your tongue in her ear and she calls the National Guard."

Frances looked up, startled. Paul was sounding very knowledgeable. He was a great student of the unconscious, however, and dedicated to the sexual origin of all behavior. Every one of his rehearsals started with a dream-clinic. She could imagine his actors sleeping at night with their faces screwed up, frowning, trying hard to make dreams for the director, the way cats catch locusts to drop at their masters' feet.

A waitress was steering the dessert-wagon down their aisle. Frances hailed her and took a piece of Nesselrode pie. Paul's eyes were still glazed and thoughtful. She could spin enough tales to see her through pie and coffee.

Paul had forgotten to shut the windows in his loft before they left. Frances went over to check the sills for built-up soot. She picked up a dirty sock and wiped off the surfaces. Then she went into the bathroom to inspect the floor. She put back all the tiny hexagonal tiles that had come out of their slots. She moistened a paper tissue with spit and began to rub at the water marks on the mirror.

Paul appeared in the doorway.

"If you're cleaning with saliva again, I'll kill you!"

She squealed but she kept on rubbing. Paul had various crotchets, but this one she disregarded. Once she had reached for his chocolate ice-cream cone to take a lick. He had howled with rage and pushed her away so she stumbled. That was how she had learned that he never shared milk products. She might lunge at his yoghurt cup with her spoon now and then, just to tease him, but she was careful not to test him any further.

Paul's kitchen was hidden inside a closet. He opened the icebox and took out a bottle of cola. He banged some ice off the freezer coils with a knife and filled two glasses. Frances took hers plain. He cut a section of lime for himself.

"Now," said Paul, as he handed Frances her drink. "The De Lessières are French hot-shots who write children's books. Who are the Wards?"

He was back to their conversation at the end of dinner. He had been so unresponsive that she'd thought he was blocking new scenes in his head. She should have known him better. The story was much too spicy.

"The De Lessières are rich," said Frances, pushing the lamp-table into neater alignment with the armchair. "They have one of those French houses where everything is done in the same pattern. You know, the walls match the bedspread matches the rug matches the slipcovers."

"Move it or lose it," said Paul. "You're like a Shakespearean messenger."

"I am trying to explain," emphasized Frances, "that Pom is a disgusting snob. She also has a perfect ear. You can always tell when the De Lessières are in from Paris. Pom can't ask if you've seen *Claire's Knee*: she has to say 'have you seen *Le Genou de Claire?*' Same thing with Toby's Brahmin aunts. She always comes back from Beacon Hill reviling the Irish."

"I'm going to bite you," warned Paul.

Frances loved to keep him in suspense. It was the only time that the balance of power shifted her way.

Then she relented. She shrugged her shoulders.

"The Wards are nobody special. They were graduate students in the M.A. program with Toby."

"Are those the only two couples, or were there more?"

She got edgy. "Why? Do you want to be put on the sign-up sheet?"

"Come on, Frances. I need to know for my art."

She relaxed. She could handle that explanation. Paul was as inquisitive as an ape, but in a higher cause. She was curious too, but she thought Pom's boasts were a figment. For one thing, Frances couldn't imagine the dialogue. How were these civilized solicitations put into language?

"O.K., let's do it," said Paul. He had closed his eyes. "I'm Jean-

Loup, or that egghead Ward, and I'm pressing up against you in
the corridor."

"Don't ask me," said Frances, who was plumping up the pillows
on the bed. "I mean, where was Toby? And where was Grisette,
or whatever her name is?"

"You are never still," said Paul. "Sit down or I'll knock you
down."

Frances slid to the floor and sat cross-legged in front of his
chair.

"You're right," she went on. "It's not logical. Jean-Loup should
say 'meet me for lunch,' or 'here is the key to my *garconnière*.'
Why drag in the others?"

"'Why' is easy." Paul became very grave. "The dramatic moment lies in 'how.'"

"Nothing is wrong between sixteen people who love each
other?" Frances killed herself laughing. She fell over on her side
and shook with laughter.

Paul refused to take part. He nudged her flank end with the toe
of his shoe. Then he nudged harder.

"Pay attention," he ordered. "I want this solved."

She just lay there, giggling and snorting. "I don't want to anymore. I'm sick of the Fosters. I'd rather do the rape in Scene
Four."

Frances had made a most unwise decision. She was used to
being a laboratory animal; but the last time they had explored the
rape it had ended badly. As part of the incest-spectrum in his play,
Paul needed to include the drunken father and the pubescent
daughter. One out of every twenty girls, he had read, is forced by
a close male relative. It was a brand new scene, and Paul had not
thought it out fully. This was the only acting-school Frances
would ever attend, so she was eager to get high marks.

Paul had put her down on the couch. "You're asleep, he wakes
you up. You think he's come to kiss you good-night, you see he's
drunk. You get scared, and you resist. The thing to remember is,
don't let him," Paul had instructed. "Do anything, use your nails,
teeth, fists, anything, but don't let him."

"He's my father," objected Frances, sitting back up. "I'd be in
shock. How could I fight?"

Paul put his palm flat on her chest and pushed her down again. He set a pillow under her head and covered her with a jacket.

"Let's do it my way now," he said. "We'll try it your way some other time."

He closed the shutters and turned off the lamp. Then he went into the bathroom and stationed himself behind the door.

Father/Paul had advanced or sneaked to the edge of the bed/couch. Daughter/Frances gave a yelp when she felt his breath on her cheek. She remembered her cue, and raised her arms for the good-night kiss. Father/Paul pulled her into his arms and reached back for her skirt. He pulled up her skirt. He started kneading her rump. She was pinned in so tight that her arms stuck out like two sticks. She could bend them part way, at the elbow, but not enough to land a solid blow. Her face was smashed into his chest. One of his buttons bit into her forehead, right on her chicken-pox scar. Father/Paul's hands stopped working for the space of a second. She heard a sharp report, like cloth ripping, and flew right out of character. She began to protest, and found she could not move her mouth. She could not form words; she could only raise a loud angry buzz. Father/Paul still deep in his role, was kneading and laughing. She lost her head. He was going too far. She could not breathe; she was choking, or thought she was. In panic she pitched herself backwards, and broke his grasp. She lay gasping and sobbing wildly, and flailing her feet. He moved over, crossed his legs, and sat there watching her. She did not like the look of his eyes; there seemed to be a film over them. Then he blinked twice, uncrossed his legs, and arched his back.

"Calm down," he said, yawning. "It wasn't a failure. I can use parts of it."

Frances gulped. Her mouth hung open in surprise. Paul had thought that she was asking him a question.

"Yeah," he answered. "That's one way to play it, where he doesn't finish. You did good," he added, and reached over to pat her hand.

He had not noticed that her collapse was real, or had just ignored it. Either way, he had not treated her like an amateur. In retrospect, Frances felt she could be proud of herself. Her memory was short; but the memory was heady. By now she saw these improvisations as tests of courage.

She got up and stood in front of his chair, a recruit at attention. "Can we start now, please?" she had asked. "I need time later to finish indexing the self-hypnosis book."

"You always want your own way." He shook his fist at her. "I'm still on the Fosters. I don't like breaking set that fast."

He was arguing for form's sake, and Frances knew it. Already he was capitulating. He was reaching into his back pocket for a miniature memo-pad. He began flipping through the pages. He jotted down ideas on tiny memo-pads in a code of glyphs. He had been refining this picture-writing since he had learned to write. The key to the code was deposited in his bank-box. He wanted his biographers to have access to his notebooks, but not other playwrights, who were larceners of ideas. For this reason he also kept his back pocket buttoned.

"All right," said Paul. "Last time we did it with you resisting."

"To the end," said Frances. "I'm a game girl, aren't I?"

"This will be easier and shorter," he said. "You just act dead."

"Dead when?" asked Frances. "After the good-night kiss?"

"No kiss," said Paul. "He gets it in while you're still asleep. Here. Take off your clothes and put on this shirt. Pretend it's a night-gown."

Frances began unbuttoning, unzipping, and untying. Her bare skin burned and shrank, as if she were stripping in front of strangers. Covered, she felt better. Paul's shirt was as long, on her, as a clergyman's cassock.

"Are you ready?" asked Paul. "You can't cop out in the middle."

"I'm O.K. Just don't cut off my breath."

This time she got into the bed and lay on her back.

"No," said Paul. She opened her eyes. "Lie on your stomach and face stage right. He'll be coming at you from stage left. It's more powerful if he turns you over. Come on. Snap to it."

She could hear Paul moving around, darkening the room. There was no light coming from anywhere, not even from underneath the blinds. There was a lump of hot lead in her stomach. A trail of ants was progressing up her thighs. They were rounding the tops of her buttocks, where there should be no nerve-ends. A good actress would be counting and emptying her mind, or relaxing the segments of her body one by one. Or thinking dead thoughts and conjuring up dead images: eyeless statues, blasted stumps, quilted satin, banks of clouds, sheets of rain. Frances was tense, not limp. She did not feel dead at all; she was feeling flayed.

She heard a skitter, like a rat across the floor. Then a creak, surely a weight lifting off the chair-springs. The bed gave: it was a knee pressing down on the mattress. She clawed the sheets, to stop her body from sliding. Any second his hand would land upon her shoulder.

She opened her eyes halfway: what made the room so black? If this were a normal rehearsal, there would be work-lights on the stage and in the hall. The lights were required by law, to prevent injuries to actors or crew. She was outside the reach of union regulations. There was no foreman from the actors' guild to voice her rights. Paul had been up before the guild that year already, on charges of exploitation. He had kept little Josey Ware going over the same long monologue for twelve straight hours. Someone had called her husband, who dragged her off the stage and carried her home. The incident had been smoothed over, and she was back on the show five days later. Paul had shrugged it off. Josey's work was much improved. "I had to break her down to help her break through": he had more confidence in means-end arguments than Joseph Stalin. Frances's reaction had been partisan and derisive. "Actors' rights," she had jeered. "Actors are children. You know their needs better than they do. They're lucky to have you!"

Now, for failing in charity, for sitting in the seat of the scornful, and for siding with Management, Frances would be punished. She was comforted to think so, at least, since it gave her a reason to stay lying face down on Paul's bed, wearing Paul's shirt, in his pitch-black room, waiting to be raped, when every other reason had deserted her.

The rape was on, and there was no saying, "oh, it's just old Paul, that big old bear, furry old funny old Paul, cries in movies, won't share milk products, locks the car doors going through Harlem, Paul's a screech, he's the universal Id, who but old Paul. . . ." It didn't work. He was someone else. He was Doctor Strangerod.

This person was working at her limbs and chest with flat, splayed palms; and Paul was as deft and steady as a fly-caster. He had left wet smears on her face; and Paul never slobbered. He pushed her legs apart at right angles, and set his knees on her thighs to hold them down. He started driving at her soft closed flesh. Whales have bones, and men do not, but he was hard as wood. Her brain was dim, like the brain of a fish, and she tried to think. *This could not happen in any theatre, there are laws and censors.* She dimmed out now, and fought back weakly to the surface. She saw some hope there, like a shaft of light through the blinds. *He can't do this on stage, so he will have to stop. He will rehearse to the brink, he won't go over. He has his marginal attention, his internal monitor, he says actors who lose themselves in their parts are just like lunatics. . . .*

Still he drove and he thrust; she was lashed to a machine. She could hear strange grunts, and Paul was always still and seemly. *This is a rape, the same as in an alley. . . .*

She felt a thud, which bounced her on the mattress. It was the impact of a fist pounding down on the bed beside her. Her thighs were free, but she found that it hurt to move them. She heard a crash, like an object breaking against the wall.

"I can't get in! You closed up like a clam! You locked me out!"

It was Paul's own voice. When the light switched on, she could see it was Paul's own form, towering over the bed in a kind of majestic snit. But peevishness is fearful in a person of such large size. When she asked to leave a movie in the middle he could look like that, or when she had a date for dinner with a girlfriend on a night when he wanted her to take rehearsal notes. Once he had seen her cat on her bed and he had yelled like that. The cat was lying on top of her pillow, curled in a circle. "You let that cat drag his anus on the sheets? I'm not sleeping in there!" They had driven back downtown to his loft, at three in the morning. Now he never spent the night in her apartment, unless she changed the bedclothes right in front of him, and locked the cat in the bathroom until they got up for breakfast the next morning.

Paul stopped towering, and began to hover anxiously.

"What's the matter? You look awful. You've lost your color."

He rubbed her cheek. She brought her knees very slowly to her chest and rolled over on one side, facing away from him. She felt bleak and empty, like the surface of the moon. She wanted to burrow her head in the pillow and sleep it off. Paul did not like it when Frances was silent and inert. It scared him. It put his universe out of whack. He wanted her up and hopping, so he poked her shoulder.

"Come on, little chicken, on your feet, nobody loves a dead person."

He poked again, and shook the shoulder for good measure.

"Do you hear me? You need a hamburger. I'll take you to Cullinan's. God damn it, Frances, if you're sick I'm going to kill you!" He bent down and pulled back her eyelid, looking for signs of life.

Frances gave up. She had enough strength to fasten her teeth onto his wrist, but not to bite down. She did not have enough strength to resist the move to Cullinan's, although she hated an actors' bar. Models named Ingrid with heart-shaped mouths would beg Pete Cullinan for introductions to Paul, because they had notions about breaking into acting, and had heard that Paul sometimes used amateurs and beginners. That was true, Paul liked to mold an actor early, the way the Jesuits like to take on a child before it is seven.

Frances let Paul stand her up. He dropped her skirt over her head and zipped up the waist, a little off-center. He stuffed her arms into the sleeves of her shirt, but he made her button it. He was too impatient. It was midnight. The action at Cullinan's had been underway for almost an hour.

Paul got out his comb and took a few swipes at her rumpled hair.

"All right, little waif, I've got you in shape. Now we have to hustle."

They rode uptown in a cab. When he wasn't taking his pulse, Paul was making notes. They were an agenda for a meeting with a rich young show-business lawyer, who might or might not be at Cullinan's that night, and might or might not be persuaded to kick some funds into the incest-play, which ate money the way a secondhand Cadillac eats gas.

Frances let her head fall hard against the seat-back, in a position portraying extreme fatigue and weakness. Her weakness was more the result of shame, than of muscles strained in the course of the rape-improv. Her body was tired, but her mind would not let her rest. *I am an underground person, I am a worm, I am less than a flea. I have no fight, girls should take contact-sports in school.*

Mother's maid, Agna, mother lost her temper, two days later a
platter got dropped, or a nightgown scorched. I want to go home,
the hypnosis index is due. I am like a sheep. I am a set of tracks to
roll over. No. I'm the roadbed. I want to see Toby. Toby is my
only male friend. He sent me that thing on the retreat house, I
wonder if they take girl-pilgrims. I want to live in silence, with
kindly nuns. . . .

"I can't," said Frances, out loud to Paul. "I feel like a piece of
Swiss cheese."

"Oh no?" he said. "Baby, that's your look-out."

They stopped for the light near the corner of Forty-fourth. She
could see Cullinan's green awning down the side street. Paul
leaned forward and told the driver her address.

"I'm getting out," he said. "You're making a big mistake."

She gave a sweet, sad smile, like the youthful Lillian Gish. She
was smiling at his back, however. He had slammed the door. Paul
had two main voices, one for pleading and one for threats. Tonight he was threatening ingénues and the hardening of his heart.
Frances was punchy from threats. She thought of Saint Sebastian.
Another arrow, to him, more or less, must have been all the same.

Even worms and fleas have an instinct for self-protection.
Frances spent the next three days working at home, ignoring the
phone. She asked her secretary to cancel her appointments, and to
tell callers she was down South with an author on a publicity tour.
She had to put herself out of touch, because Paul was a bird dog.
She had hidden out once before and he had bribed the doorman,
who let him into her apartment with a duplicate set of keys.
When he was in a hurry, and her telephone rang busy, he would
tell the operator there had been a death in the family, and break
in on her call. Frances called him the Hound of Heaven, but it
made her jumpy. If he suspected she was not down South he
might watch her building. As it was, she went out for groceries
after dark, when he was at the theatre, wearing a kerchief over her
hair, and a raincoat that was much too big on her. This bit of in-
trigue added zest to her retreat. She spread her index cards in rows
upon the rug, and spent the days happily shifting around on her
hands and knees. She loved her job, and even found virtue in the
donkey-work.

By the end of the third day she was restless nonetheless. She wanted to give Paul a healthy jolt; she did not want to lose him. She decided to answer the phone, but it would not ring.

The doorbell rang instead, and then again. Someone was pounding the door, which rattled on its hinges.

Paul stood there. He threw his arms wide open. She ran to him and he lifted her off her feet.

"Little creature," he said, "don't hate your poor bad animal."

"You forget how large and you hurt me." She sobbed, and clung to his waist.

"Look. David and Goliath." He turned her toward the mirror. "Maybe we are mismatched."

"I'm your side-kick dwarf," laughed Frances, and he squeezed her harder. Between weeping and laughing she got her spirits back. By the time she was restored, there was a large wet patch on Paul's shirt front.

"Oh, lord," she said contritely. "Do you want me to get my hair dryer?"

"No, leave it," said Paul. "You drool when you're happy too."

"How did you know I was here?" she asked.

"I pestered Ruth Anne till she told me."

"I'll get her," said Frances.

"No, you won't," said Paul. "She held out on me for three whole days. She was pretty tough." He looked proud of himself and sneaky, like a dog who was not caught sleeping on the couch.

Paul was late for the theatre. When he left, Frances tried to go back to work. She kept sitting down and stopping, or getting side-tracked by lint and cat hairs on the rug. She felt addled and light-hearted; her mind was scattered all over the room, like her index cards. For one moment she mourned the loss of her concentration, and the shape and silence of her abbreviated retreat. Paul had planted her feet back on the high road to adventure. Left to herself, she would have stuck to the side roads. She was Sancho Panza; this phase of her destiny was to be lived out as a straight man.

The windows in Toby's office looked out over the Charles River. It was a privileged view, for Toby was a Senior Editor. He was emeritus before his time, a kind of resident scholar. He had turned down the more visible post of Editor-in-Chief. "I hate budgets and personnel," he had said to Frances, "and besides, I'd have to keep my door open." "You'd be nibbled to death by ducks," she had agreed, "that's what my boss says."

The staff at Harwood had learned to approach Toby's office on tiptoe. They never marched up and knocked on his door; they hovered, and tapped. Frances had even heard Cleve Harwood, the President, whispering to an English publisher, "That's Toby Foster's door; he does our double dome books." Publishers revere academics, and Toby dealt with Professors. If he could talk to them, his colleagues reasoned, he must be their peer and rival. Hammy Griner, who was the Chief Editor, apologized to Toby for every Harwood book on the best seller list. Hammy was round and whiskery. He would hunch his shoulders forward and duck his head, reducing himself in physical stature as if to portray his distance from Toby's intellectual standards. Toby did nothing to check the course of Hammy's self-abasement. He would stand two feet away, the distance he chose for any close encounter, and let Hammy tie himself in knots and run on like a louvered-door salesman. Hammy would break down, molecule by molecule, while Toby's contours would grow sharper and sharper, like Percival as he was about to lay hands on the Grail. Frances hated to see it. She had sometimes intervened, lifted Hammy off his knees, walked him back to his office and restored him with coffee and book-chat.

It was not Toby's fault; he believed in the life of the mind. He did not see other people, except as containers of ideas. Frances hardly minded; he tuned her in and out all the time. "Small talk is fine," he liked to say, "but we have to remember it's small." Toby was restful to be with, for a man. He didn't like to touch, to emphasize a point, or from affection. He didn't flirt, unless he was flirting when his drawl got more pronounced. He sent no signals; but his heaven-blue eyes had no expression. Frances never felt like prey around Toby, and assumed he lacked the predatory instinct. She wondered, at times, about Pom and her whipstitch energies; she remembered the two blonde babies, and the picture fell into place. She thought Toby might be that rare Christian man, for whom marriage was an ethical laboratory.

Paul was suspicious of Frances's accounts of Toby. "Those simon-pure types are cesspools," he said. She would frown, but she didn't answer back. In fact, Frances had dug a pit in her excellent memory. Into the pit she had dropped Toby's sexual gossip, and his jokes about cabbage-leaves and nose-flutes, and covered it over with sod and sticks, like a bear trap. Now and then he would pass another blue remark, and she would plunge down the pit, like the bear, and remember that he had his sixth-grade tendency. He looked like a grown-up altar boy, and she appointed herself chief curator of that image.

They were sitting across from each other at Toby's kneehole desk, trading entries for the college poetry contest. There were more than a hundred poems. So far only two had reached the semifinals. If they both liked a poem, they would stop to read it aloud.

"Here's a little number called *Dominatrix*."

Toby handed Frances a coffee-colored sheet of stationery. Frances flinched. Somehow his face had widened and flattened. The pale loiterer had been snuffed out, and replaced by a sneering lecher. She understood why Dürer gave evil figures, like Christ's torturers, the monkey-features of the feeble-minded.

"Is it good?" she demanded, "or just vile?"

Toby smiled. "Some choice borrowings from Huysmans," he said.

Frances had already heard Toby's lecture on Decadence, which started out as a comparison with Symbolist diction, and spiralled down to the prevalence of corpse-passions. She had asked Toby the meaning of 'algolagnia,' and been treated to anecdotes about upside-down crucifixions, and whipping closets fitted out with slanting floors and drains. She had stopped Toby in the middle of a sentence. He accused her of denying literary masters their full humanity. She had no intention of provoking another lecture, so she slapped the poem on top of the pile of rejects.

Toby seemed to take her gesture in good part. He pulled the stack of unread entries onto his lap, and counted them to himself, moving his lips. When he looked up at Frances his face was once more beautiful. She smiled at him fondly, affirming his better self. Some part of him was stuck in puberty, that was all.

"Eighty to go," he said, ruffling the pile. "Forty tomorrow and forty Saturday."

"I told Paul I'd be back Friday. I'd better call him."

"Ask your beau to come up Saturday night. We can celebrate the end of this charade."

"Good Toby. You solve all my problems. I think he's off for the weekend."

Back in the cubicle that was her temporary Boston office, Frances sat waiting for the stage manager to call Paul to the telephone.

"Ho ho ho," he said, when she had issued the invitation. "Does that mean I get a shot at old Pom?"

"I warn you," said Frances, "if you do one over-liberated thing. . . ."

"I don't like you," said Paul. "You try to stifle my joy of life."

She was almost in tears. "Just forget it. I'll come back down."

Paul heard the break in her voice with satisfaction. It unsettled him when she was away or out of reach. When they were separated he tried to provoke her to strong emotion, to be sure she was still his creature, and under no new influence. Frances knew this pattern, but the knowledge never forearmed her. She reacted each time like a hamster to the laboratory bell.

Then Paul let her off the hook, with the tact he usually reserved for actors.

"Did you find any big talents?" he asked.

"I think so." This colleagueship pleased her. "One girl from Northeastern."

"You read her to me Saturday night," he said. "I'll meet you at the Fosters."

The rest of the conversation was easy as milk. But when Frances put down the phone, she was filled with misgivings. Did she want Pom and Toby and Paul alone together in one room? There was more wisdom in keeping these parts of her life discrete. She was not afraid Paul would shock or outrage other people; she was afraid other people would not live up to Paul. When he was around she began to see types and not individuals. The mold for Paul had been cast in Heaven, and very soon broken. Knowing the Fosters still gave her a foothold in her own tradition. If they failed her, she would have to throw safe custom aside. Nowadays Frances was measuring herself against Paul, like a child whose parents cut notches in a doorframe, to show him his height from year to year. How tall was she the last time she had measured? She wondered how long it might take before she would reach him.

Baby Joshua and little Beth had fallen asleep on the hearthrug, curled together, like puppies, with their rumps up. They were still asleep, puffing wetly through their mouths, at eleven o'clock. Dinner had been served very late, though not late according to Pom. She had spent her Junior Year Abroad in Valladolid, which allowed her to declare Spanish hours when she was behind schedule.

Paul had arrived at seven-thirty. Frances kept a wary eye on him while they sat in the living room. He had been raised by a grandmother who believed in demand feeding and a mother who fed him on a rigid program. These rival nurturers had addled his infant metabolism, and anxiety about mealtimes made him prey to a mood he called chemical anger. Frances could see he was in its grip; she knew all the signs. He was jiggling his foot, narrowing his eyes, and taking his pulse. She grew warier and warier, until she had no attention for anyone else. He drank six bottles of diet-cola and finished off a basket of humid corn chips. By ten o'clock she feared he might eat the ferns, then start on the children.

At eleven Pom was starting to serve dessert. They were having strawberries, with crème fraîche she had fermented herself. Toby and Paul were leaning back in their chairs and talking. Paul's chemical anger had been appeased by good rare beef. Frances trotted back and forth with dirty plates, while Pom chattered, and hulled and halved the berries.

"I asked her if I could make the quiche and she said I've got the quiche, so I said I'd bring the pâté and she told me she had the pâté. Then I told her I'd get the brie but oh no, she had the brie. I don't see what else I could have done, do you, Frances?"

Pom spewed and sputtered like a little teakettle. She was grieving over Mrs. Cleve Harwood's self-sufficiency. Pom wanted Toby to be the next president of Harwood. She pushed and worried the issue, and kept it right in the front of her mind. In the same vein, she would tear the cloth when she was cutting out a pattern, lacking the patience to keep opening and closing the scissors. For this reason, mainly, Frances did not believe in the Wards and the De Lessières. Yet why did Pom even hint at them? No true company wife would obstruct her own goal with scandal.

Frances took the bowl of strawberries in both hands, and set her hip against the swinging dining room door to open it. She balked at the sill. Apparently her thoughts had been partially telepathized. Paul was describing the practice of group marriage in the Sinusian Islands. Spite and mischief were upon him, the transmutation of chemical anger. He was going to smoke out the Fosters, those false polygamists.

Briefly, Frances thought of dropping the strawberries. That would halt the conversation; but would it change it? She could hear Toby's drawled responses. She was sure he had on his ape-face, the face she hated. So far, Paul was being merely anthropological. It seemed the Sinusians imitated the customs of their ancestor-gods. Group marriage, Paul expounded loftily, was of proven benefit to children, who grew up believing all men were truly brothers. These short, grey-skinned islanders had an answer that evaded civilized Westerners. As she stood there eavesdropping, Frances had to stiffen her cheeks to keep from laughing. Delight at Paul's strategy slackened all her governess-reflexes. Clyde Beatty also knew when it was useless to restrain a tiger.

Baby Joshua and little Beth were back upstairs in their cribs. To save dishes, Pom brought the coffee in styrofoam cups. Opposite one another, on facing love seats, sat Toby with Frances, and Paul with Pom. Paul had one arm stretched out behind Pom's back, like a teen-ager poised to make a snaky move at a drive-in. Frances dug well into her end of the couch, crossing her arms over her chest, and wrapping her legs around each other at the knees and ankles.

Paul still had the floor. With his high brow and his strong, clefted chin, he seemed to be in the grip of pure theory. He had a look on his face like Magellan when he was rounding Patagonia. He stood at the prow of his argument: imagine the wind in his hair, and his eyes narrowed to pierce the land mass. Imagine Suslov, the Soviet military tactician, all mind, burning behind the rimless eyeglasses. Under the force of so much intellectual rapture, Pom slid down in her seat, leaned back, and let the top of her head graze the underside of Paul's arm.

"My community of actors," Paul concluded, "is a group marriage in all but sexual practice. And many of us feel we are almost ready for that ratification."

Toby clamped the back of his hand to his mouth, as if to quell a rush of saliva.

"Literary movements also have an orgiastic, or pseudo-orgiastic, drive," he said. Frances thought he had told her his early stammer had been cured.

Paul shook his head, and smiled with sweet compassion.

"I'm talking about fellowship, and you fix on degradation."

Frances was dazzled. Paul had mastered the art of shaming intellectuals; all he did was speak the role of the natural man. He had used the same knack with the critics: if they disagreed with him, they must be deficient in human feeling. These critics, poor hydrocephalic husks, would fall to their knees, and beg to be reunited with their bodies. Paul had undertaken the rehabilitation of several of them, especially the younger ones, who wrote for *Manhattan Showcase*. His biggest success had been Marty Julius, who joined a mime troupe, foreswearing the written and spoken word forever.

Frances had never before seen Toby at a loss. He looked like a child in a Christmas pageant whose halo has slipped. He gave her a pleading glance, then addressed himself to Paul.

"You can't involve a girl like Frances in your experiment." Toby reached for her hand, or as much of her hand as she would extend, the three middle fingertips. He was trying on the cloak of womanhood's knight and champion.

"I've been in on all the planning sessions," said Frances. "I helped draw up the charter. We've even scheduled periods of abstinence, like meatless Fridays." She could see from the flash in Paul's eye that she had passed the audition.

Pom was scratching behind her ears as if she had fleas. Toby had hired a black editor and published Soviet runaways. Many full-page protest ads had appeared in the newspapers, signed by both Fosters. No one had told them about this new movement, or asked them to join. She would have to pipe up, to show that they had the credentials.

"We've been approached," said Pom, as if it were a matter of sorority bidding, "quite recently too, wasn't it, Toby? Four times, actually, I don't mean by four people, it was two couples twice. We turned them down, didn't we, Toby? We weren't sure they were really committed, Toby said they were dilettantes. Besides, they didn't have any children."

Frances spoke very carefully, because Pom did not trade in logic. "What does childless or not have to do with it?"

"You know, fellowship," said Pom brightly. She was parroting the lesson. "That was the real thing for us, to be a family."

Paul lowered his voice with a crash. "I'll bet you ran like a rabbit." He was turning mean, losing patience with the game just as Frances was learning to play.

"That's the liberal dodge," said Paul, "watching and talking. Mincing around on the edges. All talk and no action."

He got up from his seat so fast he collapsed the cushions. "On your feet, Frances. It's late. I need my sleep."

He nodded and waved, like the Queen from her carriage, as he swept her by the Fosters, the stiff-armed wave with stiff fingers, performed from the elbow. On the stairs Frances wriggled around and looked below. Pom and Toby dangled bleak in their chairs, as if their strings had gone slack.

In their room Paul fell on the bed and removed his loafers. He let them drop, one by one, on the floor. They were large, loud shoes.

"You've got no stamina for anything but art." Frances was whining. "All that great material down the drain. You could have held out one more hour."

Paul raised the window and put his head way out. He seemed to be measuring the distance from the sill to the ground.

"They're too easy," he answered, and ducked back inside. "It's like jacking off."

"We can't leave now," said Frances. "We'll go after breakfast."

"I won't sit knee to knee with those owls. Is there a clock in this room?"

"All right, all right." She pointed. "Over there. You set it for six. I can write them a nice bland note."

The moon left a broad white wake across the bed. The shades were up, because Frances could not sleep in the dark. In her own apartment, two and a half rooms and an alcove, she patrolled each night, jerking aside the clothes in the closets, and peering behind the shower curtain. She was not sure if what she feared most was burglars or vampires. She slept deeper with Paul in the bed, but she still needed light. He lay on his side and she pressed up against him, clamping her arm over his chest, fitting her knees into the bend of his legs. They came apart several times in the night, then recombined.

Paul, in sleep, was a nerveless creature. He could have slept through the battle of Midway. He had long refreshing dreams, with plots, in which he shot current enemies with machine-guns or set spectacular fires. Sometimes he dreamed a new scene for his play, and would use it, intact. Frances believed that coherent dreams were a sign of genius since her own were vague and disguised, and hung on to make her morbid all day long. No dream-symbol dictionary, popular or learned, had ever helped solve them.

What she saw, at that moment, was a normal image from her dreams. Two pale, bare figures were gliding into the room. Misty, doleful figures, holding hands at the foot of the bed. Frances blinked. The door was open, but she knew Paul had shut it. Her mind was drowsy. Perhaps it was the children, walking in their sleep or wanting a drink of water. Her eyes cleared. She jabbed Paul hard, in the kidneys. He sat up in bed and let out a strangled yelp.

"Hit the deck! They've got guns!"

He was not awake. The two ghostly figures shrank back, but they held their ground. Paul kept one hand on Frances's head, mashing her into the pillow. He thrashed at the sheets with his knees, and reached for the bed-table.

"Stay down! I've got them!"

He yanked the lamp out of its socket and hurled it. The lamp grazed Toby on one twinkling buttock as they were fleeing.

Paul bounded across the room and threw his body against the door. It slammed with a bang, but no harder than Frances was laughing. She tried to think what Paul could be dreaming: that Indians had surrounded the conestoga wagon? that the Spanish Inquisition had raided a cell of heretics?

"Wake up!" she called out. "Brave fellow!" Tears streamed down her face. She loved laughing like this, more than back-rubs and more than sex.

"I'm awake," he said. "Get up quick. Those scabby little perverts might come back."

Frances swallowed her laughter. "I thought you were dreaming about Indians!"

"Oh, no," said Paul, opening the suitcase. "I had to save face. Theirs and ours. I egged them on, after all."

"You're a very great man," said Frances.

They packed and dressed in the dark, except for their shoes, and moved out down the hallway barefoot. The house had a flight of back stairs, which did not creak. As they crossed the front lawn toward the car, Paul tripped on the sprinkler. He picked it up by the neck and spoke to it.

"I'm not finished here yet."

He went up the porch-steps and set down the sprinkler, aiming it at the door. He screwed it into the fixed position, so it wouldn't revolve. Frances did not have to wait for orders. She followed the hose to the side of the house and opened the spigot.

They watched the shower, for a moment, entranced.

"Can't we lurk across the street and watch them get it?"

Paul yanked her arm for an answer. They got into the car. With the sun coming up they left Boston, hitting seventy-five miles per hour. It was the first time Frances had ever begged Paul to drive faster.

OLD LIGHT

BARRY TARGAN

Barry Targan received the University of Iowa School of Letters Award in Short Fiction in 1975 for the collection of stories *Harry Belten and the Mendelssohn Violin Concerto*. The University of Illinois Press recently published a collection of his stories, *Surviving Adverse Seasons*, in their short-fiction series. He teaches creative writing at the State University of New York at Binghamton and makes his home in Schuylerville, New York.

We had come up to the farm for our four summer weeks, and Maine was all before us like a promise as various and new as the flow of the heavy tides. Blueberries, the sea, the pine stained air, clamming on the mud flats, black bears at the dump. And there was the ritual of memory that she turned for us, like a massy key in the lock of the door to heedless days, a gift that each year increased its value as we grew ready for it.

Her house was her studio, a contrivance of light and space around her painting. Her work was everywhere, a dominant line. Sketchbooks, canvases, tubes, bottles, jars, frames, cans of brushes, until it all joined into its own controlling logic, but she moved about in it easily enough.

She painted anything that would hold light, but she was best known, well-known, as a painter of people's faces. Not as a portraitist glorifying corporate presidents and dowager heiresses (though she had painted them all in her time), but a painter who tried to see, like her betters before her—Velasquez perhaps, Rembrandt—the soul figured forth in pigments. Her work hung in the world's great galleries and museums and private collections. And now young art historians wrote her letters and were beginning to construct treatises about her accomplishments and what they fancied was her glory.

But there was a greater glory.

"Your father slept there from the time he was twelve." She pointed through one of her large windows to a small barn-like shed. "Up top. Your grandfather and I, we slept here in the main house. And your Aunt Susan, well, we were never sure where she would turn up. With her you could never tell."

It was our delight to hear this, and our envy, I suppose. Against her indulgent but firm, creative chaos, we would compare the grumbling strictures we lived by, for our father, though an abundant man in all ways, was orderly and as accurate as one of his T-squares.

"He gets that from your grandfather. He was orderly. But about the rest—meals and beds and clothing and where the children were—he never thought much about that and I suppose I didn't either. It must have put a mark upon your father."

And then, "Tell us about John Palmer," one of us would ask. Again. As always.

"Oh, you've heard all about John Palmer," she would say. "How about Winston Churchill? Or Eisenhower?"

"No, no. Tell us about John Palmer, how you met."

"I'll tell you about Rita Hayworth or William Faulkner. I met them too. Or Enrico Fermi."

"No, no. John Palmer. You and John." And the three of us, her grandchildren, would chorus her until she was borne back into that summer, into the salt-tanged days of war and love to come.

She had just graduated from art school in Philadelphia and now, in that summer, she went back to the Atlantic City boardwalk where she had in summers past drawn quick portraits in charcoal or sepia pencil or full pastels. She worked in a boardwalk store that had been hollowed out to allow room for the twelve artists, their easels and chairs, and for the crowds who became their customers to stand behind them and watch them work. A man, Joseph Brody, owned the store—the Artists Village, he called it.

There wasn't much other work to get then, and what she had really wanted to do anyway, had wanted since childhood, was to visit Europe, to see the cathedrals, the paintings, Picasso, the Left Bank, the Paris night. But now, of course, Europe was aflame. Just weeks ago we had invaded it. Even as she drew the soldiers and their girls, many had received their orders. They would all get to Europe before her, but to a Europe she could not imagine now but could only fear for. Would the Cathedral at Ulm be standing? The Louvre. What would be left for her?

Atlantic City had been converted into possibly the world's largest military training base. All the hotels were made over into barracks, and all day soldiers would drill on the boardwalk. But at night and on weekends, even with the special precautions taken to keep the lights from shining out to sea, the city and the boardwalk turned back to play, as if the daytime business of preparing for war was just that, a business with regular hours and a set routine.

Everyone on the boardwalk then was from somewhere else, and that somewhere else was from anywhere in America—Idaho, New Mexico, Maine, the west Texas mountains, Louisiana, the cornfields of Kansas. And no one was staying. Everyone was passing through, to Europe or the Pacific. Nothing was standing still.

"Time and event was in charge of all our lives, sweeping us together and apart and yet toward a grand destiny that we all had a share in," she would tell us. "It was—the *war* was—terrible, but this, *this* was wonderful. A mad music. A heady wine."

About the end of July, maybe early August, in mid-afternoon when the temperature was very high and had driven everyone off the boardwalk and on to the beach, she and two other artists were taking their turn minding the store. It was a Monday, slow and tired after the hurtling weekend. Only Joseph Brody, from time to time, would whirl through and urge them to get up and pull someone in off the boardwalk, or maybe he even meant the beach. They paid no attention and Joseph Brody did not wait around to see if they did. This summer she was reading her way slowly through an anthology of American poetry. She had gotten to Whitman, and that day, remarkably, she had just read,

Give me the shores and wharves heavy-fringed with black ships!
O such for me! O an intense life, full of repletion and varied!
The life of the theatre, bar-room, huge hotel, for me!
The saloon of the steamer! The crowded excursion for me! The
    torchlight procession!

The dense brigade bound for the war, with high-piled military
  wagons following;
People, endless, streaming, with strong voices, passions,
  pageants . . .

when she heard this man begin to talk to her. She didn't remember him *starting* to talk, just that he was talking when she
finally heard him. He might have been talking to her for some
time.

"You're the best one, you know," he said. "I've been watching
you for two days and you are *by far* the best one. You should open
your own place, or at least you should work on your own. Is the
problem capital? There are ways around that, you know. I've been
looking around. There are three stores that would rent you space.
Here, I've got the figures." He sat down in the customer's chair
and pulled it over to her and produced a small notebook of figures
—rents, percentages, equipment, paper, mats, bags, insurance, util-
ities. He had it all worked out. On paper she could have opened
her own business in a week. She was astounded.

"Who are you?" she asked. And then, "And what's it your concern anyway?"

"I'm John Palmer," he said. "Corporal Palmer for the time
being. And there's no point in getting angry. You don't have to
open your own business just because you could. But if you ever
think about it, this is the way to do it."

Just then Joseph Brody came by and saw John Palmer sitting
close to her. "What is this, afternoon tea? You. Up," he said to
John. John got up and Joseph Brody pushed the customer's chair
back to its proper position and then he pushed John down into it.

"Now," he said. "You want to talk, so talk." To her he said,
"Draw." And then he was gone.

"Go ahead, draw," John said.

"It's o.k. You don't have to. Joseph is just a little crazy."

"No. It's o.k. Go ahead, draw my portrait."

And so she did, and as she drew he talked on and on about her
possibilities, about what she could do for herself if she wanted.
And after a time she heard that it was good talk, that there was
thought and fact and imagination to it and that what he had constructed for her was, indeed, as possible as he had claimed. Fi-

nally, when she got to his mouth, she told him he would have to stop talking so she could draw it. He stopped, but she could see that it was not easy for him, though it wasn't that he was *driven* to talk, it was only that he had so much to say.

By the time she had finished a small crowd had gathered at her back, which was what usually happened, and when John got up another person sat down.

"Here," he said, and gave her the notebook with the figures and plans.

"Thanks, it's an interesting idea but I don't want to be that permanent. I've got more to do than this. But thanks. And good luck. Goodbye."

"I'll be back," he said. And he was.

Late in the afternoon three days later he returned with a wonderfully crafted artist's easel, unique and better than anything she had ever seen like it. It was made out of a lovely mahogany, elegantly jointed, with brass fittings and wooden buttons of a contrasting wood. It had drawers and compartments and arms that slid out of slots and turned in sockets. It even had places to hold extra canvases or boards. And most incredible of all, the whole thing could fold up as if into itself and could be carried about like a suitcase.

"For you," he said after demonstrating it.

"But where ever did you get it?" she asked.

"I made it. I designed it and I made it."

"You *made* it? But I don't understand."

"I'm a carpenter. A boatbuilder, actually, but they have me a carpenter now. I'm attached to a combat engineer unit bound for somewhere. I went to the shop and worked on this until I got it right, though I can think of ways I might change it if I ever do it again. That's the way I am."

He went to her regular easel and started to dismantle it, moving the lights, the chairs, her supplies, everything. Quickly he put the new easel—more a traveling studio—in place.

"But Corporal Palmer, how can I accept this? I don't even know you."

"It's not an engagement ring," he said over his shoulder. "It's just a piece of furniture." He turned. "And I sure can't take it with me, so you either have to take it or sell it or throw it out."

"What's going on here? What is this?" Joseph Brody descended and twirled like a tornado. "What is this?" He looked at the old easel before him and the new one in its place. He spun. He didn't know what to do. "You," he said to John, "what do you want?"

"My picture. I want her to draw my picture," he said, disarming Joseph Brody, neutralizing him.

"Oh . . . well . . . so," he turned to her, "so what are you waiting for? Draw him, draw him."

And she did. Then, and again and again and again four and five or even six times almost every day or evening right through August and past Labor Day.

And she would tell on, and as in any fairy tale, the three of us bore down upon the details, waiting to savor again the familiar, excited within our expectations the way you anticipate music that you have gotten by heart. John Palmer would come by at odd times, day but mostly night. He, like many others, was in a holding pattern, past training and now waiting for the exact orders to depart. Sometimes he had duties, but often not. He would come to the Artists Village and whenever she was not busy with a customer, he would talk to her, and when Joseph Brody would swoop down on them, he would sit and be drawn.

He would talk about *going on*, she would explain to us. It was as if he did not recognize the war, overlooked it, *refused it*. It could claim his time, but that was all. He was busy with other things that he could imagine. So busy that what he imagined became real enough to live by, as if he could actually see and touch what he was looking at through the mind's eye. And, oh, he looked at everything.

He was a boatbuilder born and reared in Warren, Rhode Island. But more than a boatbuilder. He was a master shipwright, the youngest ever in Rhode Island. He was a naval architect without the title or the schooling. He had taught himself their math and had read all their books, and then he added to that what he knew in his fingers and with it all built better boats. He told her about his triumphs, about the racing victories of Palmer boats through all of the Narragansett Bay and beyond. Clear over to Martha's Vineyard.

He designed and invented and built boats to any task—for racing or fishing or hauling or just to row in. He was 25 years old but already had his own yard "stuffed with boats" waiting for his return, as he put it. But there was no arrogance to him, not a touch of it. It was confidence, rather, the self-assurance of a superb craftsman. To be so good at something that it could speak loudly enough for you, first you had to be absorbed by it, taken over and humbled by it. Finally, there had to be no room for *you* in your work. She knew what he meant. They talked about the discipline and intricacies of their respective crafts, though John did more talking than she.

And then, casually, he began to wait for her until she finished working, sometimes until one in the morning or even two on the weekends, when he would walk her home, to the room in the boarding house on a side street far from the boardwalk. But just as often they would stay on the boardwalk and walk its length talking about the things they had done with paint and wood and about the things they were going to do, the astonishing paintings, the magnificent boats. They did not talk about themselves. Or about each other, but who they were came clear, each to each, as they talked about their love of light and of straight-grained wood.

She had one day free each week, and they would go off. John was marvelous. He could produce anything. A car to take them away, a boat when they wanted, and just the right boat. He would rig a sail out of what he could find and they would poke about the sandbar islands and into the small inlets for crabs that they would eat late at night on a beach somewhere. Or he would sail them out to sea on a boat like a slab of wood with a sail not much more than a bed sheet, but he would tighten everything down and make the boat do just what he told it. She never worried then. She would have sailed around the world in those tiny boats with John Palmer at the tiller.

Those were filling days, the sea and the light bursting together, John Palmer sitting back with the mainsheet clenched in his toes like another hand, at ease in any swell, as she watched him, lean and effective, to remember and sketch later.

Sometimes a Coast Guard cutter would steam up close to them as if to board them for an inspection, but they were never stopped or questioned. The cutter would steam away, men along the rail looking at them, *glad* for them, for they were charmed.

They would fish and swim and walk through the starved sand grasses and the ground-up shells and sometimes they would walk across the sand stained with the oil from a torpedoed boat, oil that may have floated across from Portugal or hung about in the sea for years to come down finally on the beach.

And John Palmer could find anything. The moon snail alive creeping across the sand, the ripest beach plums, ghost crabs. Sometimes they would go down to Cape May, to the very point of New Jersey, and watch the birds of all sorts, and John Palmer would know them all. The birds and the stars and the trees and the curve and shape of everything and how it would weigh-out in water or air, how it would all balance.

"Gaiety," she would say to us. "It is the word I think of when I think of then."

Sometimes they would walk before the huge hotels, gray and ornate as sandcastles, with the thousands of men in them sleeping, waiting to cross the dark sea just a hundred yards away, walk in the salty night carving the air excitedly into glowing images and animate shapes so sharp and firm that she always remembered them, even as the Coast Guardsmen with dogs patrolled the beaches at the water's edge against enemies, and airplanes from the mainland droned overhead looking out.

"Oh my, oh my," she would say, "but we were affirming flames."

Once they walked right into the dawn. They were not allowed to be on the boardwalk after certain hours, but by now the patrols knew them well enough and let them be. And that night they never turned back. They clambered their way out to the end of a rocky jetty and watched the sea slowly brighten into the day.

It was the first time that John Palmer was entirely silent. They just sat there closely in the darkness listening to the sea well up and hiss through the dried seaweed. They sat quietly thinking their own thoughts but each other's thoughts, too. When he finally did speak again he said, "Maybe after the war, I'll come back here."

It was the first time he had ever mentioned the war. "Maybe I'll come back here and build boats. There are special problems to water like this, different from the Bay." And he explained the problems. "And there are advantages." The easy cedar he could get, the oak, the wider ranging markets of the Delaware and the Chesapeake. As ever, he had worked it all out first, not as a daydream but as a plan as exact as the boats that he would design even if he might never build them. John Palmer went about his life doing things one way.

"But what about your yard in Warren?"

"Oh, I could sell it off easy enough. A yard's not worth much more than the man who runs it."

"But you would be starting all over again."

"I don't see it as starting over, just as continuing in another place."

She thought he was going to say more, and she thought she knew what more he was going to say, but he had not thought her out fully enough for him to figure her into his calculations yet. Not yet, though she was sure he was working on it and the time would come. Then what would she do?

But the war came before them, swiftly. Orders. Packing up. No time for a gentle leaving. John Palmer came up to the boardwalk at a busy time. It was the Sunday of the Miss America Pageant week and she had customers waiting in line. He took his place. She did not see him until he sat down once again before her. He told her that he was leaving in a few hours. He talked on as if the audience at her back were not there. He had found a sawmill on the mainland that had stacks and stacks of perfectly dried planks waiting. He had made an informal contract with the operator. He went on as if the orders in his pocket and the ordering of his life were not in contention. He was, as always, *going on*.

But she could not put it all together as well as he, not nearly so well. The blue marine September day, Miss America in the air, the clog and density of people everywhere, the rivulets of perspiration that ran down through her charcoal-smudged face, Joseph Brody flying about like a trapped pigeon, John Palmer calmly figuring the length of his dry-dock runway against the average of the tides. And the battle lines in Normandy defined in the maps that the newspapers were now printing each day. She could not hold it together in a pattern.

Then John Palmer was gone. She had not even time for a proper goodbye. Before he left he gave her a portfolio of all the drawings she had done of him over the summer. And he would write. Make plans. Yes. But where? Where would she be? But he was gone. Someone else, another soldier, was sitting in his place. She drew him and how many others she could not tell. She saw nothing more. Not even John Palmer. Only a blankness.

Only much later that night at the bone-weary end of work did it all come together and she fell and kept falling into winter and into her life alone. The war had come suddenly true, and the fire that was John Palmer that had burned the mist of the war away was banked down now, and she grew cold.

She went back to Philadelphia and set up a studio and spent days doing nothing, hearing the radio, walking about, sitting in Rittenhouse Square for hours until it became too cold, sometimes doing freelance art work that a friend would call about. Her money was running low, but she was listless, a cork bobbing about. There were parties to go to, and young men who were interested in her, and professors whose pet she had been who were anxious that she should begin her promising career. But she could not take hold, as if she had broken without being hurt and was mending now.

She grew cold with waiting for what she did not know. Only sometimes the thought of John Palmer would warm her, his exuberance and confidence and energy would ray through her and for an hour or two or a morning she would start up, mix paint, spring at a canvas, paint at what she had talked to him about in the long summer nights and on the beaches and at sea. Then she would take courage. Make plans. But the winter wore on, bore her down in the snow and the shortness of things so that even John Palmer grew vague and thin and as fleeting as all of her life felt to her just then.

And the war bore down on her too as the terrible cost of moving the battle lines in the newspaper came clearer. By February she was as vacant as February can be, as toneless as a raw umber wash on an unprimed canvas.

And what was worse, she could not say what had happened to her. She was not suffering, exactly. She was not depressed or worried, only empty as if a plug had been pulled and she had drained out.

In late March a friend showed up at her dreary studio with a letter from Joseph Brody. She had worked for Brody too and he had sent the letter to her friend because he did not know how to reach her. She had given him no address, for she had no thought of returning to his Artists Village or to her indentured status. She had left the village. His letter thought otherwise. It was the same letter she had been receiving since her senior year in high school, a letter of instructions, work schedules, arrangement of pay. She dropped it on the table. But in his envelope there were other letters to her, six of them, from John Palmer. She opened them and arranged them in order, smoothing out the thin blue paper, and read them, long letters and thorough.

In the midst of war there was no war. Only the intimacy of personal effort and the sweep of his imagination doing this to some building or that to some machine. And the boatyard somewhere along the south Jersey coast grew more tangible in his letters even than in his talk. There were sketches, bills of particulars, lists. He even asked her to send for information from certain manufacturers whose names he included.

But he saw Europe, too, and reported to her that Chartres was intact, the Louvre undamaged though all the art was hidden away, that the Cathedral at Ulm was standing. He had remembered everything, every detail that she had told him about her European dreams and, as best he could, he had gone about seeing Europe for her. And he saw it clearly, not only the splintered streets, rubble-strewn and broken, but the spirit and the hope and the achievement of civilization. She knew enough about the destruction from the daily news. It took a John Palmer in the midst of it all to remember that there was more, and that time would come and maybe men like him to make life whole again.

She read all the letters and she read them three times again. And she stirred like life itself in March begins to stir. Who was John Palmer? She would see.

She found the portfolio of portraits she had drawn of him through the summer. She had stored them in the miraculous easel that he had built for her. Like his letters, she arranged the portraits in an order. There were 174 of them, and through that long March afternoon she watched herself as she came to know this man almost as if for the first time. And she discovered herself, too, how she had a great magic, and that she could find a person's

humor in a charcoal line, his wit and compassion and strength
and courage and fear. Through that summer she had been discovering John Palmer layer by layer. And discovering herself, too.
Though she had found neither of them until now. And now she
knew what she was supposed to do.

In the easel in which she had stored the portfolio there were
other things—her hodgepodge of art supplies, broken shells and
pieces of beach glass, sketchbooks. The easel was like opening the
summer again. There was even sand. And there was the anthology
of poetry she had been reading when John Palmer began to speak
to her. The page was marked still, the poem at which she had
stopped as he began to speak.

Give me the shores and wharves heavy-fringed with black ships!
O such for me! O an intense life, full of repletion and varied!
The life of the theatre, bar-room, huge hotel, for me!
The saloon of the steamer! The crowded excursion for me! The
    torchlight procession!
The dense brigade bound for the war, with high-piled military
    wagons following;
People, endless, streaming, with strong voices, passions, pageants,

She had fallen in love. And now what was she to do? Could she
write to the APO address on his letters? The last letter was dated
in January. She had answered none. What could he have thought?
Did he imagine she worked at the Artists Village all year long? But
of course she had told him that she would go back to Philadelphia, but she had no address to give him then. Would he understand that she was not receiving his letters even as he dutifully
went on writing them? But she decided that John Palmer would
figure out whatever was necessary if anyone could, and that what
he was doing was *going on*. The important figuring out to be done
was for her. What was she to do? And where begin?

She would write, of course, but she would go back to where she
had stepped off into nothing. She would go back to where she had
gotten off of any path. And, of course, she was going back to wait.
With the kind of faith that comes to us in life once only, when
we are young enough to believe *completely* in anything we want,
she went back to Joseph Brody's Artists Village because she *knew*

that someday John Palmer would come back there to do what he had said, and that he would come back there for her too. And that they would walk off down the boardwalk again as if time had not happened, as if the bridges of the Rhine had not happened. He would come back and they would pick up their proper lives.

But he did not. The war claimed him after all. And her story would end.

In other years her story would end and we would ask clamoring children's questions like after a tale by the brothers Grimm, intense with the child's literal necessity of where and when and what and why, until the excitement of the story wore down and we were beckoned away by other pleasures.

But we were older now. *I* was.

"That's a sad story, Grandma," I said.

"Yes," she said. She had gone to the great window above the sea and watched the snake-necked cormorants resting on the exposed reefs. "Yes, it is. Sad. But it is a lovely story, too. I've remembered, you see. And proudly. Proudly."

I came to her by the window. My sisters had gone off. There was more to the story, this part of it now, as if she had waited until I had turned, was turning, into life myself. She had waited for me to allow her to come closer.

"He was a special man, John Palmer. A gorgeous human," she said. Then, "We all need—*must have*—someone like that happen to us or else nothing will ever make enough sense. Do you understand?" She turned to me, hard and nearly vehement, but she was imploring, rather, and not angry, granting a trust now made good. "I love him still. I won't put that aside. I would not willingly lose him or give him up. Not in all these years. There's room in my life for him and your grandfather and for all of this." She waved her hand around her kingdom in and out of the house. "John Palmer made it large enough for that. I've had all the luck."

SWEET TALK

STEPHANIE VAUGHN

Stephanie Vaughn was born in Millersburg, Ohio, and grew up on army posts in the United States and abroad. She has attended Ohio State University, The University of Iowa Writers' Workshop, and Stanford University, and is currently an Ohio Arts Council Grants recipient. Her fiction has appeared in *Antaeus*, *Redbook*, and *The New Yorker*.

Sometimes Sam and I loved each other more when we were angry. "Day," I called him, using the surname instead of Sam. "Day, Day, Day!" It drummed against the walls of the apartment like a distress signal.

"Ah, my beautiful lovebird," he said. "My sugar sweet bride."

For weeks I had been going through the trash trying to find out whether he had other women. Once I found half a ham sandwich with red marks that could have been lipstick. Or maybe catsup. This time I found five slender cigarette butts.

"Who smokes floral-embossed cigarettes?" I said. He had just come out of the shower, and droplets of water gleamed among the black hairs of his chest like tiny knife points. "Who's the heart-attack candidate you invite over when I'm out?" I held the butts beneath his nose like a small bouquet. He slapped them to the floor and we stopped speaking for three days. We moved through the apartment without touching, lay stiffly in separate furrows of the bed, desire blooming and withering between us like the invisible petals of a night-blooming cereus.

We finally made up while watching a chess tournament on television. Even though we wouldn't speak or make eye contact, we were sitting in front of the sofa moving pieces around a chess

board as an announcer explained World Championship strategy
to the viewing audience. Our shoulders touched but we pretended
not to notice. Our knees touched, and our elbows. Then we both
reached for the black bishop and our hands touched. We made
love on the carpet and kept our eyes open so that we could look at
each other defiantly.

We were living in California and had six university degrees between us and no employment. We lived on food stamps, job inter-
views and games.

"How many children did George Washington, the father of our
country, have?"

"No white ones but lots of black ones."

"How much did he make when he was Commander of the Revolutionary Army?"

"He made a big to-do about refusing a salary but later presented the first Congress with a bill for a half million dollars."

"Who was the last slave-owning president?"

"Ulysses S. Grant."

We had always been good students.

It was a smoggy summer. I spent long hours in air-conditioned
supermarkets, touching the cool cans, feeling the cold plastic
stretched across packages of meat. Sam left the apartment for
whole afternoons and evenings. He was in his car somewhere,
opening it up on the freeway, or maybe just spending time with
someone I didn't know. We were mysterious with each other
about our absences. In August we decided to move east, where a
friend said he could get us both jobs at an unaccredited community college. In the meantime, I had invented a lover. He was rich
and wanted to take me to an Alpine hotel, where mauve flowers
cascaded over the stone walls of a terrace. Sometimes we drank
white wine and watched the icy peaks of mountains shimmer gold
in the sunset. Sometimes we returned to our room carrying tiny
ceramic mugs of schnapps which had been given to us, in the German fashion, as we paid for an expensive meal.

In the second week of August, I found a pair of red lace panties
at the bottom of the kitchen trash.

I decided to tell Sam I had a lover. I made my lover into a tall, blue-eyed blond, a tennis player on the circuit, a Phi Beta Kappa from Stanford who had offers from the movies. It was the tall blond part that needled Sam, who was dark and stocky.

"Did you pick him up at the beach?" Sam said.

"Stop it," I said, knowing that was a sure way to get him to ask more questions.

"Did you have your diaphragm in your purse?"

We were wrapping cups and saucers in newspaper and nesting them in the slots of packing boxes. "He was taller than you," I said, "but not as handsome."

Sam held a blue and white Dresden cup, my favorite wedding present, in front of my eyes. "You slut," he said, and let the cup drop to the floor.

"Very articulate," I said. "Some professor. The man of reason gets into an argument and he talks with broken cups. Thank you Alexander Dope."

That afternoon I failed the California drivers' test again. I made four right turns and drove over three of the four curbs. The highway patrolman pointed out that if I made one more mistake I was finished. I drove through a red light.

On the way back to the apartment complex, Sam squinted into the flatness of the expressway and would not talk to me. I put my blue-eyed lover behind the wheel. He rested a hand on my knee and smiled as he drove. He was driving me west, away from the Vista View Apartments, across the thin spine of mountains which separated our suburb from the sea. At the shore there would be seals frolicking among the rocks and starfish resting in tidal pools.

"How come you never take me to the ocean?" I said. "How come every time I want to go to the beach I have to call up a woman friend?"

"If you think you're going to Virginia with me," he said, "you're dreaming." He eased the car into our numbered space and put his head against the wheel. "Why did you have to do it?"

"I do not like cars," I said. "You know I have always been afraid of cars."

"Why did you have to sleep with that fag tennis player?" His head was still against the wheel. I moved closer and put my arm around his shoulders.

"Sam, I didn't. I made it up."

"Don't try to get out of it."

"I didn't, Sam. I made it up." I tried to kiss him. He let me put my mouth against his, but his lips were unyielding. They felt like the skin of an orange. "I didn't, Sam. I made it up to hurt you." I kissed him again and his mouth warmed against mine. "I love you, Sam. Please let me go to Virginia."

"George Donner," I read from the guidebook, "was sixty-one years old and rich when he packed up his family and left Illinois to cross the Great Plains, the desert, and the mountains into California." We were driving through the Sierras, past steep slopes and the deep shade of an evergreen forest, toward the Donner Pass, where in 1846 the Donner family had been trapped by an early snowfall. Some of them died and the rest ate the corpses of their relatives and their Indian guides to survive.

"Where are the bones?" Sam said, as we strolled past glass cases at the Donner Pass Museum. The cases were full of wagon wheels and harnesses. Above us a recorded voice described the courageous and enterprising spirit of American pioneers. A man standing nearby with a young boy turned to scowl at Sam. Sam looked at him and said loudly, "Where are the bones of the people they ate?" The man took the boy by the hand and started for the door. Sam said, "You call this American history?" and the man turned and said, "Listen, mister, I can get your license number." We laughed about that as we descended into the plain of the Great Basin desert in Nevada. Every few miles one of us would say the line and the other one would chuckle, and I felt as if we had been married fifty years instead of five, and that everything had turned out okay.

Ten miles east of Reno I began to sneeze. My nose ran and my eyes watered, and I had to stop reading the guidebook.

"I can't do this anymore. I think I've got an allergy."

"You never had an allergy in your life." Sam's tone implied that I had purposefully got the allergy so that I could not read the guidebook. We were riding in a second-hand van, a lusterless, black shoebox of a vehicle, which Sam had bought for the trip with the money he got from the stereo, the TV, and his own beautifully overhauled and rebuilt little sports car.

"Turn on the radio," I said.

"The radio is broken."

It was a hot day, dry and gritty. On either side of the freeway, a sagebrush desert stretched toward the hunched profiles of brown mountains. The mountains were so far away—the only landmarks within three hundred miles—that they did not whap by the windows like signposts, they floated above the plain of dusty sage and gave us the sense that we were not going anywhere.

"Are you trying to kill us?" I said when the speedometer slid past ninety.

Sam looked at the dash surprised and, I think, a little pleased that the van could do that much. "I'm getting hypnotized," he said. He thought about it for another mile and said, "If you had managed to get your license, you could do something on this trip besides blow snot into your hand."

"Don't you think we should call ahead to Elko for a motel room?"

"I might not want to stop at Elko."

"Sam, look at the map. You'll be tired when we get to Elko."

"I'll let you know when I'm tired."

We reached Elko at sundown, and Sam was tired. In the office of the Shangrila Motor Lodge we watched another couple get the last room. "I suppose you're going to be mad because I was right," I said.

"Just get in the van." We bought a sack of hamburgers and set out for Utah. Ahead of us a full moon rose, flat and yellow like a fifty-dollar gold piece, then lost its color as it rose higher. We entered the Utah salt flats, the dead floor of a dead ocean. The salt crystals glittered like snow under the white moon. My nose stopped running, and I felt suddenly lucid and calm.

"Has he been in any movies?" Sam said.

"Has who been in any movies?"

"The fag tennis player."

I had to think a moment before I recalled my phantom lover. "He's not a fag."

"I thought you made him up."

"I did make him up but I didn't make up any fag."

A few minutes later he said, "You might at least sing something. You might at least try to keep me awake." I sang a few Bea-

tles tunes, then Simon and Garfunkel, the Everly Brothers, and
Elvis Presley. I worked my way back through my youth to a Girl
Scout song I remembered as "Eye, Eye, Eye, Icky, Eye, Kai,
A-nah." It was supposed to be sung around a campfire to remind
the girls of their Indian heritage and the pleasures of surviving in
the wilderness. "Ah woo, ah woo. Ah woo knee key chee," I sang.
"I am now five years old," I said, and then I sang, "Home, Home
on the Range," the song I remembered singing when I was a child
going cross-country with my parents to visit some relatives. The
only thing I remembered about that trip besides a lot of going to
the bathroom in gas stations was that there were rules which
made the traveling life simple. One was: do not hang over the
edge of the front seat to talk to your mother or father. The other
was: if you have to throw up, do it in the blue coffee can, the red
one is full of cookies.
  "It's just the jobs and money," I said. "It isn't us, is it?"
  "I don't know," he said.

  A day and a half later we crossed from Wyoming into Nebraska, the western edge of the Louisiana Purchase, which
Thomas Jefferson had made so that we could all live in white,
classical houses and be farmers. Fifty miles later the corn began,
hundreds of miles of it, singing green from horizon to horizon.
We began to relax and I had the feeling that we had survived the
test of American geography. I put away our guidebooks and took
out the dictionary. Matachin, mastigophobia, matutolypea. I tried
to find words Sam didn't know. He guessed all the definitions and
was smug and happy behind the wheel. I reached over and put a
hand on his knee. He looked at me and smiled. "Ah, my little
buttercup," he said. "My sweet cream pie." I thought of my Alpine lover for the first time in a long while, and he was nothing
more than mist over a distant mountain.

  In a motel lobby near Omaha, we had to wait in line for twenty
minutes behind three families. Sam put his arm around me and
pulled a tennis ball out of his jacket. He bounced it on the thin
carpet, tentatively, and when he saw it had enough spring, he
dropped into an exaggerated basketball player's crouch and ran
across the lobby. He whirled in front of the cigarette machine and

passed the ball to me. I laughed and threw it back. Several people
had turned to stare at us. Sam winked at them and dunked the
ball through an imaginary net by the wall clock, then passed the
ball back to me. I dribbled around a stack of suitcases and went
for a lay-up by a hanging fern. I misjudged and knocked the plant
to the floor. What surprised me was that the fronds were plastic
but the dirt was real. There was a huge mound of it on the carpet.
At the registration desk, the clerk told us the motel was already
full and that he could not find our name on the advance reserva-
tion list.

"Nebraska sucks eggs," Sam said loudly as we carried our luggage to the door. We spent the night curled up on the hard front
seat of the van like boulders. The bony parts of our bodies kept
bumping as we turned and rolled to avoid the steering wheel and
dash. In the morning, my knees and elbows felt worn away, like
the peaks of old mountains. We hadn't touched each other sexually since California.

"So she had big ta-ta's," I said. "She had huge ta-ta's and a bad-
breath problem." We had pushed on through the corn, across
Iowa, Illinois and Indiana, and the old arguments rattled along
with us, like the pots and pans in the back of the van.

"She was a model," he said. He was describing the proprietress
of the slender cigarettes and red panties.

"In a couple of years she'll have gum disease," I said.

"She was a model and she had a degree in literature from Ox-
ford."

I didn't believe him, of course, but I felt the sting of his intention to hurt. "By the time she's forty she'll have emphysema."

"What would this trip be like without the melody of your
voice," he said. It was dark, and taillights glowed on the road
ahead of us like flecks of burning iron. I remembered how, when
we were undergraduates attending different colleges, he used to
write me letters which said: keep your skirts down and your knees
together, don't let anyone get near your crunch. We always
amused each other with our language.

"I want a divorce," I said in a motel room in Columbus, Ohio.
We were propped against pillows on separate double beds watch-

ing a local program on Woody Hayes, the Ohio State football coach. The announcer was saying, "And here in front of the locker room is the blue and gold mat that every player must step on as he goes to and from the field. Those numbers are the score of last year's loss to Michigan." And I was saying, "Are you listening? I said I want a divorce when we get to Virginia."

"I'm listening."

"Don't you want to know why I want a divorce?"

"No."

"Well, do you think it's a good idea or a bad idea?"

"I think it's a good idea."

"You do?"

"Yes."

The announcer said, "And that is why the night before the big game Woody will be showing his boys reruns of the films *Patton* and *Bullitt*."

That night someone broke into the van and stole everything we owned except the suitcases we had with us in the motel room. They even stole the broken radio. We stood in front of the empty van and looked up and down the row of parked cars as if we expected to see another black van parked there, one with two pairs of skis and two tennis rackets slipped into the spaces between the boxes and the windows.

"I suppose you're going to say I'm the one who left the door unlocked," I said.

Sam sat on the curb. He sat on the curb and put his head into his hands. "No," he said. "It was probably me."

The policeman who filled out the report tried to write "Miscellaneous Household Goods" on the clipboarded form, but I made him list everything I could remember, as the three of us sat on the curb—the skis and rackets, the chess set, a baseball bat, twelve boxes of books, two rugs which I had braided, an oak bed frame Sam had refinished. I inventoried the kitchen items: two bread pans, two cake pans, three skillets. I mentioned every fork and every measuring cup and every piece of bric-a-brac I could recall—the trash of our life, suddenly made valuable by the theft. When the policeman had left without giving us any hope of ever recovering our things, I told Sam I was going to pack and shower. A half hour later when I came out with the suitcases, he was still on the curb, sitting in the full sun, his cotton shirt beginning to stain in wing shapes across his shoulder blades. I reached down to touch him and he flinched. It was a shock—feeling the tremble of his flesh, the vulnerability of it, and for the first time since California I tried to imagine what it was like driving with a woman who said she didn't want him, in a van he didn't like but had to buy in order to travel to a possible job on the other side of the continent, which might not be worth reaching.

On the last leg of the trip, Sam was agreeable and compliant. If I wanted to stop for coffee, he stopped immediately. If I wanted him to go slower in thick traffic, he eased his foot off the pedal without a look of regret or annoyance. I got out the dictionary. Operose, ophelimity, ophryitis. He said he'd never heard of any of those words. Which president died in a bathtub? He couldn't remember. I tried to sing to keep him company. He told me it wasn't necessary. I played a few tunes on a comb. He gazed pleasantly at the freeway, so pleasantly that I could have made him up. I could have invented him and put him on a mountainside terrace and set him going. "Sammy," I said, "that stuff wasn't much. I won't miss it."

"Good," he said.

About three a.m. green exit signs began to appear announcing the past and the future: Colonial Williamsburg, Jamestown, Yorktown, Patrick Henry Airport. "Let's go to the beach," I said. "Let's just go all the way to the edge of the continent." It was a ludicrous idea.

"Sure. Why not."

He drove on past Newport News and over an arching bridge towards Virginia Beach. We arrived there just at dawn and found our way into a residential neighborhood full of small pastel houses and sandy lawns. "Could we just stop right here?" I said. I had an idea. I had a plan. He shrugged as if to say what the heck, I don't care, and if you want to drive into the ocean that will be fine, too.

We were parked on a street that ran due east towards the water —I could see just a glimmer of ocean between two hotels about a mile away. "All right," I said, with the forced, brusque cheerfulness of a high school coach. "Let's get out and do some stretching exercises." Sam sat behind the wheel and watched me touch my toes. "Come on, Sammy. Let's get loose. We haven't done anything with our bodies since California." He yawned, got out of the van, and did a few arm rolls and toe touches. "All right now," I said. "Do you think a two-block handicap is about right?" He had always given me a two-block advantage during our foot races in California. He yawned again. "How about a one-and-a-half-block lead, then?" He crossed his arms and leaned against the van, watching me. I couldn't tell whether he had nodded, but I said anyway, "I'll give you a wave when I'm ready." I walked down the middle of the street past houses which had towels hanging over porch rails and toys lying on front walks. Even a mile from the water, I smelled the salt and seaweed in the air. It made me feel light-headed and for a moment I tried to picture Sam and myself in one of those houses with tricycles and toilet trainers and small latched gates. We had never discussed having a child. When I turned to wave, he was still leaning against the van.

I started out in a jog, then picked up the pace, and hit what seemed to be about the quarter-mile mark doing a fast easy run. Ahead of me the square of water between the two hotels was undulating with gold. I listened for the sound of Sam's footsteps but heard only the soft taps of my own tennis shoes. The square spread into a rectangle and the sky above it fanned out in ribs of orange and purple silk. I was afraid to look back. I was afraid that if I turned to see him, Sam might recede irretrievably into the merciless gray of the western sky. I slowed down in case I had gone too fast and he wanted to catch up. I concentrated on the water and listened to the still, heavy air. By the time I reached the three-quarters mark, I realized that I was probably running alone.

I hadn't wanted to lose him.

I wondered whether he had waited by the van or was already headed for Newport News. I imagined him at a phone booth calling another woman collect in California, and then I realized that I didn't actually know whether there was another woman or not, but I hoped there was and that she was rich and would send him money. I had caught my second wind and was breathing easily. I looked towards the shore without seeing it and was sorry I hadn't measured the distance and thought to clock it, since now I was running against time and myself, and then I heard him—the unmistakable sound of a sprint and the heavy, whooping intake of his breath. He passed me just as we crossed the main street in front of the hotels, and he reached the water twenty feet ahead of me.

"Goddammit, Day," I said. "You were on the grass, weren't you?" We were walking along the hard, wet edge of the beach, breathing hard. "You were sneaking across those lawns. That's a form of cheating." I drummed his arm lightly with my fists pretending to beat him up. "I slowed down because I thought you weren't there." We leaned over from the waist, hands on our hips, breathing towards the sand. The water rolled up the berm near our feet and flickered like topaz.

"You were always a lousy loser," he said.

And I said, "You should talk."

AMANUENSIS: A TALE OF
THE CREATIVE LIFE

GAIL GODWIN

Gail Godwin, novelist and short-story writer, is the author of
*The Perfectionists, Glass People, The Odd Woman, Violet
Clay* (novels), *Dream Children* (stories), and the librettos
for three operas. Her stories and essays have appeared in
numerous periodicals. She has held a National Endowment
and Guggenheim fellowship, and taught at The Center for
Advanced Study in Urbana, The University of Iowa Writers'
Workshop, Vassar, and Columbia.

*Joylessness. Deadness. Aridity. Everything coming to a slow, dry
stop.*

And on another day, after looking out of the window for an
hour, she wrote: *The pond is beginning to freeze around the
edges. I am beginning to freeze around the edges.*

And on still another (for she forced herself to honor her work
schedule of twenty years): *Nothing.*

Then, as though keeping up the show for an invisible audience
who gathered outside her study door each morning to listen for
the sound of her electric typewriter, she began copying slyly from
books. A passage from *Death in Venice*. The first page of an Isak
Dinesen tale. Several pages from Bishop Paget's classic study on
the sin of Acedia. She typed quickly, in a parody of her old inspired rhythm. Then she would pull the sheet of purloined eloquence from the typewriter and squint at it, willing it to give up
its secret of confidence, trying to graft onto herself the feeling of

Originally published in *Cosmopolitan* as "A Tale of the Literary Life." Copyright © 1979 by Gail Godwin. Reprinted by permission of Paul R. Reynolds,
Inc.

entitlement the other writer had felt when composing this page: the priceless feeling of having the *right* to say . . . precisely what one had said.

Then she gave up that pretense, too, and simply shut the door to her study every morning at nine and sat down in front of the cold machine—a stubborn priestess guarding her altar, even though its flame had gone out.

Outside, in the real world, it was deep winter. Six snowfalls lay, one on top of the other. The trees, sheathed in ice, glittered in the cold sun. The leaves of the rhododendrons she had planted were furled tight as little green cigars. And the pond, the real pond as well as the image she had appropriated to describe the condition of her imagination was frozen hard and thick.

Her name was Constance Le Fevre. Through a combination of violent ambition and single-minded dedication to her talent, she had succeeded in imposing that name on the reading world. When still an undergraduate, she had taken her youth and offered it, without a second thought, to the Great God Art. He had accepted it. Then she began to accrue words which led to pages of what she determined would be a memorable first impression: a saga, based vaguely on her own family, Huguenots who had settled in an upstate New York village in the seventeenth century. From the beginning Constance had the knack of keeping one eye on her own soul and the other on the world's soul, and what resulted was a hefty "read" of 600 pages in which the reader was allowed intimate and detailed knowledge of how a family rose to financial and social and moral power, then fell again. A story the world never tires of. The world was pleased. And Constance had also managed to please herself: She had used this book, as she was to use most of her books, to further or balance her inner life. At twenty, her most pressing need was to discover who she was; but whereas the average twenty-year-old would have focused unhesitatingly on the navel, Constance hesitated . . . for she wanted to be extraordinary . . . and then chose to use a panoply of "historical" characters to play out the drama going on in herself where deep religious impulse warred with an attraction to frivolity, arrogance with self-doubt, a desire to be famous, notoriously famous, with the opposite desire for a private peace. Constance knew very little about her real ancestors, except for the village where they had settled. She went to that village and haunted the local Historical Society, presided over by little old ladies with old names (one of them was also a Le Fevre, but from a "better" branch); Constance didn't need much, all she needed was some convincing underpinning for the saga she would build from her imagination's needs. The most memorable character came not out of the Historical Society's files, but out of Constance's head. She labored over it, this first work of hers; she wrote and rewrote; she was a stickler for details. When the "ancestor" who had made the "family fortune" began to build his fine house, Constance sought out a young architect in the village and asked him to go through the crumbling but haughtily proportioned ruin built by one Augustin DePuy in the 1760's and tell her exactly how such a house was constructed, nail by nail, plank by plank, stone by stone. The architect fell in love with Constance's masculine mind and feminine charm. Her saga came out when she was twenty-three and enjoyed exceptional success for a first novel. Movie rights were purchased, enabling Constance to buy the old DePuy ruin and adjoining acreage, and when she returned frustrated from Hollywood a year later, after writing the screenplay that would never be needed, she married her architect, who had created out of the old ruin the exact house built by her character in her book.

Her second book was pure fantasy. It was the kind of story her working-class parents (the "fallen" Le Fevres) had neither the invention nor the time to tell her when she was a child; it was the kind of story she planned to read to her own child, as soon as it got out of the womb and became old enough to appreciate it.

Her third novel was a disillusioned account of a failed marriage and all its miscarried hopes (metaphor for Constance's lost child). It was a bit downbeat, but it restored her public's faith. They had found the "fantasy" rather cloying and self-congratulatory. This new novel spoke of the dull kind of suffering they themselves underwent daily; it did well, well enough for Constance to cash her royalty check in time to purchase a round-the-world cruise ticket for her thirtieth birthday.

The ship visited twenty-two ports. Constance talked to many passengers and crew and slept with some of them. She kept exhaustive notes. What interested her at this point in her life was the otherness of other people. She wanted to get out of herself—it was too uncomfortable being in oneself—and be able to slip into the bodies and thoughts of others, speak as they spoke, want what they wanted. She wanted to put as much distance between her writing self (which, through all, had functioned splendidly) and the self that cringed with guilt and sorrow.

Her *Ports of Folly* was proclaimed her tour de force: Twenty-two people told their stories and confessed their guilts in twenty-two chapters labeled exotically with the names of ports. "A modern *Decameron* in which the plague is the twentieth century," wrote one reviewer.

The next few years of Constance's life sped by in a blur of twenty-pound bond sheets with carbon copies. Her love affairs, her night fears, her social life, even her writing life, she fed back into the jaws of Art, often before the experiences registered fully on her own emotions. When at thirty-five she found a dead-white patch lurking beneath the glossy dark hair on the right side of her head, she covered it over hurriedly and sat down at her typewriter and began to compose *Second Thoughts*, a novel about a playwright who wakes up one day and realizes he has fed the entire first half of his life into his art and is completely drained of all memory and feeling. She produced four hundred pages of this novel and then, suddenly sickened by it, put it away in a drawer.

One of the little old ladies in the village's upper-crust Historical Society passed away. Constance was asked to take her place. Her family's ignominious descent into poverty and ordinariness had been redeemed by her own reputation, and newcomers to the village believed—were encouraged by the little old ladies to believe (for it made a better story)—that Constance lived in the imposing stone house of her *other* ancestor, the grand merchant-statesman Augustin DePuy. Constance accepted the invitation to join the Historical Society. Her new duties gave her a deep satisfaction. The very boredom of having to donate one whole afternoon of her life every week to dressing nicely and sitting behind a table with fresh flowers and asking people to be sure and sign the visitor's book appealed to her. It was healthy, traditional, this once-a-week, unselfish foray into community life. But eventually she got restless, especially when a whole afternoon would creak by without a single visitor, and she began to rifle the old records and files,

where she pounced one afternoon on the material for a sensa-
tional short novel that, if she drove herself, would coincide with
the bicentennial. *Kull's Kill* was written in a six-week burst of energy. It related in a cool raconteur's voice the depraved, incestuous
story of an eighteenth-century Dutch immigrant and his daughter
and was brought out in the spring of the bicentennial. Reporters
drove up the thruway to the little village, which was not so little
anymore since the state university had opened a large branch
there, and trudged through still-frozen fields to photograph the little *kill*, or stream, where poor "Kitty Kull" in sadistic mirth had
induced her father-lover to bash her head in; then they went down
to the Historical Society and photographed the author in pre-
Revolutionary costume and frilly white cap sitting demurely behind the desk and extending the visitor's book. Afterward, they
went through the files—which were, after all, open to the public,
and Xeroxed the old document that revealed the true name of
"Johannes Kull." When *Kull's Kill* became a best seller (Constance's first), a magazine did a feature on the historical novel
boom: Across from a close-up of Constance was a little inset of
Jonas Kip's hair-raising confession, preserved in the photostatted
diary of the judge who had sentenced him to hang. The little old
lady who was a direct descendant of the unfortunate Kip bore up
stoically; she did not, as several other Society members did, cut
Constance dead in the supermarket. Constance resigned from the
Society, pleading pressing engagements, before they could ask her
to resign. She felt a bit queasy about the whole thing, as if she
had soiled her own nest. If only she hadn't been so desperate to
get another novel out, before her public forgot her! Now her public loved her more than ever, whereas she despised it a little, for
having granted the popularity she had craved for so long to her
most vulgar work. Could it be that, for almost twenty years, she
had been courting with all the wiles of her sensitivity a lover with
a heavy, insensitive soul?

As soon as the Old Guard dropped Constance, the new local
branch of the state university picked her up. She had snubbed its
English department when, several years ago, it had approached
her about teaching a Creative Writing Seminar. (She, Constance
Le Fevre, in the same catalogue that listed such "courses" as
"Human Relations" and "Oral Communications" as fully accred-

ited *academic* subjects?) But now her pride was assuaged when she was invited to give the annual Rose Verplanck Memorial Lecture to the humanities department. She worked hard on her lecture and even drove down to New York and bought a new dress for the occasion.

A by-product of Constance's lecture was her brief affair with an associate professor in the English department named Alan Insel. Almost as soon as she was fully into it, she realized her error in judgement. But then, it took her several months to get out of it again because he had made himself so indispensible to her comforts and her vanity. Insel was an affable sort of failure who had somehow managed to erect a civilized edifice around his shortcomings. He courted Constance with formal deference. He let her know that he *knew* her financial and professional successes were far, far above him. He had tried and tried to get his novels published, he told her, in an amused tone of voice, as though laughing at himself, but he just hadn't been as lucky in his subject matter as she; and also, he didn't have her *technique*. But still, he let her know, there were a few points of good living he might be able to share with her, a few serendipitous delicacies she may, in her single-minded pursuit of her craft, have overlooked. He drove her like a princess across the Hudson in his renovated old brown Jaguar and bought her violets from a greenhouse in January; he always had tickets for interesting productions of rare Ibsen, or Pirandello; he belonged to a local vineyard cooperative, and his wine bottles bore his own signature in gold on their pretty labels; he told her she was burning the wrong woods in her massive stone fireplace and arranged with his "man" to deliver two cords of the proper ones in early spring, "so the logs will have the whole summer to season." He liked words like *season* and *subtle* and *sensual*. When they went to bed together, he made it a point of honor never to be obvious or predictable. She never knew quite what he was going to do, but the result was . . . inevitably . . . satisfactory in a languid, *soothing* way. In a sense, she could let herself go with him because he didn't matter, but also there was something rather demonic and awful about the way his pale and oddly heavy limbs engulfed her and serviced her while his thin, satiric face gleamed at her in a curious, cold complicity.

And then, abruptly, she woke up beside him in her own bed

one early spring morning and knew she loathed him and couldn't wait to get him out of the house. She felt guilty, but guilty in the way one feels guilty when about to discommode some clinging slug which has managed to attach itself to one's arm or leg. She allowed him to make their breakfast—he was an eggs-Benedict and Bloody Mary man—and, loathing him more by the minute, she sat across from him in Augustin DePuy's rustic-beamed old kitchen whose tiny windows her architect/ex-husband had enlarged to let the morning sun in, and she allowed Insel to go on one last time, in his smug "lecturing" voice, about how she, Constance, had been "lucky in her subject matter" and had mastered her "technique." "Ah, if I had your *technique*," he said, licking a tiny drop of egg yolk from where it had fallen on his fingers, "I'd be able to fly us both to Aruba . . . did you see that marvelous color ad in the last *New Yorker*, the one with the Updike story . . . now *his* technique . . ." And Constance, steeling herself for the strike, told him she had already been to Aruba, it was, if he recalled, the first port of call in her *Ports of Folly*. "But I must correct you, Alan, on one point," she went on, her voice dropping to a dangerous earnestness. "When you talk about technique, I think you are confusing it with talent. The two are not the same."

Several days later he sent her, inside an envelope, a postcard of Gustav Klimt's *The Kiss*. "All relationships need their breathing spells," he typed neatly on the back. "Perhaps you ought to call me when you feel ready to see me again." At least he was tactful. He had let her off the hook and preserved his own pride in the bargain. Once or twice in the next few weeks she was tempted to call him, when she felt like sharing the leisurely courses of a gourmet meal . . . or when she felt in need of oblivion, combined with caresses and flattery. I am too isolated, she told herself, I need to get out more; I would never have stooped to this "relationship"—how I loathe that word—had I not been too long alone all those months I was trying to write that wretched novel about the playwright who offered his youth to Art. And then, on top of that, when the old ladies snubbed me, that hurt, too; being loved and accepted by individual, discerning people in my everyday orbit is important to me; some dumb, anonymous mass that manifests itself in numbers of copies sold is not enough. No, I was at a particularly vulnerable juncture in my life when I took up with associate professor Insel with his talk of "technique." Of course, I wasn't writing. A nonwriting Constance Le Fevre is a damned Constance Le Fevre, and Alan Insel was my Satan Incarnate.

And then, providentially, the State Department invited Constance to go to South America for the entire month of May. They made up a killing itinerary for her, to speak on "Current Fiction in the United States" in fourteen cities, and she accepted with alacrity. The trip proved exhausting, not only physically but in a curious spiritual way as well, and Constance returned feeling old and rather knocked out by life, to her Dutch-and-Huguenot-settled village in early June. Sifting through the big cardboard box of mail the post office had saved for her, she plucked out a brief, urbane note from Insel, saying that he had tried to phone her to say good-by before he left to spend the summer in Greece.

Good riddance! thought Constance, and now I must really get back to what matters. It had been over a year since *Kull's Kill* had been published, and, except for a few desultory short stories, the kind she could write with the upper half of her mind, she had not been able to get into anything that lodged at the center of her inner necessities.

She completely forgot Alan Insel.

She withdrew into herself all through that summer and into the autumn and early winter; she saw no one, except for a harmless old college friend who came to visit but spent most of her time commuting to New York City for trysts with a married man. After some false starts, Constance got out all her South American notes and the State Department itineraries and began a novel about a successful American businesswoman destined to have a breakdown in Brazil. At first it went splendidly, she clocked herself at ten-page intervals and scribbled calculations: If she kept up this momentum she would be done with the book by spring! The more she thought about it, the more the idea of this novel pleased her: It was exactly right for where she was, both professionally and psychologically; it would be big and realistic and modern, to counterbalance the dark little romance of *Kull's Kill* in her public's eye; and it would be a way of averting her own "midlife crisis" (hateful word!) by foisting it more profitably on an interesting, high-powered woman character. Much more satisfactory than dealing at one remove from her sex with that tiresome male playwright. The business angle of her new novel fascinated her. She had not done so much research since her Huguenot saga . . . could it really be twenty years ago? She read up on multinationals, subscribed to three business magazines, and sat down happily on the floor every Sunday and clipped articles from the *Times* Business Section, which formerly she had dropped, along with Sports, in the wire trash bin outside the village drugstore, to keep from weighing her bicycle down.

And then, mysteriously, without any warning, her novel died on her. She knew the signs, the sickening reluctance to begin in the mornings, the dull, heavy joylessness that spread like a greasy film over the world, the feeling as if some connection had been severed between herself and the book. It was irrevocable, she knew. She had not been so sad since she had miscarried . . . could it have been fifteen years ago?

She mourned the book. She sat in her study and gazed blankly out at a world growing more still and frozen by the day and wondered, without much interest or emotion, what would happen to her next. A few days would go by and then she would be granted a flicker of false hope: Where was her courage? She must just start something new, perhaps a story, something quickly finished, to give her back her confidence. Just type a sentence into the machine, see where it led, make a story from it (after all, she was Constance Le Fevre, who had made her name from storytelling); "Once there was a spy," she typed, "who did not think of himself as a spy, but simply as a boy who had lost his parents and was good with languages . . ."

And that was the end of that. Then came the short, despairing journal-type ejaculations. And then the copying from the works of others. And then a silent Constance tending her cold altar of a typewriter whose mechanical carriage had gone sluggish from not being turned on in weeks. Constance, barred from her Art, which returns us to the deep winter morning on which this tale began.

Someone was knocking at the front door. The only people who used Constance's front door were the Jehovah's Witness lady with her little retarded girl and the United Parcel man bringing another bound galley of another first novel with the respectful editor's note clipped to the cover: "Just a few words from you would be of inestimable . . ."

Nonetheless, Constance sprang from her typing chair with shameful relief at the sound of that knock.

It was a young girl, slim and pretty in a piquant sort of way, with a pert face that looked like an acorn under the brown knitted cap pulled down over her ears. She wore a ratty full-length fox fur that must have been some woman's pride and joy in the 1930's, and heavy, round-toed boots like a man's.

"Yes?" said Constance. She saw a dilapidated old car parked in her circular drive.

"I was wondering if I could speak with you for a minute," said the girl, giving Constance a sudden disarming smile. "I'm not selling anything, I promise. I'm . . . well . . . I'm offering something for free."

"Would you like to come in?" Constance could tell from the smile that the girl thought highly of herself, that she was more often asked into places than not, and that even if Constance had turned her away she would have gone on thinking highly of herself.

"Thank you," the girl said, bestowing another smile on Constance. She had small, sturdy white teeth with little spaces between them. She thrust her cold, firm hand into Constance's as she gave her big boots one last stomp on the doormat. "My name is Jesse Newbold."

"How do you do," said Constance, already impressed by the girl's precise, confident manner. She closed the door on the cold. "Mine is Constance Le Fevre."

"Oh, I know who *you* are," said Jesse solemnly. "That's why I finally got up my courage to come over here. Wow, is that some fireplace!"

"The house is over two hundred years old. It's all been done over, of course. It was a ruin when we . . . I . . . won't you sit down?" Constance sat down first on the roomy sofa and patted a place beside her. How nice this room is, she thought. Her glance passed with fresh appreciation over the massive dark-stained beams, the walls of creamy yellow, the framed drawings and old maps, the ceiling-high shelves crammed with books. It had been weeks since she had sat in this room. The Impatiens plant, she noticed, had a whole sheaf of new pink buds. "Now, do tell me what it is you're offering me."

"Well," said Jesse, sitting erectly on the edge of the sofa and shrugging halfway out of the shabby fox coat, "I'm offering myself."

Under the coat she wore a long blue cotton dress sprigged with white flowers. She raised her eyes, which were the same blue of the dress, to meet Constance's puzzled look. Then, as if taking the lid off her proffered gift package, she snatched away her knitted cap. Two short brown-gold clumps of young hair fell neatly to either side of her innocent yet artful face. For a third time, Constance received the charming smile.

"But . . . I don't understand," said Constance. "You mean as a cleaning girl, or what?" She had tried several girls from the college in this capacity, but they had never worked out.

"Cleaning, if you want. Cooking, typing, fending off fans, answering letters, whatever you need. I have come to offer myself as your amanuensis," said Jesse, putting a lovely musical lilt into the old-fashioned word. "And I wouldn't charge a penny!"

"But why?" asked Constance, who was a firm believer in the adage *nobody gets something for nothing*. "I mean, what would you get out of it?"

"Everything!" the girl exclaimed passionately, and Constance was reminded poignantly of her own younger self and how fiercely that self had wanted things. "I'll get to see how you work, how you live . . . I'll have the satisfaction of knowing I'm freeing you from having to deal with . . . the stuff you've earned the right, through your talent, not to *have* to deal with!"

This part was probably rehearsed, thought Constance.

"Do you . . . um . . . write, yourself?" she asked, feeling depressed at the possibility that this persuasive, charming creature might write terrible prose.

"Oh, I know, I know what you're thinking," said Jesse, massaging the wool cap in her hands. "But you needn't worry, Miss Le Fevre. If you'll just give me a chance, I promise you'll never be burdened by *my* paltry efforts. I've come here to relieve your burdens, not add to them."

"But . . . I don't know, Jesse . . . and please call me Constance . . . I really don't know if there's enough for you to do.

Since I lost my last maid, I just run a dust cloth over things once a week, when I water the plants. . . . I've never been obsessive about house keeping . . . how many hours a week did you have in mind?"

"As many or as few as you need," explained the smiling girl. "Let me explain. You see, I'm only taking one course this semester, in Earth Science. I have to have one science course before I can transfer . . . I want to transfer to another college. . . . I've got all I can get from these people here. And . . . well . . . I hate wasting time, and since I think you're a great writer and that's what I want to be eventually, how could I better spend my time than being around you, seeing how you do it? I don't mean I'd be snooping over your shoulder or anything, but I could sort of observe your rhythms, maybe pick up some of your discipline by osmosis."

"I couldn't possibly let you work for nothing," Constance said, "I'd feel so guilty about exploiting you, I couldn't work." As soon as she pronounced this lie about her own "work" the impotence of her predicament hit her anew with the force of a physical blow. She found herself dreading the moment her bright visitor would get up to go. "I would insist on paying you," she added severely. As an incentive, she added, "In cash, of course. So there wouldn't be any income tax problem."

"I'll accept whatever you say," replied Jesse. "You can make all the rules. That's the point, too, you know. I can see what rules you *will* make and be educated by that, too. I will get to observe at close hand the mental processes of a successful woman."

Constance waved this last effusion aside. "Shall we say three-fifty an hour, starting tomorrow? Come about this time? I like to have the first hours of the morning for my . . ." She made a gesture with her hand, rather than pronounce the lie again.

Engagingly, the girl caught Constance's hand and pressed it warmly in both of hers. "I'm thrilled!" she cried.

They smiled at each other with the joy of mutual discoverers.

"By the way," said Constance, "how old are you?"

"Almost twenty," said Jesse.

"Ah, twenty was when it all began for me," said Constance with a sigh.

Constance spent the rest of that day walking around her house, seeing her life as the girl—Jesse—must see it. From the girl's view, it must look enviable. She turned over certain of Jesse's phrases with the relish she remembered certain of her rave reviews.

That evening, Constance rearranged her study. On one table she put all her unanswered mail, the many magazines and journals still in their brown wrappers, the piles of bound galley proofs of other people's novels, with the respectful editors' notes clipped to the covers . . . yes, anyone could see from that table that Constance Le Fevre was in demand. Yet, over the last frozen months, it had been all she could do to weed out the bills from the mass of correspondence and make sure they were paid on time.

She took a fresh manila file folder and wrote in large magic-marker letters on the front: WORK IN PROGRESS: though she had never done such a thing before in her life. She put the folder, with a dozen or so sheets of yellow paper inside, to the left of her typewriter.

Then she turned on the machine and sat in front of it for a while, listening to its hum, smiling bemusedly at her lamplit reflection on the dark glass of the windowpane.

The girl was, as ladies are fond of saying about their good servants, "a gem." Not that Jesse was a mere "servant." Rather, she made you go back and reexamine the nobler uses of the verb *to serve*. Jesse served Constance. Not only that, she had the tact of one's own shadow. She fitted her movements to Constance, who had been often annoyed by cleaning girls and women for no other reason than they impinged on her space. Jesse had arrived promptly at ten-thirty on her first day. Constance heard the old car drive up, but it had been agreed the day before that Jesse would let herself in. With an uplifted mood, Constance, in her study, heard the girl take off the heavy boots and begin padding softly about the downstairs rooms. The spraying of furniture polish. The thud-*thump*, thud-*thump* of the sponge mop. Constance, in a burst of greeting, had let loose a barrage of sentences on her spy story, which she had resumed in order to pretend she was writing something. Thus, the morning passed . . . thud-*thump* from downstairs . . . an answering rackety-rackety-rack from upstairs: like a dialogue between them.

At a little past noon, delicious lunch odors wafted upstairs.

"How did you know I adored mushroom soup?" Constance
called, coming downstairs. "Mmm! Is that grilled cheese?"

"The soup was in your cabinet," said Jesse, turning to smile at
Constance from her station at the stove. Today, she wore a long
dress of a modest squirrel gray with tiny pearl buttons all the way
down the front, and one of Constance's old aprons tied tightly
round her small waist. "And I always treat myself to a grilled
cheese sandwich when I'm in the midst of exams."

The table was laid with an indigo cloth Constance had forgotten she had. In a bud vase, Jesse had placed a cutting of the
blooming impatiens. The vivid splash of fuscia against the deep
blue cloth gave Constance pleasure. "But the table's only set for
one, Jesse, aren't you having anything?"

"Oh, I can get something for myself later. I thought you might
like to be alone with your thoughts."

"I'd much rather eat with you," said Constance.

"In that case," replied Jesse, her pert face coloring slightly
with embarrassment or delight, Constance wasn't sure which, "I'd
love to."

"Are your parents alive?" Constance asked delicately, when they
were having their soup. She was dying to find out more about her
amanuensis.

"Yes, but they've been divorced ever since I can remember. I always lived with my mother. She works for a dental surgeon in
Queens. She's not a very happy person. My father conducts these
archaeological digs. For amateurs. You've probably heard of them.
Not that *he's* an amateur. He just likes to be out in the field any
way he can." Jesse volunteered all this smoothly, rather glibly, as
though she'd come to terms with her parents ages ago.

"And do you see much of your father?"

"Not too much," said Jesse, spooning her soup thoughtfully.
"Once in a while. But we get along. He lives with someone not
much older than me. She and I get along okay. Would you like
more mushroom soup?"

Constance watched the girl's lithe gray-clad figure at the stove. *I
am old enough to be her mother,* she thought. *What would it
have been like, to have had her all these years? Would I be what I
am? Would she be as she is? Would she say, when discussing me
with others, "She's not a very happy person"?*

The two women soon settled into a routine. Jesse came, for five hours, on Mondays, Wednesdays, and Fridays. (Tuesdays and Thursdays were Earth Science days.) She cleaned a bit and prepared lunch. The lunches were always simple but comforting, the sort of food children might fix if the meals were left to them: sardines on toast; canned soups; bacon, lettuce, and tomato sandwiches; but Constance had not enjoyed her food so much in months. After lunch, they went to Constance's study and tackled the correspondence. Constance had been an antisocial "author" in the past, throwing in the wastebasket anything that did not directly further her career. Now, for Jesse's benefit, she found herself filling in the ballots for P.E.N. elections, answering the questionnaires the Authors' Guild was always sending about contracts, reprint rights, and so on; she dictated a brief but individual reply to every fan letter, every request to speak or teach at a college. When the correspondence table began to look threateningly bare, Constance resorted to the stacks of bound galleys of other people's novels. The pub dates had already come and gone for many of them. Of the ones still to come, Constance made two piles: the "trashy at a glance" and the possibilities. For the "trashy at a glance" she dictated caustic or amusing notes designed either to instruct Jesse that one couldn't be too careful about one's integrity or simply to make the girl snort with laughter. She decided to test her protégée's budding literary acumen on the "possible" ones.

"I just don't have time to read these," she told Jesse. "Why not take one or two of these *deserving*-looking ones home with you. No big deal. Skim through them if you feel like it, scribble something if they strike a chord."

The poor girl turned pale when Constance suggested this. But then she squared her shoulders and said she'd try. Off went the galleys, under the arm of her ratty fox coat at the end of the day; they were returned, in two days' time with neatly typed notes stapled to their covers. *A bit labored*, thought Constance. *Of course she was trying to impress me.* To please Jesse, she selected the less pretentious of the girl's critiques, changed a few adjectives, and told Jesse to send it off to the publisher over the signature of Constance Le Fevre. The girl seemed mildly surprised, though not as flattered as Constance would have hoped. *My pretty little acorn is*

not an easy nut to crack, thought Constance, her curiosity piqued
more each day by Jesse Newbold.

In mid-February, Constance came down with the flu. As soon
as she complained of sore throat and feverishness, Jesse made her
take her temperature. One hundred two degrees. "Why don't I
sleep over for a few days," suggested Jesse. "You go to bed and
pamper yourself."

"Dear child, you can't devote your life to me," protested Constance weakly, though the idea rather appealed to her.

"Who said anything about life? I'll just go and pick up a few
things from my place. It'll be fun for me to sleep in a two
hundred-year-old house."

Thus Constance abandoned herself to the process of her illness.
She lay under her satin comforter and felt helpless and cherished.
Jesse made tea and soup, lowered the shades, raised them again,
ran up and down the stairs bringing Constance books she asked
for. Then off the girl would go, to her Earth Science lab, to the
supermarket for more cans of soup, to the drugstore for more
throat lozenges and Kleenex, and Constance would lie watching
the light change outside her window. Already the darkness was
that of very early spring, not winter darkness anymore. In one of
the panes of glass was a tiny crack that winked like a diamond.
Constance lay with a book propped open on her knees, not reading but listening to the silence, waiting for the rattling sound of
the old car churning its way back up the icy drive. Her thoughts—
perhaps colored by her fever—turned to her old age and eventual
death. Was there any sort of afterlife of the consciousness, or did
you live on only through the minds of others? What others?
Would any of her books outlive her? Which ones? She imagined
herself leaving this house to Jesse in her will. She envisioned an elegant little memoir, published some years after her death, in
which Jesse, by then an old lady herself, would tell what it had
been like to live with Constance Le Fevre on a day-to-day basis.
She only hoped Jesse could write well enough to do justice to the
material. So far, except for the "book reports," Constance had
seen none of Jesse's writing. But then, the girl had vowed not to
burden her with any "paltry efforts."

"You'd make a great nurse, Jesse," said Constance, who by this time was merely luxuriating in sniffles. "That is, if you didn't want to be a writer. Speaking of which . . . don't you think it's time you showed me something? You must let me help you if I can. Turnabout's fair play." For Jesse had refused, absolutely, to accept one penny for nursing Constance.

"I . . . I don't really have anything ready at the moment," stammered the girl.

"Well," pursued Constance, "show me something that's not. Maybe something you're having problems with."

"I'll see what I can come up with," said Jesse, after going very quiet for several minutes.

That night Constance dreamed Jesse was in her room, down at the other end of the hall, writing a story for her. The girl's pen scratched louder and louder and Constance's sleep grew troubled. So abrasive! What was Jesse writing on? It sounded like a sharp instrument scratching on stone.

Constance woke up. She could still hear the repetitive scratching . . . only, it was coming from outside. She got out of bed and went to the window and pulled back the shade. A full moon gave the snowy landscape an eerie daylight quality. The amanuensis was skating on the frozen pond. Round and round, shoulders hunched forward, hands clasped behind her back. Constance could not make out her face under the knitted cap, but there was an intensity to her skating, as if she were working out her thoughts in the rhythm of it. *I'd give anything to know what she is thinking,* Constance thought. For one degrading moment, she was tempted to whisk down the hall to Jesse's room and go through her things. Maybe she kept a journal. Constance's heart pounded guiltily as a culprit's. No, that's not fair, she decided, perhaps she'll let me in on her life through her story she's promised to bring me. Constance went back to bed and sat in the dark, her hands laced tightly together, listening to the girl's skates cut and recut into the frozen pond.

Alas, the story Jesse brought was a disappointment. Although competently written, even with skill in places, it was weary and flat. It was about an older man, alone in some tropical climate, self-importantly reviewing his past. Also, it seemed he had lost a woman, though Constance wasn't sure whether she had left him

or died. *Oh, poor girl,* thought Constance. But I asked for it and
now I must be encouraging and also very, very careful. The man is
undoubtedly Jesse's attempt to "get into" her father, the distant
archaeologist; she's dispensed with the father's girlfriend, I see.
Besides . . . Jesse is only twenty . . . I don't want to nip any
later-blooming talent in the bud. Just because I was such a ruthless, early-blooming little go-getter: And yet, never once in my
young nights did I skate on a frozen pond in the moonlight.

"Jesse, I think it's terribly brave of you to write a story from the
point of view of a man . . . and a person of an older generation,
as well."

"You do?"

"Yes. And the prose is tight. Well, usually. You probably
worked hard on this."

The girl blushed.

"It's an arduous business we've chosen, Jesse. I once spent four
hundred pages trying to raise a character from the dead, and
failed. What I'm trying to say, my dear, is . . ." Constance
stopped. The girl's face was working in a woefully rubbery attempt to keep back tears.

"Please," whispered Jesse, "don't call me 'dear'."

"I'm sorry. But I didn't mean it as an affectation. You are dear
to me." Now it was Constance's turn to blush.

"I'm nothing," said Jesse between her teeth, her eyes brimming.
"I'm a piece of shit."

"But, Jesse, the story isn't that bad. My God, you're just beginning. And it has a certain . . ." she groped for a word and found
only the hated evasion Insel had used, "it has a certain *technique* . . ."

"Oh, I don't give a damn about the story," shrieked Jesse. She
dashed out of Constance's study sobbing. Constance listened to
her running down the hall to her room. The door slammed. Constance realized with a strange lift of heart that if Jesse were her
own daughter they might be having a scene just like this. I don't
give a damn about the story, either, thought Constance. I give a
damn about *her.*

At the beginning of March, Jesse insisted on moving back to
her own place. "I'll miss having you in the house," Constance

told her, trying to be brave, "but of course you must have your own life. I'll be all the more glad to see you on Monday, Wednesday, and Friday. And who knows, maybe next year . . . I've been thinking . . . if I knew I had someone responsible to stay in the house, I might travel a bit. I've decided I don't really get out enough."

"My plans are so uncertain," murmured the girl.

"Yes, I know. You said you might transfer. But if your new college is in easy distance, you might like to come here for weekends, or for the long vacations. You don't have to decide now. I just want you to know it's an option."

"You're great," said Jesse, but rather dispiritedly, Constance thought.

Since the day of the outburst, neither of them had mentioned the story again. Jesse arrived at the house promptly on her three working days, worked as well, or even better than before. Her demeanor had become more subdued and the little acorn face did not smile so readily, but she treated Constance in a new and tender way, with even more attentiveness than when she had had the flu: She asked Constance's advice about her clothes, about books she ought to read; she bought Constance a red carnation and put it in a vase in her study. One afternoon Constance had to go to the dentist in a sleetstorm; when she arrived home, she found a blazing fire in the big stone fireplace and Jesse had stayed late to prepare an "English tea" for them both. It was as if, thought Constance in bed one night, the tears springing to her eyes, the girl were making amends through these extra attentions for her lack of talent.

It was the end of March. The snow still lay on the ground, but there were hopeful patches of raw earth. Constance up in her study was feeling good. She could hear the drip, drip of melting snow from the gutters outside and from downstairs were beginning to emanate the signs of one of Jesse's comforting lunches. How nice *just being* is, thought Constance, listening to the girl clattering about in the kitchen. She responded via her typewriter with some clatter of her own, to keep up the dialogue. For though the "spy story" was by this time quite long, Constance knew it was not a real story: it was to convince Jesse that she was upstairs plying her Art; it was to give Jesse her reason for being *downstairs*.

A door slammed. A car started up. What had the girl forgotten this time? The child might not be the world's next Jane Austen, but she was a perfectionist when it came to her luncheon productions. Once before, she had rushed out at the last minute to purchase capers.

Constance decided to sneak down and see what was cooking. The table was covered with a clean cloth. In a small porcelain vase was the year's first crocus. On Constance's plate—she had already noticed with alarm that the table was set for one—was an envelope.

Constance picked up the knife beside her plate and slit open the envelope.

Dear Constance, it said (it was the first time she had seen the girl's handwriting, wobbly and uneven like a much younger person's), *Clam chowder on LOW. Bologna sandwich in fridge. I can't keep this up anymore. You are a really good lady and I can't take any more advantage of you. Please don't try to find me, you have better things to do with your time, and besides you won't. There is no "Jesse Newbold."*

She had first tried to sign herself Your Amanuensis, but after several spelling tries settled for Your Friend.

Nevertheless, Constance did try to find her. She went to all three instructors of the six sections of Earth Science at the college and described Jesse's appearance and her clothes. "You don't know her name?" they asked, wondering what this harassed woman was up to. "If you'd let me see your class lists, perhaps I could recognize it?" Constance pored over girls' names on computer print-outs, pouncing on the smallest clue. "How about this Jane Newburg?" she said excitedly. "No, Janie's a special student. She comes in a wheelchair."

Constance made a nuisance of herself at the registrar's office: more lists of names; Constance finally confiding in the registrar. "You might try the police," said the woman, "but otherwise, well frankly, you have so little to go on. Do you know how many students drop in and out of school these days like a country club? Your young secretary may be in California by now."

Constance phoned her researcher, a young man in New York who sometimes looked up things in the library for her; she asked him to call the offices of all the dental surgeons in Queens and find out if any woman who worked for them had a daughter of about twenty enrolled in this branch of the state university. But after a few days, he phoned back and said a lot of the women were suspicious and wouldn't answer until they knew why he was calling. "They're perfectly right," said Constance, suddenly seeing it from their side, and she told the young man to drop the research and how much did she owe him.

Please don't try to find me, you have better things to do with your time, and besides, you won't.

Okay, Jesse, you win, said Constance aloud, pacing the rooms of the big old house, finding something in every room that reminded her of her vanished amanuensis. You came out of nowhere and now you've gone back into it again. She stood looking at the bed, which Jesse herself had stripped down to the mattress, then covered neatly with a spread, when she had vacated the room. You were a gift and one has no right to report a vanished gift to the police.

The house began to seem like a mausoleum to her. She saw the years stretch out before her; she squinted at herself in the mirror and saw how she would be ten years from now, twenty, thirty. She saw herself as an old woman, dying alone in this house.

She telephoned her architect/ex-husband, who was remarried and lived in the next village over. When they had split up, she had promised him she would let him know before she ever put this house on the market.

He came by that afternoon, bringing with him his small son, who was a little afraid of Constance. He had aged well, her former husband: a slim, wiry man with shaggy gray hair, and, behind his steel-rimmed spectacles, a look of earnest absorption, as though he were making a constant effort to work out a floor plan of the world. Now that he belonged safely to another woman, Constance found him attractive again.

"You really mean to sell?" he asked. "Somehow I pictured you hanging on here to the very end."

"Thank you," laughed Constance drily. "I've just pictured it myself and it's that fate I want to avoid."

"But where will you go? Donny, please don't play with those fire tongs."

"I have decided," announced Constance with significance, "to go *out*."

"Out," he echoed testily, as he had done frequently during their marriage, playing back to Constance the last words of her more ambiguous statements.

"I mean out into the world. Just to live in it. With no ulterior motive. Let things and people come and go on their own terms, without my interference, and see where they'll go. I've decided to give myself a sabbatical from achievement."

"But won't you need a home to come back to when your 'sabbatical' is over?" he asked with genial concern.

"This has stopped being my home. It's more like an imposing shell that has begun to cut off my sensations and my oxygen. If you don't want to buy it, I guess I'll put it on the market."

"I always did love this house. You know that. Some of my best ideas went into this house."

"And your wife? Would she live here?"

"Would she! It's been the one bone of contention between us. How I was too soft and didn't fight you for it."

"Your softness is becoming to you," said Constance. "In fact, I think I'm going to develop *my* softness."

"Oh, Con," he laughed, with his old husband's knowledge of her. "You say that with such *ambition*."

Constance invested most of the house money in securities she had learned about during her research for the aborted businesswoman novel. She banked the rest, and bought a yellow Land Rover, some camping supplies, traveler's cheques, and she set off, with the tremulousness of a young girl, to see what was happening when she didn't interfere. She wanted to catch the outside world off guard before it froze into her own willed conception of it. She had many adventures, some disappointments, and a few scares. Through it all, she desisted grimly from taking a single note. The active, nomadic life toughened her body and dissembled her mind —for a while. Then she felt she had proved her point. She felt restless to make up her own world again. Her year had made her more impressionable to the great ebbs and flows of existence: She resolved to take similar excursions in the future, whenever she began to feel frozen or stale; but now, she couldn't wait to put all her fresh impressions into a huge, new fiction.

She settled down, this time in a city whose energies kept pace with her own, and began to write again. The juices flowed, crosscurrents sizzled on connection; her vitality had regenerated itself. Could that have been she, poor dried-up husk rattling around in that big old house, cringing prematurely at her own death?

It was perfectly clear now: Jesse Newbold, whatever her real name or real purpose, had been Constance's angel of release.

And Constance persisted in believing this, even after the mystery was cleared up. One day she received the bound galleys of a small novel. "Mr. Alan Insel has asked us to send you what we consider a striking first novel," wrote the editor of a second-rate publishing house. "Any comment you would care to give would be of inestimable . . ."

The novel was called *The Amanuensis*.

Constance read the novel. She recognized many things. She recognized the contents of her former medicine cabinet and waste basket. She recognized the menus. She recognized certain conversations in which her remarks were exaggerated to seem calculating or high-flown. Certain habits and gestures of hers were spotlit in a morbid, obsessive glare. She recognized in the omniscient narrator's weary, self-satisfied voice the same voice in the bad story she had once believed Jesse to have written. She did not recognize the Lesbian encounter in which the lonely and grasping woman writer, in bed with flu, seduces the reluctant young girl—who has only taken this job, secretly, as an "independent study" with an English professor who was cruelly spurned by the woman, after he had been given cause to hope. The professor has decided to teach the woman a lesson in unrequited love.

After the girl mysteriously disappears, the woman is distraught and finally kills herself.

Ah, it was a "striking" novel all right—but not in the sense of "technique."

When Constance had finished the book, she sat for a long time with her hands folded on her lap. He should have left himself and *his* motives out altogether. The story is the girl and the woman: All the necessary reflections and reverberations are contained within *them*. All this clutter about his broken heart and his "revenge" and about how the girl is practically illiterate, but needs the one English credit to pass out of two years of college to become an airline stewardess . . . that lowers the story to . . . just an embarrassing personal reality. If an artist had shaped and refined this material, ah what he might have made of it. Pity I didn't do it myself. Well, maybe I will someday. Life is long.

And also the woman shouldn't have killed herself; it's much harder to make people live.

She amused herself composing witty and malicious "blurbs" to send to Mr. Insel's editor. She even, for a minute, saw herself suing Insel, but of course that might be exactly what he was hoping for: the advance publicity. So, through herself and through Jesse, he had finally hit on a "lucky subject" and managed to get published.

In the end she opted for silence. Let his impoverished production have its short life, the poor little *clef* (so diligently compiled by Jesse) without its *roman*. Constance had her own work-in-progress and was so religiously grateful it was going well that she could pass up the triumph of having the last word. Why, in a way, she owed Insel thanks. He had, after all, provided her with her angel of release.

Had Jesse gotten the credit, the English credit she had needed for her "independent study"? The ambitious side of Constance wanted her to have gotten it; she had certainly earned it. But the spiritually concerned side of Constance prayed that the girl had told her shabby professor good-by and go to hell on the same day she had scrawled her contrite farewell to Constance.

Nevertheless, when Constance flew around the country, or between countries, plying her trade, or sometimes just taking a vacation from achievement, she always looked carefully—and rather wistfully—into the faces of the stewardesses when she entered the planes.

TRUTH OR CONSEQUENCES

ALICE ADAMS

Alice Adams grew up in Chapel Hill, North Carolina, and
graduated from Radcliffe; since then she has lived mostly in
San Francisco. Her collection of stories *Beautiful Girl* was
published by Knopf in 1979, and her fourth novel, *Rich Rewards*, will be published in the fall of 1980, also by Knopf.
This is her tenth O. Henry story.

This morning, when I read in a gossip column that a man named
Carstairs Jones had married a famous former movie star, I was
startled, thunderstruck, for I knew that he must certainly be the
person whom I knew as a child, one extraordinary spring, as 'Car
Jones.' He was a dangerous and disreputable boy, one of what
were then called the 'truck children,' with whom I had a most curious, brief and frightening connection. Still, I noted that in a way
I was pleased at such good fortune; I was 'happy for him,' so to
speak, perhaps as a result of sheer distance, so many years. And
before I could imagine Car as he might be now, Carstairs Jones,
in Hollywood clothes, I suddenly saw, with the most terrific accuracy and bright sharpness of detail, the schoolyard of all those
years ago, hard and bare, neglected. And I relived the fatal day, on
the middle level of that schoolyard, when we were playing Truth
or Consequences, and I said that I would rather kiss Car Jones
than be eaten alive by ants.

Our school building, then, was three stories high, a formidable
brick square. In front a lawn had been attempted, some years
back; gravelled walks led up to the broad, forbidding entranceway,
and behind the school were the playing fields, the playground.

This area was on three levels: on the upper level, nearest the school, were the huge polished steel frames for the creaking swings, the big green splintery wooden seesaws, the rickety slides— all for the youngest children. On the middle level older girls played hopscotch, various games, or jumped rope—or just talked and giggled. And out on the lowest level, the field, the boys prac- ticed football, or baseball, in the spring.

To one side of the school was a parking space, usually filled with the bulging yellow trucks that brought children from out in the country in to town: truck children, country children. Some- times they would go back to the trucks at lunchtime to eat their sandwiches, whatever; almost always there were several overgrown children, spilling out from the trucks. Or Car Jones, expelled from some class, for some new acts of rebelliousness. That area was al- ways littered with trash, wrappings from sandwiches, orange peel, coke bottles.

Beyond the parking space was an empty lot, overgrown with weeds, in the midst of which stood an abandoned trellis, perhaps once the support of wisteria; now wild honeysuckle almost cov- ered it over.

The town was called Hilton, the seat of a distinguished univer- sity, in the middle south. My widowed mother, Charlotte Ames, had moved there the previous fall (with me, Emily, her only child). I am still not sure why she chose Hilton; she never much liked it there, nor did she really like the brother-in-law, a profes- sor, into whose proximity the move had placed us.

An interesting thing about Hilton, at that time, was that there were three, and only three distinct social classes (Negroes could possibly make four, but they were so separate, even from the poorest whites, as not to seem part of the social system at all; they were in effect invisible). At the scale's top were professors and their families. Next were the townspeople, storekeepers, bankers, doctors and dentists, none of whom had the prestige nor the money they were later to acquire. Country people were the bot- tom group, families living out on the farms that surrounded the town, people who sent their children in to school on the yellow trucks.

The professors' children of course had a terrific advantage, academically, coming from houses full of books, from parental respect for learning; many of those kids read precociously and had large vocabularies. It was not so hard on most of the town children; many of their families shared qualities with the faculty people; they too had a lot of books around. But the truck children had a hard and very unfair time of it. Not only were many of their parents near-illiterates, but often the children were kept at home to help with chores, and sometimes, particularly during the coldest, wettest months of winter, weather prevented the trucks' passage over the slithery red clay roads of that countryside, that era. A child could miss out on a whole new skill, like long division, and fail tests, and be kept back. Consequently many of the truck children were overage, oversized for the grades they were in.

In the seventh grade, when I was eleven, a year ahead of myself, having been tested for and skipped the sixth (attesting to the superiority of northern schools, my mother thought, and probably she was right) dangerous Car Jones, in the same class, was fourteen, and taller than anyone.

There was some over-lapping, or crossing, among those three social groups; there were hybrids, as it were. In fact I was such a cross-breed myself: literally my mother and I were town people—my dead father had been a banker, but since his brother was a professor we too were considered faculty people. Also my mother had a lot of money, making us further elite. To me, being known as rich was just embarrassing, more freakish than advantageous, and I made my mother stop ordering my clothes from Best's; I wanted dresses from the local stores, like everyone else's.

Car Jones too was a hybrid child, although his case was less visible than mine: his country family were distant cousins of the prominent and prosperous dean of the medical school, Dean Willoughby Jones. (They seem to have gone in for fancy names, in all the branches of that family). I don't think his cousins spoke to him.

In any case, being richer and younger than the others in my class made me socially very insecure, and I always approached the playground with a sort of excited dread: would I be asked to join in a game, and if it were dodgeball (the game I most hated) would I be the first person hit with the ball, and thus eliminated?

Or, if the girls were just standing around and talking, would I get all the jokes, and know which boys they were talking about?

Then, one pale blue balmy April day, some of the older girls asked me if I wanted to play Truth or Consequences with them. I wasn't sure how the game went, but anything was better than dodgeball, and, as always, I was pleased at being asked.

"It's easy," said Jean, a popular leader, with curly red hair; her father was a dean of the law school. "You just answer the questions we ask you, or you take the consequences."

I wasn't at all sure what consequences were, but I didn't like to ask.

They began with simple questions. How old are you? What's your middle name?

This led to more complicated (and crueller) ones.

"How much money does your mother have?"

"I don't know." I didn't, of course, and I doubt that she did either, that poor vague lady, too young to be a widow, too old for motherhood. "I think maybe a thousand dollars," I hazarded.

At this they all frowned, that group of older, wiser girls, whether in disbelief or disappointment, I couldn't tell. They moved a little away from me and whispered together.

It was close to the end of recess. Down on the playing field below us one of the boys threw the baseball and someone batted it out in a long arc, out to the farthest grassy edges of the field, and several other boys ran to retrieve it. On the level above us, a rutted terrace up, the little children stood in line for turns on the slide, or pumped with furious small legs on the giant swings.

The girls came back to me. "Okay Emily," said Jean. "Just tell the truth. Would you rather be covered with honey and eaten alive by ants, in the hot Sahara desert—or kiss Car Jones?"

Then as now I had a somewhat literal mind: I thought of honey, and ants, and hot sand, and quite simply I said I'd rather kiss Car Jones.

Well. Pandemonium: did you hear what she said? Emily would kiss Car Jones! *Car Jones.* The Truth—Emily would like to kiss Car Jones! Oh Emily, if your mother only knew! Emily and Car! Emily is going to kiss Car Jones! Emily said she would! Oh, Emily!

The boys, just then coming up from the baseball field, cast

bored and pitying looks at the sources of so much noise; they had always known girls were silly. But Harry McGinnis, a glowing, golden boy, looked over at us and laughed aloud. I had been watching Harry timidly for months; that day I thought his laugh was friendly.

Recess being over, we all went back into the school room, and continued with the Civics lesson. I caught a few ambiguous smiles in my direction, which left me both embarrassed and confused

That afternoon, as I walked home from school, two of the girls who passed me on their bikes called back to me, "Car Jones!" and in an automatic but for me new way I squealed out "Oh no!" They laughed, and repeated, from their distance, "Car Jones!"

The next day I continued to be teased. Somehow the boys had got wind of what I had said, and they joined in with remarks about Yankee girls being fast, how you couldn't tell about quiet girls, that sort of wit. Some of the teasing sounded mean; I felt that Jean, for example, was really out to discomfit me, but most of it was high-spirited friendliness. I was suddenly discovered, as though hitherto I had been invisible. And I continued to respond with that exaggerated, phoney squeal of embarrassment that seemed to go over so well. Harry McGinnis addressed me as Emily Jones, and the others took that up. (I wonder if Harry had ever seen me before).

Curiously, in all this new excitement, the person I thought of least was the source of it all: Car Jones. Or rather, when I saw the actual Car, hulking over the water fountain or sprawled on the steps of a truck, I did not consciously connect him with what felt like social success, new popularity. (I didn't know about consequences).

Therefore, when the first note from Car appeared on my desk, it felt like blackmail, although the message was innocent, was even kind. "You mustn't mind that they tease you. You are the prettiest one of the girls. C. Jones." I easily recognized his handwriting, those recklessly forward-slanting strokes, from the day when he had had to write on the blackboard, "I will not disturb the other children during Music." Twenty-five times. The note was real, all right.

Helplessly I turned around to stare at the back of the room, where the tallest boys sprawled in their too-small desks. Truck children, all of them, bored and uncomfortable. There was Car, the tallest of all, the most bored, the least contained. Our eyes met, and even at that distance I saw that his were not black, as I had thought, but a dark slate blue; stormy eyes, even when, as he rarely did, Car smiled. I turned away quickly, and I managed to forget him for a while.

Having never witnessed a southern spring before, I was astounded by its bursting opulence, that soft fullness of petal and bloom, everywhere the profusion of flowering shrubs and trees, the riotous flower beds. Walking home from school I was enchanted with the yards of the stately houses (homes of professors) that I passed, the lush lawns, the rows of brilliant iris, the flowering quince and dogwood trees, crepe myrtle, wisteria vines. I would squint my eyes to see the tiniest pale green leaves against the sky.

My mother didn't like the spring. It gave her hay fever, and she spent most of her time languidly indoors, behind heavily-lined, drawn draperies. "I'm simply too old for such exuberance," she said.

"Happy" is perhaps not the word to describe my own state of mind, but I was tremendously excited, continuously. The season seemed to me so extraordinary in itself, the colors, the enchanting smells, and it coincided with my own altered awareness of myself: I could command attention, I was pretty (Car Jones was the first person ever to say that I was, after my mother's long-ago murmurings to a late-arriving baby).

Now everyone knew my name, and called it out as I walked onto the playground. Last fall, as an envious, unknown new girl, I had heard other names, other greetings and teasing-insulting nicknames. "Hey Red," Harry McGinnis used to shout, in the direction of popular Jean.

The next note from Car Jones said, "I'll bet you hate it down here. This is a cruddy town, but don't let it bother you. Your hair is beautiful. I hope you never cut it. C. Jones."

This scared me a little: the night before I had been arguing with my mother on just that point, my hair, which was long and straight. Why couldn't I cut and curl it, like the other girls? How

had Car Jones known what I wanted to do? I forced myself not to
look at him; I pretended that there was no Car Jones; it was just a
name that certain people had made up.

I felt—I was sure that Car Jones was an "abnormal" person (I'm
afraid "different" would have been the word I used, back then).
He represented forces that were dark and strange, whereas I myself
had just come out into the light. I had joined the world of the
normal. (My "normality" later included three marriages to increas-
ingly "rich and prominent" men; my current husband is a surgeon.
Three children, and as many abortions. I hate the symmetry, but
there you are. I haven't counted lovers. It comes to a normal life,
for a woman of my age.) For years, at the time of our coming to
Hilton, I had felt a little strange, isolated by my father's death,
my older-than-most-parents mother, by money. By being younger
than other children, and new in town. I could clearly afford nothing to do with Car, and at the same time my literal mind ac-
knowledged a certain obligation.

Therefore, when a note came from Car, telling me to meet him
on a Saturday morning, in the vacant lot next to the school, it
didn't occur to me that I didn't have to go. I made excuses to my
mother, and to some of the girls who were getting together for
cokes at someone's house. I'd be a little late, I told the girls, I had
to do an errand for my mother.

It was one of the palest, softest, loveliest days of that spring. In
the vacant lot weeds bloomed like the rarest of flowers; as I
walked toward the abandoned trellis I felt myself to be a sort of
princess, on her way to grant an audience to a courtier.

Car, lounging just inside the trellis, immediately brought me up
short. "You're several minutes late," he said, and I noticed that
his teeth were stained (from tobacco?) and his hands were dirty:
couldn't he have washed his hands, to come and meet me? He
asked, "Just who do you think you are, the queen of Sheba?"

I am not sure what I had imagined would happen between us,
but this was wrong; I was not prepared for surliness, this scolding.
Weakly I said that I was sorry I was late.

Car did not acknowledge my apology; he just stared at me,
stormily, with what looked like infinite scorn.

Why had he insisted that I come to meet him? And now that I
was here, was I less than pretty, seen close up?

A difficult minute passed, and then I moved a little away. I managed to say that I had to go; I had to meet some girls, I said.

At that Car reached and grasped my arm. "No, first we have to do it."

Do it? I was scared.

"You know what you said, as good as I do. You said kiss Car Jones, now didn't you?"

I began to cry.

Car reached for my hair and pulled me toward him; he bent down to my face and for an instant our mouths were mashed together (Christ, my first kiss!) Then so suddenly that I almost fell backward, Car let go of me. With a last look of pure rage he was out of the trellis and striding across the field, toward town, away from the school.

For a few minutes I stayed there in the trellis; I was no longer crying (that had been for Car's benefit, I now think) but melodramatically I wondered if Car might come back and do something else to me, beat me up, maybe. Then a stronger fear took over: someone might find out, might have seen us, even. At that I got out of the trellis fast, out of the vacant lot. (I was learning conformity fast, practicing up for the rest of my life).

I think, really, that my most serious problem was my utter puzzlement: what did it mean, that kiss? Car was mad, no doubt about that, but did he really hate me? In that case, why a kiss? (Much later in life I once was raped, by someone to whom I was married, but I still think that counts; in any case, I didn't know what he meant either).

Not sure what else to do, and still in the grip of a monumental confusion, I went over to the school building, which was open on Saturdays for something called Story Hours, for little children. I went into the front entrance and up to the library where, to the puzzlement of the librarian, who may have thought me retarded, I listened for several hours to tales of the Dutch Twins, and Peter and Polly in Scotland. Actually it was very soothing, that long pasteurized drone, hard even to think about Car while listening to pap like that.

When I got home I found my mother for some reason in a livelier, more talkative mood than usual. She told me that a boy had called while I was out, three times. Even before my heart had time to drop—to think that it might be Car, she babbled on, "Terribly polite. Really, these *bien élevé* Southern boys." (No, not Car). "Harry something. He said he'd call again. But darling, where were you, all this time?"

I was beginning to murmur about the library, homework, when the phone rang. I answered, and it was Harry McGinnis, asking me to go to the movies with him the following Saturday afternoon. I said of course, I'd love to, and I giggled in a silly new way. But my giggle was one of relief; I was saved, I was normal, after all. I belonged in the world of light, of light-heartedness. Car Jones had not really touched me.

I spent the next day, Sunday, in alternating states of agitation and anticipation.

On Monday, on my way to school, I felt afraid of seeing Car, at the same time that I was both excited and shy at the prospect of Harry McGinnis—a combination of emotions that was almost too much for me, that dazzling, golden first of May, and which I have not dealt with too successfully in later life.

Harry paid even less attention to me than he had the day before; it was a while before I realized that he was conspicuously not looking in my direction, not teasing me, and that that in itself was a form of attention, as well as being soothing to my shyness.

I realized too, after a furtive scanning of the back row, that Car Jones was *not at school*, that day. Relief flooded through my blood like oxygen, like spring air.

Absences among the truck children were so unremarkable, and due to so many possible causes, that any explanation at all for his was plausible. Of course it occurred to me, among other imaginings, that he had stayed home out of shame for what he did to me. Maybe he had run away to sea, had joined the navy or the marines? Cold-heartedly, I hoped so. In any case there was no way for me to ask.

Later that week the truth about Car Jones did come out—at first as a drifting rumor, then confirmed, and much more remarkable than joining the navy: Car Jones had gone to the principal's office, a week or so back, and had demanded to be tested for entrance (immediate) into high school, a request so unprecedented (usually only pushy academic parents would ask for such a change) and so dumbfounding that it was acceded to. Car took the test and was put into the sophomore high school class, on the other side of town, where he by age and size—and intellect, as things turned out; he tested high—most rightfully belonged.

I went to a lot of Saturday movies with Harry McGinnis, where we clammily held hands, and for the rest of that spring, and into summer, I was teased about Harry. No one seemed to remember having teased me about Car Jones.

Considering the size of Hilton, at that time, it seems surprising that I almost never saw Car again, but I did not, except for a couple of tiny glimpses, during the summer that I was still going to the movies with Harry. On both those occasions, seen from across the street, or on the other side of a dim movie house, Car was with an older girl, a high school girl, with curled hair, and lipstick, all that. I was sure that his hands and teeth were clean.

* * *

By the time I had entered high school, along with all those others who were by now my familiar friends, Car was a freshman in the local university, and his family had moved into town. Then his name again was bruited about among us, but this time as an underground rumor: Car Jones was reputed to have "gone all the way"—to have "done it" with a pretty and most popular senior in our high school. (It must be remembered that this was more unusual among the young then than now). The general (whispered) theory was that Car's status as a college boy had won the girl; traditionally, in Hilton, the senior high school girls began to date the freshmen in the university, as many as possible, as often. But this was not necessarily true; maybe the girl was simply drawn to Car, his height and his shoulders, his stormy eyes. Or maybe they didn't do it after all.

The next thing I heard about Car, who was by then an authentic town person, a graduate student in the university, was that he had written a play which was to be produced by the campus dramatic society. (Maybe that is how he finally met his movie star, as a playwright? The column didn't say.) I think I read this item in the local paper, probably in a clipping forwarded to me by my mother; her letters were always thick with clippings, thin with messages of a personal nature.

My next news of Car came from my uncle, the French professor, a violent, enthusiastic partisan in university affairs, especially in their more traditional aspects. In scandalized tones, one family Thanksgiving, he recounted to me and my mother, that a certain young man, a graduate student in English, named Carstairs Jones, had been offered a special sort of membership in D.K.E., his own beloved fraternity, and "Jones" had *turned it down.* My mother and I laughed later and privately over this; we were united in thinking my uncle a fool, and I am sure that I added, Well, good for him. But I did not, at that time, reconsider the whole story of Car Jones, that most unregenerate and wicked of the truck children.

But now, with this fresh news of Carstairs Jones, and his wife the movie star, it occurs to me that we two, who at a certain time and place were truly misfits, although quite differently—we both have made it: what could be more American dream-y, more normal than marriage to a lovely movie star? Or, in my case, my marriage to the successful surgeon?

And now maybe I can reconstruct a little of that time; specifically, can try to see how it really was for Car, back then. Maybe I can even understand that kiss.

Let us suppose that he lived in a somewhat better-than-usual farm house; later events make this plausible, his family's move to town, his years at the university. Also, I wish him well. I will give him a dignified white house with a broad front porch, set back among pines and oaks, in the red clay countryside. The stability and size of his house, then, would have set Car apart from his neighbors, the other farm families, other truck children. Perhaps his parents too were somewhat "different," but my imagination fails at them; I can easily imagine and clearly see the house, but not its population; brothers? sisters? probably, but I don't know.

Car would go to school, coming out of his house at the honk of the stained and bulging, ugly yellow bus, which was crowded with his supposed peers, toward whom he felt both contempt and an irritation close to rage. Arrived at school, as one of the truck children, he would be greeted with a total lack of interest; he might as well have been invisible, or been black, *unless* he misbehaved in an outright, conspicuous way. And so he did; Car yawned noisily during history class, he hummed during study hall, and after recess he dawdled around the playground and came in late. And for these and other assaults on the school's decorum he was punished in one way or another, and then, when all else failed to curb his ways, he would be *held back*, forced to repeat an already insufferably boring year of school.

One fall there was a minor novelty in school: a new girl (me), a Yankee, who didn't look much like the other girls, with long straight hair, instead of curled, and Yankee clothes, wool skirts and sweaters, instead of flowery cotton dresses worn all year 'round. A funny accent, a Yankee name: Emily Ames. I imagine that Car registered those facts about me, and possibly the additional information that I was almost as invisible as he, but without much interest.

Until the day of Truth or Consequences. I don't think Car was around on the playground while the game was going on; one of the girls would have seen him, and squealed out, "Oooh, there's Car, there *he is!*" I rather believe that some skinny little kid, an unnoticed truck child, overheard it all, and then ran over to where Car was lounging in one of the school busses, maybe peeling an orange and throwing the peel, in spirals, out the window. "Say Car, that little Yankee girl, she say she'd like to kiss you."

"Aw, go on."

He is still not very interested; the little Yankee girl is as dumb as the others are.

And then he hears me being teased, everywhere, and teased with his name. "Emily would kiss Car Jones—Emily Jones!" Did he feel the slightest pleasure at such notoriety? I think he must have; a man who would marry a movie star must have at least a small taste for publicity. Well, at that point he began to write me those notes: "You are the prettiest one of the girls" (which I was not). I think he was casting us both in ill-fitting roles, me as the prettiest, defenseless girl, and himself as my defender.

He must have soon seen that it wasn't working out that way. I didn't need a defender, I didn't need him. I was having a wonderful time, at his expense, if you think about it, and I am pretty sure Car did think about it.

Interestingly, at the same time he had his perception of my triviality, Car must have got his remarkable inspiration in regard to his own life: there was a way out of those miserably boring classes, the insufferable children who surrounded him. He would demand a test, he would leave this place for the high school.

Our trellis meeting must have occurred after Car had taken the test, and had known that he did well. When he kissed me he was doing his last "bad" thing in that school, was kissing it off, so to speak. He was also ensuring that I, at least, would remember him; he counted on its being my first kiss. And he may have thought that I was even sillier than I was, and that I would tell, so that what had happened would get around the school, waves of scandal in his wake.

For some reason, I would also imagine that Car is one of those persons who never look back; once kissed, I was readily dismissed from his mind, and probably for good. He could concentrate on high school, new status, new friends. Just as, now married to his movie star, he does not ever think of having been a truck child, one of the deprived, the disappointed. In his mind there are no ugly groaning trucks, no hopeless littered playground, nor squat menacing school building.

But of course I could be quite wrong about Car Jones. He could be another sort of person altogether; he could be as haunted as I am by everything that ever happened in his life.

THE PRIEST'S WIFE:
Thirteen Ways of Looking at a Blackbird

JOHN L'HEUREUX

John L'Heureux, from South Hadley, Massachusetts, is a
contributing editor of *The Atlantic* and associate professor
of English at Stanford University, where he also is director
of the Writing Program. "The Priest's Wife" will appear in
his next collection of stories, *Desires*.

1

The priest and his wife were seen skiing together before they were
married; or, rather, she was seen skiing and he was around, somewhere.

She took the lift to the slope reserved for advanced skiers. She
was wearing a black parka and formfitting ski pants, also black.
Her blond hair hung loose and straight.

Those who watched with binoculars from the deck of the lodge
said it was an exercise in discipline. She allowed herself none of
the indulgences of the advanced skiers. She plunged straight down
vertical slopes, shooting off at an angle over horizontal ones,
slaloming between invisible poles even when her momentum
would seem to indicate certain disaster. She never shifted weight
suddenly from one leg to the other. She never skidded, never fell.
She crouched, swerved, straightened, her body always completely
in control.

An exercise in grace, someone said. No one could take eyes off
her and so no one was sure who said it. It may have been the
priest.

Snow had begun to fall so they all went indoors for hot but-

tered rum and a little fooling around by the fireplace. Every now
and then somebody would look out the window and see her
mounting once more that precipitous slope, and then the lightning descent, the perfect turn around the invisible poles.

Among twenty snowy mountains she was the only moving
thing.

2

After he met her the priest was of three minds regarding what he
ought to do. After he watched her skiing on the slopes he was of
one mind. He wanted to be a poet and write perfect love songs.
For God, naturally. And then eventually perhaps for publication.
And finally just to create a good thing. To make something. He
was of one mind about that.

With such an attitude, it was inevitable that in time he got out
and left behind him the order, the priesthood, and—he sometimes
thought—common sense. Burdened with an artist's drive and a
priest's training, he did what anyone would do. He married her
and became a teacher of high school English.

3

She had a face like a woman in a novel. Her grandfather said that
to her once when she was nine or ten, and it pleased her. It gave
her an existence out there, in the real world, in a book.

She was Katharine Stone, age nine or perhaps ten, and she was
called Kate. Her father was a psychiatrist and her mother was a
psychiatric nurse; they employed a cleaning woman, a part-time
gardener, and a part-time cook. These people, and her German
shepherd, Heidi, were her serious world. Her play world was at
school where nothing was serious, really, not for a girl who had a
face like a woman in a novel.

When Kate grew up she scrutinized novels, old ones particularly, in an effort to discover what her grandfather had meant.
When she grew up some more, she turned to psychology in an
effort to discover which woman in which novel she might be. In
time she came to know certain women well, in and out of novels.

Even though she knew she was not beautiful, she worried that she might be Anna Karenina, a woman she knew by instinct, a woman she feared. Anna, with her red leather bag, getting on the train at the beginning; Anna, with that same red leather bag, plunging beneath the train's wheels at the end. Why the red leather bag? Why the train? Surely Anna's fate was in some way connected to the fact of her face. Surely one day she would unravel what that mysterious connection might be.

Perhaps she should write a novel of her own, as Cora had told her to. Perhaps she would someday. In the meanwhile she entered the convent. It was autumn, and as the sisters walked in twos from chapel to school, the wind caught their veils and whirled them about so that they flapped like the wings of blackbirds.

4

Cora Kelleher had been the cleaning lady for the Stones ever since Kate's birth. She had seen Kate Stone grow up plain and skinny, she had seen her enter the convent, and she had seen her come out ten years later, blond and beautiful. In jig time Kate had gotten herself a husband, a job with IBM, and had taken up skiing, would you believe. There was no sign Kate was pregnant or about to be. Cora herself had had seven.

"I don't see she's pregnant," Cora said to Eunice, the part time cook.

"Who would that be, now?" Eunice said, moony as ever.

"Kate Stone that was." She snorted. "The priest's wife."

"A lot of them today use the Pill."

"A lot of them today use a lot of things."

"She's a beautiful girl, though." Eunice stopped peeling potatoes and gazed out the window dreamily. "And her a nun once."

"Her a nun and now that marriage. There's no luck on that marriage, let me tell you that."

"He teaches school," Eunice said, peeling again.

"Only high school. For all his priest education, he only teaches high school."

"She's a beautiful girl, though."

"Well, she was a plain stick of a thing when she was little. I remember once when she was no bigger than this, she says to me, giving herself airs, she says, 'Grandpa said I have the face of a woman in a novel.' 'And why is he telling you grand things like that?' I says. 'Because I asked him if he thought I was pretty,' she says. So I told her, I says to her, 'Well then, you'll have to write it yourself. There are no novels about skinny little things like yourself,' I says."

"Beautiful hair she has," Eunice said, peeling.

"She was always uppity. Another time, after her grandpa died it was, she said to me, all serious and with her eyes big, she says, 'I'm going to practice dying. Like Grandpa. I'm going to spend my whole life getting ready.' 'Are you, now!' I says to her. I says, 'Well, you're going to die anyway, ready or not, once it's your time.' Uppity she was and uppity she is."

"And her a nun once," Eunice said. "I could have been a nun once. Of course it's too late now." And she ran the water loudly, so Cora Kelleher had to shout.

"There'll be no luck to that marriage, you mark my words! A man and a woman are one thing. But a priest and a woman? It's like having a buzzard sitting right square on your tombstone."

5

It had been one hell of a day for him at school. The kids had been maliciously thickheaded and they had talked all through his exposition of Yeats's "Second Coming." So what was the use? And in the two hours before Kate got home from her office, he had accomplished absolutely nothing. The poem simply wouldn't come right, he just didn't have it, he wasn't a poet.

"You are a poet," she said, "you're a wonderful poet. Why don't you let me take a poet to dinner? Anywhere you want. Or you take me. Either way I get to dine with a poet. Bewitching."

So they went out to dinner and afterward to a movie and by then he'd cheered up and they made love. Kate had office work to do but she kept quiet about it and, for his sake, pinched and poked him until he felt like doing it again. After the second time they lay, exhausted, staring at the ceiling.

"I'm going to take one more try at that poem," he said.

"Good for you," she said. "And I'm going to take a shower and fix you a nice drink—I won't disturb you—and then I'll go do a little work too."

He heard the water come on and the glass doors slide closed. She was being awfully good; she always was. And he knew what a bore he must be, what a pain in the ass about being a failed poet. And God knows, he didn't mean to rage; he just couldn't help it. He'd make it up to her and surprise her in the shower.

He opened the bathroom door softly, though there was no need for stealth since the water was running wildly. He was about to slide open the glass doors to the shower when he saw—as if in a film—the long line of her body, complete, perfect. She had her head back so that the water struck her full in the face. He traced the long neck to where it disappeared in the rise of her small breasts. And then the rib cage and her little belly and the long severe thighs. Perfection.

He sat down on the toilet seat, his head in his hands.

"Will I ever know her?" he whispered, and then again, "Will I ever know her?" He had folded that body so completely into his own so many times now during these past three years, and still he had never seen her . . . he could not find the words . . . her naked face. "I will never know her," he whispered, but already he was thinking something else. He was thinking, I will never be a poet. Never.

He left the bathroom, angry, and went to his little study off the kitchen. Kate had shopped everywhere to get him just the right desk and she had decorated the study according to his instructions, but still he never used it. His desk was heaped with books and papers, so there was no room to write. He wrote either at the dining table, which he also kept heaped with books, or sitting in his easy chair. You don't need a study if you can't write anyhow, he had told her, though it was he who had insisted on the study in the first place.

He could hear her tiptoeing around the kitchen as she got his drink ready. How could he concentrate knowing she might interrupt him at any second? "I don't want to bother you but . . ." He sat there, daring her. She glided into the room on her soft slippers and placed the drink on a coaster near him, patting him twice on the shoulder.

"Goddamnit," he shouted, "I'm trying to write. Is there no place in this goddamned apartment I can work in peace?"

"I didn't say anything," she said, defensive, used by now to these outbursts. "I just gave you your drink."

"You bumped me on the shoulder. You poked me twice. I was just getting it right and you interrupted and now it's gone." He looked at her with hatred and then took a good slug of his drink. "I'm sorry. I hate to sound like a bastard, but Jesus Christ!" He had been penitent for a second and now he was furious all over again. He slammed down the glass and the liquor sloshed onto his papers. "You always do this! You always ruin it! You always . . ." But she had gone. He followed her into the bedroom where she had her papers spread on the bed. She bent over the papers, not looking at him.

"Don't," she said. "Not again. I can't take it."

"Sometimes I detest you," he said. "Sometimes I curse the day I ever laid eyes on you."

She stared back at him in silence. And then she said, "Someday you'll say one thing too many. I give you warning. Now."

He backed out of the room. Several drinks later he woke her up. "Forgive me, sweet. Katie, forgive me, please," he said, and buried his head in her breasts.

"I know," she said. "It's all right. I love you."

"Friends?" he said.

"Friends," she said.

And so it was over, this time.

6

They had been married five years now, and it was winter. Icicles filled the long window that looked out over the ruined garden. It was evening and shadows in the garden and shadows in the living room flickered as Kate moved back and forth in front of the light, watering the indoor plants. She wore a red gown, knotted at the neck and waist, and it created for her a mood in which she could feel withdrawn but not unpleasant. Her husband sat with his chin in his hands, watching her, watching the shadows she cast. He had just despaired, yet again, of ever being a poet. And besides, he had a terrible sore throat. And so they had their last fight.

It was about her habit of visiting her widower father, that bastard, every Saturday, and about her job at IBM. And it was about her way of being vague with him, as if what he said required only half her attention, as if he didn't really matter. And it was about his failure as a writer.

Five years of this and now, at last, she had had enough.

"I can't live your life for you," she said. "There are some things you've got to do for yourself. You've got to breathe, you've got to eat, you've got to crap, and goddamnit, you've got to live. If you hate your job, then do something about it. And if you resent mine, which you do, then why don't you . . ."

"Go ahead, say it! Say it! You've been wanting to."

But she didn't say it. She went to bed and he went to the kitchen for a drink. He had a second and a third and then he went in to wake her but she wasn't asleep yet anyhow. He apologized and she apologized and it was almost over.

Deliberately he looked at her hand. He had had a sort of vision once of who she was and how she loved him and it had split him down the middle. He had thought at the time that he had become two people, both of them crazy. And all because of her hand. She had placed it on his knee during a quarrel—afterward he could not remember what the quarrel was about—and he had watched it crumple and break like an autumn leaf, while his words continued angry and smooth and satisfying. In those days he had had all the words. And then, as the hand fell from his knee, he stopped and said to her, "I'm not a good person. I'm not like you." He cried then, and he had not cried in fifteen years. That was during the first week of their marriage.

Now, five years later, he sat on the edge of the bed looking at her hand, white and small with long tapered fingers, trying to make it happen again, that vision.

But nothing happened.

"Friends?" he said.

"Friends," she said.

In bed, they both pretended to sleep. After a long while she got up and poured herself a drink and sat in the dark living room. She finished it and poured herself another. Then, not really knowing what she was going to do, she put on the light and got out a pencil and a legal pad and wrote, "I want out. I want a divorce." She stared at the words for a long time, and then she wrote them again. And then again. She found a peculiar satisfaction in form-

ing the letters, in putting down on paper those words that finally
said the unsayable. "I hate him. I hate what he turns me into. I
hate the way he hates himself." She made a list of the things she
could not say, and she said them. She wrote out their most violent
quarrels, including in parentheses the words she had not said because they might kill him. ("You'll never be a poet." "You have a
gift for words but no gift for poetry." "You're wrecking your life
and you're trying to wreck mine, but I'm not going to let you."
"Why didn't you stay in the priesthood and just drink yourself to
death?") And it was astonishing. Words did not kill, at least not
on paper. Rather, they gave her a wonderful feeling of release, of
freedom. She got herself another drink and went on writing until,
hours later, she had run out of things she was angry at. Without a
pause she moved into a description of how she had first met him,
her husband now, in the train station. The strap had broken on
her red leather tote bag and he had offered to help her with it.
But the bag was square, and with his hands occupied with skis
and his own suitcase, he hadn't been able to get a good grip on it;
he dropped it and it opened and spilled out keys and makeup and
God knows what else. She had laughed at him then and he had
laughed too.

She stopped writing—these notes, in time, would find their way
into her first novel—and looked out at the garden where the sun
was just touching the silver branches of the trees. A single black-
bird lit on the end of a branch, making it bend, sending down a
thin sifting of snow. Smiling to herself, she recited the
Magnificat, as she had done every morning for the past twenty
years.

And so the divorce was put off for eleven months.

7

During those eleven months they often walked by the river together. And they often dined out. He appeared to be the more
talkative but in public she did most of the talking. If the marriage
was not a happy one, they at least put a good face on it, and five
years is a long time to put a good face on anything.

Acquaintances who had known them off and on for years said
that marriage made them both merely conventional. His wild

imagination and flights of whimsy disappeared altogether, replaced by a kind of watchfulness and a mildly sardonic humor. She talked politics a lot and, when the conversation turned to religion, she avoided discussion of how much she still believed, dismissing the topic with a remark about how bored she was with Sunday sermons.

Friends of hers who visited from the convent said the couple was supremely happy. She had taken to wearing high-fashion clothes, finding it necessary to be more feminine now that she had so many males directly responsible to her. She had a big job with big obligations. Friends of his who visited from the monastery said she had done wonders for him. He had put on weight and he was no longer so volatile. He had settled down to being a high school teacher; her big job with IBM obviously posed no ego problems for him.

They had private jokes and sometimes on the street they were caught laughing immoderately. They held hands at these times. They also held hands in restaurants, though not so frequently as on their walks. This was not natural in people married so long; it was probably a cover-up for something.

After eleven endless months they separated.

8

In the two years of their separation he had seven job promotions with his ad agency and she wrote two novels, both of them flops.

He had moved to New York, and by some fluke, or by talent, managed to put together a trendy portfolio. In no time he was making as much money as Kate, and by the end of the two years he was making a great deal more. He was happy and fulfilled, except of course that he missed her. He was a different man now. It was the writing that had made him so miserable. She'd see. Would she take him back? Would she agree to drop the divorce business and give the marriage another try? And, ahem, would IBM be willing to transfer her from her new job in Gaithersburg to a newer one in New York?

She smiled. She would think about it. But he'd better be clear on one thing; she was fiddling around with a novel and she didn't intend to give it up for anybody. Got that?

The first two novels were mistakes, no doubt about it. She had begun with a description of their meeting in the train station, a nice, tightly written scene, but when read aloud it sounded so like a murder mystery that she decided to turn it into one. She killed herself off in the first chapter and then . . . well, it didn't work out. Her murders were clumsy and her murderers uninteresting; she was more preoccupied with psychoanalyzing the bereaved than with moving the damned plot along. Five publishers turned it down before she realized that it was a mistake, that she just didn't know anything about murders and didn't care much either.

With the second novel she decided to stick to what she knew: life in a convent. She put in the mistress of novices and her more colorful teachers and her eager and ambitious nun friends, all of them meticulously drawn. She had gotten down every revealing gesture, every idiosyncrasy of speech and behavior, and yet somehow nobody came alive. The book was a jumble of real people rather than fictional characters, and it was rejected everywhere.

Her next novel, the one she wouldn't give up for anybody, would be different. She would write about what she knew as if she didn't really know it. And she would put herself in it. One thing was certain: whatever it was that she knew and was able to get down on paper, she herself was involved in it.

Meanwhile she would think about dropping the divorce suit. She might even think about requesting a transfer.

9

In Utica, New York, the priest's mother heard the following established facts at the Lady's Guild.

1. Katharine Stone had grown up in Utica and moved to Boston when she was five. She was an airline stewardess for seven years and often flew back and forth between Boston and upper New York State. Now that she was separated she had gone back to United. She had been seen in her uniform only last week. In Utica. Many people in Utica knew her well.

2. Kate Stone was a staff editor of *Ms.* magazine and had formerly been a fashion model. She was six feet tall and beautiful. She dated married men.

3. Katharine Stone was a former nun who grew up in D.C. but

who lived, at the time of her marriage, in Baltimore. She was from a distinguished family of doctors in which all the men went to Harvard and all the women to Radcliffe. She was, despite this, not the least bit snobbish and was quite content teaching high school English. Her family would never permit a divorce.

4. A friend of the guild's president's daughter had gone to Noroton with Kate Stone and there they had both known the Ford girls, Anne and Charlotte. They, the four, had not been close since she entered the convent. Kate Stone, of course. Anne Ford had not entered the convent and neither had Charlotte.

5. Kate Stone had been a dancer until she broke her foot. Since then she had worked for IBM and spent all her free time skiing. She was going to get a divorce and then marry her ski instructor.

The priest's mother went home and cried until ten, when *Kojak* came on.

10

In the spring of that year they both got transfers to Boston, where they bought a house and took up where they left off, only a lot better. Kate was involved in writing her novel and her husband was all worked up over a new ad campaign, and so they were happy. They even put in their names to adopt a child.

That summer they drove to Baltimore to visit Kate's friends in the convent. Kate was all in white and very tanned though it was still only the end of June. He was wearing his white suit and his white shoes, too summery perhaps, just this side of affectation. They knew they looked good.

Kate's friends came to the visiting parlor in twos and threes. Visits were not so exciting as they had been years ago, before the cloister had moved into the world. These days a visit from outside meant little. Still, everybody was curious to see the couple now that they were reconciled. How long would it last? Kate looked wonderful, but he was putting on weight. He was polite, said very little. Whenever they asked about him, he answered briefly and directed the conversation back to Kate and her friends. There was no telling from the way he acted whether or not he'd take off again for New York. Poor Kate.

At noon some of the sisters went to chapel for midday meditation. Kate and her husband went for a walk around the grounds. Hand in hand they walked down the long slope of grass to the lake. A small dirt path ran around the lake and they followed it for a while, disappearing among the overhanging willows and high swamp grass. There were pine needles everywhere. He wanted to lie down on them but she said no, it was time to turn back. They lay down for a little while anyway.

As they came out from under the trees, they paused and looked across the lake. The sun turned the water green and cast a green reflection on their faces and clothes.

The sisters, coming out of chapel, paused on the cloister walk to gaze out over the lake. The sisters saw the man and woman, their hands joined together, their clothes of dazzling white drenched green in the reflection from the lake. Just those two white figures, joined, against the world of green.

Someone cried out in disbelief.

11

And so she finished the damned book, as she said, and got a publisher, and sold 1600 copies of it. The New York *Times* said it was a promising start and the *New Republic* said it was witty and disturbing. Nobody else said anything about it.

What she wrote was, in actuality, a pack of lies about her friends at IBM and about her husband and—in a peculiar way—about herself. The characters numbered thirteen and they were as diverse in their morals and desires and preoccupations as even God or nature would have made them. There was a man who was so insecure he dared to communicate with his employees only when he had worked himself into a rage. There was a man whose sole love was for machines and who had cut himself off from human intercourse completely. There was a housewife whose loneliness and vulnerability drove her into affairs with any man who presented himself. And another who wanted to write poetry and instead was drinking herself to death. And a woman executive who made passionate love to her husband each night, moaning and tearing at his flesh, and then went to the bathroom where she calmly and coldly masturbated before the full-length mirror. They were unscrupulous people and hateful people and pitiful people. And all of them, so her husband recognized, understanding at last, were Kate Stone. In some way, at some moment in the story, they all wore her face.

He was grateful for the book. She existed now, in reality, for him.

She was grateful too. The book was done, some kind of awful duty was discharged, and she felt no desire to write another. All she wanted to do now was to take up skiing once again and to conquer at last the dark fear of hers that plunging down that slope was somehow entering the valley of the shadow of death.

12

It was their anniversary and she gave him a card she had made herself. Inside it she had written, "This river that carries us with it, out of control, out of any control, at least carries us together."

He did not know what she meant, he never knew what she meant, but it no longer mattered because he had seen her naked face and loved her.

13

Time passed for them. There may have been children, a boy and a girl, adopted. There may have been a dog. There may have been . . . but the snow falls and everything recedes into uncertainty, except that we die and we do not wish to die.

"It's snowing," she said.

"And it's going to snow," he said.

The light on the snow had been pale purple all afternoon and, though it continued to snow, she insisted nonetheless on going skiing.

They were seen leaving the lodge where everyone was sitting around drinking hot buttered rum by the fireplace and they were seen again later taking the lift to the highest slope. Slowly at first, and then with lightning speed, they descended, two black figures against the white snow, darting across one another's path, plunging straight down and then veering off at an angle, dodging invisible poles. For a long while people from the lodge watched them, but then the sun dipped behind the trees. Nonetheless they went on ascending and descending that hill.

In the first dark an owl hooted and some winter bird shifted on his perch in the cedar limbs.

THE PITCHER

ANDRE DUBUS

Andre Dubus was born on August 11, 1936, in Lake
Charles, Louisiana. He has published a novel, *The Lieu-
tenant* (1967, Dial), and collections of stories: *Separate
Flights* (1975, David Godine) and *Adultery And Other
Choices* (1977, Godine). "The Pitcher" has also appeared
in a recent collection of stories published by Godine.

They cheered and clapped when he and Lucky Ferris came out of
the dugout, and when the cheering and clapping settled to spo-
radic shouts he had already stopped hearing it, because he was
feeling the pitches in his right arm and watching them the way he
always did in the first few minutes of his warm-up. Some nights
the fast ball was fat or the curve hung or the ball stayed up
around Lucky's head where even the hitters in this Class C league
would hit it hard. It was a mystery that frightened him. He threw
the first hard one and watched it streak and rise into Lucky's mitt;
and the next one; and the next one; then he wasn't watching the
ball anymore, as though it had the power to betray him. He
wasn't watching anything except Lucky's target, hardly conscious
of that either, or of anything else but the rhythm of his high-kick-
ing windup, and the ball not thrown but released out of all his
motion; and now he felt himself approaching that moment which
he could not achieve alone: a moment that each time was granted
to him. Then it came: the ball was part of him, as if his arm
stretched sixty feet six inches to Lucky's mitt and slammed the ball
into leather and sponge and Lucky's hand. Or he was part of the
ball.

First appeared in *The North American Review*. Copyright © 1979 by the
University of Northern Iowa. Reprinted by permission.

Now all he had to do for the rest of the night was concentrate
on prolonging that moment. He had trained himself to do that,
and while people talked about his speed and curve and change of
pace and control, he knew that without his concentration they
would be only separate and useless parts; and instead of nineteen
and five on the year with an earned run average of two point one
five and two hundred and six strikeouts, going for his twentieth
win on the last day of the season, his first year in professional ball,
three months short of his twentieth birthday, he'd be five and
nineteen and on his way home to nothing. He was going for the
pennant too, one half game behind the New Iberia Pelicans who
had come to town four nights ago with a game and a half lead,
and the Bulls beat them, Friday and Saturday, lost Sunday, so that
now on Monday in this small Louisiana town, Billy's name was
on the front page of the local paper alongside the news of the war
that had started in Korea a little over a month ago. He was ready.
He caught Lucky's throw, nodded to him, and walked with head
down toward the dugout and the cheers growing louder behind it,
looking down at the bright grass, holding the ball loosely in his
hand.

He spoke to no one. He went to the far end of the dugout that
they left empty for him when he was pitching. He was too young
to ask for that, but he was good enough to get it without asking;
they gave it to him early in the year, when they saw he needed it,
this young pitcher Billy Wells who talked and joked and yelled at
the field and the other dugout for nine innings of the three nights
he didn't pitch, but on his pitching night sat quietly, looking neither relaxed nor tense, and only spoke when politeness required it.
Always he was polite. Soon they made a space for him on the
bench, where he sat now knowing he would be all right. He did
not think about it, for he knew as the insomniac does that to give
it words summons it up to dance; he knew that the pain he had
brought with him to the park was still there; he even knew it
would probably always be there; but for a good while now it was
gone. It would lie in wait for him and strike him again when he
was drained and had a heart full of room for it. But that was a long
time from now, in the shower or back in the hotel, longer than
the two and a half hours or whatever he would use pitching the
game; longer than a clock could measure. Right now it seemed a

great deal of his life would pass before the shower. When he trotted out to the mound they stood and cheered and, before he threw his first warm-up pitch, he tipped his cap.

He did not make love to Leslie the night before the game. All season, he had not made love to her on the night before he pitched. He did not believe, as some ballplayers did, that it hurt you the next day. *It's why they call it the box score anyway,* Hap Thomas said on the bus one night after going hitless; *I left me at least two basehits in that whorehouse last night.* Like most ballplayers in the Evangeline League, Thomas had been finished for a long time: a thirty-six year old outfielder who had played three seasons—not consecutively—in Triple A ball, when he was in his twenties. Billy didn't make love the night before a game because he still wasn't used to night baseball; he still had the same ritual he'd had in San Antonio, playing high school and American Legion ball: he drank a glass of buttermilk then went to bed, where for an hour or more he imagined tomorrow's game, although it seemed the game already existed somewhere in the night beyond his window and was imagining him. When finally he slept, the game was still there with him, and in the morning he woke to it, remembered pitching somewhere between daydream and nightdream: and until time for the game he felt like a shadow cast by the memory and the morning's light, a shadow that extended from his pillow to the locker room, when he took off the clothes which had not felt like his all day and put on the uniform which in his mind he had been wearing since he went to bed the night before. In high school, his classes interfered with those days of being a shadow. He felt that he was not so much going to classes as bumping into them on his way to the field. But in summer when he played American Legion ball, there was nothing to bump into, there was only the morning's wait which wasn't really waiting because waiting was watching time, watching it win usually, while on those mornings he joined time and flowed with it, so that sitting before the breakfast his mother cooked for him he felt he was in motion toward the mound.

And he had played a full season less one game of pro ball and still had not been able to convince his mind and body that the night before a game was far too early to enter the rhythm and concentration that would work for him when he actually had the

ball in his hand. Perhaps his mind and body weren't the ones who
needed convincing; perhaps he was right when he thought he was
not imagining the games, but they were imagining him: benevo-
lent and slow-witted angels who had followed him to take care of
him, who couldn't understand they could rest now, lie quietly the
night before, because they and Billy had all next day to spend
with each other. If he had known Leslie was hurt he could have
told her, as simply as a man saying he was beset by the swollen
agony of mumps, that he could not make love on those nights,
and it wasn't because he preferred thinking about tomorrow's
game, but because those angels had followed him all the way to
Lafayette, Louisiana. Perhaps he and Leslie could even have
laughed about it, for finally it was funny, as funny as the story
about Billy's Uncle Johnny whose two hounds had jumped the
fence and faithfully tracked or followed him to a bedroom a few
blocks from his house, and bayed outside the window: a bedroom
Uncle Johnny wasn't supposed to be in, and more trouble than
that, because to get there he had left a bedroom he wasn't supposed to leave.

Lafayette was funny too: a lowland of bayous and swamps and
Cajuns. The Cajuns were good fans. They were so good that in
early season Billy felt like he was barnstorming in some strange
country, where everybody loved the Americans and decided to
love baseball too since the Americans were playing it for them.
They knew the game, but often when they yelled about it they
yelled in French, and when they yelled in English it sounded like
a Frenchman's English. This came from the colored section too.
The stands did not extend far beyond third and first base, and
where the first base stands ended there was a space of about fifty
feet and, after that, shoved against each other, were two sections of
folding wooden bleachers. The Negroes filled them, hardly noticed beyond the fifty feet of air and trampled earth. They were
not too far down the right field line: sometimes when Billy ran
out a ground ball he ended his sprint close enough to the bleachers to hear the Negroes calling to him in French, or in the
English that sounded like French.

Two Cajuns played for the Bulls. The full name was the Lafayette Brahma Bulls, and when the fans said all of it, they said
Bremabulls. The owner was a rancher who raised these bulls, and

one of his prizes was a huge and dangerous-looking hump-necked bull whose grey coat was nearly white; it was named Huey for their governor who was shot and killed in the state capitol building. Huey was led to home plate for opening day ceremonies, and after that he attended every game in a pen in foul territory against the right field fence. During batting practice the left handers tried to pull the ball into the pen. Nobody hit him, but when the owner heard about it he had the bull brought to the park when batting practice was over. By then the stands were filling. Huey was brought in a truck that entered through a gate behind the colored bleachers, and the Negroes would turn and look behind them at the bull going by. The two men in the truck wore straw cowboy hats. So did the owner, Charlie Breaux. When the Cajuns said his first and last names together they weren't his name anymore. And since it was the Cajun third baseman, E.J. Primeaux, a wiry thirty year old who owned a small grocery store which his wife ran during the season, who first introduced Billy to the owner, Billy had believed for the first few days after reporting to the club that he pitched for a man named Mr. Chollibro.

One night someone did hit Huey: during a game, with two outs, a high fly ball that Hap Thomas could have reached for and caught; he was there in plenty of time, glancing down at the pen's fence as he moved with the flight of the ball, was waiting safe from collision beside the pen, looking now from the ball to Huey who stood just on the other side of the fence, watching him; Hap stuck his arm out over the fence and Huey's head; then he looked at Huey again and withdrew his arm and stepped back to watch the ball strike Huey's head with a sound the fans heard behind third base. The ball bounced up and out and Hap barehanded it as Huey trotted once around the pen. Hap ran toward the dugout, holding the ball up, until he reached the first base umpire who was alternately signalling safe and pointing Hap back to right field. Then Hap flipped him the ball and, grinning, raised both arms to the fans behind the first base line, kept them raised to the Negroes as he ran past their bleachers and back to Huey's pen, taking off his cap as he approached the fence where Huey stood again watching, waved his cap once over the fence and horns, then trotted to his position, thumped his glove twice, then lowered it to his knee, and his bare hand to the other, and crouched.

The fans were still laughing and cheering and calling to Hap and Huey and Chollibro when two pitches later the batter popped up to Caldwell at short.

In the dugout Primeaux said: "Hap, I seen many a outfielder miss a fly ball because he's wall-shy, but that's the first time I ever seen one miss because he's *bull*-horn shy." And Hap said: "In this league? That's nothing. No doubt about it, one of these nights I'll go out to right field and get bit by a cottonmouth so big he'll chop my leg in two." "Or get hit by lightning," Shep Caldwell said. In June lightning had struck a centerfielder for the Abbeville Athletics; struck the metal peak of his cap and exited into the earth through his spikes. When the Bulls heard the announcement over their public address system, their own sky was cloudy and there were distant flashes; perhaps they had even seen the flash that killed Tommy Lyons thirty miles away. The announcement came between innings when the Bulls were coming to bat; the players and fans stood for a minute of silent prayer. Billy was sitting beside Hap. Hap went to the cooler and came back with a paper cup and sat looking at it but not drinking, then said: "He broke a leg, Lyons did. I played in the Pacific Coast League with him one year. 'Forty-one. He was hitting three-thirty; thirty-something home runs; stole about forty bases. Late in the season he broke his leg sliding. He never got his hitting back. Nobody knew why. Tommy didn't know why. He went to spring training with the Yankees then back to the Pacific Coast League, and he kept going down. I was drafted by then, and next time I saw him was two years ago when he came to Abbeville. We had a beer one night and I told him he was headed for the major leagues when he broke his leg. No doubt about it. He said he knew that. And he still didn't understand it. Lost something: swing; timing. Jesus, he used to hit the ball. Now they fried him in front of a bunch of assholes in Abbeville. How's that for shit." For the rest of the game most of the players watched their sky; those who didn't were refusing to. They would not know until next day about the metal peak on Lyons' cap; but two innings after the announcement, Lucky went into the locker room and cut his off. When he came back to the dugout holding the blue cap and looking at the hole where the peak had been, Shep said:

"Hell, Lucky, it never strikes twice." Lucky said: "That's because it don't have to," and sat down, stroking the hole.

Lafayette was only a town on the way to Detroit, to the Tigers; unless he got drafted, which he refused to think about, and thought about daily when he read of the war. Already the Tiger scout had watched Billy pitch three games and talked to him after each one, told him all he needed was time, seasoning; told him to stay in shape in the off-season; told him next year he would go to Flint, Michigan, to Class A ball. He was the only one on the club who had a chance for the major leagues, though Billy Joe Baron would probably go up, but not very far; he was a good first base-man and very fast, led the league in stolen bases, but he had to struggle and beat out drag bunts and ground balls to keep his av-erage in the two-nineties and low three hundreds, and he would not go higher than Class A unless they outlawed the curve ball. The others would stay with the Bulls, or a team like the Bulls. And now Leslie was staying in this little town that she wasn't sup-posed to see as a town to live in longer than a season, and staying too in the little furnished house they were renting, with its rusted screen doors and its yard that ended in the back at a woods which farther on became a swamp, so that Billy never went off the back porch at night and if he peered through the dark at the grass long enough he was sure he saw cottonmouths.

She came into the kitchen that morning of the final game, late morning after a late breakfast so he would eat only twice before pitching, when he was already—or still, from the night before—concentrating on his twentieth win; and the pennant too. He wanted that: wanted to be the pitcher who had come to a third place club and after one season had ridden away a pennant winner. She came into the kitchen and looked at him more seriously than he'd ever seen her, and said: "Billy, it's a terrible day to tell you this but you said today was the day I should pack."

He looked at her from his long distance then focused in closer, forced himself to hear what she was saying, felt like he was even forcing himself to see her in three dimensions instead of two, and said: "What's the matter, baby?"

"I'm not going."

"Not going where?"

"San Antonio. Flint. I'm staying here."

Her perspiring face looked so afraid and sorry for him and determined all at once, that he knew he was finished, that he didn't
even know what was happening but there would never be enough
words he could say. Her eyes were brimming with tears, and he
knew they were for herself, for having come to this moment in the
kitchen, so far from everything she could have known and predicted; deep in her eyes, as visible as stars, was the hard light of
something else, and he knew that she had hated him too, and he
imagined her hating him for days while he was on the road: saw
her standing in this kitchen and staring out the screen door at the
lawn and woods, hating him. Then the picture completed itself: a
man, his back to Billy, stood beside her and put his arm around
her waist.

"Leslie?" and he had to clear his throat, clear his voice of the
fear in it: "Baby, have you been playing around?"

She looked at him for such a long time that he was both afraid
of what she would say, and afraid she wouldn't speak at all.

"I'm in love, Billy."

Then she turned and went to the back door, hugging her
breasts and staring through the screen. He gripped the corners of
the table, pushed his chair back, started to rise, but did not; there
was nothing to stand for. He rubbed his eyes, then briskly shook
his head.

"It wasn't just that you were on the road so much. I was ready
for that. I used to tell myself it'd be exciting a lot of the time, especially in the big leagues. And I'd tell myself in ten years it'd be
over anyway, some women have to—"

"*Ten?*" Thinking of the running he did, in the outfield on the
days he wasn't pitching, and every day at home between seasons,
having known long ago that his arm was a gift and it would last
until one spring when it couldn't do the work anymore, would become for the first time since it started throwing a baseball just an
ordinary arm; and what he could and must do was keep his lungs
and legs strong so they wouldn't give out before it did. He surprised himself: he had not known that, while his wife was leaving
him, he could proudly and defensively think of pitching in his
early thirties. He had a glimpse of the way she saw him, and he
was frightened and ashamed.

"All right: fifteen," she said. "Some women are married to

sailors and soldiers and it's longer. It wasn't the road trips. It was when you were home: you weren't here. You weren't here, with me."

"I was here all day. Six, seven hours at the park at night. I don't know what that means."

"It means I'm not what you want."

"How can you tell me what I want?"

"You want to be better than Walter Johnson."

From his angle he saw very little of her face. He waited. But this time she didn't speak.

"Leslie, can't a man try to be the best at what he's got to do and still love his wife?" Then he stood: "Goddamnit, who *is* he?"

"George Lemoine," she said through the screen.

"George *Lemoine*. Who's George *Lemoine*?"

"The dentist I went to."

"What dentist you went to?"

She turned and looked at his face and down the length of his arms to his fists, then sat at the opposite end of the table.

"When I lost the filling. In June."

"June?"

"We didn't start then." Her face was slightly lowered, but her eyes were raised to his, and there was another light in them: she was ashamed but not remorseful, and her voice had the unmistakable tone of a woman in love; they were never so serious as this, never so threatening, and he was assaulted by images of Leslie making love with another man. "He went to the games alone. Sometimes we talked down at the concession stand. We—" Now she looked down, hid her eyes from him, and he felt shut out forever from the mysteries of her heart.

All his life he had been confident. In his teens his confidence and hope were concrete: the baseball season at hand, the season ahead, professional ball, the major leagues. But even as a child he had been confident and hopeful, in an abstract way. He had barely suffered at all, and he had survived that without becoming either callous or naive. He was not without compassion when his life involved him with the homely, the clumsy, the losers. He simply considered himself lucky. Now his body felt like someone else's, weak and trembling. His urge was to lie down.

"And all those times on the road I never went near a whore-house."

"It's not the same."

He was looking at the beige wall over the sink, but he felt that her eyes were lowered still. He was about to ask what she meant, but then he knew.

"So I guess when I go out to the mound tonight he'll be moving in, is that right?"

Now he looked at her, and when she lifted her face, it had changed: she was only vulnerable.

"He has to get a divorce first. He has a wife and two kids."

"Wait a minute. *Wait* a minute. He's got a wife and two *kids?* How *old* is this son of a bitch?"

"Thirty-four."

"God*damn*it, Leslie! How dumb can you be? He's getting what he wants from you, what makes you think he won't be smart enough to leave it at that? God*damn*."

"I believe him."

"You believe him. A dentist anyhow. How can you be married to a ballplayer and fall for a dentist anyhow? And what'll you do for money? You got that one figured out?"

"I don't need much. I'll get a job."

"Well you won't have much either, because I'm going over there and kill him."

"Billy." She stood, her face as admonitory as his mother's. "He's got enough troubles. All summer I've been in trouble too. I've been sad and lonesome. That's the only way this could ever happen. You know that. All summer I've been feeling like I was running alongside the players' bus waving at you. Then he came along."

"And picked you up."

He glared at her until she blushed and lowered her eyes. Then he went to the bedroom to pack. But she had already done it: the suitcase and overnight bag stood at the foot of the bed. He picked them up and walked fast to the front door. Before he reached it she came out of the kitchen, and he stopped.

"Billy. I don't want you to be hurt; and I know you won't be for long. I hope someday you can forgive me. Maybe write and tell me how you're doing."

His urge to drop the suitcase and overnight bag and hold her and ask her to change her mind was so great that he could only fight it with anger; and with the clarity of anger he saw a truth which got him out the door.

"You want it all, don't you? Well, forget it. You just settle for what you chose."

Scornfully he scanned the walls of the living room, then Leslie from feet to head; then he left, out into the sun and the hot still air, and drove into town and registered at a hotel. The old desk clerk recognized him and looked puzzled but quickly hid it and said: "Y'all going to beat them New Iberia boys tonight?"

"Damn right."

The natural thing to do now was go to Lemoine's office, walk in while he was looking in somebody's mouth: *It's me you son of a bitch* and work him over with the left hand, cancel his afternoon for him, send him off to another dentist. What he had to do was unnatural. And as he climbed the stairs to his room he thought there was much about his profession that was unnatural. In the room he turned off the air conditioning and opened the windows, because he didn't want his arm to be in the cool air, then lay on the bed and closed his eyes and began pitching to the batting order. He knew them all perfectly; but he did not trust that sort of perfection, for it was too much like confidence, which was too much like complacency. So he started with Vidrine, the lead-off man. Left-handed. Went with the pitch, hit to all fields; good drag-bunter but only fair speed and Primeaux would be crowding him at third; choke-hitter, usually got a piece of the ball, but not that quick with the bat either; couldn't hit good speed. Fastballs low and tight. Change on him. Good base runner but he had to get a jump. Just hold him close to the bag. Then Billy stopped thinking about Vidrine on base. Thing was to concentrate now on seeing his stance and the high-cocked bat and the inside of the plate and Lucky's glove. He pushed aside the image of Vidrine crouching in a lead off first, and at the same time he pushed from his mind Leslie in the kitchen telling him; he saw Vidrine at the plate and, beyond him, he saw Leslie going away. She had been sitting in the box seat but now she walked alone down the ramp. Poor little Texas girl. She even sounded like a small town in Texas: Leslie Wells. Then she was gone.

The home run came with one out and nobody on in the top of the third inning after he had retired the first seven batters. Rick Stanley hit it, the eighth man in the order, a good field no hit third baseman in his mid-twenties. He had been in the minors for seven years and looked like it: though trimly built, and the best third baseman Billy had ever seen, he had a look about him of age, of resignation, of having been forced—when he was too young to bear it well—to compromise what he wanted with what he could do. At the plate he looked afraid, and early in the season Billy thought Stanley had been beaned and wasn't able to forget it. Later he realized it wasn't fear of beaning, not fear at all, but the strain of living so long with what he knew. It showed in the field too. Not during a play, but when it was over and Stanley threw the ball to the pitcher and returned to his position, his face looking as though it were adjusting itself to the truth he had forgotten when he backhanded the ball over the bag and turned and set and threw his mitt-popping peg to first; his face then was intense, reflexive as his legs and hands and arm; then the play was over and his face settled again into the resignation that was still new enough to be terrible. It spread downward to his shoulders and then to the rest of him and he looked old again. Billy wished he had seen Stanley play third when he was younger and still believed there was a patch of dirt and a bag and a foul line waiting for him in the major leagues.

One of Billy's rules was never to let up on the bottom of the batting order, because when one of them got a hit it hurt more. The pitch to Stanley was a good one. Like many players, Stanley was a poor hitter because he could not consistently be a good hitter; he was only a good hitter for one swing out of every twelve or so; the other swings had changed his life for him. The occasional good one gave the fans, and Stanley too by now, a surprise that always remained a surprise and so never engendered hope. His home run was a matter of numbers and time, for on this one pitch his concentration and timing and swing all flowed together, making him for that instant the hitter of his destroyed dream. It would happen again, in other ball parks, in other seasons; and if Stanley had been able to cause it instead of having it happen to him, he would be in the major leagues.

Billy's first pitch to him was a fast ball, waist high, inside corner. Stanley took it for a strike, with that look on his face. Lucky called for the same pitch. Billy nodded and played with the rosin bag to keep Stanley waiting longer; then Stanley stepped out of the box and scooped up dust and rubbed it on his hands and the bat handle; when he moved to the plate again he looked just as tense and Billy threw the fast ball; Stanley swung late and under it. Lucky called for the curve, the pitch that was sweet to-night, and Billy went right into the windup, figuring Stanley was tied up tightly now, best time to throw a pitch into all that: he watched the ball go in fast and groin-high, then fall to the left and it would have cut the outside corner of the plate just above Stanley's knees; but it was gone. Stanley not only hit it so solidly that Billy knew it was gone before looking, but he got around on it, pulled it, and when Billy found it in the left-centerfield sky it was still climbing above James running from left and LeBlanc from center. At the top of its arc, there was something final about its floodlit surface against the real sky, dark up there above the lighted one they played under.

He turned his back to the plate. He never watched a home run hitter cross it. He looked out at LeBlanc in center; then he looked at Harry Burke at second, old Harry, the manager, forty-one years old and he could still cover the ground, mostly through cunning; make the pivot—how many double plays had he turned in his life? —and when somebody took him out with a slide Billy waited for the cracking sound, not just of bone but the whole body, like a dried tree limb. Hap told him not to worry, old Harry was made of oiled leather. His face looked as if it had already outlived two bodies like the one it commanded now. Never higher than Triple A, and that was long ago; when the Bulls hired him and then the fans loved him he moved his family to Lafayette and made it his home, and between seasons worked for an insurance company, easy money for him, because he went to see men and they drank coffee and talked baseball. He had the gentlest eyes Billy had ever seen on a man. Now Harry trotted over to him.

"We got twenty-one outs to get that back for you."

"The little bastard hit that pitch."

"Somebody did. Did you get a close look at him?"

Billy shook his head and went to the rubber. He walked the fat

pitcher Talieferro on four pitches and Vidrine on six, and Lucky
came to the mound. They called him Lucky because he wasn't.

"One run's one thing," Lucky said. "Let's don't make it three."

"The way y'all are swinging tonight, one's as good as nine."
For the first time since he stepped onto the field, Leslie that
morning rose up from wherever he had locked her, and struck
him.

"Hey," Lucky said. "Hey, it's early."

"Can't y'all hit that fat son of a bitch?"

"We'll hit him. Now you going to pitch or cry?"

He threw Jackson a curve ball and got a double play around the
horn, Primeaux to Harry to Baron, who did a split stretching and
got Jackson by a half stride.

He went to his end of the bench and watched Talieferro, who
for some reason pronounced his name Tolliver: a young big left-
handed pitcher with the kind of belly that belonged to a much
older man, in bars on week-end afternoons; he had pitched four
years at the local college, this was his first season of pro ball, he
was sixteen and nine and usually lost only when his control was
off. He did not want to be a professional ballplayer. He had a job
with an oil company at the end of the season, and was only
pitching and eating his way through a Louisiana summer. Billy
watched Lucky adjust his peakless cap and dust his hands and
step to the plate, and he pushed Leslie back down, for she was
about to burst out of him and explode in his face. He looked
down at the toe plate on his right shoe, and began working the
next inning, the middle of the order, starting with their big hitter,
the centerfielder Remy Gauthreaux, who was finished too, thirty
years old, but smart and dangerous and he'd knock a mistake out
of the park. Low and away to Gauthreaux. Lucky popped out to
Stanley in foul territory and came back to the dugout shaking his
head.

Billy could sense it in all the hitters in the dugout, and see it
when they went to the plate: Talieferro was on, and they were off.
It could be anything: the pennant game, when every move
counted; the last game of the season, so the will to be a ballplayer
was losing to that other part of them which insisted that when
they woke tomorrow nothing they felt tonight would be true; they
would drive home to the jobs and other lives that waited for

them; most would go to places where people had not even heard
of the team, the league. All of that would apply to the Pelicans
too; it could be that none of it applied to Talieferro: that rarely
feeling much of anything except digestion, hunger, and gorging,
he had no conflict between what he felt now and would start feeling tomorrow. And it could be that he simply had his best stuff
tonight, that he was throwing nearly every pitch the way Stanley
had swung that one time.

Billy went to the on-deck circle and kneeled and watched Harry
at the plate, then looked out at Simmons, their big first baseman:
followed Gauthreaux in the order, a power hitter but struck out
about a hundred times a year: keep him off balance, in and out,
and throw the fast one right into his power, and right past him
too. Harry, choking high on the bat, fouled off everything close to
the plate then grounded out to short, and Billy handed his jacket
to the batboy and went through cheers to the plate. When he
stepped in Talieferro didn't look at him, so Billy stepped out and
stared until he did, then dug in and cocked the bat, a good hitter
so he had played right field in high school and American Legion
when he wasn't pitching. He watched the slow easy fat man's
wind-up and the fast ball coming out of it: swung for the fence
and popped it to second, sprinting down the line and crossing the
bag before the ball came down. When he turned he saw Talieferro already walking in, almost at the third base line. Harry
brought Billy's glove out to the mound and patted his rump.

"I thought you were running all the way to Flint."

In the next three innings he pitched to nine men. He ended the
fifth by striking out Stanley on curve balls; and when Talieferro
led off the sixth Billy threw a fast ball at his belly that made him
spin away and fall into the dust. Between innings he forced himself to believe in the hope of numbers: the zeroes and the one on
the scoreboard in right-center, the inning number, the outs remaining for the Bulls; watched them starting to hit, but only one
an inning, and nobody as far as second base. He sat sweating
under his jacket and in his mind pitched to the next three Pelicans, then the next three just to be sure, although he didn't believe he would face six of them next inning, or any inning, and he
thought of eighteen then fifteen then twelve outs to get the one
run, the only one he needed, because if it came to that, Talieferro
would tire first. When Primeaux struck out leading off the sixth,

Billy looked at Hap at the other end of the bench, and he wanted to be down there with him. He leaned forward and stared at his shoes. Then the inning was over and he gave in to the truth he had known anyway since that white vision of loss just before the ball fell.

Gauthreaux started the seventh with a single to right, doing what he almost never did: laid off pulling and went with the outside pitch. Billy worked Simmons low and got the double play he needed, then he struck out the catcher Lantrip, and trotted off the field with his string still going, thirteen batters since the one-out walk to Vidrine in the third. He got the next six. Three of them grounded out, and the other three struck out on the curve, Billy watching it break under the shiny blur of the bat as it would in Flint and wherever after that and Detroit too: his leg kicking and body wheeling and arm whipping around in rhythm again with his history which had begun with a baseball and a friend to throw it to, and had excluded all else, or nearly all else, and had included the rest somewhere alongside him, almost out of his vision (once between innings he allowed himself to think about Leslie, just long enough to forgive her); his history was his future too and the two of them together were twenty-five years at most until the time when the pitches that created him would lose their speed, hang at the plate, become hits in other men's lives instead of the heart of his; they would discard him then, the pitches would. But he loved them for that too, and right now they made his breath singular out of the entire world, so singular that there was no other world: the war would not call him because it couldn't know his name; and he would refuse the grief that lurked behind him. He watched the final curve going inside then breaking down and over and Lucky's mitt popped and the umpire twisted and roared and pointed his right fist to the sky.

He ran to the dugout, tipping his cap to the yelling Cajuns, and sat between Hap and Lucky until Baron flied out to end the game. After the showers and goodbyes he drove to the hotel and got his still-packed bags and paid the night clerk and started home, out of the lush flatland of marsh and trees, toward Texas. Her space on the front seat was filled as with voice and touch. He turned on the radio. He was not sleepy, and he was driving straight through to San Antonio.

THE CINDERELLA WALTZ

ANN BEATTIE

Ann Beattie was born in Washington, D.C., and now lives in Connecticut. She has previously published a collection of stories, *Secrets And Surprises*, with Random House, which recently published her new novel.

Milo and Bradley are creatures of habit. For as long as I've known him, Milo has worn his moth-eaten blue scarf with the knot hanging so low on his chest that the scarf is useless. Bradley is addicted to coffee and carries a thermos with him. Milo complains about the cold, and Bradley is always a little edgy. They come out from the city every Saturday—this is not habit but loyalty—to pick up Louise. Louise is even more unpredictable than most nine-year-olds; sometimes she waits for them on the front step, sometimes she hasn't even gotten out of bed when they arrive. One time she hid in a closet and wouldn't leave with them.

Today Louise has put together a shopping bag full of things she wants to take with her. She is taking my whisk and my blue pottery bowl, to make Sunday breakfast for Milo and Bradley; Beckett's "Happy Days," which she has carried around for weeks, and which she looks through, smiling—but I'm not sure she's reading it; and a coleus growing out of a conch shell. Also, she has stuffed into one side of the bag the fancy Victorian-style nightgown her grandmother gave her for Christmas, and into the other she has tucked her octascope. Milo keeps a couple of dresses, a nightgown, a toothbrush, and extra sneakers and boots at his apartment for her. He got tired of rounding up her stuff to pack for her to take home, so he has brought some things for her that can be left. It annoys him that she still packs bags, because then he has to go around making sure that she has found everything before she goes home. She seems to know how to manipulate him, and after the weekend is over she often calls tearfully to say that she has left this or that, which means that he must get his car out of the garage and drive all the way out to the house to bring it to her. One time, he refused to take the hour-long drive, because she had only left a copy of Tolkien's "The Two Towers." The following weekend was the time she hid in the closet.

"I'll water your plant if you leave it here," I say now.

"I can take it," she says.

"I didn't say you couldn't take it. I just thought it might be easier to leave it, because if the shell tips over the plant might get ruined."

"O.K.," she says. "Don't water it today, though. Water it Sunday afternoon."

I reach for the shopping bag.

"I'll put it back on my windowsill," she says. She lifts the plant out and carries it as if it's made of Steuben glass. Bradley bought it for her last month, driving back to the city, when they stopped at a lawn sale. She and Bradley are both very choosy, and he likes that. He drinks French-roast coffee; she will debate with herself almost endlessly over whether to buy a coleus that is primarily pink or lavender or striped.

"Has Milo made any plans for this weekend?" I ask.

"He's having a couple of people over tonight, and I'm going to help them make crêpes for dinner. If they buy more bottles of that wine with the yellow flowers on the label, Bradley is going to soak the labels off for me."

"That's nice of him," I say. "He never minds taking a lot of time with things."

"He doesn't like to cook, though. Milo and I are going to cook. Bradley sets the table and fixes flowers in a bowl. He thinks it's frustrating to cook."

"Well," I say, "with cooking you have to have a good sense of timing. You have to coördinate everything. Bradley likes to work carefully and not be rushed."

I wonder how much she knows. Last week she told me about a conversation she'd had with her friend Sarah. Sarah was trying to persuade Louise to stay around on the weekends, but Louise said she always went to her father's. Then Sarah tried to get her to take her along, and Louise said that she couldn't. "You could take her if you wanted to," I said later. "Check with Milo and see if that isn't right. I don't think he'd mind having a friend of yours occasionally."

She shrugged. "Bradley doesn't like a lot of people around," she said.

"Bradley likes you, and if she's your friend I don't think he'd mind."

She looked at me with an expression I didn't recognize; perhaps she thought I was a little dumb, or perhaps she was just curious to see if I would go on. I didn't know how to go on. Like an adult, she gave a little shrug and changed the subject.

At ten o'clock Milo pulls into the driveway and honks his horn, which makes a noise like a bleating sheep. He knows the noise the horn makes is funny, and he means to amuse us. There was a time just after the divorce when he and Bradley would come here and get out of the car and stand around silently, waiting for her. She knew that she had to watch for them, because Milo wouldn't come to the door. We were both bitter then, but I got over it. I still don't think Milo would have come into the house again, though, if Bradley hadn't thought it was a good idea. The third time Milo came to pick her up after he'd left home, I went out to invite them in, but Milo said nothing. He was standing there with his arms at his sides like a wooden soldier, and his eyes were as dead to me as if they'd been painted on. It was Bradley whom I reasoned with. "Louise is over at Sarah's right now, and it'll make her feel more comfortable if we're all together when she comes in," I said to him, and Bradley turned to Milo and said, "Hey, that's right. Why don't we go in for a quick cup of coffee?" I looked into the back seat of the car and saw his red thermos there; Louise had told me about it. Bradley meant that they should come in and sit down. He was giving me even more than I'd asked for.

It would be an understatement to say that I disliked Bradley at first. I was actually afraid of him, afraid even after I saw him, though he was slender, and more nervous than I, and spoke quietly. The second time I saw him, I persuaded myself that he was just a stereotype, but someone who certainly seemed harmless enough. By the third time, I had enough courage to suggest that they come into the house. It was embarrassing for all of us, sitting around the table—the same table where Milo and I had eaten our meals for the years we were married. Before he left, Milo had shouted at me that the house was a farce, that my playing the happy suburban housewife was a farce, that it was unconscionable of me to let things drag on, that I would probably kiss him and say, "How was your day, sweetheart?," and that he should bring home flowers and the evening paper. "Maybe I would!" I screamed back. "Maybe it would be nice to do that, even if we were pretending, instead of you coming home drunk and not caring what had happened to me or to Louise all day." He was holding on to the edge of the kitchen table, the way you'd hold on to the horse's reins in a runaway carriage. "I care about Louise," he said finally. That was the most horrible moment. Until then, until he said it that way, I had thought that he was going through something horrible—certainly something was terribly wrong—but that, in his way, he loved me after all. "*You don't love me?*" I had whispered at once. It took us both aback. It was an innocent and pathetic question, and it made him come and put his arms around me in the last hug he ever gave me. "I'm sorry for you," he said, "and I'm sorry for marrying you and causing this, but you know who I love. I told you who I love." "But you were kidding," I said. "You didn't mean it. You were kidding."

When Bradley sat at the table that first day, I tried to be polite and not look at him much. I had gotten it through my head that Milo was crazy, and I guess I was expecting Bradley to be a horrible parody—Craig Russell doing Marilyn Monroe. Bradley did not spoon sugar into Milo's coffee. He did not even sit near him. In fact, he pulled his chair a little away from us, and in spite of his uneasiness he found more things to start conversations about than Milo and I did. He told me about the ad agency where he worked; he is a designer there. He asked if he could go out on the porch to see the brook—Milo had told him about the stream in the back of our place that was as thin as a pencil but still gave us our own watercress. He went out on the porch and stayed there for at least five minutes, giving us a chance to talk. We didn't say one word until he came back. Louise came home from Sarah's house just as

Bradley sat down at the table again, and she gave him a hug as well as us. I could see that she really liked him. I was amazed that I liked him, too. Bradley had won and I had lost, but he was as gentle and low-key as if none of it mattered. Later in the week, I called him and asked him to tell me if any free-lance jobs opened in his advertising agency. (I do a little free-lance artwork, whenever I can arrange it.) The week after that, he called and told me about another agency, where they were looking for outside artists. Our calls to each other are always brief and for a purpose, but lately they're not just calls about business. Before Bradley left to scout some picture locations in Mexico, he called to say that Milo had told him that when the two of us were there years ago I had seen one of those big circular bronze Aztec calendars and I had always regretted not bringing it back. He wanted to know if I would like him to buy a calendar if he saw one like the one Milo had told him about.

Today, Milo is getting out of his car, his blue scarf flapping against his chest. Louise, looking out the window, asks the same thing I am wondering. "Where's Bradley?"

Milo comes in and shakes my hand, gives Louise a one-armed hug.

"Bradley thinks he's coming down with a cold," Milo says. "The dinner is still on, Louise. We'll do the dinner. We have to stop at Gristede's when we get back to town, unless your mother happens to have a tin of anchovies and two sticks of unsalted butter."

"Let's go to Gristede's," Louise says. "I like to go there."

"Let me look in the kitchen," I say. The butter is salted, but Milo says that that will do, and he takes three sticks instead of two. I have a brainstorm and cut the cellophane on a leftover Christmas present from my aunt—a wicker plate that holds nuts and foil-wrapped triangles of cheese—and, sure enough: one tin of anchovies.

"We can go to the museum instead," Milo says to Louise. "Wonderful."

But then, going out the door, carrying her bag, he changes his mind. "We can go to America Hurrah, and if we see something beautiful we can buy it," he says.

They go off in high spirits. Louise comes up to his waist, almost, and I notice again that they have the same walk. Both of them stride forward with great purpose. Last week, Bradley told me that Milo had bought a weathervane in the shape of a horse, made around 1800, at America Hurrah, and stood it in the bedroom, and then was enraged when Bradley draped his socks over it to dry. Bradley is still learning what a perfectionist Milo is, and how little sense of humor he has. When we were first married, I used one of our pottery casserole dishes to put my jewelry in, and he nagged me until I took it out and put the dish back in the kitchen cabinet. I remember his saying that the dish looked silly on my dresser because it was obvious what it was and people would think we left our dishes lying around. It was one of the things that Milo wouldn't tolerate, because it was improper.

When Milo brought Louise back on Sunday night they were not in a good mood. The dinner had been all right, Milo said, and Griffin and Amy and Mark had been amazed at what a good hostess Louise had been, but Bradley hadn't been able to eat.

"Is he still coming down with a cold?" I ask. I was still a little shy about asking questions about Bradley.

Milo shrugs. "Louise made him take megadoses of Vitamin C all weekend."

Louise says, "Bradley said that taking too much Vitamin C was bad for your kidneys, though."

"It's a rotten climate," Milo says, sitting on the living-room sofa, scarf and coat still on. "The combination of cold and air pollution . . ."

Louise and I look at each other, and then back at Milo. For weeks now, he has been talking about moving to San Francisco, if he can find work there. (Milo is an architect.) This talk bores me, and it makes Louise nervous. I've asked him not to talk to her about it unless he's actually going to move, but he doesn't seem to be able to stop himself.

"O.K.," Milo says, looking at us both. "I'm not going to say anything about San Francisco."

"*California* is polluted," I say. I am unable to stop myself, either.

Milo heaves himself up from the sofa, ready for the drive back to New York. It is the same way he used to get off the sofa that last year he lived here. He would get up, dress for work, and not even go into the kitchen for breakfast—just sit, sometimes in his coat as he was sitting just now, and at the last minute he would push himself up and go out to the driveway, usually without a goodbye, and get in the car and drive off either very fast or very slowly. I liked it better when he made the tires spin in the gravel when he took off.

He stops at the doorway now, and turns to face me. "Did I take all your butter?" he says.

"No," I say. "There's another stick." I point into the kitchen.

"I could have guessed that's where it would be," he says, and smiles at me.

When Milo comes the next weekend, Bradley is still not with him. The night before, as I was putting Louise to bed, she said that she had a feeling he wouldn't be coming.

"I had that feeling a couple of days ago," I said. "Usually Bradley calls once during the week."

"He must still be sick," Louise said. She looked at me anxiously. "Do you think he is?"

"A cold isn't going to kill him," I said. "If he has a cold, he'll be O.K."

Her expression changed; she thought I was talking down to her. She lay back in bed. The last year Milo was with us, I used to tuck her in and tell her that everything was all right. What that meant was that there had not been a fight. Milo had sat listening to music on the phonograph, with a book or the newspaper in front of his face. He didn't pay very much attention to Louise, and he ignored me entirely. Instead of saying a prayer with her, the way I usually did, I would say to her that everything was all right. Then I would go downstairs and hope that Milo would say the same thing to me. What he finally did say one night was "You might as well find out from me as some other way."

"Hey, are you an old bag lady again this weekend?" Milo says now, stooping to kiss Louise's forehead.

"Because you take some things with you doesn't mean you're a bag lady," she says primly.

"Well," Milo says, "you start doing something innocently, and before you know it it can take you over."

He looks angry, and acts as though it's difficult for him to make conversation, even when the conversation is full of sarcasm and double-entendres.

"What do you say we get going?" he says to Louise.

In the shopping bag she is taking is her doll, which she has not played with for more than a year. I found it by accident when I went to tuck in a loaf of banana bread that I had baked. When I saw Baby Betsy, deep in the bag, I decided against putting the bread in.

"O.K.," Louise says to Milo. "Where's Bradley?"

"Sick," he says.

"Is he too sick to have me visit?"

"Good heavens, no. He'll be happier to see you than to see me."

"I'm rooting some of my coleus to give him," she says. "Maybe I'll give it to him like it is, in water, and he can plant it when it roots."

When she leaves the room, I go over to Milo. "Be nice to her," I say quietly.

"I'm nice to her," he says. "Why does everybody have to act like I'm going to grow fangs every time I turn around?"

"You were quite cutting when you came in."

"I was being self-deprecating." He sighs. "I don't really know why I come here and act this way," he says.

"What's the matter, Milo?"

But now he lets me know he's bored with the conversation. He walks over to the table and picks up a *Newsweek* and flips through it. Louise comes back with the coleus in a water glass.

"You know what you could do," I say. "Wet a napkin and put it around that cutting and then wrap it in foil, and put it in water when you get there. That way, you wouldn't have to hold a glass of water all the way to New York."

She shrugs. "This is O.K.," she says.

"Why don't you take your mother's suggestion," Milo says. "The water will slosh out of the glass."

"Not if you don't drive fast."

"It doesn't have anything to do with my driving fast. If we go over a bump in the road, you're going to get all wet."

"Then I can put on one of my dresses at your apartment."

"Am I being unreasonable?" Milo says to me.

"I started it," I say. "Let her take it in the glass."

"Would you, as a favor, do what your mother says?" he says to Louise.

Louise looks at the coleus, and at me.

"Hold the glass over the seat instead of over your lap, and you won't get wet," I say.

"Your first idea was the best," Milo says.

Louise gives him an exasperated look and puts the glass down on the floor, pulls on her poncho, picks up the glass again and says a sullen goodbye to me, and goes out the front door.

"Why is this my fault?" Milo says. "Have I done anything terrible? I—"

"Do something to cheer yourself up," I say, patting him on the back.

He looks as exasperated with me as Louise was with him. He nods his head yes, and goes out the door.

"Was everything all right this weekend?" I ask Louise.

"Milo was in a bad mood, and Bradley wasn't even there on Saturday," Louise says. "He came back today and took us to the Village for breakfast."

"What did you have?"

"I had sausage wrapped in little pancakes and fruit salad and a rum bun."

"Where was Bradley on Saturday?"

She shrugs. "I didn't ask him."

She almost always surprises me by being more grownup than I give her credit for. Does she suspect, as I do, that Bradley has found another lover?

"Milo was in a bad mood when you two left here Saturday," I say.

"I told him if he didn't want me to come next weekend, just to tell me." She looks perturbed, and I suddenly realize that she can sound exactly like Milo sometimes.

"You shouldn't have said that to him, Louise," I say. "You know he wants you. He's just worried about Bradley."

"So?" she says. "I'm probably going to flunk math."

"No, you're not, honey. You got a C-plus on the last assignment."

"It still doesn't make my grade average out to a C."

"You'll get a C. It's all right to get a C."

She doesn't believe me.

"Don't be a perfectionist, like Milo," I tell her. "Even if you got a D, you wouldn't fail."

Louise is brushing her hair—thin, shoulder-length, auburn-colored hair. She is already so pretty and so smart in everything except math that I wonder what will become of her. When I was her age, I was plain and serious and I wanted to be a tree surgeon. I went with my father to the park and held a stethoscope—a real one—to the trunks of trees, listening to their silence. Children seem older now.

"What do you think's the matter with Bradley?" Louise says. She sounds worried.

"Maybe the two of them are unhappy with each other right now."

She misses my point. "Bradley's sad, and Milo's sad that he's unhappy."

I drop Louise off at Sarah's house for supper. Sarah's mother, Martine Cooper, looks like Shelley Winters, and I have never seen her without a glass of Galliano on ice in her hand. She has a strong candy smell. Her husband has left her, and she professes not to care. She has emptied her living room of furniture and put up ballet bars on the walls, and dances in a purple leotard to records by Cher and Mac Davis. I prefer to have Sarah come to our house, but her mother is adamant that everything must be, as she puts it, "fifty-fifty." When Sarah visited us a week ago and loved the chocolate pie I had made, I sent two pieces home with her. Tonight, when I left Sarah's house, her mother gave me a bowl of jello fruit salad.

The phone is ringing when I come in the door. It is Bradley.

"Bradley," I say at once, "whatever's wrong, at least you don't have a neighbor who just gave you a bowl of maraschino cherries in green jello with a Reddi Wip flower squirted on top."

"Jesus," he says. "You don't need me to depress you, do you?"

"What's wrong?" I say.

He sighs into the phone. "Guess what?" he says.

"What?"

"I've lost my job."

It wasn't at all what I was expecting to hear. I was ready to hear that he was leaving Milo, and I had even thought that that would serve Milo right. Part of me still wanted him punished for what he did. I was so out of my mind when Milo left me that I used to go over and drink Galliano with Martine Cooper. I even thought seriously about forming a ballet group with her. I would go to her house in the afternoon, and she would hold a tambourine in the air and I would hold my leg rigid and try to kick it.

"That's awful," I say to Bradley. "What happened?"

"They said it was nothing personal—they were laying off three people. Two other people are going to get the axe at the agency within the next six months. I was the first to go, and it was nothing personal. From twenty thousand bucks a year to nothing, and nothing personal, either."

"But your work is so good. Won't you be able to find something again?"

"Could I ask you a favor?" he says. "I'm calling from a phone booth. I'm not in the city. Could I come talk to you?"

"Sure," I say.

It seems perfectly logical that he should come alone to talk—perfectly logical until I actually see him coming up the walk. I can't entirely believe it. A year after my husband has left me, I am sitting with his lover—a man, a person I like quite well—and trying to cheer him up because he is out of work. ("Honey," my father would say, "listen to Daddy's heart with the stethoscope, or you can turn it toward you and listen to your own heart. You won't hear anything listening to a tree." Was my persistence willfulness, or belief in magic? Is it possible that I hugged Bradley at the door because I'm secretly glad he's down and out, the way I used to be? Or do I really want to make things better for him?)

He comes into the kitchen and thanks me for the coffee I am making, drapes his coat over the chair he always sits in.

"What am I going to do?" he asks.

"You shouldn't get so upset, Bradley," I say. "You know you're good. You won't have trouble finding another job."

"That's only half of it," he says. "Milo thinks I did this deliberately. He told me I was quitting on him. He's very angry at me.

He fights with me, and then he gets mad that I don't enjoy eating dinner. My stomach's upset, and I can't eat anything."

"Maybe some juice would be better than coffee."

"If I didn't drink coffee, I'd collapse," he says.

I pour coffee into a mug for him, coffee into a mug for me.

"This is probably very awkward for you," he says. "That I come here and say all this about Milo."

"What does he mean about your quitting on him?"

"He said . . . he actually accused me of doing badly deliberately, so they'd fire me. I was so afraid to tell him the truth when I was fired that I pretended to be sick. Then I really *was* sick. He's never been angry at me this way. Is this always the way he acts? Does he get a notion in his head for no reason and then pick at a person because of it?"

I try to remember. "We didn't argue much," I say. "When he didn't want to live here, he made me look ridiculous for complaining when I knew something was wrong. He expects perfection, but what that means is that you do things his way."

"I *was*. I never wanted to sit around the apartment, the way he says I did. I even brought work home with me. He made me feel so bad all week that I went to a friend's apartment for the day on Saturday. Then he said I had walked out on the problem. He's a little paranoid. I was listening to the radio, and Carole King was singing that song 'It's Too Late,' and he came into the study and looked very upset, as though I had planned for the song to come on. I couldn't believe it."

"Whew," I say, shaking my head. "I don't envy you. You have to stand up to him. I didn't do that. I pretended the problem would go away."

"And now the problem sits across from you drinking coffee, and you're being nice to him."

"I know it. I was just thinking we look like two characters in some soap opera my friend Martine Cooper would watch."

He pushes his coffee cup away from him with a grimace.

"But anyway, I like you now," I say. "And you're exceptionally nice to Louise."

"I took her father," he says.

"Bradley—I hope you don't take offense, but it makes me nervous to talk about that."

"I don't take offense. But how can you be having coffee with me?"

"You invited yourself over so you could ask that?"

"Please," he says, holding up both hands. Then he runs his hands through his hair. "Don't make me feel illogical. He does that to me, you know. He doesn't understand it when everything doesn't fall right into line. If I like fixing up the place, keeping some flowers around, therefore I can't like being a working person, too, therefore I deliberately sabotage myself in my job." Bradley sips his coffee.

"I wish I could do something for him," he says in a different voice.

This was not what I have expected, either. We have sounded like two wise adults, and then suddenly he has changed and sounds very tender. I realize the situation is still the same. It is two of them on one side and me on the other, even though Bradley is in my kitchen.

"Come and pick up Louise with me, Bradley," I say. "When you see Martine Cooper, you'll cheer up about your situation."

He looks up from his coffee. "You're forgetting what I'd look like to Martine Cooper," he says.

Milo is going to California. He has been offered a job with a new San Francisco architectural firm. I am not the first to know. His sister, Deanna, knows before I do, and mentions it when we're talking on the phone. "It's middle-age crisis," Deanna says sniffily. "Not that I need to tell you." Deanna would drop dead if she knew the way things are. She is scandalized every time a new scene is put up in Bloomingdale's window. ("Those mannequins had eyes like an Egyptian princess, and *rags*. I swear to you, they had mops and brooms and ragged gauze dresses on, with whores' shoes—stiletto heels that prostitutes wore in the fifties.")

I hang up from Deanna's call and tell Louise I'm going to drive to the gas station for cigarettes. I go there to call New York on their pay phone.

"Well, I only just knew," Milo says. "I found out for sure yesterday, and last night Deanna called and so I told her. It's not like I'm leaving tonight."

He sounds elated, in spite of being upset that I called. He's happy in the way he used to be on Christmas morning. I remember him once running into the living room in his underwear and tearing open the gifts we'd been sent by relatives. He was looking for the eight-slice toaster he was sure we'd get. We'd been given two-slice, four-slice, and six-slice toasters, but then we got no more. "Come out, my eight-slice beauty!" Milo crooned, and out came an electric clock, a blender, and an expensive electric pan.

"When are you leaving?" I ask him.

"I'm going out to look for a place to live next week."

"Are you going to tell Louise yourself this weekend?"

"Of course," he says.

"And what are you going to do about seeing Louise?"

"Why do you act as if I don't like Louise?" he says. "I will occasionally come back East, and I will arrange for her to fly to San Francisco on her vacations."

"It's going to break her heart."

"No it isn't. Why do you want to make me feel bad?"

"She's had so many things to adjust to. You don't have to go to San Francisco right now, Milo."

"It happens, if you care, that my own job here is in jeopardy. This is a real chance for me, with a young firm. They really want me. But anyway, all we need in this happy group is to have you bringing in a couple of hundred dollars a month with your graphic work and me destitute and Bradley so devastated by being fired that of course he can't even look for work."

"I'll bet he is looking for a job," I say.

"Yes. He read the want ads today and then fixed a crab quiche."

"Maybe that's the way you like things, Milo, and people respond to you. You forbade me to work when we had a baby. Do you say anything encouraging to him about finding a job, or do you just take it out on him that he was fired?"

There is a pause, and then he almost seems to lose his mind with impatience.

"I can hardly *believe*, when I am trying to find a logical solution to all our problems, that I am being subjected, by telephone, to an unflattering psychological analysis by my ex-wife." He says this all in a rush.

"All right, Milo. But don't you think that if you're leaving so soon you ought to call her, instead of waiting until Saturday?"

Milo sighs very deeply. "I have more sense than to have important conversations on the telephone," he says.

Milo calls on Friday and asks Louise whether it wouldn't be nice if both of us came in and spent the night Saturday and if we all went to brunch together Sunday. Louise is excited. I never go into town with her.

Louise and I pack a suitcase and put it in the car Saturday morning. A cutting of ivy for Bradley has taken root, and she has put it in a little green plastic pot for him. It's heartbreaking, and I hope that Milo notices and has a tough time dealing with it. I am relieved I'm going to be there when he tells her, and sad that I have to hear it at all.

In the city, I give the car to the garage attendant, who does not remember me. Milo and I lived in the apartment when we were first married, and moved when Louise was two years old. When we moved, Milo kept the apartment and sublet it—a sign that things were not going well, if I had been one to heed such a warning. What he said was that if we were ever rich enough we could have the house in Connecticut *and* the apartment in New York. When Milo moved out of the house, he went right back to the apartment. This will be the first time I have visited there in years.

Louise strides in in front of me, throwing her coat over the brass coatrack in the entranceway—almost too casual about being there. She's the hostess at Milo's, the way I am at our house.

He has painted the walls white. There are floor-length white curtains in the living room, where my silly flowered curtains used to hang. The walls are bare, the floor has been sanded, a stereo as huge as a computer stands against one wall of the living room, and there are four speakers.

"Look around," Milo says. "Show your mother around, Louise."

I am trying to remember if I have ever told Louise that I used to live in this apartment. I must have told her, at some point, but I can't remember it.

"Hello," Bradley says, coming out of the bedroom.

"Hi, Bradley," I say. "Have you got a drink?"

Bradley looks sad. "He's got champagne," he says, and looks nervously at Milo.

"No one *has* to drink champagne," Milo says. "There's the usual assortment of liquor."

"Yes," Bradley says. "What would you like?"

"Some bourbon, please."

"Bourbon." Bradley turns to go into the kitchen. He looks different; his hair is different—more wavy—and he is dressed as though it were summer, in straight-legged white pants and black leather thongs.

"I want Perrier water with strawberry juice," Louise says, tagging along after Bradley. I have never heard her ask for such a thing before. At home, she drinks too many Cokes. I am always trying to get her to drink fruit juice.

Bradley comes back with two drinks and hands me one. "Did you want anything?" he says to Milo.

"I'm going to open the champagne in a moment," Milo says. "How have you been this week, sweetheart?"

"O.K.," Louise says. She is holding a pale-pink, bubbly drink. She sips it like a cocktail.

Bradley looks very bad. He has circles under his eyes, and he is ill at ease. A red light begins to blink on the phone-answering device next to where Bradley sits on the sofa, and Milo gets out of his chair to pick up the phone.

"Do you really want to talk on the phone right now?" Bradley asks Milo quietly.

Milo looks at him. "No, not particularly," he says, sitting down again. After a moment, the red light goes out.

"I'm going to mist your bowl garden," Louise says to Bradley, and slides off the sofa and goes to the bedroom. "Hey, a little toadstool is growing in here!" she calls back. "Did you put it there, Bradley?"

"It grew from the soil mixture, I guess," Bradley calls back. "I don't know how it got there."

"Have you heard anything about a job?" I ask Bradley.

"I haven't been looking, really," he says. "You know."

Milo frowns at him. "Your choice, Bradley," he says. "I didn't ask you to follow me to California. You can stay here."

"No," Bradley says. "You've hardly made me feel welcome."

"Should we have some champagne—all four of us—and you can get back to your bourbons later?" Milo says cheerfully.

We don't answer him, but he gets up anyway and goes to the kitchen. "Where have you hidden the tulip-shaped glasses, Bradley?" he calls out after a while.

"They should be in the cabinet on the far left," Bradley says.

"You're going with him?" I say to Bradley. "To San Francisco?"

He shrugs, and won't look at me. "I'm not quite sure I'm wanted," he says quietly.

The cork pops in the kitchen. I look at Bradley, but he won't look up. His new hairdo makes him look older. I remember that when Milo left me I went to the hairdresser the same week and had bangs cut. The next week, I went to a therapist who told me it was no good trying to hide from myself. The week after that, I did dance exercises with Martine Cooper, and the week after that the therapist told me not to dance if I wasn't interested in dancing.

"I'm not going to act like this is a funeral," Milo says, coming in with the glasses. "Louise, come in here and have champagne! We have something to have a toast about."

Louise comes into the living room suspiciously. She is so used to being refused even a sip of wine from my glass or her father's that she no longer even asks. "How come I'm in on this?" she asks.

"We're going to drink a toast to me," Milo says.

Three of the four glasses are clustered on the table in front of the sofa. Milo's glass is raised. Louise looks at me, to see what I'm going to say. Milo raises his glass even higher. Bradley reaches for a glass. Louise picks up a glass. I lean forward and take the last one.

"This is a toast to me," Milo says, "because I am going to be going to San Francisco."

It was not a very good or informative toast. Bradley and I sip from our glasses. Louise puts her glass down hard and bursts into tears, knocking the glass over. The champagne spills onto the cover of a big art book about the Unicorn Tapestries. She runs into the bedroom and slams the door.

Milo looks furious. "Everybody lets me know just what my

insufficiencies are, don't they?" he says. "Nobody minds expressing himself. We have it all right out in the open."

"He's criticizing me," Bradley murmurs, his head still bowed. "It's because I was offered a job here in the city and I didn't automatically refuse it."

I turn to Milo. "Go say something to Louise, Milo," I say. "Do you think that's what somebody who isn't brokenhearted sounds like?"

He glares at me and stumps into the bedroom, and I can hear him talking to Louise reassuringly. "It doesn't mean you'll *never* see me," he says. "You can fly there, I'll come here. It's not going to be that different."

"You lied!" Louise screams. "You said we were going to brunch."

"We are. We are. I can't very well take us to brunch before Sunday, can I?"

"You didn't say you were going to San Francisco. What *is* San Francisco, anyway?"

"I just said so. I bought us a bottle of champagne. You can come out as soon as I get settled. You're going to like it there."

Louise is sobbing. She has told him the truth and she knows it's futile to go on.

By the next morning, Louise acts the way I acted—as if everything were just the same. She looks calm, but her face is small and pale. She looks very young. We walk into the restaurant and sit at the table Milo has reserved. Bradley pulls out a chair for me, and Milo pulls out a chair for Louise, locking his finger with hers for a second, raising her arm above her head, as if she were about to take a twirl.

She looks very nice, really. She has a ribbon in her hair. It is cold, and she should have worn a hat, but she wanted to wear the ribbon. Milo has good taste: the dress she is wearing, which he bought for her, is a hazy purple plaid, and it sets off her hair.

"Come with me. Don't be sad," Milo suddenly says to Louise, pulling her by the hand. "Come with me for a minute. Come across the street to the park for just a second, and we'll have some space to dance, and your mother and Bradley can have a nice quiet drink."

She gets up from the table and, looking long-suffering, backs into her coat, which he is holding for her, and the two of them go out. The waitress comes to the table, and Bradley orders three Bloody Marys and a Coke, and eggs Benedict for everyone. He asks the waitress to wait awhile before she brings the food. I have hardly slept at all, and having a drink is not going to clear my head. I have to think of things to say to Louise later, on the ride home.

"He takes so many *chances*," I say. "He pushes things so far with people. I don't want her to turn against him."

"No," he says.

"Why are you going, Bradley? You've seen the way he acts. You know that when you get out there he'll pull something on you. Take the job and stay here."

Bradley is fiddling with the edge of his napkin. I study him. I don't know who his friends are, how old he is, where he grew up, whether he believes in God, or what he usually drinks. I'm shocked that I know so little, and I reach out and touch him. He looks up.

"Don't go," I say quietly.

The waitress puts the glasses down quickly and leaves, embarrassed because she thinks she's interrupted a tender moment. Bradley pats my hand on his arm. Then he says the thing that has always been between us, the thing too painful for me to envision or think about.

"I love him," Bradley whispers.

We sit quietly until Milo and Louise come into the restaurant, swinging hands. She is pretending to be a young child, almost a baby, and I wonder for an instant if Milo and Bradley and I haven't been playing house, too—pretending to be adults.

"Daddy's going to give me a first-class ticket," Louise says. "When I go to California we're going to ride in a glass elevator to the top of the Fairman Hotel."

"The Fairmont," Milo says, smiling at her.

Before Louise was born, Milo used to put his ear to my stomach and say that if the baby turned out to be a girl he would put her into glass slippers instead of bootees. Now he is the prince once again. I see them in a glass elevator, not long from now, going up and up, with the people below getting smaller and smaller, until they disappear.

ALL THE PELAGEYAS

MILLICENT G. DILLON

Millicent G. Dillon was born in New York. She has previously published a book of short stories, *Baby Perpetua And Other Stories* (1971), and a novel, *The One In The Back Is Medea* (1973). Her most current work, a biography of Jane Bowles, *A Little Original Sin*, will be published by Harper & Row. She works as a writer for Stanford University News and Publications.

At the lectern Professor Felsovanyi began her introduction. "She speaks for all women in her revolt against the patriarchy." A stiffness in the way Professor Felsovanyi held her head and a stiffness in the way she pursed her lips made Kay suspect her of intellectual pretensions. Kay looked at Adrienne Rich, sitting in a straight chair, and saw how she bent her head and looked at the floor. When the applause came, she rose and bowed hurriedly. She went to the lectern and waited, unsmiling.

"I've been walking around this beautiful serene university campus," she began quietly. But then her tone changed as she turned from the peaceful campus to the "violence being perpetrated in our names," to the sense of "rage and impotence many of us feel."

"Suppose we were to try to discover the source of that violence in ourselves, in the life we live. . . . Let me suggest the parallel of rape. A man or two men or a group of men rape a woman, then strangle her, then repeatedly stab her. Now this is not so exceptional a type of crime. And it pervades both men's and women's sexual fantasies far more than maybe people like ourselves care to admit.

"The fantasy of raping or being raped, the connection of sex with violence, is one of the primal facts underlying a patriarchal culture . . ."

Listening, Kay felt herself on the edge of rage. There was something infuriating in the poet's voice, something rancorous yet intimate, something appropriating. As Adrienne Rich began to read from her work, Kay tried to reason with herself. It's only that she's being too insistent, making outside the same as inside, making what happens there the same as what happens here, that's what's getting to me. Yet she felt as if there were something more, something oddly personal.

She turned as if for reassurance to those around her. In their faces she saw eager agreement to what they were hearing. They were leaning forward as if something in them were being unloosed. And she felt herself slouching, feeling the level of the anger in the room rise as if in grateful response to an order given by Adrienne Rich.

The poet stopped and asked for a glass of water. Professor Felsovanyi left through a side door. She returned at once carrying a red plastic pitcher and a glass. As Adrienne Rich drank, Kay got up. "Excuse me—sorry," she said as she pushed past the knees of those beside her to get to the aisle. She did not feel her going was a statement. The going was only for herself. She was refusing to participate. Or have I participated, she wondered, by refusing?

At the top of the stone staircase, looking out over the live oak in the plaza, she tried to calm herself. She knew enough of her own anger to know how it muddled things up. In there what happened is only part of the times, she told herself. What did you expect? talk of doing good? gentleness? That's not the way things are. For all your complaints, for all your bleatings, she said to herself, as if it were the cry of a small animal she were stifling as she descended the stone staircase into an afternoon that seemed too bright.

That night Kay dreamed she was walking down a street and in the dream she explained to herself the principle of a dream. I am not really here, she said to herself, though I feel here. Therefore I may do whatever I want without shame. Am I sure of this? she wondered, looking ahead of her and around her. Thought, as much as act, can be the invitation to attack. And I could be attacked at any moment.

No, she said to herself suddenly, harshly, this is not my dream. I dream the dreams of Adrienne Rich.

And almost awake, she saw that the window of her room was not closed, that there was a great hole in it.

Once Kay had had a theory about story, essay, and dream. (Or rather the beginning of a theory. For though she had an endlessly theorizing mind, her pursuit of any particular theory was often blocked by her misgivings about the very worth of theorizing itself.) When she was a student, she had discussed this theory with Dr. Harkavy. "The author of a story is at two different distances from the reader simultaneously, the distance of feeling and the distance of thought. And those two distances shift and change, together and separately." "I'm not sure I know what you're talking about," Dr. Harkavy said. "Look," she persisted, "you can think of a story as an essay and a dream." She tried to show him what she meant by the beginning of "Gooseberries".

> The whole sky had been overcast with rain clouds from early morning; it was a still day, not hot, but heavy, as it is in gray dull weather when the clouds have been hanging over the country for a long while, when one expects rain and it does not come. Ivan Ivanovich, the veterinary surgeon, and Burkin, the high school teacher, were already tired from walking, and the fields seemed to them endless . . .

"Do you see," she told him, "how even in that beginning are elements of essay and dream, how Chekov is sometimes closer, sometimes further away, how the movement of feeling and the movement of thought are not the same?" She tried to explain to Dr. Harkavy, but her words and her thoughts became as muddy as the ground of Alehin's mill, where, in the story, Ivan Ivanovich, Burkin, and Alehin swim. Dr. Harkavy looked at her as if impatient or embarrassed and changed the subject.

Dr. Harkavy was a mournful man of many silences. When he grew silent about her theory, when he changed the subject, she began to doubt herself. Only later did she remember something he had once said in class about "Gooseberries": "To me Pelageya is the most beautiful woman in all of literature."

How can that be, Kay had asked herself, when she is only mentioned a few times in the story? "Beautiful Pelageya, looking refined and soft, brought them towels and soap . . . lovely Pelageya, stepping noiselessly on the carpet and smiling softly, handed them tea and jam on a tray . . ." That was the most beautiful woman in all literature?

When Dr. Harkavy said that about Pelageya, she had let it pass, though she felt a certain contempt for that silently serving figure. She didn't challenge him because of that terrible awkwardness of his that now and then slid into brusqueness. She responded to his awkwardness awkwardly, and to his brusqueness with hurt or resentment. But then she recalled his mournfulness and she felt a small self reproach. Of course she also felt a certain awe of his position, which she never got over even when she met him some years later in the street with his wife and daughter. His wife was large and pleasant. His daughter was slight with prominent eyes and her chin was drawn back to her neck. They chatted and Dr. Harkavy called her Kay. He asked her what she had done with her life. She could not call him Morris. Nor did she mention that she still had her notes for her unfinished theory in a box in the closet, put away as one might put away a well-liked but outdated dress with the thought that it might come back into style. (Yet as years went by and now and then she would take the dress out something had happened to it in the closet. It had changed. It was not quite right.)

Now after the lecture, after the dream Kay thought once more of her theory and she remembered again what Dr. Harkavy had said about Pelageya. The most beautiful woman in all of literature? Even in retrospect she felt a twinge of resentment, some sense of having been passed by, of having let herself be passed by. She should, after all, have said something to him. But what did all this have to do with Adrienne Rich and the lecture and her anger? Like the discarded dress, the theory and Pelageya—yes, she too— were out of style . . . No man would dare speak of the most beautiful woman in all of literature now without knowing he would have to justify himself. Well, what did it matter? Whatever her anger had been at Adrienne Rich and what she said, luckily the dream had absorbed it.

One evening, three or four months later, the telephone rang. "How are you? How are things?" It was Mike Askine, a teacher at the local community college. He chatted about his teaching, about his new house, about his family. "Everything," he said, "is just great." Kay knew him well enough to know that he would go roundabout, that he needed to set the scene before he said what he had to say and revealed his latest enthusiasm. She remembered how he had been disappointed in the past. Nothing was ever what he hoped it would be. Yet that didn't stop him. With his tall thin frame and his long grey hair flying, he walked as if he were bending into the wind, eager, searching for the next, the best hope. It's not my business to remind him of the past, she reminded herself.

Finally he came to the point. "It's unbelievable what's happening among the women. It's like an explosion. They've got this whole new thing and they want to talk about it and write about it, but they don't know how to do it. It's all too new. They need encouragement and support. They need to see that other women are going through the same thing.

"I finally got the college going on this. We've set up a conference on sex roles and writing, not just for the women but for men too. You know when you have a feeling that the time is right?"

He stopped and Kay waited.

"We'd like you to come and give one of the talks. I was thinking maybe you'd talk about Adrienne Rich."

After a small silence, she said, "I disagree with a lot that she says."

"That's fine. It doesn't make any difference. I don't insist that you agree with her. I just think that what she has to say is important. She speaks to the young women, but she also opens up new possibilities for everybody."

Kay thought of saying no, but then she chided herself. It's wrong to turn things down when they come like this. One ought to submit to coincidence. Sometimes that in itself points the way to—to meaning. Yet she sensed a small malevolent urge in herself, a disposition to revenge. Revenge for what? Or am I jealous, she asked herself, of Adrienne Rich, the public figure who has her finger on the pulse of the nation while I, an unknown part-time essayist, have mine on a corpse or a child not yet born?

Quit that, she said to herself, and she told Mike she'd give the talk. But I'm not going to attack, she warned herself. The whole point is to come to some understanding about her anger and my anger, and the anger of all those other people in the room. Maybe that dream had not absorbed everything, after all.

The community college union was built into the slope of a hill. Kay entered at the top and descended a staircase to the main floor. There, the large room which was ordinarily a cafeteria had been converted into an auditorium. A great number of people were milling about. So Mike had been right in what he said: it was the right time. At that moment she saw him pass by, his body bent forward, papers clutched in his hand, his hair flying, intent, in his eagerness and excitement.

Kay went to the front of the room and sat in a chair at the end of the first row. She pulled out her notes, then set them down. She knew all that she had to say. The windows in front of her were two stories high, looking out over a grassy slope to a steep hillside. The sky was still, hanging heavy, casting a mouldy light. In the room there was the smell of food cooked for a long time in great steel vats, though the doors to the kitchen were closed. In the corner on a table were some dirty dishes that had not been cleared away.

Mike hurried to the lectern and asked everyone to be seated. His voice hoarse, he made a series of announcements about the program for the next few days. He seemed a slight figure, standing with his back to the huge window. Kay looked around her and behind her. There were many more women than men, many more young women than old. Though she recognized some of those in the audience, they seemed at the moment at a great distance from her, as if they'd been absorbed into a foreign mass. As Mike introduced her, she had the sudden presentiment that they were not going to listen to what she had to say. But she felt, at the same time, an obligation to go on, a moral stricture, no matter how much she was out of step with the times.

As she walked across the floor to the lectern, she noticed that the papers in her hand were trembling. At the lectern the microphone was too high. She tried to lower it, but it would not move.

"Wait a minute," a young man with a large head called out, as he came down the center aisle. He walked with a sidewise limp that made his going slow and painful. He adjusted the microphone and stood to the side, watching. Kay put her notes on the lectern and faced the audience. The large window behind her cast a cold light on those before her and she found no single face to focus on. Her voice strained, as if she'd been holding it down for a long time, she began, "We are all familiar enough with anger. But in Adrienne Rich's anger in her essays and her recorded conversations, there is something unfamiliar and disturbing."

There was an echo in that high ceilinged room. By the slightest lapse, her voice was being returned to her, barely amplified. "At some crucial point her anger is disjointed. It is as if she misses something in a necessary sequence yet runs ahead. So reading her essays, you cannot help but wonder about her anger and its reasons."

"We can't hear," someone yelled.

The young man with the large head and the sidewise limp appeared again. He tried to adjust the microphone; he fiddled with the amplifier. "This does this sometimes," he said. "All of a sudden it just stops working. It's rotten equipment. I keep telling them and telling them, but they don't do anything. Go ahead, try it again."

"When she speaks of breaking the hold of the past that derives from man's power over women—"

"We still can't hear," someone shouted from the back.

"I'll tell you what to do. Hold the microphone in your hand," the young man said.

". . . when she says connections have finally been drawn between our sexual lives and our political institutions, she is taking a leap—"

"Louder!" came another shout from the back.

Mike came up and he too fiddled with the amplifier. "I think you're just going to have to do without it. You'll just have to shout."

"Yeah, yell," said the young man with the large head.

"Should I start all over again?" Kay asked.

"Just go on from there," Mike said.

She felt a terrible dismay that the sequence she'd prepared so carefully had been disrupted. Still she went on, shouting about Adrienne Rich's early work, how it had been praised for its modesty and sweetness, then shouting about the poet's recanting of that modesty and sweetness. She shouted as she quoted her: "'To be a female human being trying to fulfill traditional female functions in a traditional way is in direct conflict with the subversive function of the imagination.'"

More and more as she shouted her sequence, she felt a detachment, a sense that she had been left behind to carry out an order, to finish what had been determined but was no longer appropriate. On the page, as she had prepared her notes, everything was clear and logical. But now, as she shouted, nothing was clear—only the obligation to persist. She had been left with words: she was shouting them and they were being hurled back in the echo from the high ceilinged room.

Still she kept shouting. She shouted about Adrienne Rich's leap from the private to the public world, about her will to change. "'There is no private psyche,' Adrienne Rich says. The cause of her anger becomes the solution to her anger. And she insists on her answer as the answer for all women . . ."

At the end there was polite applause. Kay went to her seat feeling relief. At least the shouting was over. From the back Mike made a brief announcement about the next session. People got up, talked, walked around. Kay stood awkwardly. A few acquaintances nodded and smiled as they passed by. She turned and picked up her notes from the chair. She felt herself turning away in response to a turning away in them.

At the door Anna Marie Peck, large, energetic, and direct, stopped her. "Where do you think you're going?"

"I'm going home."

"Oh no. You're not going to get away with that. Not after that attack. We're having a discussion upstairs on women and writing and there are a few questions we want you to answer."

Perhaps it was the staleness and the flatness that Kay felt that decided her, the feeling that something else was needed to make an ending. "All right," she agreed.

"I'll be right up," Anna Marie told her.

Upstairs in the student lounge, Kay sank into a dark leather chair. "Not after that attack," Anna Marie had said. What attack? It wasn't an attack. She got up and went to the bathroom at the back of the lounge. At the sink she poured cold water into her cupped hands, then bent over and put her face into the water.

"You probably don't remember me," she heard a woman say. As Kay straightened up, some water dripped down her neck.

"You were a student of my father's, Professor Harkavy."

Yes, Kay remembered that meeting on the street, those curiously prominent eyes, that chin pulled back stiffly into her neck.

"How is your father?"

"He retired last year."

"I didn't know."

"He says he misses the teaching, but then he used to say he was fed up with it. You know how he is."

Do I know how he is? Kay asked herself, remembering that mournful and distant man.

"I'm so nervous," Professor Harkavy's daughter went on. "I'm supposed to be part of that panel in there. This is the first time I've ever done anything like this."

"Once you get started, you'll forget you're nervous," Kay reassured her, drying her face and hands on a paper towel.

"I hope so." She smiled hesitantly. "I guess I'd better get in there. They may be getting started." At the door she turned. "Some time I'd like to talk to you about your lecture. I don't agree with a lot that you said, but maybe I misunderstood it."

In the lounge the four panelists, sitting on straight chairs set in a row, introduced themselves: Anna Marie Peck, Judith Harkavy Brody, Bob Keller, and Alice Goudge. Kay slipped into a deep leather chair and looked at Judith Harkavy Brody. Her eyes were shining. She smiled and bit her lip. Kay thought of Dr. Harkavy. Did he pull his chin back like that? Surely she would have noticed.

"This is going to be very informal," said Keller, a balding young poet. "We're just going to kick around the whole question of sex roles in writing. I'd like to get the ball rolling by saying something about your talk." He turned to Kay. "I feel you haven't been fair to the whole body of Adrienne's work. You've picked on only a few things and neglected the entire body of her work."

"I wasn't talking about the entire body of her work. I—"

A young woman in the audience interrupted. "You've put a black value on anger, but anger can lead to a cleansing." There was a murmuring of agreement.

"I do think it's important," Keller went on, "that anger be expressed. The women now are much clearer about their anger than the men are. I feel that we men have to be grateful for that."

From deep inside the leather chair, pulled down as she tried to pull herself up, Kay began to talk about transcendence, about the transcendence of anger in art.

"I don't believe in transcendence," Keller said. "That art is separate from life is an esthetic left over from the nineteenth century. It just doesn't work any more, if it ever did. We live in a different kind of a world. We can't fool ourselves with transcendence. In fact, if you look carefully, you'll see that what really holds this world together, what everything else is based on, is economics. Rich's real error is in not seeing that the real dynamic force in this society is the economic one. That's what shapes everything else. That's what determines men's roles and women's roles."

"Ah, come on," Anna Marie said. "I thought we'd gone beyond that shit."

Alice Goudge interrupted to say that the role of women was determined entirely by society. She was pale and thin and had long pale brown hair and when she spoke her voice was so quiet, Kay had to strain to hear her.

A young man with a beard insisted on being recognized. "It's not just the women who are angry. The men are angry too. The women are angry because they've been giving too much for too long and they're resentful. The men have been taking things for too long unfairly and that brings its own guilt. When you carry around that kind of guilt, you can't help being angry."

"You're saying anger is not nice," Judith Harkavy Brody said, turning to Kay, "but it's necessary."

"Nice!" Anna Marie said and laughed out loud. "You heard what Auden said about Rich's early work. He said it was nice. And Jarrell said it was sweet. No wonder Rich was enraged."

"Nice, yes we were always told to be nice," a middle-aged

woman at the back said. She was wearing a South American poncho. Her face was lined and her expression was very intent.

"Yes. Be nice for this. Be nice for that. That's what we were always told. The only time I can remember not having to be nice was when I was in the bathroom," Anna Marie said.

"I don't remember being told to be nice," Kay said, but after she'd said it, she didn't know if it was true or not.

From his straight chair Keller said, "But what you're all talking about is the niceness of the middle class, whereas actually—"

"I know about that middle class niceness. When I was a young woman, I got that whole bit in spades," the woman in the poncho said. "I got away from it by going abroad, to South America, but there I was trapped in an even more sexist culture."

"The trouble is that we've been shoved around and mistreated and we didn't even know it," someone said.

"And still are—"

A pretty young woman with dark hair got up. Her voice was shaking as she began to speak. "I was living with this guy for two years. Things kept getting worse, but I couldn't tell what was happening. All the time I kept blaming myself. Finally, after two years, I realized it wasn't me, it was him. He was fucking me up with all that power shit and I didn't even know it. I told him last week he had to get out. And now I'm going to understand what happened. That's what I want to write about."

"Right on," someone said.

"We're still prisoners. There's no use pretending it's not so," said Judith, her voice trembling. "We're prisoners even—especially—in the literary world. I've just been reading a paper on sexist criticism. The woman who wrote it pointed out how most of the words in literary criticism are masculine words. They talk about a line not being sharp or clear or tight. The worst thing is for a line to be flaccid or limp, or for an author's tone to be soft instead of hard. All the feminine characteristics such as roundness or softness are despised. They only like things with vertical lines. And the climax, the way they talk about climax—" She threw up her hands.

Everyone laughed.

"The point is that they only praise literature that has the shape of the male experience. Even that word you used," she turned to Kay, "transcendence, that's a male word."

For a moment Kay couldn't say anything. She remembered how nervous Judith had said she was, in the bathroom, yet here she was opening up, attacking—yes, it was an attack. She tried to be calm and patient as she responded to her. She appealed to her as she'd once appealed to Dr. Harkavy. She pointed out those writers, men writers, who had written of women with understanding and compassion. "Take Tolstoi, in *Anna Karenina*."

"Tolstoi? Tolstoi was a sexist. Look what he did to Anna, how he killed her off for what she did, for having an affair outside of marriage."

"I was just thinking about the bind we're all in," the woman in the poncho interrupted. "Men have never been able to feel what we feel, yet they tell us what we're feeling. Is it any wonder that we're angry? Isn't that what Adrienne Rich is talking about?"

"Let's try to focus this discussion," Keller said. "We want to talk about sex roles in writing. Are women different or not different in what they have to say and in the forms they must use? We need to start being more concrete."

Alice Goudge thrust back her long pale hair and spoke softly. "I think the most important thing is that we must have a sense of solidarity with women all over the world. I identify with women everywhere. I've just written a poem about a farmer's wife in Africa, about her feelings as she works the land . . ."

Suddenly Kay felt an enormous sense of constriction, a choking, a sense of being held back and of holding herself in at the same time. She felt as if she were on an edge, as if she could not contain herself one more minute. She was sitting with the others yet she'd been separated off and become some kind of totem in her "reason." In some way that she could not understand, her talk had given impetus to what they were saying. In listening to her they had heard only the words of Adrienne Rich, the words she had shouted. The others had not followed her sequence by sequence to her ending, but had left her on the way. And now she was isolated, the defender of reason, she who had so many doubts about reason herself.

At the back of the room she saw the young man with the large head. He was standing, listening; when he saw her look at him he grinned sheepishly. Then Kay heard Judith say, "I remember when I was pregnant with my first child. I remember I thought it was going to be a boy. And I felt as if I were carrying the Messiah. I thought I was crazy to be thinking such a thing, so I never told anyone. But since then, only recently, I have heard other women say they felt the same thing. If I had only known then . . ."

That night Kay had a dream. In the dream she was walking down University Avenue. On a corner she saw Professor Harkavy. With him was his daughter, only it did not look like her; it looked like Alice Goudge. "They do not help others the way they used to," Dr. Harkavy said brusquely. "Even if you ask them, they don't do anything." His daughter nodded, her long pale hair flying. Kay tried to protest, but he stopped her. "All the Pelageyas know that," he snapped at her and hurried off, with his daughter running behind. Watching him go down the street, Kay felt a sense of horror, for she knew that by "Pelageya" he meant "whore." "Wait! Listen!" she tried to shout. And she awoke, making strange sounds like the bleating of a small animal.

I never should have stayed, she told herself the next morning as she sat at her desk. She tried to put everything into sequence that had happened, but nothing fell into place. She thought of Judith Harkavy and what she had said about carrying the Messiah. She thought of Alice Goudge. Her and her solidarity. What did she know of a farmer's wife in Africa? Kay looked at her lecture notes, but the words on the page seemed inert and tedious. Put it away, don't look at it now, she told herself. She went into the kitchen and made herself some tea. Sitting at the kitchen table, she saw through the window the dense leaves of the plum tree, dark and wet. Why "all the Pelageyas?" she asked herself. She decided she needed to get out, to get away from the house.

Outside the ground and pavement were wet. An unseasonal rain had left a curious smell in the air, as if the vegetation were rotting in the unaccustomed moisture. Kay got in the car and drove westward, out of the built-up flatland toward the hills. Even they seemed to be sodden in the murky air.

She followed the familiar turns of Page Mill Road up to Foothills Park, then drove in and parked near Boronda Lake. She walked past bay laurels and buckeyes to Wildhorse Valley, then up to the Sunrise Trail. In the mild, too moist air she had a sense of incipient release. Lulled in the repetitive motion of climbing, she felt that she did not need to struggle for understanding of the dream or of all the sequences that had come before, that she only needed to wait and she would eventually know what they meant. On the crest of a hill she stopped and thought of the words of the dream: "They do not let others help them the way they used to," and "All the Pelageyas know that."

She looked east over the built-up flatland to the Bay and then to the salt hills on the other shore. To the north was a bridge and beyond that another bridge and even further north, though it was not visible, was the city. A terrible judgment had been made. It was her dream. She had made it, but she was also one of the judged. It was as if the others, previously unjudged, had been joined to her in judgment.

Descending past red-barked madrone, past scrub oak, past poison oak with shiny new leaves, she felt suddenly a release from her own surveillance. It was as if a muscle too long contracted had finally let go and she could breathe calmly, gently, as she followed the shifting surface of the firebreak back down to Wildhorse Valley.

At the edge of Boronda Lake she stopped near the "No Swimming" sign. The mallards rushed up out of the water onto the bank, making a great quacking sound. Behind them came the black coots, their water bodies awkward on their green feet, running silently with an almost human twist of their torsos.

"Sorry birds, poor birds," she said, and she reminded herself that the next time she came, she must bring them some old bread.

AN INFLUX OF POETS

JEAN STAFFORD

Jean Stafford was a short-story writer and novelist whose
Collected Stories won her a Pulitzer Prize in 1969. She was
born in Covina, California, in 1915, but moved with her
family to Colorado, where she grew up and later graduated
from the University of Colorado at Boulder. Miss Stafford
was a regular contributor to such periodicals as *The New
Yorker, Partisan Review, Kenyon Review,* and *Harper's
Bazaar.* She died in March of 1979 after a long illness.

That awful summer! Every poet in America came to stay with us.
It was the first summer after the war, when people once again had
gasoline and could go where they liked, and all those poets came
to our house in Maine and stayed for weeks at a stretch, bringing
wives or mistresses with whom they quarrelled, and complaining
so vividly about the wives and mistresses they'd left, or had been
left by, that the discards were real presences, swelling the ranks,
stretching the house, *my* house (my very own, my first and very
own), to its seams. At night, after supper, they'd read from their
own works until four o'clock in the morning, drinking Cuba
Libres. They never listened to one another; they were preoccupied
with waiting for their turn. And I'd have to stay up and clear out
the living room after they went soddenly to bed—sodden but not
too far gone to lose their conceit. And then all day I'd cook and
wash the dishes and chop the ice and weed the garden and type
my husband's poems and quarrel with him. I had met Theron
Maybank in Adams, Colorado, five years earlier at a writers' conference at Neville University, where, as a graduate student, I was

serving on the arrangements committee. Theron had left his native Boston for his first trip West in order to meet the famous and reclusive American poet Fitzhugh Burr, who had agreed to make a rare public appearance on the campus. I found Theron's brilliant talk and dark good looks somehow reminiscent of the young Nathaniel Hawthorne. We were married in Adams a few weeks after the conference ended, and left one week later for Baton Rouge.

On the Labor Day weekend the well went dry: a death rattle shook every pipe in the house, there was a kind of bleating sound, and then a sigh. Three poets—one with a wife—were in residence at the time, and so was Minnie Rosoff, just divorced from Jered Zumwalt, the bard of Harvard, Canarsie-born. The well went dry, and Evan and Lucia Bronson left the next day, taking Harry Matthews with them back to Princeton. They had been guests for three full weeks, and the reading of poetry had been perpetual. Lucia and I were kept at our typewriters typing Evan's and Theron's poems as they wrote them; it seemed to us they wrote at the speed of light, but this was not so. They were snail-paced (oh, I admit they were brilliant poets, if you happen to be interested in that sort of thing), but if they changed an "a" to a "the" the whole sonnet had to be typed over again. And I grant that such a change can make all the difference in the world (if, that is, you happen to be a poet or a lover of poetry), but why couldn't the alteration be made by hand? Meanwhile, down in the finished room in the lower part of the barn, Harry Matthews, whose precocious glitter eventually came to nothing—he was forgotten soon after his first book appeared—really *was* writing like greased lightning.

And then at night the ladies of the house sat in my pretty parlor (*my* parlor! My own! I bought the house, I bought the furniture, the student lamps, the cachepots, the milk-glass bowls I used for water lilies from the lake—Theron and I had got to Maine before the antique dealers, and there were still big old ramshackle firetraps called "secondhand stores," generally owned by men whose real income came from undertaking), listening to the poets listen to themselves and not to one another. What Lucia thought about I couldn't guess; we did not know each other as friends— only as the wives of young poets—but I know that my own mind strayed, browsing in fields far distant from those bounded by the barbed-wire fences (some of them electric) of my marriage. I was a child back in Missouri, in my grandfather's Sunday punishment room, listening to Foxe's "Book of Martyrs," scared and rebellious and disloyally bored. Usually, to be sure, I took a drink as the poetry was read, but drink didn't help; if I'd been out in the kitchen by myself, drinking that emetic compound of rum and Coca-Cola, I would have been at peace, staring into space and dreaming of what my life could have been if I had married someone else, or what it still could be if Theron drowned, perhaps, in the lake behind my house or in the tidal river in front of it. But I was in this throng of litterateurs (three poets in one medium-sized room constitute a multitude), enjoying nothing. I never did, even afterward, know what Lucia was thinking. But Minnie Rosoff was agape, adoring and adorable, loving them all, especially my husband, and, because she was so obvious, mendaciously flattering me.

I had been in Boston the day Minnie came to begin her visit with us; the Bronsons had gone down the coast to stay with friends for a few days. (They came back to us, of course—there was more poetry in *our* house, and they would be there when the well gave up the ghost.) Just back from Nevada, where she had divorced Jerry Zumwalt, Minnie had been moving slowly down the coast of Maine, alighting like a bird to charm and sing in other houses, making her carefree passage in other people's motorcars and other people's boats. She came to us, quixotically and at the expense of her last host, in a Piper Cub, landing on an island in Hawthorne Lake, behind us, flown there by a Seabee so stricken with her that he loitered in the village several days afterward. If I had been there when she came, the outcome of my marriage would, I daresay, have been the same, but the end of it would probably not have come so soon. Certainly it would not have been so humiliating, so banal, so sandy to my teeth. But I was not there on that beautiful afternoon when her blithe plane banked and came bobbing to rest on Loon Islet and she came swimming to our landing.

I'd gone to Boston two days before to try to learn the reason for the headaches that daily harrowed me. I knew they came from something more than rum, and I knew—although I did not want to know—that I could not honestly attribute them to too many

iambs and too many dithyrambic self-congratulations by the baby
bards. (Though they were no longer enfants terribles, the blood of
despots was in their veins and they would very soon usurp their
elders' thrones and their dominions.) When I came back to Edwards Mills, depleted by the dark and heavy heat of Boston, dirty
from the train, I found Minnie and Theron sitting in the garden in
the perishing day like a Watteau summer idyll, already so advanced in their lore (infatuation acquires its history and literature
in minutes) that they were beyond the need of language and were
listening, as they drank mint juleps from my silver goblets, to the
phonograph playing in the living room, playing Scarlatti sonatas,
my favorites, which Theron theretofore had barely tolerated, pre-
ferring the music of Beethoven, which, he said, showing off, was
"impeccably flatulent—all bawdy hoydens and horny knaves,"
adding, "He's the Bruegel of music."

I did not at that moment apprehend the reason for their blissful circumstance; I saw only that they *were* blissful, and I envied
their simple pleasure in the cool air and the light waning to violet
and the smell of the flowers and the feeling of the icy dew on the
goblets they held, all bespangled with the wit of the harpsichord.
Soon there would be fireflies.

As I paused at the door without their knowledge of my looking
at them, I saw Theron not as the husband I loved to despair and
hated to the point of murder—the man I wanted to flee because,
in failing to commit myself entirely to him, I knew he would not
commit himself to me; I saw him only as a thin, dark, tall, large-
headed genius, complementing by his differences of stature and
structure the pretty, small, dark, *zaftig* girl who was luring and
foiling my silver tabby cat with a piece of string to which she had
tied a small green pinecone. At first the tableau—except for the
gentle swinging of the impromptu toy and the contraction of my
cat's withers as she prepared to spring, the scene was motionless—
eased me, made me think, "I'm not done for yet if I can still get
this far outside myself to be made so happy by so slight a scene,"
and then, suddenly, I sickened and felt gross and smutted, alien,
and I remembered the blunt, brusque doctor, prejudiced against
me by my having come to him at the apex of the humid day, saying to me without compassion and without interest, "Considering

your symptoms and your history, I can do nothing but advise you
to see a psychoanalyst."

I had not expected Minnie until dinnertime. All the way from
Boston on the East Wind, steeling myself with drink (and, as I
steeled, softening my headlong nerves), I had planned how I
would tell Theron of Dr. Lowebridge's recommendation, one that
I knew he would greet with an admixture of contempt and com-
placence, for while he despised psychiatry—he despised medicine
in general—he had many times ended our vicious quarrels with
the reminder that if what I had told him about my father (whom
he had never met) was the truth, my mental heritage was doubt-
less suspect and I was *immoral* not to be examined by someone
competent to navigate the eccentric meanders of my mind.
("What meanders?" I demanded. He would only smile and roll
back his eyes, and I would go mad with rage and terror.) I
dreaded equally his satisfaction and his indifference: whether he
crowed or shrugged, he would undermine me, he would cripple
me and make me mute, for latterly I had so feared the smile that
when I sensed it coming I would say nothing more and bear his
scorn, his lofty, hidebound disapproval, as if I were an uppity field
hand getting what was coming to me.

Dr. Lowebridge's prescription for me was, I thought, appalling;
it had taken my breath away. How could these brutish headaches
and this lurching nausea have their genesis in my mind? It was
preposterous. Still, there had been compensations in the advice—
if, that is, I decided to follow it—and I had dimly seen a way that
it might suspend my struggle with Theron for a while. He was, despite his eccentricities and his rebellion, an intransigently conventional man; thus his diehard repudiation of psychiatry as pop-
pycock, a Viennese chicanery devised to bilk idle women and
hypochondriacal men. After accepting Dr. Lowebridge's diagnosis,
Theron was almost bound to send me to New York lest the news
that I was "mental" be noised about in Boston, and such a separation, justified and temporary, was what I had prayed for all these
stewed and sleeplessly stewing nights of summer.

I meant (this had been my plan on the train) to come to him
suppliantly with the news, to come in such humility and courage
that he could not fail to console and support me and, seeing my
need, would leave off his snobberies. I had intended to be wifely

and womanly, freshly bathed and wearing my most floating dress when I appeared, my hair done blamelessly and as he liked it, in braids around my head, my external integument past any criticism. I would jocosely take his side against me; I would seriously assume all responsibility for our antagonisms and would hold out hope (I had no hope at all) for their extirpation. Simply to be away from him, I thought, would signal the beginning of the end of my nightmare. I was glad that our conversation would not be long but must be suspended with Minnie's arrival and with the proprieties of dinner, to which I had invited three guests. I had got home in good time, just after five, for an hour of dress rehearsal, but Minnie's being there already, and as if she'd been there for weeks, or even years, deflected the course of my strategy and sent me astray into a wilderness of confusion and shame and embarrassment.

I stepped down into my own garden as if I were a guest, related only by the kind amenities of my hostess to the cat, to the roses, and to the man—who, barely looking at me, said, "I called off dinner because I knew you'd be tired. Besides, Minnie didn't want to dress."

Perhaps my deepest, longest lingering dismay began then, in that kind of panoramic view of his whole history which is supposed to flash before the eyes of a man drowning or hurtling to his death from a great altitude. I gasped, looking at Minnie Rosoff in her sleek, chic negligee of white linen shorts and a long-sleeved pale-blue shirt with bogus-emerald Chanel cufflinks; my city black was wrinkled, ash-smudged, my hands were swollen and red from the heat and black from the train, too clumsy for the cat's casual and elegant toy (Colette would have devised such a thing) or for the silver goblets. My smile for this woman became a green schoolgirl's grin; I blushed, I stumbled toward a canvas chair, and when Minnie Rosoff said, "Theron, do make a drink for your poor exhausted wife," I felt like a traveller who had just debarked from steerage and who, through some unthinkable mistake, had got into the first-class customs line.

With his back to me, as if he could not bear the sight of me, my husband said, "You don't mind that I called off dinner?"

I minded very much, but I smiled, and, for the sake of our

guest, I was polite and thanked him warmly, and I said, "In that case, we can have our supper on trays out here."

"Minnie would like to take a picnic to Loon," he said. "She wants to see the Cub Scout again."

"*Piper Cub*, you goose!" cried Minnie, and laughed the infant, fluting laugh that had heretofore enchanted me as it had everyone she knew. "But Cora doesn't know how I got here! I flew down from Castine in a *wee* plane, like a kite exactly. With such a sweet boy, and the plane is still on that *tiny* island. The moon will be full—it's summertime! Say that you want a picnic, sweetie!"

Theron gave me no chance to sanction or to veto the picnic, which I did not want—which seemed to me unbearably boisterous. He said, "Cora can't row and can't swim, and she's got a thing about small boats."

"Oh, poor lamb," said Minnie. "But with two of us to save you you'll be perfectly safe." And she tried to persuade me with those arguments, logical and sensible, with which people who are not sufferers themselves try to subdue a phobia in someone else. "But it's only a garter snake," they say. "It can't possibly hurt you." And the ophidiophobe repeats that his horror comes not from the venom or the size of the snake but from the movement and the shape and the especial *essence* of the creature, and that he recognizes but cannot help his irrationality. Thus, my fear of water (not of drowning, not of what the water would do to me, but an aboriginal, a prehistoric fear, but prehistoric in the present tense, of the nature of water and its antiquity and its secrecy) could in no way be diminished by Minnie's assurances that the lake was not deep at our end, that she had had experience in giving artificial respiration, that our dory was as safe as houses (so they'd been rowing earlier among the lily pads?), that she could have the pilot of the Piper Cub bring over a Mae West for me. The more she tried to persuade me, the more stubbornly I resisted, until finally I was angry, protective of this neurosis—which, in point of fact, had been a nuisance and an impediment to me all my life and one I would have given anything to be delivered from.

Theron remained silent, and while once I might have been grateful that he did not add to my discomfort by teasing me, now I was suspicious: his faint smile, the way in which his gaze followed the capers of the cat and never fell on me, although occasionally it did on Minnie, still moving the pinecone like a pendulum, baffled me. I had often thought that when I was out of his sight I was literally out of his mind, that he never imagined me as I might be in a train or in a strange hotel, as I always imagined him when he was away from home. I had never felt myself to be so far away from him—as if we were separated by many actual miles—as I did this early evening when I sat opposite him in the garden, three feet away, conjoined by our house (mine! Remember, Cora Savage, if you forget all else, that this is *your* house), our cat, and the inveigling voice of Minnie Rosoff. I did not understand his silence; I was alarmed, for in my misery I was wholly egocentric and looked on every act as being related in some way to me. What was the motive that caused him to hold his peace instead of bolstering Minnie's arguments with impatient ones of his own? And what on earth possessed him, when at last she gave up and he went in to make me a drink, to make it double strength, when all summer he had denied or rationed me with public frowns and headshakes that had made my blood boil? "What the bleeding hell?" I'd yell at him. "You drink as much as I do. You drink more!" and he'd reply, "A difference of upbringing, dear—no more than that. I learned to drink at home in the drawing room, so I know how. No fault of yours—just bad luck. You don't drink well, dear. Not well at all."

When he gave me my triple hemlock on crushed ice, bedizened with a spray of mint, he said, "Minnie and I will have our picnic. You can stay here. Will you make us some sandwiches, Cozy Cora? Please? Pretty please with sugar on it?"

I put my drink down on the grass beside my chair and stood up and took my cat into my arms and buried my face in her satiny flank. She was bored with the game anyhow, and when I sat down again she curled serenely into my lap.

"You are my cat," I said. "You are my personal cat." At the sound of my voice she looked up and blinked her Mediterranean green-blue eyes. Always literary, Theron had named her Anna Livia Plurabelle, and she was known as Livvy for short. "You are my cat," I repeated, "and from now on your name is Pretty Baby."

After Minnie and Theron had gone down through the meadow with their picnic basket and a bottle of wine I had brought up from the well, I sat for some time in the garden, unthinking, trying to count the short, soft beams of the magic fireflies. (Each Fourth of July night at Granny Savage's house in Missouri, before we moved to Colorado, my father had caught fireflies in one of Mama's hairnets and draped it over my older sister Abigail's head. The green, and sometimes blue and sometimes violet, lights went on and off among her dark-red curls and, to please her idol, she would twirl around, swoop down, and then rise up on her toes. "By George, what's this we have?" exclaimed my father. "Queen Mab herself! Titania!" Mama laughed and clapped, and my younger brother, Randall, giggling and howling like a wolf, would chase her. We'd see them weaving in and out among the willow trees and the acacias. The trapped fireflies attracted others, and my brother and sister were enveloped in a mist of stars. I wanted a halo, too, but there was no other hairnet, and when I stamped my foot and shouted, "It isn't *fair!*" Mama tried to soothe me, saying, "Never mind. You can put it on when Abigail is through.") I postponed going to bed, the more to savor the sleep I knew awaited me. For a long time now, I had not been able really to sleep unless there was a moon. I could not close my eyes until the fallow light overtook the serious country darkness on the windowpanes and consolingly revealed to me familiar objects in the room —my wrapper thrown over the blue velvet slipper chair, the silver-birch logs lying across the andirons on the tiny hearth, the Quimper pitcher on the mantelpiece which I kept full of wild flowers. And then, almost at once, after this last look, my eyelids would close, cherishing the warmth and love of sleep, my breathing would deepen, I could feel myself falling headlong into the most delectable condition on earth. Only thus could I escape Theron the poet, and Theron the poet's poet friends. He was beside me and they were in all the rooms around me and in the barn, but I was dead to their world, and they, thereby, were dead to mine.

Pretty Baby was mewing in the living room and, knowing that she would be moving her kittens and, liking to watch the curious ritual scene-shifting, I went into the house and saw her carrying the runt of the litter, all black, across the carpet from the nest she had made for them behind the sofa to the basket beside the fireplace, where they properly belonged. The other three were there already, and I wondered if she had taken the runt last because she liked him least or because she feared his fat siblings would smother him. They were still blind and she was still proud, cosseting them with her milk and her bright, abrasive tongue and the constant purr into which, now and again, she interjected a little yelp of self-esteem. When she was nestled down, relaxed amongst her produce, I knelt and strongly ran the knuckle of my thumb down the black stripes that began just above her nose and terminated in the wider, blacker bands around her neck, and then I left her to her rapturous business of grooming her kittens, nursing in their blindness and their sleep.

I turned out all the lights but one—one to guide back to shore the Loon Islet revellers who did not fear the water. I did not doubt that Minnie would at some time sing "Over the sea to Skye," one of her specialties. Her voice was as high and as clear as a blockflöte. How gifted was this little minx, raven-tressèd, damask-skinned, by turns so sharp-witted as a critic that critics cringed when she attacked them in the pages of the leading intellectual quarterly, The Divergent, and as moon-eyed and adoring as a daft maiden when she was in the presence of a poet. Still, she was not feared by the poets' wives, because her unchivalric and murderously moody husband, Jered Zumwalt, had broadcast wide, in disgraceful but convincing detail, the news that she was as cold as stone. Theron, respectful of Jerry, who with much éclat had published several books and was generally regarded as the most gifted of the young Cambridge poets (Theron was moving steadily up in the race but he had not yet published a book), had fretted with Jerry over Minnie's defection through cases of beer and quarts of blended whiskey in our apartment on Kirkland Street. Quite often, too drunk to go home, Jerry spent the night on the sofa in the living room, where I would find him in the morning on my way to Miss Heath's School, where I taught English. His ruptured loafers, bloated and stained with rain and snow and mud, lay always at some distance from each other—one by the chair where he had been having his last swallow, the other halfway across the room where he had walked out of it on his way to the short, slippery leather sofa on which now he lay as contorted as an old windworn tree, his left hand clenched under his chin, the right resting on a stiff round pillow atop his head. I had one time seen a photograph of him and Minnie taken in the early days of their marriage: so similar were their textures and their values, so clear their grave innocence and so concealed their wit and wisdom, that they could have been two star-crossed, moon-struck lovers—Romeo and Juliet, Aucassin and Nicolette, Floris and Blanchefleur. Soon those sweet and plaintive images shattered: Jerry grew generally drunk, maudlin, and bilious by turns, and Minnie, in Nevada for the divorce, was, we gathered from letters to us and to other friends, having a ripsnorting romp, learning to ride a cow pony and to sing cowboy songs and, most rambunctious of all, working as a shill in a gambling house. When Jerry told us of this last improbable lark, Theron, heavily Bostonian in his sarcasm, said, "After the battle royal, taper off on fun and games, what?," and Jerry, drinking dollar sherry straight from the bottle, then drawing on his five-cent cigar (his bad habits were so inappropriate to his Donatello looks that I never could take them seriously), said, "The only reason she's a shill in the Big Bonanza is that she didn't happen to think of going to Virginia City to be Lucius Beebe's printer's devil."

Now she was back at her old post, beguiling poets. There was an influx of poets this summer in the state of Maine and ours was only one of many houses where they clustered: farther down the coast and inland all the way to Campobello, singly, in couples, trios, tribes, they were circulating among rich patronesses in ancestral summer shacks of twenty rooms, critics on vacation from universities who roughed it with Coleman lamps and outhouses but sumptuously dined on lobster and blueberry gems, and a couple of novelists who, although they wrote like dogs (according to the poets), had made packets, which, because they were decently (and properly) humble, they were complimented to share with the rarer breed. As Mr. Zumwalt worked his way north, so the former Mrs. Z. was migrating south, and we, the Maybanks, and Eliza and her critic husband, Andrew Brandt, in the middle, had tidings from several longitudes and latitudes. So far, the paths of the disaffected had not crossed, and there were jubilant and studious speculations on what would happen if they did. It was the fashion to use Freud's works as a recipe book and to add garnitures from Henry James and Proust.

Standing still in the dim-lit living room, I shuddered suddenly, aware of my dishevelment and remembering the brusque doctor on Commonwealth Avenue who had made my headaches a disgrace and counselled me to go and be shriven of my mortal sins by a psychoanalyst. How would I tell Theron? And when? The poets Bronson and Matthews and the poem-typist Lucia would soon be back and now that Minnehaha was here, the fly-by-nights who had seen Jerry at Isle au Haut or in Aroostook would come flocking in to spy and gabble and prophesy. I would have a ton of fish to fry and bake and poach, a rod of shoe-peg corn to shuck, a gross bushel of salad to harvest and wash and tear and slice and dress, a floe of ice to chop for Cuba Libres. Although the war was over, we were still rationed; for some while to come, I must postpone my shameful revelation to my husband while I hatched up means to disguise horsemeat.

This was not the way I had planned the summer. We had limped painfully through the fifth year of our marriage, having changed the scene of our travail each year from the beginning. Cambridge was no better than New York, New York no better than Connecticut, Connecticut no better than Louisiana or the mountains of Tennessee. But we often limped on different routes, shedding our blood on sand and rocks miles apart. When we did meet in some kind oasis or quiet glade, we were at first shy and infatuated and glad, but the reunion did not last, the shade and water were part of a mirage, lightning smote and burned the hemlocks of our forest sanctuary.

Theron, who had found Catholicism shortly after he found me, ran to Father Bernard—our spiritual adviser in Cambridge—and came back whimpering "*Mea maxima culpa*" so heartbrokenly that I crept from the hiding shadows to console him with old running jokes, and for a while we played again, two precocious, oafish six-year-olds. The blood of the Salem witch-burners scalded the walls of Theron's veins and so, perforce, did that of the Salem warlocks; and I was hot to the touch where I had been scoured and curried with Ayrshire brimstone. We baffled Father Bernard, who had not been trained to crack the whip over wayward rowdies. Surely he must have dreaded Theron's abstruse and convoluted confessions, he must have longed to shut the wicket against those pedantic admissions of frailty and pad softly home to tea and a scone.

Actually, save for the sin of pride, Theron was a blameless man. I was the lost one, for I did not believe in any of it—not in the Real Presence, not in the Immaculate Conception, not in God—and, to compound my perfidy, I received the Host each Sunday and each day of obligation and did not confess my infidelity. Not to Father Bernard and no longer to Theron. In the beginning, I had tried, but he, rapt in his severe belief, had brushed me aside and called my doubt a temporary matter. "But it isn't *doubt!* It's positive repudiation!" I'd cry. We talked like that, in our frustration forgetting to be colloquial, in our insanity forgetting to be sane. Theron once told me that I was going through the dark night of the spirit and I should meditate and read John of the Cross. I did, with a certain kind of recognition, read St. John's friend Teresa's "Interior Castle," and one morning in the shallow sleep just before awakening I dreamed I got a penny postal in the mail which read, "Dear Cora, I keep out. Love, Teresa of Avila." I was fond of my dreams, particularly of brief verbal ones like this, but Theron scorned them and said they had no style.

Long before Theron had thought of Catholicism, long before we had met and I was eighteen, I had been instructed by Father Strittmater in the Sacred Heart Church in Adams, and had been baptized and had once and once only received the wafer. My mission had not been accomplished, despite my fervor and my need. Later on, from time to time, I tried again in different churches of different towns at different seasons of the year and different hours of day and night. But I was God-forsaken; the shepherd could not hear my bleating, for I was miles astray in the cold and the dark and the desert. And at last I vanished without a trace; with a faint shiver and a faint sigh, I gave up the Ghost.

Half a year after we were married, Theron, immersed in the rhythms of Gerard Manley Hopkins the poet, was explosively ignited by Gerard Manley Hopkins the Jesuit, and, as my mother would have said, he was off on a tear. We were in Louisiana then —in steaming, verminous fetor; almost as soon as the set of Cardinal Newman's works arrived from Dauber & Pine, the spines relaxed, for the Deep South cockroaches, the size of larks, relished the seasoned glue of the bindings and banqueted by night. Like Father Strittmater, Theron's instructor was Pennsylvania Dutch— a coincidence that only mildly interested me but one by which my husband set great store: Our Lord (he adopted the address with ease) had planned likenesses in our experience. Father Neuscheier wore the miasmas from the bayous like a hair shirt, having chosen Baton Rouge out of many possibilities because it afforded him so excellent a chance to chasten his chaste flesh. Air-conditioning was in its infancy—not even the movie houses had it, or the saloons—but in most buildings of a public nature there were those large, romantic ceiling fans, whirling and whirring quietly, at a slow speed, resembling animated daisies with petals made of wood. But there was no fan in the nave of Our Lady of Pompeii, and Father Neuscheier must have suffered as the wet air thickened and warmed, but not a bead of sweat shone on his perfectly round face or his perfectly bald head. His austerity was right up Theron's alley, and before I knew what had happened to me, I had been dragged into that alley which was blind.

Theron had promised at the start that he would not impose his old-time religion on me, but within a week after he was confirmed I found myself being remarried in the Catholic Church, and a week after that I was going to daily Mass at seven in the morning, before I taught my first class at eight, and to benediction in the late afternoon; together we told two Rosaries a day, and we replaced our reproductions of "A Little Street in Delft" and "La Grande Jatte" with black-and-white photographs of Bellini's "St. Francis Receiving the Stigmata" and Holbein's "Thomas More." There would be, so did declare the head of the house, no sacrilegious jokes: we did not even laugh one rainy Sunday when Father Neuscheier announced at Mass that if anyone had sneakily or even accidentally caught some raindrops on his tongue, thereby breaking his fast, he would not be eligible to receive Communion.

What had become of the joking lad I'd married? He'd run hell-bent for election into that blind alley—that's what had become of him—and yanked me along with him, and there we snarled like hungry, scurvy cats. If I had stubbornly withstood him from the beginning, or if I had left him when he left me for the seraphim

and saints—but I had tried to withstand and had got for myself
only wrath and disdain. Leaving him had not really occurred to
me, for I had married within my tribe, and we were sternly monog-
amous till death. Supinely I endured and made out lists of things
while Mass was being sung—the cities I had traversed by bus on
journeys from east to west and west to south, the names of the
buildings on Neville's campus, all the people I knew whose given
name was John. In each new place we lived and I taught, as soon
as I had got my house in order and my schoolwork planned I called
at the rectory of the church Theron had selected as home base
and, depending on the nature of the man of God I found, humbly
declared my doubts or concealed them and invited him to tea.

In Cambridge, Father Bernard, an innocent, tired, and affectionate old man, had befriended me and had done so at a time
when I was needier than I had ever been before. Somewhere—on
a park bench in the Common, in a bar-and-grill in Scollay Square,
on the steps of Widener—Theron had met up one day with a fa-
natic who convinced him that the only godly way was a life of
holy poverty, and we were to move to a mission house in Dorchester and live on turnips and bean soup. We would sleep on the
floor and, I gathered, prowl the slums barefoot in the snow on the
lookout for derelicts sleeping off their Tokay sprees in sub-zero
temperatures. We were to give away our clothes and furniture—
one of the first things to go was my engagement ring, which had
belonged to Theron's great-aunt Charity Nephews, who had the-
atrically widowed her husband when she contracted dengue fever
at the opening of the Panama Canal. Although Theron appeared
to have repudiated all the luxuries and the limitations of his Bostonian breeding and totems, he had not in fact done so at all: he
was as vain as a peacock that Copley had painted his distant
Cousin Augustus' family and that Great-Aunt Charity had died
while she was acting as foreign correspondent for the Boston *Evening Transcript*. (T. S. Eliot, whose poem of that name he would
have liked me to embroider as a sampler, was then one of his
muses.) We were to give away the Nephews diamond, beset with
the palest of pink pearls, and, as well, a silver tea service bought in
Rangoon by Theron's father, the Captain, and disliked by his
mother for its showy bosses of birds and beasts and octopoid

goddesses. But we could not be all spirit (if we were, we would not have the means to be Lord and Lady Bountiful as well as Samaritans), so I was not to give up my job of teaching at Miss Heath's. And while I taught subjunctives to the bonny, snobby girls, Theron would write psalms and hymns and Christmas carols. "Quid pro quo," said he, his eyes rolled back so that the pupils rested on the optic thalamus. "Quid pro quo and tit for tat," I said to myself, thinking how I might set this to a simple tune to sing to a friendly cat.

If it had not been for Father Bernard, I am quite sure I would have taken on this graceless, humbug role of holy poverty. But Father Bernard, who in looks and in deportment resembled the dog named after his patron saint, was fond—perhaps profanely so—of creature comforts, and when one day I went to call on him to tattle on Theron and his latest excess, he took my side. Indeed, although he endeavored to maintain serenity, he showed his consternation—or, rather, his embarrassment—by giving his attention to a jardiniere planted with mosses and small ferns and keeping his back to me. Kind as he was, and affectionate, Father Bernard had not been cut out for the role of spiritual adviser; because he was humorless, he was vulnerable, and complicated emotional troubles upset his bowels. Theron mightily dismayed him, pestering him with abstruse exegeses of the sacraments as they might be applied to the modus vivendi of the New England transcendentalists, complaining of his failure to dislodge his mother from her Unitarianism, demanding that I be brought to book for my failure to obey the letter of the law. (One time I had eaten a Salisbury steak on a Friday when we took the Merchant's Limited from New York to Boston; Theron maintained that the journey was too short to justify such a dispensation.)

I very rarely called on Father Bernard, but because the rectory was on Irving Terrace, nearby our apartment building, on Kirkland, I often ran into him on the street and sometimes at the greengrocer's, where he liked to browse among the lettuces and roots; he loved all vegetables that grew underground, and the closest he ever came to making a joke was when, while fondling a turnip which was especially white and had especially pretty lilac markings, he said, "Do you think I am a *radical?*" Occasionally he would invite me to tea and, snug beside his fire, we talked over

our good strong brew and Peek Frean shortbread biscuits. But on
the day I sought his counsel on how to avoid a life of evangelical
destitution, I made an appointment. I was as shy as he, for I was
no better equipped to be the recipient than he to be the donor of
marriage guidance. For some minutes he fiddled with his ter-
rarium while I stroked his marmalade tom, whose name, curiously
enough, was Moses; this golden robust fellow, gleaming on an ot-
toman before the hearth, was the extension of his master—well
fed and safe, immune to disarray. At last, having waited in vain
for the arrival of the tea cart and then remembering that this was
Thursday and was therefore the housekeeper's afternoon off, I
spoke to Father Bernard's back.

"Oh, my!" said the auntly priest. "Oh dear! I'm all for lay
apostolates, you understand. Third orders do grand things with
soup kitchens and warm clothes for the poor—I say, Mrs. Maybank, I'm afraid there isn't any tea today. Would you like a glass
of sherry? Or of whiskey? I think I may have gin, too."

And so it was that Father Bernard and I, sipping some very old
bourbon neat from some very old topaz Sandwich tumblers, came
upon a possible solution to my dilemma. I could tell—by the
lacunae during which we blew our noses (we both had awful head
colds, and our affliction made the prospect of holy poverty the
more discomfiting) and by certain near slips of the tongue—that
impassioned converts were less to his liking than impenitent
thieves. I told him how all my life I had been making houses for
myself—in a corner of the attic in my parents' house in Missouri,
in clearings among lodgepole pines in the Adams foothills, in
offices I shared with other teachers. My nesting and my neatening
were compulsions in me that Theron looked on as plebeian, anti-
intellectual, lace-curtain Irish; he said I wanted to spend my life
in a tub of warm water, forswearing adventure but, worse, forswearing commitment. My pride of house was the sin of pride. I
took no stock in this, I knew it to be nonsense, but I did not
know how to defend myself against his barbs, the cruellest of
which was that I could not sin with style; as my dreams were
wanting in vitality, so was my decoration of houses wanting in
taste. (God almighty! Never was a man so set on knocking the
stuffing out of his bride!)

Blessed Father Bernard pointed out to me and I was to point

out to Theron that churches were made magnificent because they were the domiciles of God, and, since the sacrament of Holy Matrimony was exalted by God, it, too, should be enshrined as beautifully as possible. As for holy poverty, well, *that*, in his opinion, was a way of living that required a vocation, a clear call, and he did not think it was one I was likely to receive. I was so happy at that moment that if I had heard not a clear call but a clarion shout from the skies, "Discalce thyself! Be host to lice! Eat maggots without salt!" I would have refused the bidding and dismissed it as a prank of the Auld Clootie.

I wanted to hug and kiss my savior. Instead, I hugged and kissed Moses, who, ruffled by my forward demonstration, left a lawn of tawny fur on my midnight-blue wool skirt. Father Bernard and I were a little snugly tipsy. Or perhaps it was our head colds as much as the whiskey that made us giggle foolishly as we shook hands and said goodbye.

I thought I had won that bout, but by the time I got home my whimsical consort had changed his tack. This time, he'd met some guy on the Pepperpot Bridge while slogging across it in a blizzard (for no good reason that I could see) who was down on cities. They had spent the afternoon in a Scollay Square pub-crawl talking about getting through to reality by means of Nature, and now there was nothing for it but that we move to some remote outpost of the Laurentians or to the nine hundred and ninety-ninth of the Thousand Islands. (This new preacher was himself aiming for Mangareva, a French island in the South Pacific, at the bottom of the world, where a solitary ship called once a year. That was too Spartan even for my poet, who was dependent on the mail, which brought us *The Divergent* and several other quarterlies, as well as letters from poets and from pen pals he had picked up on retreats.) But our move to the wilderness depended on where I could get a job, because except for a trust fund that paid Theron —depending on the welfare of A.T. & T., the Boston & Maine, and other sobersided companies—about thirty-two dollars a month, I was the only means, visible or covert, of our support. I did not wholly rejoice in the thought of rural life (Thoreau had never fully captivated me), but it was so glamorous an alternative to a pious doss house in Dorchester that I set about at once writing letters to boards of education in the province of Quebec.

At Christmastime that year, the only miracle of my life befell me—a miracle so amazing and so magically well timed that I almost came to believe in Heaven as a place whence miracles were sent. My twin aunts Amy and Jane McKinnon had, after the death of my grandfather, fled Missouri and had gone to New South Wales, where both of them almost at once found prospering husbands; both of them were barren and—poor, pretty dears— loved children. Their disappointment led them to good works among the aborigines, but when the chips were down for Aunt Jane and she commenced to die of cancer, loyalty to her own Gaelic clan atavistically returned, and in her will, besides endowments to charitable institutions for the needy of the bush, she remembered her nieces and nephews. She had been widowed for several years by the time she died, and her estate was considerable. Her bequests to my cousins and to Abigail and me (my brother had been killed in the war the year before, in Normandy) vexed my father and mother, because, not to put too fine a point upon it, as they iteratively implied they did not, they were far more sorely pinched than we were and could have used a helping hand. My father, with one of his bootless and wicked tricks of legerdemain, tried to dissuade us from accepting the money, because the individual sums were small—five thousand apiece, but there were nine of us!

Five thousand dollars! The evening of the day I got the news, Theron and I went to Locke-Ober for dinner and, although we both hated it, we drank champagne. We were charming to each other, and when I proposed that with my windfall we buy a simple cabin somewhere near a country public school, Theron was so bowled over with enthusiasm that he ordered another bottle of champagne. The next day we were as sick as dogs, our stomachs churning with simonpure hydrochloric acid.

And so, when I had taught my last class at Miss Heath's, we rented our apartment and went to Maine for the summer, working our way slowly down the coast from Eastport, looking for a house to buy. We were so happy! We were so fond! Once again in love, we fell in love with Stonington, where we wanted to spin out the rest of our days, Theron as a commercial fisherman and I as a teacher and a respected small-town matron. I saw myself, in the autumn of my life, retired, putting on a pair of white gloves at three o'clock in the afternoon and putting on a hat and going to the public library to borrow a Ouida novel. But there were no houses for sale.

We finished out the summer in Rankin Harbor, and just before Labor Day, too late for me to find a job, we discovered the house —*my* house—in Edwards Mills; I bought it, paying for it with a check.

For a few weeks, back in Cambridge, we remained friendly. I made a trip back to Maine in October and with no trouble at all got a job teaching at the high school beginning the following year. But the delay took the snap out of Theron's fancy for rural rides, and by Christmas of that year (no manna from Aunt Jane's Heaven this time) I was a witch again, and all day and all night my God-fearing yokemate burned me at the stake in Salem. He was right. I make no plea for myself, for I had the tongue of an adder and my heart was black with rage and hate.

Unpeopled and at peace, my little country drawing room bewitched me because it was part of the house that belonged to me, and while everything in it was a castoff from my Maybank in-laws or something I had bought at a secondhand store or on the cheap at Filene's, and while it was a far cry from being all of a piece, it had for me a flawed and solacing enchantment. I was thirty now, and I had achieved at last what I had striven for from the beginning: a house and a lawn and trees. I had seen Father Bernard more often than before in Cambridge during the winter, and because he, too, was a nester he could revive my flagging spirits simply by asking me if I thought lightning rods would be necessary or if I planned to put a weathervane on the barn that was attached to the house.

On weekends in the spring, I went up to check on the progress of the workmen. Honoring my marriage by making this temple for it, my acolytes—the carpenters and the electricians, the chimney sweep and the plumber—became my friends and allies. We were together in a blameless conspiracy to overwhelm my husband. They worked with uncommon fidelity (the postmistress, who was an outlander like myself, assured me of this), and each time I unlocked my front door and was greeted with the smell of sawdust and of paint and the litter everywhere of tag ends of hardware and snarls of frayed old electric wires and heaps of plaster commingled with bent and rusted nails, I was delirious. For the last week of March and the first of April, I was in residence during the spring holiday from Miss Heath's. Theron was making a retreat with the Trappists in New Jersey, and I was therefore free to be absorbed completely in washing the windows and hanging the Swiss-organdie glass curtains and, beside them in the living room, the red velvet draperies. (Oh, how sumptuous I thought they were, poor skimpy things!) When the mossy carpet came from Boston, I could not sleep at all that night but kept going downstairs, walking on it in my bare feet; in the morning my bed sheets were downy with green lint from my excursions, and they were rumpled from my excited leapings out of bed.

Where now were my beatitudes? From my darkened living room, I could no longer see the sunlight on the hay and lilies and could only sense the folds and the effluvia of night, and instead of birds saw snakes and instead of grass saw pestilential ooze. Supperless and sleepless, I went up to our bedroom, taking a bottle of whiskey and a dagger of ice in a glass; as I chipped it off the block, I thought how proud I had been to find this huge old ice chest for two dollars and a half.

I drank, stared into space, connived. Some accident befell Theron and Minnie on the lake and they never came back; honorably widowed, I was free. Or they fell in love and their adultery exonerated me of all my capital crimes and all my peccadilloes and all my hypocrisies and self-indulgences. I was in love with their sinful love and saw them doomed, like Paolo and Francesca, to an eternity of passion and of loathing. Theron Maybank the watchful, jealous Salem Puritan, the watchful, zealous Roman Catholic catechumen turned overnight into the most banal kind of sinner even before the baptismal water was dry upon his forehead! Dishonored, I would ascend refreshed, putting aside the ruin of this marriage shattered so ignominiously by *the other woman*, by that most unseemly of disgraces, above all by something *not my fault*, giving me the uncontested right to hate him. And I would come eventually into a second marriage: I saw my husband and I saw my sons. But the house I saw was this house, bought with Aunt Jane's legacy; I saw my fireplaces and I saw my barn until my tears erased them and I sobbed into the pillow as if, already deprived and homeless, I lay alone on stones.

At last, dead drunk, I slept.

There is no advice sounder than this, and none, I daresay, so difficult to follow: Be careful what you wish for, be wary of the predicates of your fantasies and lies. So ignorant and sheeplike is my flesh that if, at the eleventh hour, I telephone my hostess to say that I cannot come to her party because I have a headache, at the twelfth hour a fang of pain strikes deep within my skull, and by the time the party is over and the guests are at home in bed asleep, I am haggard with suffering, doomed to twenty hours of the blindness and throbbing of a migraine. It is not prudent to say, "I would rather break an arm than keep this appointment with the dentist." The hyperbolic substitute we devise in this offhand fashion, if it is realized, does not circumvent but only postpones, so we are doubly burdened by the headache or the broken arm and by another party and a later appointment with the dentist. So when I wished that Theron and Minnie Rosoff would enter upon an outrageous affair, I was safeguarded against the calamities it would sow in me because it seemed an impossibility (as does the migraine or the fractured humerus)—something too good to be true, a fictional expedient having its initiation only in my mind. Because it could not happen, it did not occur to me that it *might* happen and that I *would* be dishonored by it, I *would* taste the vilest degradation, the bitterest jealousy, the most scalding and vindictive rancor.

The daydream was still with me in the morning, and it lasted that day and the next and more days thereafter. Blinded by my wish for the farthest-fetched, the most grotesque product of the former Mrs. Zumwalt's visit, I never dreamed, despite the obvious testimony before my eyes, that it had already come true (and that, indeed, at least so far as Theron was concerned, it had come true about the time my train was pulling out of Portland the day I was homeward bound from Boston). In consequence, I urged Minnie to prolong her stay with us, and, until the Bronsons and Harry Matthews came back, I excused myself from their society by saying that I must prepare for my classes at the high school, so that they could be free to go sailing and swimming and fishing

without me. I helped in every way to make the match, which was
already a fait accompli and which, when I discovered that it was,
was to hurtle me off the brink on which I had hovered for so long
into a chasm.

It was true that Theron's attendance on Minnie puzzled me a
little, for she was not the kind of woman he liked; she was flirtatious, competitive, argumentatively political. Her taste was modern, and he repudiated as soulless or dull or ugly everything that
had been built or painted or written (except for certain poetry
and the prose of certain contemporary English divines) after 1850.
Moreover, he was, by heritage and by instinct, anti-Semitic, and
soon after we met Jerry Zumwalt, he dumbfounded me by saying,
"I would never have a Jew as a close friend." And they never had
been close—not in the way he was close with friends from
boarding-school and college days.

The sensible and wifely side of me looked on his games with
Minnie with pleasure: I was glad he was having fun, and perhaps
his attraction to her meant that he was relaxing his rigidity. The
hermit side of me, the secret boozehead side, looked on the alli-
ance with even greater pleasure: I was blissfully addicted to the
fantasies the genie of the bottle contrived for me each night they
went for a late swim in the lake, each day they went clamming on
the mud flats of the tidal river.

Because now there was no longer anything for us to say to each
other, we sat in separate cars on the train from Camden to Boston, but we did so with discretion, and with explanations ready on
our tongues lest we encounter anyone we knew. We were so in
concord in this desire to keep up appearances that it had not been
necessary for us to plan our behavior before we boarded the train.
Until Wiscasset we sat together in a parlor car, and for the benefit
of the ticket-taker and the porter and for the passengers Theron
listed again to me (as he had done to everyone in Edwards Mills,
down to the cretinous child who peddled his mother's homemade
bread) the reasons we had decided, after all, not to live in Maine.

So on the train, among the travellers returning from Mt. Desert
and Blue Hill, heedless of everything but the boats they had
stored and the pleasures and problems of the city season they were
now confronting, my husband, unknown to them, loudly ad-

dressed congratulations to us both on our sensible leave-taking. And when the derelict schooner in the Sheepscott at Wiscasset loomed forth, he felt he had said enough, and, turning to me with a perfect imitation of solicitude, even bending forward to look into my face, he said, "You look worn out. Don't you want a drink?"

I nodded, accepting his signal, and gathered together my purse and scarf and book (I had not understood a printed word for months) and, matching my manners to his for the sake of those total strangers, I said, "You needn't come. I know you want to work."

"You're a dear," he said and picked his briefcase up off the floor, opening it to show a Loeb "Confessions of St. Augustine," distended with sheets of onionskin on which for a year or so he had made fine notes, cryptic and self-centered, in black ink, which, however, dried as purple, giving the pages a schoolish look. "I'll join you when I've finished Monica's death."

Liar, I thought. Swindler. Ten minutes before the North Station you'll come into the club car, where you'll find me drunk; the sight of you will drive me wild, for I will know what you have been doing, with your eyes so piously attentive to the Latin of your little book. You will have been dreaming, mooning, delighting yourself with thoughts of your reunion with Minnie, your playmate, this very night. (He had dismissed me with that word. "I don't want a wife," he had said, "I want a playmate.")

I could not help myself. I said, "Where will you have din-din tonight with your playmate?"

My question enraged us both, and I got up before he could answer. As I left the car, I looked back; apparently deep among the Manichees, he was thinking of his doll-sized, doll-dressed doll with her bisque-doll skin.

The bar car was empty except for two Army officers recollecting D Day. It was not necessary for me to be surreptitious as I took a phenobarbital before I started to drink my lulling drink, but even so, having asked the waiter for a glass of water, I explained, with Theron's kind of insistence, that I was taking a headache pill, and I was careful not to say aspirin, fearing he might observe how small the pellet was. Like Theron, I stared at the pages of a book; like his, my mind was far.

We would say goodbye at the North Station and I would then go to the South and take a train for New York, where I had an appointment with a psychoanalyst two days hence.

We had killed Pretty Baby and killed her kittens. Theron himself had put them in a gunnysack and weighted it with stones and had rowed halfway out to Loon Islet and dropped them among the perch and pickerel.

He beached the boat. I was waiting for him on the front stoop; I had already locked the door. The idling of the motor in the waiting taxi was the only sound that broke the silence of that absolutely azure and absolutely golden early autumn day.

MAGAZINES CONSULTED

Antaeus
    Ecco Press, 1 West 30th Street, New York, N.Y. 10001
Antioch Review
    P.O. Box 148, Yellow Springs, Ohio 45387
Apalachee Quarterly
    P.O. Box 20106, Tallahassee, Fla. 32304
Appalachian Journal
    P.O. Box 536, Appalachian State University, Boone, N.C.
    28608
Ararat
    Armenian General Benevolent Union of America, 628 Second Avenue, New York, N.Y. 10016
Arizona Quarterly
    University of Arizona, Tucson, Ariz. 85721
Ascent
    English Department, University of Illinois, Urbana, Ill.
    61801
Aspen Anthology
    P.O. Box 3185, Aspen, Col. 81611
The Atlantic
    8 Arlington Street, Boston, Mass. 02116
Bachy
    11317 Santa Monica Boulevard, Los Angeles, Calif. 90025
Bennington Review
    Bennington College, Bennington, Vt. 05201
Bloodroot
    P.O. Box 891, Grand Forks, N.D. 58201
Boston University Journal
    704 Commonwealth Avenue, Boston, Mass. 02215
Brushfire
    c/o English Dept., University of Nevada, Reno, Nev.
    89507
California Quarterly
    100 Sproul Hall, University of California, Davis, Calif.
    95616

Canadian Fiction Magazine
    P.O. Box 46422, Station G, Vancouver, B.C., Canada
    V6R 4G7
Canto
    11 Bartlett Street, Andover, Mass. 01810
Carleton Miscellany
    Carleton College, Northfield, Minn. 55057
Carolina Quarterly
    Box 1117, Chapel Hill, N.C. 27515
The Chariton Review
    Division of Language & Literature, Northeast Missouri
    State University, Kirksville, Mo. 63501
Chicago Review
    Faculty Exchange, Box C, University of Chicago, Chicago,
    Ill. 60637
Christopher Street
    Suite 417, 250 W. 57th St., New York, N.Y. 10019
Cinemonkey
    P.O. Box 8502, Portland, Ore. 97207
Colorado Quarterly
    Hellums 134, University of Colorado, Boulder, Col.
    80309
Confrontation
    English Department, Brooklyn Center of Long Island Uni-
    versity, Brooklyn, N.Y. 11201
Cornell Review
    108 North Plain Street, Ithaca, N.Y. 14850
Cosmopolitan
    224 West 57th Street, New York, N.Y. 10019
Crucible
    Atlantic Christian College, Wilson, N.C. 27893
Cumberlands
    Pikeville College, Pikeville, Ky. 41501
Cutbank
    c/o English Dept., University of Montana, Missoula,
    Mont. 59801
December
    P.O. Box 274, Western Springs, Ill. 60558

The Denver Quarterly
    Dept. of English, University of Denver, Denver, Col.
    80210
Descant
    Dept. of English, TCU Station, Fort Worth, Tex. 76129
Dog Soldier
    E. 323 Boone, Spokane, Wash. 99202
Epoch
    254 Goldwyn Smith Hall, Cornell University, Ithaca, N.Y.
    14853
Esquire Magazine
    488 Madison Avenue, New York, N.Y. 10022
Essence
    1500 Broadway, New York, N.Y. 10036
Eureka Review
    Dept. of English, University of Cincinnati, Cincinnati,
    Ohio 45221
The Falcon
    Bilknap Hall, Mansfield State College, Mansfield, Pa.
    16933
Fantasy and Science Fiction
    Box 56, Cornwall, Conn. 06753
The Fault
    33513 6th Street, Union City, Calif. 94538
Fiction International
    Dept. of English, St. Lawrence University, Canton, N.Y.
    13617
Fiction Magazine
    c/o Dept. of English, The City College of New York, New
    York, N.Y. 10031
The Fiddlehead
    The Observatory, University of New Brunswick, P.O. Box
    4400, Fredericton, N.B., Canada E3B 5A3
Fisherman's Angle
    St. John Fisher College, Rochester, N.Y. 14618
Forms
    P.O. Box 3379, San Francisco, Calif. 94119
Forum
    Ball State University, Muncie, Ind. 47306

Four Quarters
    La Salle College, Philadelphia, Pa. 19141
The Gay Alternative
    252 South St., Philadelphia, Pa. 19147
Georgia Review
    University of Georgia, Athens, Ga. 30602
GPU News
    c/o The Farwell Center, 1568 N. Farwell, Milwaukee, Wis. 53202
The Great Lakes Review
    Northeastern Illinois University, Chicago, Ill. 60625
Green River Review
    Box 56, University Center, Mich. 48710
The Greensboro Review
    University of North Carolina, Greensboro, N.C. 27412
Harper's Magazine
    2 Park Avenue, New York, N.Y. 10016
Hawaii Review
    Hemenway Hall, University of Hawaii 96822
The Hudson Review
    65 East 55th Street, New York, N.Y. 10022
Iowa Review
    EPB 453, University of Iowa, Iowa City, Iowa 52240
Kansas Quarterly
    Dept. of English, Kansas State University, Manhattan, Kan. 66506
Ladies' Home Journal
    641 Lexington Avenue, New York, N.Y. 10022
The Literary Review
    Fairleigh Dickinson University, Teaneck, N.J. 07666
The Little Magazine
    P.O. Box 207, Cathedral Station, New York, N.Y. 10025
The Louisville Review
    University of Louisville, Louisville, Ky. 40208
Mademoiselle
    350 Madison Avenue, New York, N.Y. 10017
Malahat Review
    University of Victoria, Victoria, B.C., Canada

The Massachusetts Review
> Memorial Hall, University of Massachusetts, Amherst, Mass. 01002

McCall's
> 230 Park Avenue, New York, N.Y. 10017

MD
> 30 E. 60th St., New York, N.Y. 10022

Michigan Quarterly Review
> 3032 Rackham Bldg., The University of Michigan, Ann Arbor, Mich. 48109

Midstream
> 515 Park Avenue, New York, N.Y. 10022

Mother Jones
> 607 Market Street, San Francisco, Calif. 94105

The National Jewish Monthly
> 1640 Rhode Island Avenue, N.W., Washington, D.C. 20036

New Boston Review
> Boston Critic, Inc., 77 Sacramento Street, Somerville, Mass. 02143

New Directions
> 333 Sixth Avenue, New York, N.Y. 10014

New Letters
> University of Missouri–Kansas City, Kansas City, Mo. 64110

New Mexico Humanities Review
> The Editors, Box A, New Mexico Tech, Socorro, N.M. 57801

The New Renaissance
> 9 Heath Road, Arlington, Mass. 02174

The New Republic
> 1220 19th St., N.W., Washington, D.C. 20036

The New Yorker
> 25 West 43rd Street, New York, N.Y. 10036

Nocturne
> P.O. Box 1320, Johns Hopkins University, Baltimore, Md. 21218

The North American Review
    University of Northern Iowa, 1222 West 27th Street, Cedar Falls, Iowa 50613
Northwest Review
    129 French Hall, University of Oregon, Eugene, Ore. 97403
Northwoods Journal
    Route 1, Meadows of Daw, Va. 24120
The Ohio Journal
    164 West 17th Avenue, Columbus, Ohio 43210
Ohio Review
    Ellis Hall, Ohio University, Athens, Ohio 45701
The Ontario Review
    (temporary address) 9 Honey Brook Dr., Princeton, N.J. 08540
Paragraph: A Quarterly of Gay Fiction
    Box 14051, San Francisco, Calif. 94114
The Paris Review
    45-39–171st Place, Flushing, N.Y. 11358
Paris Voices
    37, rue de la Bucherie, Paris 5, France
Partisan Review
    128 Bay State Rd., Boston, Mass. 02215 / 552 Fifth Avenue, New York, N.Y. 10036
Perspective
    Washington University, St. Louis, Mo. 63130
Phylon
    223 Chestnut Street, S.W., Atlanta, Ga. 30314
Playboy
    919 North Michigan Avenue, Chicago, Ill. 60611
Ploughshares
    Box 529, Cambridge, Mass. 02139
Prairie Schooner
    Andrews Hall, University of Nebraska, Lincoln, Neb. 68588
Prism International
    Dept. of Creative Writing, University of British Columbia, Vancouver, B.C., Canada V6T 1WR

Quarterly West
> 312 Olpin Union, University of Utah, Salt Lake City, Utah 84112

Quartet
> 1119 Neal Pickett Drive, College Station, Tex. 77840

Quest/79
> 1133 Avenue of the Americas, New York, N.Y. 10036

Redbook
> 230 Park Avenue, New York, N.Y. 10017

Remington Review
> 505 Westfield Ave., Elizabeth, N.J. 07208

Rolling Stone
> 625 Third Street, San Francisco, Calif. 94107

The Saturday Evening Post
> 110 Waterway Boulevard, Indianapolis, Ind. 46202

The Seneca Review
> P.O. Box 115, Hobart and William Smith College, Geneva, N.Y. 14456

Sequoia
> Storke Student Publications Bldg., Stanford, Calif. 94305

Sewanee Review
> University of the South, Sewanee, Tenn. 37375

Shenandoah: The Washington and Lee University Review
> Box 722, Lexington, Va. 24450

The South Carolina Review
> Dept. of English, Clemson University, Clemson, S.C. 29631

The South Dakota Review
> Box 111, University Exchange, Vermillion, S.D. 57069

Southern Humanities Review
> Auburn University, Auburn, Ala. 36830

Southern Review
> Drawer D, University Station, Baton Rouge, La. 70803

Southwest Review
> Southern Methodist University Press, Dallas, Tex. 75275

Steel Head
> Knife River Press, 2501 Branch St., Duluth, Minn. 55812

Story Quarterly
> 820 Ridge Road, Highland Park, Ill. 60035

The Tamarack Review
    Box 159, Postal Station K, Toronto, Ont., Canada M4P
    2G5
Tri-Quarterly
    University Hall 101, Northwestern University, Evanston,
    Ill. 60201
Twigs
    Pikeville College, Pikeville, Ky. 41501
Twin Cities Express
    127 N. 7th St., Minneapolis, Minn. 55402
University of Windsor Review
    Dept. of English, University of Windsor, Windsor, Ont.,
    Canada N9B 3P4
U.S. Catholic
    221 West Madison Street, Chicago, Ill. 60606
Vagabond
    P.O. Box 879, Ellensburg, Wash. 98926
The Virginia Quarterly Review
    University of Virginia, 1 West Range, Charlottesville, Va.
    22903
Vogue
    350 Madison Avenue, New York, N.Y. 10017
The Washingtonian
    1828 "C" St., N.W., Suite 200, Washington, D.C. 20036
West Coast Review
    Simon Fraser University, Vancouver, B.C., Canada
Western Humanities Review
    Bldg. 41, University of Utah, Salt Lake City, Utah 84112
Wind
    RFD Route 1, Box 809, Pikeville, Ky. 41501
Woman's Day
    1515 Broadway, New York, N.Y. 10036
Writers Forum
    University of Colorado, Colorado Springs, Col. 90907
Yale Review
    250 Church Street, 1902A Yale Station, New Haven,
    Conn. 06520
Yankee
    Dublin, N.H. 03444